# SEVEN BIRDS

*a novel*

*Amy Sargent Swank*

ISBN: 1545164932
ISBN-13: 9781545164938

*This book is for you, Mom; you've been gone a long time and I miss you.*

One for sorrow,
Two for joy,
Three for girls,
Four for boys,
Five for silver,
Six for gold,
Seven for a secret
Never to be told.
Eight for a wish,
Nine for a kiss,
Ten for a bird
You must not miss.

*English nursery rhyme*
*about counting crows*

# CHAPTER 1

# FESSENDEN

I slowly opened my eyes and sat up at my desk, a sharp pain radiating down my neck. One of my arms, a bony, lumpy makeshift pillow, tingled from bearing the weight of my head. I reached across my laptop for my phone to check the time: 2:13 a.m. I opened the laptop I had fallen asleep on, and up sprang my document, the unfinished chapter that was haunting me. I needed to finish writing this book. I needed to because it was overdue, and I needed to because I needed the advance. But panic was overtaking diligence.

I noticed I had a missed text from William, which filled me with the usual dread, but I opened it anyway: *Fez, please call back. I'm so sorry about this. At least let me come down and help you pack up the house. I'm trying to make this right. I really am. Please.*

I snorted at the phone. Too late, William. Way, *way* too late.

His text was an unpleasant reminder of what lay ahead today. I should have started packing and getting organized days ago, but I hadn't, and I was certain that Hazel hadn't started packing, either. Jesus! Hazel! When did she get in? Did I hear her come in? I was drawn to go check on her, but even more drawn to climb into bed and get at least a few more hours of sleep, without which facing tomorrow—or rather later today—was going to be all but impossible.

A few short hours later, I woke up again, drenched with sweat, disoriented, and tightly wrapped in a twisted, damp knot of sheets. I heard the crows screeching their gritty, raspy calls. I reflexively reached for William, but his side of the bed was cool, crisp, and empty, something I was still not used to, even after all these months.

I pulled back my hand, untangled my feet from the sheets, and rolled over onto my right side to face the window toward Crow's Pond. The sky was hazy, the water still and pale; it was already hot. As the fog of sleep began to lift, something ominous started to creep in: a slow, dark, thick feeling of dread, and then, within a minute, I was fully engulfed. Today was, in all likelihood, our last day in this quirky, wonderful house. Three generations of my family here, and it all ended now when I would pack up the house and go, leaving a set of keys for a white-haired, ruddy-skinned real estate agent named Janet who was going to sell this house, *my* house. Thinking of this filled me with such a wave of fury at William that I wanted to throw something. *How could he have done this to us?* It's a question I've asked myself too many times to count.

I kicked the covers onto the floor as I abruptly stood up. I went into the bathroom, put on my blue terrycloth bathrobe, rust-stained from the hook, and headed out to wake up Hazel and remind her to start packing. In the light of day, I clearly recalled that she did not check in last night as she was supposed to, but I admonished myself not to bring it up. It was going to be a hard enough day without starting an argument and eye-rolling, which is how way too many days this summer had begun.

I walked down the stairs, the white-painted wood floors gritty from sand. Framed photographs lined the stairway wall. Already feeling nostalgic in anticipation of our departure, I stopped and looked at them. In one, Hazel, at the age of three, was sitting in a skirted bathing suit, on the little beach out back, plastic shovel in her hand. William's protective hand was on her tiny shoulder. Hazel was staring straight at the camera, serious and focused, without a trace of a smile, her head cocked as if she was about to ask something. William was looking at her and saying something consoling or instructive, his tanned broad shoulders reflecting the bright, warm sun. In the background, a lime-green plastic pail, filled with sand, water, and skittering hermit crabs. My shadow evident on the sand, stretched thin and long.

I went down another step and looked at the next photograph, a formal family portrait taken in the living room here, circa 1969: my dear grandparents; my mother; my father; my aunt Bunny and her husband, Buck; and me—the entire family. All the women sitting stiff and erect, their identical bony, sun-freckled legs running parallel, primly crossed ankles, on straight-backed Hitchcock chairs. My beloved grandpa, my father, and Uncle Buck standing behind them with their hands resting on their spouses' shoulders. Me, aged seven, looking restless and uncomfortable, sitting on Bunny's lap. Two golden retrievers lying in front of Mimi on the threadbare needlepoint floral rug. Everyone was looking straight at the camera with faint smiles except my mother, who must have moved her head at just the wrong moment. Her face was a blur.

I moved down the creaking steps and out through the kitchen to head up the small hill to check on Hazel. The screen door slammed behind me, narrowly missing my heel. I could smell the heat, the dry, sandy dirt, and the black-eyed Susans as I traversed the slate stepping-stones.

I carefully pushed open the screen door to the Halfway House, our tiny guest cottage on the property, and saw Hazel sleeping on her side in one of the twin beds, the popcorn-crocheted coverlet pulled up to her chin, her dark hair a sweaty tangle around her pillow, a few stray strands stuck to her damp face. Her mouth agape, she was clearly sleeping deeply. I marveled at how young and sweet she looked.

On the bedside table, there was a photograph of her, taken a few summers ago. She was sitting at the kitchen table, holding one red, steamed lobster with a big smile on her tanned face. I picked up the small, framed picture and held it in my hand. Hazel was alone in almost every picture we had of her. We tried so hard to give her a sibling, but miscarriage after miscarriage before she was born, and also after her, stole those hopes. The last loss and the most devastating was when Hazel was four. I was six months pregnant, well past any date of worry, when I stopped feeling the baby kicking and shifting. I went to the doctor, fighting panic as he ran his ultrasound wand over and over my swollen belly, over the still heart, the lifeless baby, until he finally looked at me and said with sincere sadness, "Fez, I'm so sorry." Even twelve years later, I felt that pain on a visceral level, as if it were some dense thing I carried in my gut, like a stone.

I had hated being an only child and wanted a big family so badly. I had begged my parents for a sibling, specifically a sister, whom I had imagined staying up late with and giggling with in this very room, but the mere request sent my mother sighing and slumping out of the room and garnered a set reply from my father: "Oh Fez, you funny thing. That ship has sailed." I set the picture of smiling Hazel back on the bedside table.

A pile of clothes was on the floor: black T-shirt, faded black jeans, intentionally holey and worn, black underwear and bra on top, everything inside out and balled together as if she had peeled it all off in one rolling motion. I picked them up to move them and found they were damp. A fine film of sand fell to the floor. Obviously she'd been to the beach, but alone? She had no friends here last night. As safe as our little neighborhood was, I told Hazel I didn't like the idea of her wandering around by herself, and I certainly didn't like the idea of her swimming alone.

I sat on her small bed, the old springs screeching loudly in protest, but she didn't stir, which gave me the chance to stare at her sleeping face, something I have loved to do since the day she was born.

I remembered one summer when she was eight or nine and had been having nightmares for weeks. During this period, I would stay next to her until she fell asleep. One night, she awoke with a start shortly after she had fallen asleep.

"Mommy!" she said, scooting closer to me.

I stroked the soft hair out of her eyes. "Yes, lovey, what is it?"

She pressed herself into my lap as she recalled her dream, her voice raspy and soft. "I was sitting in a classroom, maybe in the science building or someplace like that, all ready to take the test." She rubbed at her eyes. "I had my pencils sharpened and all in a row on my desk. You know the yellow pencils?"

"Yep. The yellow ones. Ticonderogas." I nodded.

"Yes, those. Well, I don't know what happened, but all of a sudden, I was naked in class." She turned to look at me, actually mortified that she was unclothed in the dream. "Naked! I mean, I looked around the room and Janie and Gordon and Moira were all sitting at their desks, and they were wearing regular clothes, you know, school uniforms. Then when I looked at them, in all their school clothes, they noticed me, and I was really naked and they knew it and then I knew it and it was so, *so* bad. I couldn't believe I had forgotten to get dressed! It felt so real, Mom."

I pulled her closer, nuzzling against her silken hair that smelled like the baby shampoo she still loved to use. "I think, maybe, just maybe, you're a little worried about the coming year. About being a fourth grader? Could that be it?"

She nestled further into my neck and murmured a hushed "maybe" and quietly drifted back to sleep.

That little girl had changed recently. The dutiful, hardworking child, always diligent and thoughtful, had become distant and detached. Her grades this past semester had dipped a bit to Bs, which shouldn't have seemed like a problem except this was *Hazel*.

She had always gotten straight As with both raw intelligence and hard work, and William and I worried that a grade slip was worthy of our concern. In May when we got her report card, we asked her about her falling grades. She said that the schoolwork was just harder, more intense, and she was taking all honors and APs now, and that was *college level* and that she'd be back on track for junior year, when in her words, "stuff started to matter." We agreed; schoolwork *had* started to intensify, and Bs were still excellent. College-level courses as a sophomore! Of course she didn't have to get As. We let it go.

I gently nudged her. "Haze," I whispered. She didn't move. I put my hand on her shoulder, bony and sharp under the coverlet. "Haze, time to wake up." Nothing. Louder. "Hazel, we've got to pack, honey." She slowly opened her eyes and groaned.

"Mom, what *time* is it?" First sentence of the day, and I could see that she was already annoyed.

"It's about eight, but I want to go for my walk, and then we have to pack up the house and hit the road." I had decided that I wouldn't tell Hazel about having to sell the house until we had a deal in place. I didn't want her summer clouded by the news, especially with the separation.

"Shit," she said. "Really?"

"Yep, sorry, last day of the summer. I'm heading down to the beach. I'll be back in about an hour. Can you get started with your stuff and then help me in the main house when I'm back?" I leaned down to kiss her cheek and smelled two things instantly: smoke and the sickly-sweet smell of a hangover. Metastasizing sugar. I pulled back. "Hazel, what did you do last night?"

She looked at me and narrowed her eyes. "Nothing, why?"

"What did you do last night?" I repeated slowly, a feeling of dread building.

"Nothing, just hung out on the beach with friends."

"Which friends?"

"Ty and Bex." These were newer friends from a different crowd at school. They were around a lot this summer, but I didn't know them well. They never came into the house, neither in Boston nor here.

"Hazel, were you drinking?"

"Just a little. Nothing big. Just a beer." Could one beer explain that smell?

"Just a beer? *Really?*"

"Yes, Mom. *Really.* I don't even really like drinking. I just kinda had one so I wouldn't look like a loser." She looked right at me, and I could tell she was being sincere.

"OK. OK. Were you smoking? I smell smoke."

"No. Jesus, Mom, relax. We just had a little bonfire. We all probably smell like smoke. It was the end-of-summer party. Remember?" She looked straight at me. "Don't worry, Mom. OK? You're gonna make yourself crazy."

It's true. I felt crazy. Every time I worried about Hazel and her behavior, every single time I accused her of something related to parties, drinking, or smoking, she would deny it, and William would side with Hazel, thereby confirming my "crazy behavior" with comments like, "She's just a teenager. She's not doing anything we didn't do at her age. Remember?" It was true. Both William and I drank at her age. We went to parties. We smoked a little pot. But it felt different when it was my own child, my own little girl.

I looked at her closely. "OK, Hazel, but just so you know, I'm *never* going to stop worrying. *Never.* Especially with our family history. You understand that, right?"

She nodded, and then rolled over with her back to me, ready to settle back into more sleep.

I headed back out to the beach path, feeling a twinge of guilt. Though I walked for an hour each and every morning of the summer, rain or shine, a ritual maintained for more than twenty years, today it felt like an indulgence. I should use this hour to work on my book, a last-ditch effort to meet my Labor Day deadline. I had been working hard this summer, really hard, but I seemed to be in a holding pattern, unable to finish, unwilling to stop the edits and the rewrites. My agent, Caroline, who was always patient and understanding, was neither of these things now.

Last week, she'd left me a stern phone message. "Fez, I know you are swamped. I know it's a bad time, but I really need to see what you've got. I don't care what shape it's in. I know *you* care, but I really don't." She took a breath and then added with emphasis, *"Don't let perfect be the enemy of good."*

I knew what she meant. I *was* buried in the writing and the edits. I was adding new chapters, which may or may not have been necessary. I was making changes in the basic structure and layout of the book at this late date. I was, possibly, so buried in my edits, I was at risk of overediting, overthinking, and muddying what was once a clear and riveting biographical storyline.

In a message from earlier in the summer, she said, "I'm wondering if you're worried about the gap between books, but don't be. Maybe expectations will be high after a ten-year book gap, but you really have something here, and I think readers' morbid fascination with the story of this *gruesome mariticide* will be enough." She loved using that expression. *Gruesome mariticide.*

"The readers want to know Agnes Williams Black and her story. It's titillating. It's awful. It's completely engaging. And you're so close. So just write, edit, and send. Soon."

I wasn't ready, and I didn't want to send crap. I needed to make sure I earned a handsome advance from this book. I just needed another week, maybe two. When I was back home in Boston and Hazel was back in school, I could focus. But first I had to pack my clothes, toiletries, and all the food in the fridge and pantry. I had to clean the kitchen and bathrooms. I had to dust. I had to sweep and vacuum. I hadn't cleaned the house well in the three months Hazel and I had been here. I had to put away clutter, so Janet could straighten up and "prepare, rearrange, tidy, organize, and *stage*" the house for going on the market. I was annoyed and overwhelmed just thinking about it.

But before any of that, I would walk. It was more important today than ever. When I got out to the beach, I turned back to face the old shingled house: the big picture window facing Crow's Pond, the grassy back terrace with its uneven pale-red bricks creating a makeshift seating area, the scrub pines, large hydrangeas and rugged rosa rugosa framing the yard. My grandparents' beautiful landscaping vision, colorful and stunning.

My grandparents bought this house and property back in the mid-1930s within a year of the completion of the Sagamore Bridge, which connected "mainland Massachusetts" to Cape Cod. My grandparents were young, gay, and excitable (Mimi's words), and Grandpa's inherited steel business was just beginning to boom. They were nearly untouched by the Depression thanks to a great deal of wealth set aside on both sides by careful and prudent parents and grandparents. They were not ostentatious in lifestyle but deeply embedded in generations of Episcopalian propriety and Boston Brahmin associations; no one misunderstood their breeding. When Grandpa showed Mimi the shingled home, sitting up high, overlooking Crow's Pond in Chatham on the elbow of lovely Cape Cod, she gasped and said, "Darling, it's perfect." And that was that. As a nod to the Anglo house-naming tradition, they named the house the Crow's Nest, partially due to its elevation and partly due to the thickly populated black bird population throughout the property. There were two other small houses on the property as well: the Halfway House and Quail House (also known as "Q"), another tiny cottage set up the hill from the main house. It was behind Q, high on the hill, in a little clearing overlooking Crow's Pond, where we scattered my grandparents' ashes one warm summer morning in 1978, both Mimi and Grandpa dying of different cancers, just four months apart. She died first, and I guess he just couldn't live without her.

From my vantage point, I could see the circle of faded yellow lounge chairs, rusted and sand- and salt-encrusted patio furniture from the 1970s, the plastic woven straps fraying and stringy. I could never bear to get rid of those relics from my childhood, so they sat, old and tired on that bumpy brick patio.

An image came back to me suddenly and strongly: my mother lounging on one of those chairs, some forty years ago. Her cotton blue floral bathing suit faded and bleached from the sun and salty air, her skin ruddy and freckled, slippery with baby oil, and a plastic cup, wet with condensation, under her seat, partially hidden in the basket-weave shadows of the chair, the pale amber liquid just visible below the melting cubes. She was fast asleep, passed out from a cocktail hour that had started at breakfast. I was reading *The Secret Garden* at her feet when my grandfather walked past and stopped to stare down at her, in her oily, slick stupor.

"She'll wake up soon," I said, feeling a need to defend her. "She promised to take me clamming."

His hands gripped the coil of rope he was holding, his knuckles white and sharp. He looked sadly at me, then back at my mother and just shook his head and walked away. I will never forget the pained expression on his face.

It was later that summer, the one I turned twelve, when two important things happened. One, I realized my mother was a drunk. Not the kind who sat red-faced and bulbous-nosed, menacing and swollen at local bars, shouting at the Bruins games, although that would have been kind of fun. And not the kind who sat primly in the gleaming waxed mahogany bars of the city's elegant boutique hotels, sipping whiskey sours while enjoying some quartet playing nostalgic tunes. And not the kind who drank too much Suave Bolla at the dinner table, argued about the state of the Cold War and

Richard Nixon, and then went to work the next day smelling sweet and stale. No, my mother was just *out*. Listless. Slothful. *Torpid.*

She was the sort of alcoholic who drank vodka or scotch quietly all day long, every single day, out of a lovely plain crystal highball, right in her drapery-drawn bedroom. The highball had been handed down through generations of Brahmins before her who probably enjoyed their own sort of mind-numbing drinks. Mother smoked Salem mentholated cigarettes throughout the day, leaving her dry pink lipstick prints on the filters. Tiny crinkled piles of paper and plastic and tiny stubs of cigarettes smashed and broken in the glass saucer. It was a quiet, sad, tragic love affair, my mother and her refreshments. No yelling. No shouting. No friends. No revelers. Just her daily quiet decline into a fuzzy, muffled gray sort of place.

From what I could gather, my mother's drinking had begun when I was a baby, or it had worsened after my birth sometime. I always wondered if perhaps *I* was the disappointment that had set her on her course. The black-and-white photos of my mother before 1962 showed a woman smiling, laughing, in a group, with my father, with friends, on a sailboat, on the beach. They were married for nearly fourteen years before they had me. Mother never told me if she had miscarried or if they had simply waited to conceive or if they had never intended to have children. Maybe something she had hoped I would give her or bring her hadn't happened.

The other thing that happened that summer: my father left us.

He had met someone else. Her name was Rosie. She was blond, fiercely energetic, and sober. It was not lost on me that these were all the things my mother wasn't. They started their new life over together in a glassy condominium in Scottsdale, playing golf and tennis on the weekends and cloistering themselves from their disappointing past lives.

I guess Dad just hit the wall. Days and months and years of dealing with my mother must have felt like a never-ending loop of despair, disappointment, joylessness. Finally, after the exhausting task of enabling, fixing, cleaning up, and *carrying on*, he walked. I understood then and still do why he did it. I even understood his leaving her for someone else, but I never fully forgave him for leaving me behind. I couldn't see around his decision to leave a twelve-year-old in a house alone with a woman who couldn't get her own sorry ass out of bed except to replenish the scotch bottle under the nightstand, and the Salem cigarette cartons from the old, cracked walnut-and-gild dresser.

After Dad left, he tried to stay connected. I had to hand it to him; he really did. I guess maybe he felt bad about the way things turned out. He sent letters and birthday cards; I rarely read them. He left phone messages on holidays; I didn't always pick up. After I graduated from college and settled in Boston, I did see him nearly every June, when he came to town for an annual insurance conference. We would have awkward, stilted dinners at the Copley Hotel restaurant, or the Ritz's Tea Room, when he would update me on his and Rosie's activities, their shiny new friends, their trips to Palm Springs and Sarasota and Santa Barbara. He would ask me about my work, my friends, but he never once asked how I felt, or how I was coping, or how I got by. We had these summer dinners until Rosie called me one night, a few months after William and I got married, in 1989, to say her beloved Sully had cancer. He died four months later from a melanoma, received in part, from that new hot and sunny outdoor lifestyle he so enjoyed.

I shook my head as if to erase the memories and turned away, plowing swiftly though the thick sand, away from the house and the past.

Usually, during my morning walks, often in the early hours, the light was new and butter yellow. The shadows were long and the world sleepy and quiet, giving me the sensation that I was somehow ahead of something. Today, though, the sun was brighter, whiter than usual, and the glare was causing me to squint and intensified the slight pinching headache right behind my eyebrows.

My eyes were drawn to something glinting and winking from the sand. An empty bottle of Popov Vodka, its red square label bright against the sea grasses, the clear plastic sparkling, twinkling, promising. Could this be a remnant of Hazel's night? I picked up the bottle staring at it, my heart beating thickly in my throat.

Just seeing that bottle brought back another flurry of memories; I had spent my childhood searching for my mother's half-filled scotch and vodka bottles and emptying them down the kitchen sink drain in some stupid, wishful ritual. I wondered if I was to be picking up bottles after Hazel now. Maybe Hazel's burgeoning problems had brought my mother up in my mind, or maybe it was the thoughts of selling the house, but she had become a milky specter this summer, more present than she had been in many, many years.

There were some wonderful memories in this house, but some hard ones too. It occurred to me, a tiny fleeting thought, that maybe it wasn't an altogether bad thing that we were selling the house, but I still couldn't forgive William. I thought back to last fall, what I ruefully think now as the beginning of the end, when William began to work much longer hours. He was gone before I woke up, and he returned long after I went to bed. He was stressed, frazzled, and exhausted. I, of course, assumed the worst: an affair. Little did I know that that would have been preferable to the truth, which I eventually discovered when I demanded that once and for all he explain his months of distraction, moodiness, and absence.

We sat down at the kitchen table one night when Hazel was out. I had poured each of us a fortifying glass of wine, which I had a sense I would need. "William, we need to talk. I need to know what the hell is going on."

William was thin, and the gray circles under his eyes were darkening. He didn't look well. He held his wine glass between two hands and looked down.

"Are you having an affair?" I knew the answer. Of course he was.

He looked up at me and started to say something. "What—"

I interrupted. "Please don't lie. I don't know what else to think. You're never fucking home. You say you're working all the time, but I just don't buy it." My voice was rising in volume despite my vow to stay calm.

In our Back Bay brownstone, on that beautiful day, with the maple trees' new citron leaves outside our windows making the world aglow in a cheery spring light, he told me what he had done. I saw the words leaving his mouth as if in a dream, spilling out messy and muted, nonsensical and confusing.

He explained that his advertising agency, the one he started fifteen years prior, the one in his own name, the one bound to succeed and thrive, was in fact failing. Fast. In September, he lost his two biggest clients. He had let people go then. He had taken out business loans to pay bills, and he had been doing all of this for nine months. The decline continued, and he panicked. In an attempt to save the agency, he had put our Chatham house, *my* Chatham house, my beloved Crow's Nest up for collateral against a loan, solely for the purpose of saving his dying company. He had forged my signature on the loan. He didn't tell me because he was afraid. He was ashamed of his failure. He thought he could turn things around. Then by March it was clear that the influx of money hadn't worked to fix the problems. The company continued to lose revenue. There was another series of unfortunate client departures, a dip in the economy and some uncharacteristically poor business decisions by William himself, which had all resulted in the precipitous decline of his once-promising business.

The large loan he took out against the Crow's Nest was a short-term fix, which, of course, had not worked. And now, *we* were in debt and unable to pay for the taxes, upkeep, and bills related to the Crow's Nest, which were significant, and ever-increasing. And despite my constant requests for him to dump the company and go back to work at an established agency with a guaranteed salary, he was still working laboriously to save that quickly sinking ship.

In the aftermath of his confession, my extreme disappointment, my rage, his shame, our burgeoning fights over money and bills grew, until, as my father had done years before, William left. He had to. I wanted him to. I was so angry I could not and *would not* speak with him, let alone figure out how we could fix our marriage, if that was even possible. He packed a few bags and moved in with his brother and sister-in-law in Wellesley. Hazel was standing with me when he left, stone-faced and grim.

"Jesus, Mom. Really? You're making him go?" I started to respond to Hazel, but she ran after William and hugged him on the sidewalk. She yelled up at me, now standing on the front stoop. "Have you ever heard of forgiveness?" Forgiveness? After nine fucking months of lies and deceit and failure? No, no forgiveness. How else was I supposed to react? I was furious, and I had every reason to be. The things I loved best about him, his stability and reliability, were gone, and with them, my family's home.

And now, all summer, in myriad text messages and phone calls, he was begging me to forgive him, begging for me to move past this, begging for me to somehow forget what he had done and have us come back together as if nothing had happened. Well, something *had* happened, and I knew I would never forgive him. And even if I could, how could I ever trust him again?

About a mile and a half down the beach was an old wooden dilapidated rowboat with aged, chipped turquoise and orange paint on its hull. It was turned upside down about fifteen yards past the high tide mark. The name on the boat was barely visible: *Turnabout*.

I always thought that old boat was the perfect marker for the half-way point of my walk. I touched the boat and its old khaki fraying bowline, and then turned around from there. I looped back toward home, the sun higher, the sky hazier, the gulls now dropping clams on the shore, diving down to collect the gooey meat from the fractured shells. Sometimes, during this second half of my walk, I would feel peaceful and light, almost floating, but today, as I approached the house, I started to feel tight and constricted.

I looked up and saw Nancy Knight coming down onto the beach from her house. I didn't want to see anyone, least of all her, the town gossip. She held up a hand to stop me.

"Fessenden!" She was wearing an old bathing suit and one of those bathing caps with rubber flowers flopping all over it. I could see a little of her short, white hair peeking out from the edges. She had the rubber strap clipped under her chin—for security, I guess.

"Hi, Nancy," I said through gritted teeth as she came closer. She had tried very hard to be friends with my elegant, understated grandmother, but Mimi never cared for her; she felt Nancy was both a snoop and a social climber. "Going for your swim?" I asked.

"Yes, dear, I am. You know me! Have to have my morning swim! It's how I keep my girlish figure!" She chuckled to herself as she looked down at her bony body. She shielded her eyes from the glare and quickly changed her expression to one of deep concern. "Fessenden, dear, did I hear a terrible rumor about the Crow's Nest?"

Last night's spaghetti churned in my stomach. "Um, yeah. We are listing the house this fall." I looked down at the watermelon-pink nail polish on her crinkly brown toes.

She rested her spotted hand on my forearm. "Oh dear, oh dear. This is just a travesty. Such a shame, such a terrible shame."

"Yes, yes it is," I agreed. I wanted to leave this conversation immediately and get back home. I didn't need Nancy Knight reminding me how fucking sad it was to sell this place.

"I just can't imagine how your grandmother would feel. Oh, and your grandfather. My gracious, they adored this place."

Thanks a lot, Nancy, I thought. Thanks a fucking lot. I wanted to look right into her pale gray-blue eyes set in her deeply wrinkled, tanned WASP-y face and say, "Shut the fuck up, Nancy," but instead I breathed in deeply through my nose, exhaled loudly and said, "Yes, well, it's disappointing for all of us." This was taking an enormous amount of restraint.

She furrowed her brow as if struggling with her next thought. "And I hear it's due to some…financial troubles?" She said the last two words in a loud whisper. I would have laughed at the theatrics if I weren't so pissed off.

I narrowed my eyes, looked at her, shaking my head, and said, "Yep. You heard right." And then I couldn't stop. I thought about stopping, but I couldn't. I raised my voice and continued, "You know what, Nance? Here's the whole story: William *fucked* up at work so badly we have to sell this house just so we can continue to stay in the brownstone and pay Hazel's tuition and eat organic food instead of Costco crap, and then William moved out, which *totally* sucks but was totally necessary because of the fuckup and all, and we're struggling to stay afloat and the Volvo needs new tires and something's up with Hazel and I can't finish my fucking book and we're probably all going to die of shame and poverty." There. Yes. Done. That felt *really* good. I nodded my head for emphasis, turned on my heel, and left her standing there slack-jawed and silent.

Fueled by my righteous indignation, I marched past the main house and up to the Halfway House. It was clear Hazel hadn't stirred, and my fury at Nancy was redirected at my daughter, who should have been packing by now.

"*Hazel, wake up!*"

She rolled over slowly, sliding something under her pillow. "Fuck, Mom, relax. I'm up."

"We have to get out of here. We have to beat the traffic, and I have stuff to do in Boston, and there's so much to do here. Pack, pack, pack!"

"Calm down, Mom. Jesus, you're always panicking. Just relax."

"Haze, what did you just slide under your pillow?"

She looked squarely at me and let out a dramatic sigh. "My journal, Mom. Very private. We're supposed to keep a summer journal for English."

"Oh, OK," I said, relieved and sorry I had even asked. I didn't want to be the paranoid person I was becoming. "Do you need help packing?"

"Nope." Then she gave me an empty, blank look before she started furiously tapping at her phone keyboard. This change in her, this growing separation and worsening connection between us, made my heart ache. It physically hurt. I wanted so desperately to reach her, to connect somehow, to have even the smallest and most benign of interactions. When she turned her back to me, I stared at her spine, tiny lumps of stacked bone, and realized our small conversation was finished. I left her and her phone.

I went into the main house, the screen door slamming again, this time catching me on the heel with a painful jab. I let out an angry, "Ow," just as my phone buzzed loudly in my pocket. I expected to see William's name on the screen, which I would have put through to voice mail, but it was Richard Lowell, a dear old friend of my mother's and a family tax attorney who assisted me in all things legal, financial, tax-related, and especially Chatham-house-related. His father (Richard Lowell, senior) had been a great help to my grandparents in the same capacity.

"Hi, Richard," I said. "Just packing up and heading back to Boston today. How are you? I don't think we've spoken since April fifteenth. Sorry about that. Enjoying your Sunday?"

"Uh, yes I am. All is good. I'm fine," he said perfunctorily. There was a long pause and a deep exhale. "Listen, Fez, I need to

talk with you about something rather sensitive. It's really important. Any way you could meet me in my office…soon?"

"Um, OK. I have a few minutes to talk now." I assumed it was
about the house sale—William must have called him—and I wanted to get it over with. A tiny part of me even indulged a child-
ish fantasy that he was calling me with a solution that had been
worked out without me even knowing it.

"Actually, this one needs to be face-to-face," he said solemnly.

My stomach clenched. "All right…is tomorrow morning OK?
Hazel and I are closing up Chatham today, and I'm not sure I'll be
up for a meeting tonight."

He paused and took a deep breath. "Sure. Come by the office
around nine o'clock, and we'll talk."

"OK, see you then." I hung up, dropped the phone on the bed,
and threw myself into a frenzy, a whirlwind of frenetic cleaning,
sorting, and packing that wouldn't leave me time to contemplate
Richard's mysterious call, or the state of my marriage, or that this
was our last day in this house.

As I brought the last bags and supplies up to the car, I started
to move heavily, slowed by the surging wave of dread and sadness
that began to fill me and weigh me down. After I put the last duffel
bag in the back of my gray Volvo, and I looked back at the Crow's
Nest, the lovely little shingled Cape Cod house, I waved a little
wave. My eyes were hot and filling when Hazel came out of the
Halfway House with her two bags.

"This is it, Hazel. This is it," I said, the emotion stuck in my
throat.

"OK, Mom." Her voice was flat. I hoped she was more tired
than coldly uncaring. Usually, she was emotional about the end of
summer; now, she just looked bored.

I closed the latch of the tailgate, our sandy bags piled up, and
pulled away, Hazel slumped down next to me and was fast asleep
by the time we reached Route 6.

That night, in the stale and dusty air of our Boston brownstone, the pigeons cooing and rattling on the eaves, after Hazel and I dumped every bag from the car onto the floor by the front door, I collapsed in bed, physically and mentally exhausted, and I was quickly overtaken by an unsettling dream.

I stood on the top step of a steep wooden staircase, my bare feet small and far beneath me, my toes curled over the lip of the step. Ready to dive, I bent my knees, leaned forward, and launched off the step, taking off with my arms splayed like Superman.

I immediately soared out straight, then dipped down low to follow the angle of the staircase. At the bottom of the stairs, the front door smoothly opened for me by an unseen doorman, allowing in neon-yellow sunlight, so bright I had to squint, as I soared out through the doorway and up, higher and higher. I looked over at my arms, which were now covered with beautiful overlapping glossy blue-black feathers, my sharp black beak visible straight ahead as I cut through the air.

I flew high up over the house, circling above the gray shingled roof, then out back over the grassy rectangle of a backyard, the sandy, dark beige beach, the dock, the float, and dipped down toward the bay.

The water was dark blue, almost navy, but sparkling with thousands of bright diamonds, winking and blinking and dancing in the morning sun. I saw something in the water, right in the middle of the small bay. Something white, ethereal, and delicate. I circled lower and lower until I could see it clearly. It was a nightgown, white and lacy, the sheer tissue fabric beginning to rot. I flew down quickly, diving steeply, and I pinched the nightgown with my beak and pulled upward. But it was wrapped around something…a body, reed thin, warm, newly dead, pale blue as sky. Black eyes stared out of a narrow, wan face, her throat rotted and chewed, a hollow spot where her neck should have been. My mother. She looked right at me and started to speak, but all that came out was a gurgling sound and a rush of foaming, black, salty water from her pale lips.

# CHAPTER 2

# HAZEL

Tonight was gonna be epic. It had to be; it was the last night of the summer, a pretty shitty summer, actually. It was so boring down here on the Cape, but it was awesome when Ty and Bex came to chill, like tonight. I planned to go out with a bang before I had to go back to school, the dreaded junior year with all that homework, SATs, field hockey, my mom breathing down my neck. All the bullshit made me sick just thinking about it.

Ty and Bex were driving down from Boston; I'm pretty sure Ty doesn't even have his license yet. Not even his permit, I don't think. I haven't seen it anyway. But his parents are always traveling for work, so he can sneak out and use one of their cars practically whenever he wants. He doesn't give a shit about rules or all the stuff you're supposed to do. He just lives his life in his own way, and I love that about him.

Ty FaceTimed. "We're close."

"Cool," I said. I was looking at his face on my phone. He was in profile; I guess Bex was holding the phone. Then he looked right at me and blew out a perfect, solid ashy-gray smoke ring. He did his sexy smirk thing, and I was in awe of his effortless cool.

"Be there in like ten minutes, I think," he said.

Bex giggled and turned the phone on herself. Her face filled the screen—pale face, black eye shadow and thick liner, her trademark dark-red lipstick I could never in a million years pull off, even if my mom would let me. "See you soon, Hazy," Bex cooed, then dramatically air-kissed the phone. I wondered if they were already drunk.

"We're thirsty. You got everything, right?" Ty asked.

"Me too. And yeah, got just the thing." I tried to echo his cool, throaty voice, but it came out stupid. "Hey, did you remember the stuff?" I asked.

He glanced at the phone, then back at the road. "Wait, you finished the ones I gave you already?"

"Yeah, I shared a bunch," I lied.

"OK, yeah, I've got more here. Gotta go, see you soon," he said.

"Ciao!" Bex called out, and then she said something I couldn't hear, and they laughed before the screen went black.

We were gonna meet on the beach cuz I didn't want to deal with Mom's bullshit. She'd be all like, "Who are your nice friends?" And it's not like they were in a hurry to hang out with my mom, either. It was about a ten-minute walk, and I didn't want to keep them waiting, but I also decided I hated what I was wearing. I tried on three more outfits before finally deciding that an EDC black T-shirt and jeans was the hip-without-trying look I was going for. But now I was gonna be late. *Shit.*

One cool thing about our house on the Cape was that there was this sorta guesthouse, and that's where I stayed this summer. I begged my mom to let me have it all to myself. I told her I needed some space, and God, did I. But still I was surprised when she agreed. It was called the Halfway House cuz it was halfway into the driveway between Crow's Pond Road and the main house. I actually heard about kids going to halfway houses, and now that things were different for me, it was fucking hilarious to be staying in a place called the Halfway House. Mom didn't even get how fucking *ironic* or *fitting* or whatever the whole thing was. I don't think she even knew what a halfway house was. Anyway, it felt like my own place. It was up the hill and a little walk from the main house, so I got to have some privacy, which was good. *For once.* I barely had any privacy at home in Boston, which totally sucked.

I walked out of my little house and down the hill to the main house. I stood at the screen door at the kitchen and listened. I could hear the printer spewing out pages. No surprise there—Mom had been working nonstop on her book pretty much all summer. Not that I wanted her to be all up in my business, but I barely saw her. Meanwhile, back in May, she was all pumped about the "quality time" we were gonna have this summer. I guess because my dad didn't come this year, she thought we were gonna be all *Gilmore Girls*, but that's not how it turned out. Which was fine by me.

I pushed open the door really slowly so the springs didn't squeak. I had to stop pushing just before the end of the inside door-mat. Now I was in the kitchen, the door still in my hand. Slowly, slowly I closed it, letting it rest quietly on the frame. I stopped and listened again, my breath heavy in my ears. I heard her padded footsteps upstairs, the creaking of the old wooden floors, and that soft scuffing sound. Shit. Was she coming down the stairs? I held my breath and waited. No, she was walking across the room to the printer. Picking up pieces of paper from the printer tray. I could picture her in her faded blue bathrobe, sighing, cocking her head, shuffling the papers, biting her bottom lip, which she always did when she was thinking.

The dirty plate from her spaghetti dinner was on the counter, the tomato sauce dark red and hardening, the fork stuck to the plate, the remaining strands of pasta dry and brown. The silver pot on the stove had more spaghetti and red sauce in it. There was another clean plate on the counter. I guess I was supposed to come for dinner. I couldn't remember if she had specifically asked me, or if she had assumed I would just come down at some particular time. I don't remember talking about dinner. I wasn't hungry anyway, even though I couldn't remember when I last ate. *Breakfast?*

I went to the fridge, took out the carton of OJ, and dropped it into my backpack next to the large bottle of vodka I'd had hidden under my bed. I heard the comforting sound of sloshing. I opened the bag and added in three red Solo cups.

Turning around to go back out the screen door, I almost tripped over them. There on the floor, right next to the door, were Dad's leather flip-flops, side by side, still sandy from last summer. Like he was going to come right back and put them on and go down to the beach and go swimming. His fishing rod was leaning up against the corner too. Had these things been here all summer and I hadn't noticed till now? Why didn't Mom put these things away? Fucking reminders everywhere.

I opened the door really fast and almost forgot to catch it on the other side, remembering a split second before the loud clack would have ruined everything.

I could feel my heart pumping in my throat, thick and whooshing as I tiptoed though the narrow backyard, over the bumpy bricks of the back terrace, along the path, down the five wooden steps, right onto the beach, and over to the sandy spot where we met last time. Out of view from the main house and Mom's vision, if she even thought to look out the window. I smelled them before I saw them. Then there was the orange tip of the joint like a beacon. As I got closer, I could see Ty's beautiful face lit up behind it, his cheekbones high and pronounced. Bex was pulling her shirt straight—laughing at some joke between them. I fought the sinking sensation of feeling like a third wheel.

"Hey, happy last night of summer," Ty said to me, smiling. "I can't believe we have to go back to school next week...totally sucks." He passed the joint to Bex and laid out a blanket. She took a deep drag and looked up at the sky and slowly exhaled the pale-gray smoke. The blanket smelled like mothballs, attics, old people.

"I guess it's pretty obvious I stole this from my grandmother," Ty said, as if reading my mind.

"Yeah," I said. "It kinda smells like it." We all sat cross-legged on the scratchy wool blanket, facing one another. I took out the cups, the vodka, and the orange juice and made screwdrivers. I felt pretty cool making drinks for my friends. I was hosting this little gig, and they were there to be with me.

I took a few quick swallows from my cup, relieved that I had made them strong but not totally gross. I felt the familiar warm flush in my belly, which, for some reason always took me back to the first drink I ever had. It was only last year. I was a "good girl" until then; I never even snuck a sip from my dad's brews. Then last fall, I went to this senior party with my friend Janie because she really liked Malcolm, this kid from our school who was throwing it. He was really cool and hot too, so I didn't think we lowly sopho- mores were gonna get into his party. But we did. Mostly cuz Janie was totally gorgeous with her wavy blond hair and her big boobs, which she was totally showing off that night. I didn't want to go, and I felt pretty stupid being her wingman, but she talked me into going anyway.

We walked there from my house on Marlborough Street, and the cool fall air was starting to smell a little like smoke and dried leaves. Fireplaces were already going in Back Bay, and the leaves were starting to turn from orange and red to rust and brown. "I really don't want to go," I told Janie again, scuffing my ballet flats along the sidewalk.

"I know, Haze, I know. You've made that abundantly clear."

"I feel so stupid, and I'm gonna feel worse when they tell us to leave. We're such idiots." I felt nervous and dumb. "You totally owe me," I reminded her.

"I know. I do." But she wasn't really looking at me, and I don't think she felt she owed me anything. I knew I was just her prop. She started walking faster as she took her pink lip gloss and sponged it onto her pretty, pouty lips, then slid it back into the back pocket of her tight designer jeans.

I looked down at my old, scuffed shoes and dropped back a few paces behind her.

We arrived five minutes later at an imposing brownstone on Beacon Street with music thumping out of the open front door, kids spilling onto the front porch. I spotted Monica Jenkins, by far the most popular girl in the senior class. She threw her head back and laughed and then took a sip from a big plastic cup. I was sick with nerves.

"Shit," I said to Janie.

"Oh, be quiet, Hazel, and try to have some fun." We walked in together, pushing our way through the sweaty bodies. I lost Janie right as we entered the house. She got swept up by some group of kids I didn't even know, and I just stood there all nervous and awkward, my hands at my sides, watching her disappear.

Then Tyler Standish came up to me. He was in my class, but in a totally different group. He was in the stoner crowd. I guess they all got high on the lot behind school every afternoon. At least that was the rumor. He handed me a red Solo cup just like I had in my hand now.

"Uh, hey," I said. I sniffed the cup of warm beer and my stomach turned. "I don't really—"

"Just shut up and drink it," he said, smirking. "Or just hold it so you don't look like such a dork."

"OK, uh, yeah…I'm Hazel, by the way…"

"I know you're Hazel. Hazel Bradlee."

"Yeah." I couldn't believe he knew my name.

"I'm Ty." Duh. Everyone knew who Ty was and what he was: gorgeous and really, *really* wealthy.

He raised his cup and tapped mine, and I tipped back my cup and drank the whole thing. I don't know why, but I totally chugged it. Tyler looked impressed and went to get me another, and then another. After that, things got a little fuzzy, so I'm not exactly sure about the deets, but I had a total and complete blast. And not just cuz I was drinking. I was laughing and hanging out with all these totally cool people I didn't even know but who I thought were so *bad* before, and they seemed to really like me and give a shit about what I was saying.

About an hour after we got there, Janie found me. "This party stinks. C'mon, let's go."

"I think I'm gonna stay for a while," I said, taking a sip from my cup. She stared at me like she didn't get what I was saying. She looked at Tyler and the other people in our little conversation circle. Then she kinda snorted and turned around and left.

I knew she was pissed at me, but for once, I actually had a good time, and I didn't give a shit that I didn't leave with her. I know that sounds bad, but I actually had some kind of weird epiphany that night. It's like I started to realize what fun looked like, and plus I was so fucking sick of being whoever I had been before. Not to mention, for once, all that pressure and craziness of school and college prep and bullshit with my parents just started to melt away a little.

Janie would die if she knew how much Bex and Ty and I hung out this summer, but I pretty much don't see her anymore. She got really judgy about my new friends and some of our "activities." She actually used the word "activities." It's like a grandma word. Jesus. I told her I had enough parenting, thank you very much, and by Christmas, we were pretty much not friends anymore.

Tyler went to roll another joint. I watched him take out the Ziploc bag and tap out the weed into the rolling paper, cradled perfectly in his smooth, tanned fingers. His fingertips moved so fast. I shielded the wind with my cupped hand so nothing would blow away, and he smiled at me. Everything felt so good right now.

I watched him lick the paper with his pointy tongue and roll a perfect, smooth joint. I could tell he was getting a pretty good buzz on cuz he had this weird smile and he just looked so damn happy. Same here.

He put the joint in my mouth and lit it, and I inhaled deeply, feeling the thick smoke singe my lungs. I smirked at Ty as I held in the smoke then laughed as I exhaled. "Nice," he said. "Now me." We passed it around and around, until the tiny roach burned the tip of Bex's finger.

We started making plans for the fall. Asher, a kid from our class, was having a back-to-school party and his parents were "cool," meaning we could have drinks there. And we were gonna take road trips up to another kid's house in Concord, New Hampshire, and another kid's house in Pemaquid, Maine. We were gonna get outta town a bunch of weekends. *We* were psyched to be making plans. I was part of that *we*. That was awesome.

I remember pouring the last dregs of vodka into our cups. I remember Bex looking at the empty bottle and saying, "That sucks." I remember us all stripping off our clothes and swimming in the bay. It's all like cool snapshots in my mind: the moon shining on the water, Bex's thick bangs slick and plastered to her face, Tyler's lanky but strong arms pulling me into the cool, salty water.

After we dried off and got dressed, Tyler handed me a little plastic bag with the long, yellow tablets inside. "There you are," he said. "Go slow this time. You're freaking me out a little." Which was weird because he wasn't ever freaked out by anything.

"It's Xanax, not heroin, Ty," I said, rolling my eyes. I reached into my jeans pocket and handed him two twenties.

"You know there's four doses a pill? You know you're supposed to break them up...right?"

I loved that he was being protective.

"Yeah, Ty, obvi." I looked at him like he was a fucking idiot. The first time Ty gave me a Xanax, back in the spring, he said it was gonna turn everything quiet and sleepy, that it was like pot but so much better in a way. He was totally right.

He shrugged as I slipped the little plastic bag into my sweat-shirt pocket. I was already planning to take one as soon as I woke up in the morning. It would at least make packing up the house and the drive back to Boston bearable.

The last thing I remember is the sky turning a light lavender and then getting up to walk up the hill to my little house, my Halfway House. I must have stumbled when I was walking away because I think I heard Ty say, "You OK, Haze?" and I think I said, "Fuck yeah. Never better." And we all cracked up. I'm pretty sure I laughed the whole way up to my bed because I was so fucking happy. Maybe it was an OK summer after all. Maybe the school year would be OK. Maybe it would all be OK. I was just so fucking happy.

# CHAPTER 3

# PENELOPE

I woked up at six on Friday, August 23, when the yellow chicken next to my bed made the funny chicken sounds. *Cockadoodleedoo* was what the funny chicken said in the morning times. And it was good the chicken maked the sounds cuz I'd sleep long, long times and miss getting to my job at the hostipal. My slippers were right next to my bed on the carpet. Two fuzzy slippers. Side by side but not touching, just how I like. I slid my feets right into them like every morning, and I sat up and tried to make my head straight cuz it was always sleepy and foggy in the morning times. And then I walked down the hall past Dottie's bedroom and into the pink-and-white bathroom where I keeped my pink toothbrush in the pink plastic toothbrush holder. Dottie's toothbrush was green. Like a lime, not like an olive.

I put on the sparkedly blue toothpaste in a little line, not a big line like I used to do before Dottie taught me not to make a big line of toothpaste, and I brushed my teeth til the foam came out of my mouth and dribbled down my chin into the sink. Then I spat it out of my mouth—*piew, piew*—and slurped the water in the little paper cup from the wall and then spat that out too. Dottie said it's not good to swallow toothpaste cuz you could get sick.

After I brushed my teeths, I turned the water to the middle part so it's both hot and cold at the same time, and I put the smallest cloth in the water and squeezed out the water so it's not too much, and then I wiped all the sleepies off my face. Then I dried off my face with the middle-size towel and went into my bedroom and looked at my clothes for the week. Dottie helped me with my clothes every week so everything was matching. Dottie called it a theme.

This week's theme was red, white, and blue. Last night, she painted my fingernails with a shiny, shiny red polish to match the theme. Today's clothes was navy-blue slax and a red-and-white-flowered top and white sneakers made by a company called Candies, but they were not anything like candy. All the underpants and bruzeers were white, and so that was easy. I hung my pajamas on the pajamas hook and put on the white underpants and white bruzeer and then pulled up my blue, stretchy slax with elastic at the tummy and then the big flowered shirt with the teeny tiny buttons, and I put on my white socks and my white shoes, and I brushed my hair, which is yellow, and I made my bed all tight and right. That's what the peoples at the hostipal where I works call it: *tight and right.* No wrinkles. All the sheets were straight and neat and tucked in real good. I was so good at *tight and right.* And then I walked out of my room to go see my bestest friend and roommate, Dottie, for breakfuss.

Here was something so essiting I was thinking about: Dottie's birthday was coming up. In twenty-five days, she was going to be sixty-one years old. I was sixty-four years old. We loved our birthdays so, so much cuz birthdays are the bestest days of the years. And I was thinking and thinking about what to do for Dottie's birthday, which was such a fun, fun thing to think about, and it gots me to thinking about all the birthdays we had together, which is thirty. Thirty birthdays together. My birthday is extra special because it's also Christmas. I was born on December 25, 1949, at

3:47 p.m. A special girl born on a special day. That's what all the peoples say: *Penny is a special girl.* And Dottie is special like me.

I may be *special*, but I is also *smart* too, not about all the things but about some things like when I was little and I saw that I was getting Christmas presents and birthday presents together on the same day, and I asked my mommy if I would get *more* presents if my birthday and Christmas was on two different days, and my mommy said, *Well, yes, Penny, I think you might get more presents if your birthday and Christmas were on two different days,* so I switched my birthday right then, and my mommy said, *OK.* I liked the 25 part, but I didn't like the December part, and so I picked May 25 cuz I liked May, and that's when everything is warm and smells like flowers and grass and ice cream. So that's what I picked for my birthday.

When I was all done in the bathroom with my bathroom chores, I came out into the kitchen room. Dottie was already up and making breakfuss. Sometimes I has to wakes her up, and sometimes she just gotted up by herself. Today she gotted up by herself. She was better than me at breakfuss stuff. Like a few times I dropped a bowl and it broked on the floor; and sometimes I dropped a spoon on the hard, hard floor and it made a big clatter; and sometimes I poured too, too much Lucky Charms into the bowls and Dottie would say, *Penny, that's too much Chahms.* And I don't even want to talk about the juice pouring. That was not so good. Very splashy and sticky. Dottie was just better at breakfuss, and so she did it for both of us. I was better at beds, but Dottie was better at breakfuss.

Dottie was walking real slow over to the kitchen table with two plastic cups of apple juice. She started putting my juice in a cup with a top and a straw cuz I was kinda spilly with my drinking. Her cup was plastic too but didn't have a top or a straw.

*Dottie,* I said.

*Yuh,* she said cuz she didn't talk so good sometimes.

*I's gonna surprise yous for your birthday. OK?*

*K,* Dottie said cuz she said things real quick.

*It's gonna be a big surprise, Dottie, and you're gonna love it!* And then I said, *Want me to tell you the surprise, Dottie?*

And Dottie got so essited then. She shook her head real fast and said, *No, no, no tell!* And then she kinda grunted funny.

So I didn't tell Dottie nuthin about her birthday surprise. She was just gonna have to wait. That made me feel happy inside. Like yellow sunshine in my belly.

We ate our Lucky Charms for breakfuss. The TV used to say they was magically delicious, but now the TV said they marshmallowy delicious. So that was a new, new thing. New things are hard. Maybe them charms weren't so magic anymore. But in the TV, the kids always were chasing the magic green boy with the green hat and the funny talk, and they always gots his box of Lucky Charms. Them kids was lucky too. Like Dottie and me. Cuz we got to eat the cereal too, and if we didn't eat so fast, the milk turned pretty colors from the magic marshmallows, and I liked that.

After we cleaned up our two bowls and our two spoons and our two cups and my top and my straw, we threw away the paper nakkins. They was my favorite nakkins cuz they was white with yellow flowers, and yellow is my favorite color. After cleanup time, we had to go down to the bus stop. First Dottie went to the bathroom and flushed her business and washed her hands and dried them, and then she got her white purse by the door. I just waited at the door cuz my chores was all done. *You ready for the bus, Dottie?* I asked.

*Yeh,* she said and looked down at her shiny white purse with the silver snaps while I opened the door. Dottie taked the bus to her job in the factery. She did something with dog food cans. I don't member everything, but there was a lot of cans in her job. She been doon it for a lot of years. I been doon my job for a lot of years too.

I wasn't aposta to drive a car because of my special-ness. So I took the P-97 bus. I had a job, and the peoples was very nice to me at my job. I worked in the Marion Kent Hospital in Marion,

Massachusetts, 02738, on 1500 General Carver Boulevard, and I did important things. I was a *candy striper*. There was stripes, but there wasn't no candy. That's just what the peoples called it. Every morning, I woked up, and I made my bed very tight. Then I woked up my bestest friend and roommate, Dorothy, and told her to make her bed really tight, but she don't make her bed as good as I do. Sometimes I told her, *Dottie, go make your bed really tight like I do it*, and she gots cranky and shaked her head real fast and funny. Sometimes I just looked at her messy bed and shaked my head real funny and don't say nothing. I maked my bed much, much better than Dottie do it.

We both walked to the bus stop, which was 127 steps from the front door of our building. It was a bright, sunny day, and Dottie's little white hairs was fluttering in the breeze.

*You gonna have a nice day at work, Dottie?* I took hold of her hand. It was small and cool.

*Yeh, I is*, she said. *You?*

*Yeah, Dottie, I is too.* She was kinda squinting into the sun. She squeezed my hand real strong when she saw the bus coming.

*Here's the bus, Penny.*

*Yep, here's the bus, Dottie.*

We both tooked the same P-97 bus to work, but Dottie's stop was before my stop, and the driver, Betty, was real nice and waited to be sure Dottie was going the right way before she drived away. I waved bye-bye to Dottie and gave her a big happy smile, but I always got real sad when the bus drived away and I saw Dottie kinda bent over holding her big bag and walkin to the factery. I felt like I was hungry, but it was not in my stomach but kinda in my neck. I didn't like when Dottie went to the factery, but in seven stops I got off the bus and goed to the Marion Kent Hospital on 1500 General Carver Boulevard, and everybody was real nice to me and said, *Hello, Penny,* and *How are you, Penny?* and *Did you have your Lucky Charms, Penny?* and things like that. I had a hook with my name,

Penny, on it, and I put my sweater or my heavy coat or my shiny raincoat on it and put on my apron, and it was really pretty stripes like red and pink and white, like a candy cane at Christmastime. I liked when my fingernails had colors on them like my apron.

I went to go to get the bedsheets. Marsha—she's a nurse, and kinda the boss to me—said, *Penny, do you remember where to get the sheets?*

*Yes,* I said, *in the linen closet,* and she smiled with her head kinda crookedy. Anyway, the door said Linen Closet right on it in case I forgotted where the sheets were. I can read. Maybe the peoples forgot that I can read. I had my own silver, shiny cart with wheels, and I put the sheets in the cart, and I looked at my chart on my own clipboard that said Penny on it, and I went to the rooms that had numbers written down on my piece of paper. I remembered where the rooms were. They had numbers, and everyone said I was really smart with numbers. It's true I am. If you told me your birthday and time of your birthday and your day and month and year, I would remember forever. I would never forget. *Marsha,* I said, *your birthday is January 12.*

*My, my, my, Penny, you are correct,* she said real loud and essited. *You certainly have the memory of an elephant!* She looked pretty happy about my memory, but I didn't feel so great about the elephant thing. I looked at her. She looked kinda confused and started to say something about elephants having really good memories, and then she said, *Never mind, it's a good thing, though.* Whatever, Marsha. I didn't want nothin to do with your big old elephants.

I was taking my cart of sheets to make the beds in A-17, A-18, and A-19. Sometimes the cart had a squeaky wheel but not today. This cart was quiet. There was a new nurse working today. Her name was Shannon. I didn't like her too good. She had skin the color of peaches. I don't like peaches. I didn't not like her cuz she had the skin the color of peaches; I didn't like her cuz she whispered about me when I walked by. And I gots good, good hearing.

Real good. When I walked by, I heard her say to Alice, who was another nurse, *She's the special needs one, right? How does she even know what to do?* Then she said something about *dumb as aboxarox.* I don't know nothing about *aboxarox,* but I know alls about dumb, and that's not good, and it's mean, and when she said that thing to her new friend, Alice, they was looking square at me and laughin and laughin, but then they looked away and was actin like they wasn't laughin at me. *Don't crash that special cart, rox,* Shannon said all quiet and mean to Alice. Like *rox* was my name or something. And like I couldn't hear or nuthin. I don't like no one doon no whispering. It's rood. You don't need to be whispering nothing about me. I knows I's special. I knows it for a while.

A long, long time ago, when I was a little, little girl, I membered Mommy and Daddy telling me that I had to go to a special school far, far away cuz I was special and had special knees. I member feeling so, so scared and not wanting to go and Daddy saying, *Yes, Penny, it's good for you, and they can meet your special knees at this school.* I started patting my knees, and I asked him about my special knees, and he said, *No, sweetheart, not your knees, your special* needs, and I liked having special knees better than special needs, so I stopped listening so good. But I felt so sad cuz Daddy was all pink in his head and crying so hard with his eyes all wet, and Mommy was kinda quiet and said no things and just stared out the window while Daddy did all the talking about all the special things. Mommy just looked at me all broken and like she was asleep with her brown eyes kinda open, though. And I felt real scared inside, and I could tell Daddy and Mommy was all scared inside. And then the next morning when I woked up, my daddy and me packed up a pink suitcase filled with my clothes and my pajamas cuz I was gonna be sleeping at the special school, and it was far, far away, so I wouldn't be home a lot, and I had to pack my little sparkly toothbrush with the fairy on it, and I didn't need no soap cuz the special school had soap. I brought my stuffed bunny rabbit and my doll Dolly and my blankie with the soft stripe at the top, and Daddy zippered the top up of my little purple bag, and he helped me carry it down even though I was a big girl even then. I had to wear my plaid coat cuz it was cold. It was October 13, 1954. I was four.

Mommy wasn't anywhere when Daddy and I left, but when I got into the back seat of the car, with the shiny, slippery red seats, and I looked up at our house to wave bye-bye to Mommy and I saw her all bent over on the upstairs window, she didn't wave or nothing. She just stood there with her hand on her mouth like she was surprised, but I don't think she was so surprised. She looked like she was really scared and sad at the same time.

After we drove a long time and I fell asleep on my blankie with my fingers in my mouth, Daddy woke me up and said we were at the special school, and an old lady in a flowery dress came and smiled real nice at Daddy and gave me a scrunched-up smile and kinda grabbed my hand hard and said, *OK now, Penelope, let's say bye-bye to Daddy,* and then I got real scared real fast, and I didn't want to go with the scary lady in the flowery dress with the thin lips and the lines on her face. I didn't mean to do it, but right there I threw up all my toast and juice right on the lady's black shoes and the ground and the grass and the dead leaves and all over the place.

Daddy rubbed my back and said, *Oh, Penny,* and he looked kinda sick too, but he just rubbed my back.

Then the scary lady said, *Mister Wright, I think the best thing in these situations is just to leave rather quickly with a fast goodbye, and you'll see it's really best for the child.*

Daddy didn't look so sure about all that, but he nodded kinda quiet and patted my back and said, *OK, OK,* and he kissed my forehead. Cuz of the throw-up on me and my dress, he couldn't hug me cuz he woulda got it on him too, and he just got into the car and drove away. And that's when I went to my special school. I member that day real, real good.

I went to a whole bunch of different special schools. Some bad things happened and some scary things, and when those things happened, I went to different places. At the first place I ever went to with the mean lady, there was too many kids there; and too many little peoples were sleeping in the same rooms; and everyone was crying and hollering and had green stuff coming out of their noses; and nobody never showed up so much; and the babysitter peoples was so cranky; and I gots real sick one time and no one even knowed I had a high, high fever; and one time Daddy came to visit me on my seventh birthday, May 25, 1957, and my diaper pants had been on so long I had a really bad rash in my privates; and that wasn't so good and we was all so sad. Daddy said to the same scrunchy-faced lady really, really loud, *I am* ab-so-loot-lee *appalled at the conditions here.* The scary lady just stared at my father and was making her mouth into a tiny circle and trying to say something back, and Daddy said, *To think, we trusted you with the care of our Penelope!* He was all red in his face with madness. Boy, was Daddy mad on that day, and I was glad he was mad cuz I hurted from my bad, bad bottom rash.

Then, my daddy moved me to another place where nuns worked in Passcoke, Road High Land. I member there was lots of nuns in long black robes and white stripes at the top where their necks was, and that place wasn't so good cuz they used rulers to remind us not to do stuff, and my hands was always red and sore cuz of all the ruler slapping and on accounta my being a little bit sassy. That's what the nuns said: *Penny, you're sassy. Penny, you're fresh. Penny you're* im-pew-dint. Slap, slap, slap, slap, slap. My daddy didn't like the rulers there, and so then when I was thirteen years old, I went to another place that was OK, but then the place couldn't stay open no more cuz there was no moneys from the state, and then when I was almost twenty-one, Daddy tooked me to a brand new place called Community Workshop Living Center, where we met Paul and, of course, I met my bestest friend, Dottie.

I member the day I met Dottie. It was January 8, 1971, when I went to the Community Workshop Living Center in Marion, Massachusetts, 02738. First thing I did was ask her when she was borned. She said, *September 17, 1954.* She was really funny and liked cheese fondue and talked really, really fast. And she had size 4 1/2 shoes, and she was tiny like a doll, but she wasn't a doll. She was real.

Turns out my daddy didn't come to see me no more cuz he stopped living with my mommy, and he moved to a house in the desert far away by a airplane, and he lived with a lady named Rosie who sure liked keeping Daddy close by. I think she got ascared when Daddy wasn't with her or somethin. He sent letters sometimes and pictures of their white puppy, Crystal, and him and Rosie and even a big picture of a cactus out their window called a saguaro. The picture made me sad cuz the sky was kinda dark and the saguaro looked like a prickly man shouting with his hands up but no head, and that made me sad. When Daddy said he wasn't gonna be visiting so much now that I was all settled and since he was so far away in the desert with the pointy, screaming plants, my tummy went all flippy floppy, and I felt kinda sick like when I was a little throw-up girl.

Anyway, Dottie and I was bestest friends right away, and when we graduated from the Community Workshop Living Center on July 1, 1985, to live in our own growed-up apartment, Dottie and I wanted to live together cuz we was best friends and practickly sisters. The nice man Paul from the Community Workshop Living Center helped us get started, but we did a really, really good job getting moved into our place, and then he helped us so we both got jobs...Dottie at the factery and me at the hostipal. So Paul said we was success stories of Community Living Workshop Center, and he was really proud to us.

I looked at my pretty sparkedly watch, and it said 3:57, and I had to work until 5:00, and I was done with my jobs at the hostipal, but I wasn't aposta leave until my watch said 5:00. I really, really missed Dottie, and I wanted to go home and see Dottie and have supper and watch TV. But I had to stay and keep pushing my cart around and asking the nurses if they needed anything. So I walked over to the nurses' station and saw Marsha sitting behind the desk.

*Marsha, you got more for me? I finished my chores.* I just wanted her to say I could go home and see Dottie.

*Did you make all the beds up in those discharged patients' rooms?*

*Yup,* I said, *all the A-rooms is done.*

*Did you tidy up the linens closet?*

*Yup. I refolded the sheets on that one shelf you asked me to do.*

*Did you put those towels from A-23 in the laundry room?*

*Yup.* I was getting tired of saying yup.

Marsha looked down at her clipboard and said, *Well, then, I think you can probably go. You were especially fast today!*

Right then, the new nurse Shannon and her new nurse friend, Alice, came down the hallway real slow. Walking with their hips going back and forth. Shannon just looked at me and made a funny face, like she knew more than me. Which she didn't.

*Whatchu lookin at, Shannon? I ain't special, and I's mad to you for talkin sass to me.* I was so mad to her.

*What are you talking about? I ain't doing nothing, Penny. You just overheard nothing.* Her arms were crossed in front of her big round boobs. She was smiling mean.

Marsha made squinty eyes and said to Shannon, *That's enough. That's enough.* Then she looked at me. *Don't you worry about a thing, Penny, OK?*

I looked right at Shannon when I answered Marsha, *I ain't worried about nothin.*

The only thing I was worried about was getting home and seeing Dottie and watching our TV.

Dottie and I did everything together essept work cuz our works was different. And we always did the same things and spent all our times together, and I think if we didn't have each other, we'd be so sad. I just started rocking if I missed her too much in one single day.

I took the P-97 home and was home for one hour and seventeen minutes before Dottie came home. As soon as I heard her key inside the door, I ran to the door to open it. Usually I could open the door before she could get her key to work. Sometimes it took her a few minutes to get the door to open. I think her key got stucked a little bit. Sometimes her pretty blue glasses slipped off her nose when she was looking down at the key. That coulda been the problem too.

I had put some saltine crackers and American cheese slices on a paper plate for us to snack on. She loved cheese so much. *How was work, Dottie?*

*Good*, she said. She looked tired. Her eyes were kinda droopy, and she walked real slow to the sofa and sat down all heavy. *I's tie-tie. My head smahts.*

*I's tie-tie too, Dottie. I sorry to your head hurting. Shannon is the worstest person ever, and I ain't never gonna speak to her again*, I said.

Dottie reached over to the coffee table and ripped a slice of American cheese into four perfect squares. She carefully put one square on top of a saltine. *Who Shannon? Why she worstest?* She put the whole cracker in her mouth, and it made her cheek come out all pointy.

*Cuz she said I was all special needs and dumb and somethin about aboxarox, and then she was actin all cool with Alice, and I ain't special needs. I's special. We's special, but we ain't got no needs. Right, Dottie?*

She slowly wiped a saltine crumb off of the corner of her mouth. *Dat's right, Penny. You's the specialest. Ever.* Her mouth was full of cracker, and she blew out some crumb dusts when she was talking.

*You too, Dottie. We's lucky.* And we is.

I turned on the TV for Dottie and me. We was gonna watch *Three's Company,* which is this really funny show about a funny guy and his two roommates and their silly, silly landlord who is skinny and has big teeth and his wife who wears long flowing flowery robes. One of the roommates has yellow hair and one has brown hair. I liked the yellow girl. The show is the funniest show, and there's laughing in the show, so we know it's really funny cuz of the other people laughing on the TV. Then the bestest thing happened! We saw on the TV my *favorite* commercial about a place called *BeautifulBoston.* That's what the TV said. *BeautifulBoston* in a pretty kind of loopy writing, and there was pictures of a green, green grass park and boats shaped like pretty swans and tall buildings made of mirrors and bright-blue skies with puffy, white clouds.

The first time I saw the commercial for *BeautifulBoston,* exactly twenty-three days ago, I got so essited because then I knew exactly what I wanted to do for Dottie for her birthday. As soon as I saw the commercial, I thought to myself, BeautifulBoston *sure looks pretty, and what if we visited Boston with those boats shaped like swans and the green, green grass and the white clouds in the bright-blue sky?*

I musta gotten all squirmy in my seat cuz Dottie said, *Why you so essited, Penny?*

I said, *Nothin, Dottie,* but that was a fib cuz now I knew what was going to happen for Dottie's birthday, and we was gonna do it together, and nobody was gonna say we couldn't.

But before I got even more essited, I had to ask Richard, who is this nice man who works right *in BeautifulBoston* who kinda takes care of all the moneys. When my mommy died, she gave me moneys, but I can't has it without Richard saying, *OK, you can has it.* He was a friend to my mommy and her mommy and daddy, and he helped them with their moneys and tackses. I always had to check with Richard if I was going somewhere or if I needed moneys to do something. He checked in on us too and made sure I was membering how to send checks to the places for the things we bought, like TV time and heating and lights and foods.

I always said, *Richard, member how I'm so good at numbers?*

And he said, *Yes, Penelope, I remember.*

So I took the phone and sneaked out of the TV room and into my bedroom and shut the door so Dottie wouldn't hear nothing, and I called Richard's number, which was in my mind cuz I am so good at membering numbers, and I dialed 16175551369, and I told Richard all about the TV show about *BeautifulBoston* and the pictures and all the swans and the boats and the grass and how me and Dottie wanted to take a trip to the building made of blue mirrors cuz it was so clean and sparkly.

And Richard said, *Well, Penny, it all sounds pretty exciting,* and he said it in a kinda growed-up way like I'm really little, which *I am not.* Then Richard paused and took a long breath and a sip of something, and he said, *Penny, I feel that you and Dottie taking a visit to Boston* (I told him it is *BeautifulBoston*) *is not such a great idea. It's a big city, and if you want I can come pick you up and escort you all around Boston, but I can't do it for a little while because my work is very busy right now.* When Richard stopped talking, I felt so, so mad. I felt like I wanted to throw something and scream and kick and punch a hole in my yellow, yellow wall. I'm not a baby. I didn't like that he thought he was the boss to me. I didn't like that one bit. *I am not a baby.* I bet my mommy or daddy would have let me go to *BeautifulBoston,* but my mommy was dead, and my daddy was dead too. So I had to listen to stupidhead Richard, and it made me feel hot and mad inside.

Sometimes it didn't bother me that I was special. Dottie and I just went about our days. We made our breakfuss, we went on the bus, we ate boloney sandwiches on Wonder Bread with yellow and red and blue polka dots on the plastic bag. We made swiggly lines on our baloney with yellow squeezy mustard. We took the bus home. We made dinner in the hot, hot microwave, and we never put something shiny in the microwave or the microwave would essplode. We knowed how to send checks to all the peoples. We were doing goodly. I didn't like to think of Richard thinking about me like a teeny tiny baby and making me feel little. I was a big growed-up lady, and so was Dottie. So when Richard said his a lot of words, I just listened real quiet. I was chewing a saltine cracker, and then I started chewing real slow, and then I said, *OK, Richard.* That's all I said cuz I knew it didn't matter what I said cuz I was special. It didn't matter. So I just said, *OK, Richard,* and I hung up the phone.

Dottie said, *Penny, was that Richard?*

And I said, *Yeah, but I's mad to him, and he ain't the boss to me.* I was mad, and I was talking in a mad, mad way. The cheese and crackers was all gone now, so Dottie went to get a bag of potato chips out of the cupboard.

She sat down next to me and opened the crinkly bag. I looked at her real slow and quiet, and she said, *Oh, you's mad to Richard?* She reached her little fingers into the bag of Ruffles-have-ridges potato chips and started chewing some potato chips. Just like me. Kinda slow.

*Yes, I is,* I said to Dottie, but then I had to stop talking cuz of the surprise and all.

So after Richard said no and he was too busy to *escort* us, I got to thinking about Shannon and all the whisperers, and I didn't want no more peoples talking *about me behind my back.* That maked me so, so mad I could scream and throw things and break things. So I decided something: No more Richard. No more *talking* and special decisions. *No, no, no, no, no.* I wanted to go to *BeautifulBoston,* and I didn't want *nobody* to tell me I couldn't do it. So on this day, I said to Dottie, *Dottie, that's it. It's jus you and me and no more everybody else.*

Dottie just kinda looked up at me real slow, chewing those Ruffles-have-ridges, and said, *OK, Penny,* and that was that. *We were going to visit* BeautifulBoston. *No matter what.*

And when I made that decision, I was so essited. And kinda like there were little critters crawling around in my tummy. Little mice and cute little critters squiggling really fast. And I was gonna make a big plan for Dottie and me to go to *BeautifulBoston,* and I was gonna surprise Dottie for her birthday when I had it figgered out. I got kinda scared too cuz I don't know why. I jus did.

So I sat on the couch and did my rocking cuz it always maked me feel real quiet and happy inside, and all the special teachers at my special schools always said if there's something that made you feel quiet and happy, you should go ahead and do it, so I did it. I rocked for a while thinking about the blue, blue sky and white, puffy clouds in *BeautifulBoston.* Then I saw that Dottie had falled asleep in her chair with the blanket folded on the back, and so I shooked her real gently like she might break if I did it any harder. She was real, real sleepy now, and didn't walk so good anymore, and sometimes she'd say, *Penny, I gots to sit. My head smahts.* Poor Dottie had her head smarting all the times now.

I said, *Dottie, it's bedtimes,* and so she wiped the water off her chin, and she checked the locks on the door, and I turned off the lights and folded the blankets on the couch and turned off the TV that was kinda loud, and Dottie went into her room real slow and wavy, and I went into my room and put on my flowered pajamas. Tomorrow I was gonna figger out our *BeautifulBoston* plan, and I was gonna surprise Dottie. For her birthday.

I climbed into bed and put all the covers right up under my chin, and I stretched out my toes way to the bottom of the bed, and I said through the walls, *Nigh nigh, Dottie.*

And she said, *Nigh nigh, Penny,* real quiet and sleepy, and I turned off the light next to my bed.

The last thing I did cuz it made me feel so happy and special inside was unwrap one gold plastic wrapper from the Werthers Original Candy Like Grandma Used To Make; and I put it right in the middle of my tongue; and I fell asleep with the sugary, buttery candy making me feel good insides. I had always done it as long as I could member, and I knew that soon I would have to get plastic teeth cuz the dentist who I do not like at all said so. He said, *Penny, you must not sleep with candy*, but I'm not gonna listen to him no more. And I'm not listening to Shannon. And I'm not gonna listen to mean, mean Richard no more cuz he said no, and he wasn't the boss to me, and he made me feel like a tiny baby, and I's *not* a tiny baby. I's a big growed-up lady.

# CHAPTER 4

# FESSENDEN

I was racing around the kitchen trying to get ready for my meeting with Richard, looking for my wallet, my handbag, and any non-flip-flop footwear. I was already late, and I had a twenty-minute walk ahead of me. Nothing was where it should have been; everything was in a damp heap on the living room floor where I dumped it after returning from Chatham yesterday afternoon. I came in the door, dragging the bags and dumping them all about six feet from the front door. I had to wear flip-flops because it's all I could find and going upstairs to find real shoes was not going to happen. I headed out and was starting to sweat profusely as I was locking the door. It was hot and sunny. As I turned to go down the front steps, my cell phone buzzed in my bag, and I saw it was Ellie.

"Hi, El!"

"Happy Monday! What, are you at the gym or something? Why are you breathless? It's nine twenty, for God's sake! Are you back? Please tell me you're back. I am *beyond* sick of these faraway, long-distance summers. Those few weekend visits were not enough." She had a way of starting conversations very enthusiastically in a jumble of thoughts and questions.

I laughed. "I'm back. I'm definitely not *exercising*, but I am racing over to the accountants to meet with Richard about some mystery thing." I was race-walking now and breathing heavily. I felt the sweat dripping down my back. I could feel it pooling just above my waist of my pants. My underarms had already sweated through the dress shirt I was wearing. I think I had forgotten to put on deodorant too. Damn. I really had to get my shit together.

"Ooh, good, I love mysteries."

"Me too. We'll talk about it later. When are we getting together? We have *so much* to catch up on."

"I know. A lot."

"What's new with William? Was it weird being in Chatham without him?"

"It *was* weird, actually. He kept sending texts apologizing and wanting to help, but whatever. The damage is done. He doesn't just get to have everything be OK just because he feels shitty."

"I know, Fez, but I think he does feel really bad. It's so out of context for him to have done that. I'm sure he's genuinely sorry. Are you going to see him at the meeting this morning?"

"Nope. Richard just said he wanted to talk with me, which means it doesn't concern income, money, or taxes. Which makes it an even bigger mystery."

"Yes it does! And how is my gorgeous goddaughter?"

I sighed. "I think we need to talk about that too. I'm not quite sure what's going on with her. She's seems different."

"How? Did she go out a lot this summer? Like with her summer friends?"

"Yes, but I don't think she's hanging with the same crowd. There's a couple of new friends, I think."

"Hmm...Could just be she's entered the ol' tunnel of adolescence. Could be something else."

"I know. This summer was weird and sad, for a million obvious reasons. And I want to talk about it more, but I really have to go.

I'm sweating and gross, and I'm almost at the office. I want to try to cool down before I meet with him."

"Good thinking. Call me when you get back home. I'm *so* coming over."

"OK. I will. Love you. El."

"Love you too. Fez."

⇒⟨—⟩⇐

Richard's office was in a blue glass tower in the heart of Boston's financial district. After submitting my license and posing for a photographic identity badge, I entered the polished chrome elevator bank and was whisked up to the fifty-third floor. It had been years since I had been here; Richard had been meeting with us at our house lately. I felt like I was seeing this office building for the first time.

Juxtaposed with the building's gleaming modern exterior, Lowell & Lowell's offices were traditionally appointed: walnut-paneling throughout the foyer and the waiting room. The office chairs were dark-brown leather with decorative brass nailheads. Persian carpets in dark reds and royal blues were scattered throughout the space. The air was chilled and whisper-quiet. The receptionist, Darlene Capell, whose name was in a brass block upon her high-fronted desk, was a pointy-featured vole with dark-brown eyes. She was dressed in a pale-gray suit and cream-colored blouse with a large bow at the throat. Large pearls at the lobes, burgundy red lipstick. It was immediately apparent by her icy demeanor and blank stare that she was joyless. In my quietest voice, I whispered that I had a meeting with Richard at around nine o'clock.

She looked up at the wall clock behind me. "It is nine forty-three."

"Yes, I know. I'm sorry. I was running a little late this morning," I said, feeling like a chagrined schoolgirl.

"Well, have a seat." She pulled the sides of her lips up into a forced smile as she dismissed me.

I used tissues from the sitting area to try to absorb some of the sweat, which was still rolling down my face and neck. As I had suspected, my shirt had sweated through in several areas and the light, cool color of the fabric only highlighted the discoloration. Darlene sporadically looked at me with derision as I swabbed. Within a few minutes, Richard came out into the waiting room to receive me. He hugged me warmly and shepherded me back to his office. I looked back at Darlene and smirked as if to say, "*He* likes me."

"Well, well, well, my dear Fez, it is so good to see you. You look well. Rested and brown as a berry," he said with a warm smile. "Oh, and a bit warm." He handed me another tissue to mop the sweat beads from my upper lip.

"I know. Sorry, I rushed over…and anyway…You look great too, Richard. Busy summer?" His phone buzzed.

"Sorry, Fez, one sec." He picked it up. "Yes, Darlene…OK, put him through," he said, putting his index finger up to indicate a short call. I looked around his office. His two windows facing east and south were nearly floor to ceiling, allowing huge parallelograms of bright, clean light into his space, bleaching out the dark wooden walls and the red-and-blue carpet. His glass and chrome desk was gleaming and sparkling in the white morning sunshine.

Richard looked good, I thought. He was aging well. I guessed he was in his mid-seventies. His gray hair was wavy and a bit long, touching the top of his white collar. His skin was the warm brown of a recent summer vacation. I thought he might be closing in on retirement soon, but maybe he was going to work well into his eighties as his father had done.

He had been more like an uncle to me over the years than a family tax attorney. He had been especially doting after my mother had died when I was still in college. After William and I married, Richard and I had stayed in touch but with a little more space between calls and visits. While he knew my mother and her parents his entire life, I think he understood her failings as a mother and didn't try to inject his sense of nostalgia or warm memories onto me, which earned my gratitude. He understood that my memories of my mother were mostly unhappy and unpleasant, and that when she died, I felt both an icy distance from her and a genuine relief in her passing.

What the hell was I doing here? I would have thought that if William had shared the news of our financial status, Richard would have acknowledged it over the phone. What was going on? What other secrets or surprises could there be?

He rolled his right hand in a circle showing me that he was as eager to end this call as I was, and a minute later, he expedited the hang-up, repeating, "Well, OK," and "We can discuss this later," and finally, "Walter, I really must go."

I was staring out the window, thinking about Chatham. Wondering how the next few months were going to go. Formulating the words to explain to Richard what was happening, in case William hadn't yet.

Richard hung up and leaned over the desk, "Fez, are you OK?"

"Oh yes, sorry," I said, shaking myself out of my reverie. "I'm just not sure why I'm here, but I'm guessing that William called to…" He was looking at me quizzically.

"What?" he asked. "What about William?"

"Wait, William didn't call you yet?"

"No, Fez, what is going on?"

I couldn't believe he didn't know, and that I was going to have to tell him. What a fucking coward William was. I specifically asked him to handle this. Jesus. I launched right in, letting the words stumble fast and awkwardly out of my mouth. I told him everything that had happened since May, and even back to September. "I asked him to call you sometime this summer and explain. I'm sorry he didn't. Needless to say, we have to sell the Crow's Nest."

"Fez, wow, this is a lot to take in. I can take a look at all the numbers, but I'm sure you're right…It does sound like you'll have to sell the house. I am so terribly sorry. I know how much that house means to you."

"Yeah, well, I just don't know what else to do. Anyway, I gave the real estate agent, Janet Nickerson, your contact information, so you guys can maybe figure out the logistics together." I think Richard thought I was going to cry, so he handed me another tissue, but I waved it away. "So, wait, why did you want me to come in?"

"Well, I didn't ask you here to talk about the Crow's Nest, that's for sure. Actually, I guess you really can't imagine why I asked you here." He sighed deeply.

His eyebrows were furrowed, and my heart started beating faster.

"What is it, Richard?"

"OK, Fez. Here it is, and I don't know how else to say this, but OK, well, *you have a sister.*" I looked at him, and he was so serious and earnest, but I thought he might be making a weird, confusing joke. I burst into a loud, boisterous laugh.

"Jesus, Richard, you *really* had me there. It's not like you to joke!" His face was blank and slack-jawed. "C'mon, why am I here… really?" I asked, still recovering from my laughter.

"Fez, I am completely serious." He reached over and grasped my hands. "In 1949, a little over twelve years before you were born, your mother and father had a daughter. She was a gorgeous little pink thing, well, actually a gorgeous *big* pink thing, nearly nine pounds, howling and healthy, ten fingers and ten toes with a big, round blond head of hair and dark navy-blue eyes." He unclasped my hands and reached into his top desk drawer, pulled out a file, opened it, and handed me a black-and-white square photograph of a chubby, light-haired baby. The picture's edges were scalloped. A black date on the side of the photograph: February 21, 1950. "This is your sister, Penelope."

I stared silently, agape. I wasn't laughing now. *"Seriously? What?"* The air had been sucked out of the room. The maelstrom of thoughts and questions were speeding around my head so fast I couldn't grab onto anything. I put both hands on the desk and pressed down. I focused on Richard's eyes and tried to stop the spinning.

He continued, "Everything was absolutely perfect for the longest time. She was a bit cranky, fussy, but nothing odd, and she was absolutely *beautiful*. It wasn't until she should have been crawling, and then walking and then cooing and learning words, sounds, mimicking. She seemed to be missing all of the progress dates. That's what they used to call them: *progress dates*. She was late, *very late* to begin doing these things, and then as if frustrated herself, she began having these extreme temper tantrums. Not just crying, but head banging and high, high screeching, and she became totally, *completely* inconsolable. I remember being at the house one day, meeting with your parents on some tax and estate issues, and your sister was in a playpen, howling. I'm thinking she was about two or three. I mean she was *screeching*, and your parents looked like they didn't know what to do. I think I may have even made a comment about your sister's set of lungs. Now that I know what was really happening, it breaks my heart.

"Your parents were so confused and scared and finally, *finally* when she was just about three, they went to some specialists at Mass General Hospital. After a number of days of tests, they said they believed she was born mentally retarded, probably from a lack of oxygen during the birth process. They assessed her IQ at about sixty-five."

He looked at me seriously. At some point, my hand had moved to cover my mouth. He was speaking to me, but the words were ghostly, and all I could think about was that my mother, a much younger version of *my mother*, had a girl, and I could see them together almost. Mom holding her up in the air. Dad picking her up from the playpen when he came back from work. Her little blond head. I was seeing a vision of some other more beautiful and elegant family from an old movie with Grace Kelly and Clark Gable. Richard's words came through the fog.

"Knowing what we know now about your mother's drinking, I suspect perhaps fetal alcohol syndrome could have been a factor as well. Just guessing. Maybe the baby was just sluggish coming out or something. I don't know. But your sister has no genetic issues. Only environmental."

Everything started buzzing and humming in my ears, as if the air conditioning was turned up and fans were blowing. I could see Richard's lips moving, and I could hear him as if he were very, very far away at the end of some sort of tinny, wet tunnel. He dialed the intercom on his phone. "Darlene, please come in."

Darlene arrived swift and smooth. "Yes, Richard?"

"Could you please get Fessenden some cool water. She's looking a bit pale. Yes, bottled is fine. Thank you, Darlene."

Darlene returned quickly and delivered a bottle of water, her lacquered red nails square and perfect on the bottle. Fiji, a water bottle in a square shape, which made no sense to me. Why did a company make water bottles square when all the cup holders in the world were round? The square shape didn't feel good in my hand. I looked at the tropical image on the square bottle and took a sip of the cool clear water, and I could feel my heart pounding, my stomach constricting, a spinning sensation.

"OK," I managed. "Please continue." I could only imagine my mother making this decision to put my sister in an institution, allowing herself to continue drinking herself to sleep every day and night.

"OK, well then," he started again, looking at me warily. "Things happened pretty fast after that. Your grandparents were told about your sister's condition, and they got involved in discussing the best care for her. I think your mother and father were still in shock, to be honest. Absolutely numb. I saw them both a few weeks after the diagnosis, and they both looked lost. So your grandmother got involved in her ever-efficient way, God rest her soul, and found a suitable place for your sister to go."

"What do you mean, a place for her to go?" I asked.

"Well, your grandmother thought it was best, given the circumstances, for your sister to be in an institution that could best meet her needs."

"It was Mimi's idea? Not Mom's?" Richard nodded his head.

I remembered every summer in late August Mimi would drive me to the Children's Shop, an elegant children's clothing store in the center of Chatham. She would sit in the corner of the shop on a wooden chair, her basket purse on her lap, and watch me model back-to-school clothes. "Now, try on that sweet dress, dear, the navy one with the red apple appliquéd on the front. It's darling." The saleslady, a gray-haired local named Gretchen, would bring in piles and piles of clothes for me to try on, always Mimi's choices. "Now let me see, Fessenden. Come model those darling dresses." I would come out of the dressing room and spin for my grandmother, my fingers pulling out the skirt of the dress like a princess. "Perfect!" she would exclaim, telling the salesgirl to put that enormous pile of clothes in tissue and bags. "We'll take them all. Nothing's too good for my darling Fez."

I was trying to reconcile this Mimi from the one Richard was now describing. "But wasn't my sister only *four* at this time?" I asked, confounded.

"Yes, that's right, just about four. And within a month of her diagnosis, in December of 1953, your father drove her to a home for children with mental retardation, near Providence."

I started to think about my own daughter at four. A tiny little thing with round cheeks and chubby little fingers and still smelling sweet like a baby, powdery and clean. Soft fine hair, wispy and light. Innocent and little. I tried to imagine my drunk, my *stupidly* drunk, Valium-addicted mother somehow *unaware*, sleeping through all the things that mattered in her life, and my father taking over, doing the chores, out of duty, keeping the household running, and not brave or strong enough to say no to his quietly powerful and convincing parents-in-law. My grandparents convinced them to institutionalize this little girl. Then I was trying to see my mother as influenced by her own mother. Could she have felt uncertainty about her baby's departure? Pressured by her own mother? How must my mother have felt?

I don't think my mother would have even known *how* she felt. My broken, stupid mother. She was a selfish, hedonistic, helpless, and utterly useless woman. She gave up on her daughter. She couldn't cope, so she threw her daughter away. I knew I was far from perfect, but I would *never, ever, ever* give up on my child, my Hazel. I can't imagine how my mother could have done that.

"But Richard, she was *four*."

"I know, Fez, and it seems unfathomable now in this day and age, but in 1953, if you had the means, people would institutionalize their children with these issues. I think Mimi felt it would be best for everyone, including your sister, but especially for your mother who was unable to cope with the entire situation. Your mother, and of course your father, but your mother especially, did not seem capable of handling this situation in any way. So Mimi took over, and your parents agreed that this was the right path."

"That is absolutely heartbreaking," I managed to say. I looked past Richard at the sparkling, gleaming city of Boston. "I have so many questions I'm not quite sure where to start."

"OK, Fez, shoot. There's more I have to say too, but ask away."

"OK, for starters, why is this the first time I have heard of her? That's a pretty obvious question, but really…I can't imagine…why?"

"Good question. After Penelope—she's called Penny—after Penny went to Rhode Island, your mother and father had a terrible, *terrible* time of it, especially your mother. I cannot even tell you the stories, but knowing your mother as you did, I think you can imagine. It terrified your grandmother to see her child so broken, so she and your father and your grandpa all agreed the very best course of action was to let your sister go. To not speak of her, not visit her, so that your mother could move on."

"That's ridiculous," I said, knitting my brow, my disbelief turning into anger. "Who thinks that way?"

"Well, you know how Mimi always worried about your mother?"

I nodded slowly.

"Well, I think Mimi wanted us to feel that this was about your mother moving on. Forgetting. Mimi trying to get her and your father to a place where your mother could start over. I always felt that Mimi knew your mother couldn't possibly handle raising Penny. At first I thought this was all about your grandmother being somewhat consumed with her heritage and her Boston Brahmin connections, her place in the Social Register. That she would have done *any*thing to cover up something that might have detracted from her proud image of the family and its place in Boston society, but in fact, I think your grandmother simply knew your mother wasn't up to the task of raising Penny.

"Anyway, in retrospect, as flawed a plan as that now seems, the idea of Penny going away, that's what happened. Over the years, your father used to visit her before he moved away and remarried. Never your mother, never your grandparents. I've been checking in with Penny periodically, doing her taxes, assisting her with her bills and helping her whenever she has questions, which is actually quite infrequently. She has a friend named Paul who lives near her in her apartment building and really helps her and her roommate out. He ran the center where they lived before and now he manages their independent living in an apartment."

He looked at me apologetically and continued, "I am so sorry, but I was sworn to secrecy, and I simply had to keep to that. There were times I thought I could or should tell you, especially in the period after your mother died in 1980, but I thought it would all be too much for you to handle. You were so young, and I thought the best thing was for you to just have your college experience without all of this shocking and confusing new information. Then I thought about telling you again after your father died, but I just couldn't. I just didn't. I'm sorry; I've really wrestled with this."

I looked at him seriously. "Richard, it would have been really nice to know I had a sister. I've had no family for so long—"

"Fez, I know," he interrupted. "I'm so sorry. I've been incredibly conflicted. I've hated keeping this news from you."

I watched him shift in his chair, clearly uncomfortable in the moment. "Richard, it's all right. It is what it is. Please just tell me more about Penny."

As Richard started discussing the hospital where my sister worked and the apartment where she lived, I started to feel as if I were dreaming. I was trying to remember if there had ever been any indication ever from my parents of an older sibling: any photographs lying around in bedside table drawers, some coded expressions I missed, some mistaken assumption, some drunken slip, a hint from Mimi or Grandpa, a pregnant pause at reunions, a teary reminder at Christmas. But nothing came to mind. This huge gaping secret. I was utterly confused, and there was another familiar feeling brewing: anger. There were all those opportunities to share this information, either on purpose or by accident, and as far as I could remember, in that moment in Richard's gleaming office, Penelope's existence had been in a vacuum. It was yet another thing to avoid, clean up and from which to disengage. I wondered what other secrets were hiding in the murky mire of my family history.

"Richard," I said with a louder voice than I intended. "I cannot get over the whole 'letting go' piece. God, that is so, so awful," I said, shaking my head. "So why are you telling me all of this? Why now?"

"That," said Richard "is the other thing I need to discuss with you."

My throat was tightening. I tried to breathe deeply. All I could think was, I have a sister named Penny. I have a sister named Penny. *I have a sister named Penny.*

"Well, Fez." Richard took a deep breath. "Penny lives in Marion, Massachusetts, just about an hour south of here, and she's been living in an apartment with her roommate Dorothy, or Dottie." Richard paused. "Very, *very* sadly, Dottie passed away last week. A heart attack, evidently. She was almost sixty."

"Oh God, that's terrible," I said.

"It *is* terrible. Dottie and your sister have been living together for about thirty years, and they were dear, inseparable friends. I really don't know how Penny must be feeling. From our brief conversation, I couldn't get a read on her emotions. I'm not quite sure how she processes feelings, especially something as complicated and layered as grief and mourning."

"That poor thing," I said. "What will Penny do now? Can I see her?"

"Well," said Richard very seriously. "This is the situation: I don't think Penny will be happy living alone. She relied quite heavily on Dottie to help her with things. While Dottie also had a very low IQ, and a diagnosis of mental retardation perhaps also from oxygen deprivation, she was a little better at managing the household, and of course, she was a huge comfort to Penny as both a roommate and a friend."

He reached over and took my hand again. "Fez, I am very worried about Penny and what she must be feeling at this difficult time. She had known Dottie for most of her adult life, and she had lived with her for decades. I don't know how she's feeling or what she needs, but I *don't* want her to be living alone in her apartment, and I also *don't* want her to go back to the center where she lived before. It's a wonderful place, but the last time she was there, many years ago, she was with Dottie. They did everything together. Absolutely everything. I just feel it would be best for her to be with someone who could really care for her and focus on her needs. You're her sister. You're her family. I would really like you to consider taking her in with you and your family. I know this is a lot of information to hear all at once. I'm just trying to do the right thing for Penny."

Did he *really* just say that? I stared at his face as he stared at mine. I couldn't believe what he was asking me. Less than a half hour ago, I didn't even know I had a sister, and now he was asking me to take care of her? I felt sheer panic, a strong fight-or-flight adrenaline rush. My heart was pounding fast and loud. I could feel the heat coming into my cheeks. I wanted to run out that walnut door, through the hushed carpeted hallways, and down the muffled and swift elevator to my freedom. I was trying to think what to say, and the words kept catching in my throat. I was shaking my head slowly.

"Richard," I finally got out. "This is going to sound really, *really* terrible, and I apologize, but I *really* can't do this right now. This is the worst possible timing, just terrible timing. I can't even believe this is happening. I know I'm supposed to say, 'Of course! A sister! Have her come live with me! The more the merrier!' But I just can't right now." I dropped my voice down to a whisper. "William and I aren't even living together right now."

Richard said, "Oh, Fez, I'm so sorry. I had no idea."

I replied, "Well, the financial situation…you know…anyway, we've been keeping it very quiet, but he's been staying with his brother in Wellesley since May. It's been very difficult." Everything felt too warm. I could feel my throat tightening. There wasn't enough oxygen in this office. "I'm really sorry. I don't know what to say. I really don't. There is no possible way I can take Penny into my house right now. *No possible way.*"

Richard looked at me for a long time. He looked very tired. He looked sad and worse, disappointed. "I understand, Fez, and

I cannot imagine what you're feeling at this time. This is a lot to digest all at once."

"Richard, I want to reiterate that this...taking care of Penny... is not something I can do *well* right now. I don't even know quite how I feel about all this...but I don't want to be a selfish little shit, either." I said slowly, "Let me talk to William and Hazel and figure this out. It's going to rock a few boats though. How long can Penny stay where she is?"

"The apartment has been rented month-to-month, and the lease would expire at the end of September. But I worry about Penny on her own, and I don't know how she is going to be without Dottie. I can only imagine she'll be scared and lonely and confused. I spoke to Paul this morning, and he said he would stay with Penny until she moves out, either to a new facility or with you.

"There's a little service for Dottie at the chapel on Wednesday in the hospital where Penny works. I'm planning to attend the service, and I'll have a talk with Penny about her options. I just ask that you please get back to me as soon as possible so I can help Penny understand what's going to happen next.

"Fez, if you decide to take Penny in, I am going to help you through this. You are not alone. I'm not saying this will be easy. I just want to remind you what Penny has been through in her life. I really hope you and your family can find a way to accommodate her."

"I just don't know," I said. I looked down at my hands and interlaced my fingers.

"I have a box of papers and documents pertaining to Penny and her diagnosis, her history in the institutions, starting from 1953 right up until now. I think at this time, regardless of your decision, it might be better for you to have this. It might help you to better understand Penny and where she's been."

Richard stood up, and came around his desk to give me a hug, though I was barely able to stand up. "I don't know whether to say 'I'm sorry' or 'good luck' or 'how nice for you to have a sister.'"

"I know. I'm at a loss. I can't quite figure out my feelings at the moment, either. Overwhelmed might be the best. Or numb." I looked at him imploringly. I just felt bad.

Richard handed me a medium-size brown cardboard box of papers, not too heavy, about half-full. This small box contained the story of Penny. I took it from him, said a quiet goodbye, and headed out the door.

I turned around at the threshold of his office. "I'll call you soon, either way." He nodded, and I turned away and walked slowly to the lobby.

I felt Darlene's eyes focused on the back of my skull. Mercifully, the elevator was quick to arrive. I pushed the lobby button, and as soon as the chrome doors shut, I felt the strong, hushed pull of gravity. I tried to calm myself down, to think clearly, to figure out some sort of plan, but the only thoughts I had were an awful combination of truths, all knitted together: I had a sister I didn't know; I had a sister who needed to come stay with me; I had a husband who lived elsewhere; I had a daughter who was drifting slowly but surely away.

The elevator doors opened onto the white, bright light of the blue glass building lobby on that beautiful crystal-clear September morning. As I stepped outside onto Clarendon Street, I put my sunglasses on, cutting the glare, and dialed William's cell.

He answered on the second ring. "Fez."

"Hey, William. Can we talk? I have some news."

"Sure, I wanted to see Haze tonight anyway. I'll come by after work." He seemed to be in a hurry to get off the phone.

I texted Ellie and asked her to call me back as soon as possible. She would be a great sounding board for this incredible new development, my newly discovered sister. As I was walking home, I started to really think about Penny, my sister, my family. I thought about growing up as an only child, about my loneliness, my isolation, and my frequent requests for a sibling from my parents and then their sad, resigned replies of no. "No, Fez. No sibling." I remembered *specifically* asking for a sister. My parents must have been crushed hearing my pleas, knowing what they knew and having to go on every day, acting exactly like there wasn't another Wright daughter, living in a sterile, institutional home somewhere in Rhode Island or Cape Cod or wherever she was in those years.

# CHAPTER 5

# PENELOPE

Yesterday was the worstest day ever. Ever, Ever, Ever. The worstest day that could ever, ever be. Yesterday was the day I was gonna tell Dottie my whole birthday plan for her birthday on September 17. I was gonna wait until her axual birthday, but I decided I was too essited to wait. Plus, if we was gonna go on a trip, we was gonna have to tell our bosses at the hostipal and the factery. So yesterday I was gonna tell Dottie the essiting news about going to *BeautifulBoston* for her birthday prezzie and how we wuz gonna axually go there and everything. I decided I didn't need Richard's OK cuz I could do it on my own, with my own moneys from my job and not even Mommy's moneys. I woked up essited like Christmastime, and I got out the Lucky Charms for breakfuss cuz they're magically delicious. And the leprakon was always running from those hungry kids. And the leprakon was funny and fast, and the kids always got their breakfuss.

Usually Dottie was up before me and getting out the breakfuss foods, but she wasn't there, so I went into her bedroom real quiet, tiptoeing, and I said, *Dottie, Dottie, time for breakfuss,* which I hardly ever have to do cuz she's almost always up before me, and I said, *Dottie, Dottie,* and she was in her bed, and her eyes was closed, and she was sleeping real quiet and no water on her chin or nothing. I put my hand on her little polka-dotty arm and said, *Dottie, Dottie,* and she didn't move or nothing. So then I got kinda scared cuz she wasn't moving or nothing, and she felt like all hard and quiet. I called Paul on his telephone, 6175553078, and said, *Paul, Dottie's all quiet and hard*

And Paul said, *Now what do you mean, Penny?*

And I said it again: *Dottie's all quiet and hard.*

And Paul said, *I'm coming up there to see for myself. OK, Penny?*

And I said, *OK, Paul.*

Paul came upstairs into our apartment, 3-C, cuz he lived downstairs in 1-A. He went into Dottie's room and felt her arm all polka-dotty from sunshine, and he said, *Oh no, Penny, I'm going to call a doctor.* He went out to the hall and called a number for the doctors to come, and he came back and said, *They're coming, Penny.* And then we waited for a little while, and Paul sat next to me on my sofa with his elbows on his knees and his hands on his scratchy cheeks. After a little while, we heard heavy clanging steps, and the doorbell rang.

A man doctor and a lady doctor not in white coats but more like fire-engine coats came into the apartment, and Paul showed them where to go to make Dottie all better, and they told Paul and me, *Thank you very much.*

And I said, *Dottie's sleeping in her bed.*

They did the crookedy head thing. *OK, all right,* they said, and they went in to make Dottie all better. But I had a tummy ache all of a sudden, and I started my rocking on the yellow sofa.

Paul reached over and patted my knee and said, *OK, Penny, let me tell you some stories,* and then he started talking about the funny, funny things he had ever seen in all of his years of working at the Community Workshop Living Center. That's where I first met Paul. He was my friend there, and he's still my friend. He talked about the time a squirrel got into the cafeteria and how all the peoples were screaming and howling on top of their eating chairs and everything was all crazy and loud, and I member when this happened.

I said, *I member, Paul. That was summertime in 1984. August 4, 1984.*

Paul shook his head smiling and said, *You're probably right, Penny,* and patted my knee again. Then Paul said, *And how about that time in activities class when big Bruce was learning how to make the pot holders, and he had to use those big soft cloth rubber bands to weave, and he didn't like the colors in the box, and he started getting sad about the colors, and remember how you found him all the blue bands, and he was so happy about the blue bands and his blue pot holder that he started doing the silly dance and singing,* I love blue so much? *And that's when you got the Kindness Award. Remember?*

*I member,* I said, and I laughed a loud laugh and said, *February 19, 1980! That was a special day, Paul.*

Paul smiled a big smile, and then he said, *Do you remember the time Old Lady Gracie wouldn't take her meds?*

And I said, *Yes, Paul, I member cuz the nurses was so mad and cranky and saying,* Gracie, you gotta take your meds, *and Gracie stomped her funny big feet in the big brown suede shoes and pulled at her flowery big dress with the pockets and the buttons and said,* Nuh hunh, I ain't taking those pills no more, *cuz Gracie sometimes got kinda crank, and the pills made her real nice and quiet, and the nurse Mary said,* Now, Gracie, you know these pills are good for you, *and Gracie said,* You're not the bossa me, *and they got in a big funny fight, and then they dragged Gracie right out of the room like she was a big old sack of potatoes, and I guess she took those pills cuz then she was real quiet again. Right, Paul? That time?* I was smiling cuz that memory was kinda funny, and it made me happy cuz Dottie and me laughed so, so hard that day. That day, when we was laughing, Dottie snorted so hard, and milk came right outta her nose. I was smiling just membering that, even though I was real scared and sad about Dottie's hardness.

*Yep,* Paul said kinda quiet and looking off, and just then, the man doctor and the lady doctor came out of Dottie's bedroom and looked at Paul and said, *Could we have a word with you?* But I thought they was gonna have more than one word with him cuz one word's not so many words to say.

They looked at me out of the sides of their eyes, and Paul said, *Well, OK,* and the three of them went out of our apartment into the hallway.

I moved from the sofa to the kitchen chair. I'm not sure why. I just did. I had to do something. I got to rocking pretty good then cuz I started rocking the legs of the chair back and forth and making scratching noise on the white speckled floor cuz the metal legs was banging back and front and back and front, and the yellow, plastic seat sounded kinda crunchy. The front door was cracked open, and I could see Paul talking to the doctor people with their backs all to me all bent over and all hushy, and I kept on rocking. I kept rocking even when they turned around and slowly, slowly walked their feets over to me, and I said, *Is Dottie feeling all better?*

And the lady doctor said, *We have some very sad news, miss.*

Then Paul stood in front of the lady doctor and looked at her and then at me kinda slow, and he took my hands in his and said, *Penny, Dottie has passed away. The doctors think it might have to do with her heart, maybe a heart attack, or maybe a stroke, but we're not quite sure yet. We'll know more later. The doctors are going to take Dottie and do some tests and get some answers.*

I don't member what happened then, but I think I threw up all over the floor. Sometimes I did that. Sometimes I threw up on the floor. I just member Paul mopping with my gray, stringy mop back and forth and back and forth and me in my yellow, plastic chair not rocking no more and the man doctor and the lady doctor sitting on both sides and saying, *I'm so sorry,* and stuff like that.

Paul and the man doctor and the lady doctor asked me if I wanted to say goodbye to Dottie, and I said, *OK, I'll say bye-bye to Dottie,* and they walked me in to Dottie's bedroom, and Paul held my right elbow, and the lady doctor held my left elbow cuz I think they thought I was gonna throwed up again or fall down on the slippery floor or something, and so we all walked in together, and the window was dark cuz the shade was pulled down, and I pulled on the shade and the shiny white shade went up really fast and around and around all rolly spinny, and then I looked at Dottie, and she was sleeping pretty good.

Then Paul said, *Do you want to be alone with Dottie?*

And I said, *OK.*

The lady doctor pulled over Dottie's little brown desk chair next to the bed, and I sat down, and the lady doctor and Paul left the room, but I knew they were right in the TV room next door cuz I could hear them whispering. I patted Dottie's polka-dot arm, and I said, *Dottie, I know you's sleeping pretty good now, and I hope nothin smarts you, and I so sad you's too sleepy to come to* BeautifulBoston *with me. Member we saw all these pictures on the television? All the pictures of the white boats and the green, green grass and the sparkedly buildings and the bumpy, bumpy streets? Member how we loved it? Well I's still gonna go there, for both of us, K?* Well, Dottie didn't say nothin, and so I just patted her arm and said, *Dottie, I hopes you has a good sleeps.* And I brushed away her funny curly gray hair from her face, and I kissed her soft, puffy, white cheek, and I said, *Sleeps real good, Dottie.*

# CHAPTER 6

# FESSENDEN

I t was insanity. Absolute insanity. My mind was racing all the way home, and I couldn't stop the frenetic succession of thoughts. At home, I climbed the stoop steps, went straight back into the kitchen, put the box of Penny's papers on the island, and made another cup of coffee. No one else was home; Hazel was at school, the first day of her eleventh-grade year. William was probably in some pointless Monday morning meeting, vainly attempting to save his anemic company. The house was quiet; I could only hear the soft clicking of the kitchen clock. I paced back and forth in the kitchen, from side to side, wiping counters over and over again with a damp rag. I sat on a stool by the island, my hands wrapped around the mug, my head down, trying to imagine how I was going to bring up this Penny conversation with William and Hazel. I was worried about how the conversation was going to go; we already had so many changes in our lives. How was I going to share this information? What the hell was I supposed to say? What would William and Hazel say?

Hazel, I thought, would probably say very little. That's all she said about anything lately. And William, our conversations were already severely strained. I couldn't imagine how the subject of

Penny coming here could be anything but another trigger point. I knew it didn't really matter what he thought, but I also didn't want any more fights. I was so tired of the discord. This conversation was sure to bring up all of our issues: our money problems, our combative marriage, his dying company, my struggles to write and finish my book, our worries about Hazel. Then again, I thought brightly, maybe William would surprise me. Maybe he would be big enough to embrace this new idea, this idea of my sister. He was close with his brother. He understood the value of family. He even expressed sorrow at times that I didn't know what it was like to have a sister or a brother. Who knows, maybe this Penny news could actually be what we needed; we could break out of the morass of our self-absorbed dramas and tensions and focus on helping Penny. At that thought, I started to feel a bit lighter, and my foggy thoughts dissipated a little. In my own mind, I started to clarify how I was feeling and what I thought I wanted to have happen, regardless of anyone's response.

A strong gust of cool wind through the open kitchen window blew a large pile of bills, notes, and loose sheets of paper onto the floor, sending them everywhere. Seeing the papers scattered all over my kitchen floor, I was taken back in time to the day I met William, in a coffee shop, on Newbury Street, right here in Boston. I was two years out of Amherst College, newly working for *Boston* magazine, writing their monthly "Around Town" column, a summary of all the cultural events happening throughout the city. I was on a deadline and under tremendous pressure to hand in the copy and impress my fastidious editor. I was nearly done. I looked up at one point as the waitress refilled my coffee cup. I saw a man about my age, sitting at an adjacent table in an expensive navy-blue suit, Brooks Brothers striped blue shirt, and bright-red tie. Dark-brown, wavy hair, piercing blue eyes, tanned skin. He looked up and met my gaze. I could feel a warm blush spreading up my face, heating my cheeks, and I looked back down to finish writing, but

I was aware of his eyes fixed on me. When I was finished with the piece, I stood up quickly to pack up my things and head back to the office to hand in my article, but when I did, I knocked over the small pedestal table, sending my pile of papers flying all over the floor, and knocking over and breaking the porcelain coffee cup and saucer. The waitress looked over at me and then said something to the cook behind the counter. They laughed, and I saw her go get a broom and dustpan.

"Oh my God," I whispered to myself. "I am such an idiot."

The blue-eyed man was squatting down next to me, picking up the papers, putting them into neat piles while I picked up the broken shards of my coffee cup. He handed me my stack of papers. "Here you go."

I put the pile of broken china on the table, and I took the paper pile from him. "Oh God, thanks. I feel so dumb."

"Nah, happens all the time." I looked at him, and he exuded order.

"Not to you, maybe."

He stood up. He had an amused look on his face. "Well, no worries. Have a great day. Try not to spill anything else today." He smiled broadly and exited the glass-and-stainless-steel door.

On his way past the window, where I was stuffing the papers into a manila folder, he tapped on the glass. I looked up. He mouthed the words, "I come here every day."

⇒┼┼⇒

I knew I had to talk to everyone as soon as possible; everything was happening so fast, and as Richard explained, Penny couldn't be alone for long, and Paul couldn't stay with her forever. But as I started to imagine even formulating the words, and initiating these conversations, nothing came to me.

William texted: *What time will H be back from field hockey?*

I texted William: *5:30.*

I would speak with Hazel after I spoke with William.

I decided to open Penny's box of papers. There was her birth certificate and files from each of the four places where she lived: a place in Providence called the Harvey House; then a Catholic institution in Pascoag, Rhode Island, called Saint Catherine's; then a state-run hospital in Worcester called the Massachusetts Center for the Disabled; and finally in Plymouth, Massachusetts, a place called the Community Workshop Living Center. All of these changes and all of these moves. She "graduated" from the last place in 1985 and moved into an apartment with Dottie in Marion, Massachusetts.

The most remarkable thing about Penny's box was its lack of information. It was just a small box with a few files, organized by residential facility, thinly representing the entirety of her sixty-five years. How sad to have the entirety of the papers of your life be such a thin stack. I saw an envelope with "Penelope Wright" written in my father's unmistakable and tiny handwriting, in his favorite writing implement, a navy-blue fountain pen. I picked up the yellowed envelope and stared at it. I turned it over and pulled out the monogrammed notecard from the torn envelope.

*September 1, 1975*
*Dearest Penelope,*

 *I'm so glad you are still enjoying your new home, and that you and Dottie are well. I am very glad you have found each other and are able to help each other in your daily lives. I'm also glad to hear Paul is of great help to you. I liked him the minute I met him, and I know you feel the same way.*

 *Remember I told you about my friend Rosie? Well, I wanted to let you know that we will be moving to Arizona at the end of this month and hoping to be married shortly after we settle down. I'll be working in a new office there. We have bought a nice modern*

*condominium in Scottsdale (lots of windows!) and we are look-ing forward to playing golf and enjoying a quiet life together. As I told you before, Rosie likes things pretty quiet, and that sounds pretty great to me now too. I'm sorry that I won't be able to visit as much as I did before. (Scottsdale is a four-hour airplane ride from Boston!) I'll keep writing to you though, and know that I love you and think about you every day.*
*I send you all my love,*
*Daddy*

She must have given the letter to Richard to hold for her. She must have been so sad. It sounded like yet another abandonment. Did he ever visit her after this? Did she feel sad he left? Had she met Rosie? I couldn't imagine what she thought or how she thought. Had she seen my mother after 1953? Had Mom visited Penny? Richard didn't think so, and knowing my mother, I had to guess no, she probably never visited her. There's no way. Penny was left alone over and over again.

This was surreal. How could this be true? How could I have had a sister my entire life? All these seconds, minutes, days, weeks, months, years, decades, all this time, all of my life, I have had a sister who was breathing and eating and thinking and feeling. *All this time.* I had to figure this out. I needed to do the right thing.

I put Penny's light box of papers on the floor and turned my thoughts to my book. Despite my preoccupation with my newly discovered sister and my need to find a delicate, appropriate way to discuss her with my family, I couldn't wait any longer to write; I promised myself I would work on and finish the book during the hours Hazel was in school. Maybe I could have it written, edited, and totally completed by Christmas. Three months late.

I spent the rest of the day organizing my thoughts and writing notes and outlines. My first novel, published a decade prior, was about a highly intelligent and successful woman, a psychiatrist, who suffered years of physical and emotional abuse by her husband, became addicted to the pain medication she was prescribing, crashed and burned, and ultimately triumphed through rehabilitation, recovery, and the satisfaction of seeing her husband and abuser ultimately punished. The *New York Times* gave it a pretty good review, the *Boston Globe* loved it, and *O* magazine raved, and while I didn't win any literary prizes, the book put me on the map and legitimized me as a decent, even good writer. After the mild success of that book and the corresponding short book tour, I couldn't seem to come up with any interesting ideas for a next novel; I wrote articles. I started writing several books but abandoned them within months. Then, about five years ago, I wrote a long article, published in the *New Yorker* (a huge coup) about Agnes Williams Black, the infamous murderess, and that article was morphing into a full-blown, roughly 125,000-word biography. I had spent hours and hours *and hours* this summer lost in the research and development of this book. Hours researching Agnes Williams Black and her background, her ancestry and family history, her childhood, her marriage to the alcoholic and brutal John Cabot Black, her burgeoning belligerence, her increasing erratic behavior, her well-documented public rantings, her alleged insanity or dementia, and the horrific and brutal murder of her husband. My agent, Caroline, thought the story was immensely interesting in its terrifying and macabre detail and that the book, once written, would be picked up quickly by a major publishing house. Caroline had even run the synopsis by her publisher friend, and he was already asking for a first draft for review.

But at the moment, after nearly six months of intensive research and book outlines, I had written so much, but I was still mired in the piles of data, information, newspaper reports, police reports. I could not find a way to organize all of these nearly three hundred pages of notes into a meaningful and cogent story.

I was seated in the loveseat in the front bay of the living room, staring at my laptop, eating a late lunch of cheese and crackers, procrastinating by looking at e-mails, surfing the web, unsubscribing from junk e-mails received over the summer. Not writing. Not editing. Not organizing.

I heard the key in the front door clicking open and the second door pushed open and the thud of a heavy backpack on the floor. Hazel was home. I looked at the clock on my laptop: 3:47. How did this entire day melt away? I never got to the grocery store or the drugstore; I hadn't done any of the errands I had planned. Why could I never seem to get things done?

"Hi, Haze," I said, turning toward her as she came in the front hall.

"Hey."

"No field hockey today? How was your first day?"

She shrugged. "No and OK."

"Just OK?"

"Yup."

When she started kindergarten and I asked her how her day was, she'd just say, "Good."

And I'd say, "Like how good? What happened today, honey?" and she'd shrug. So we started playing a game called "five things." She'd have to answer my five questions about the day so I could get more details. We still did it.

"Five things, Haze."

"Mom, not this year."

"Yep, five things."

"Nope."

"Yes, Haze. Not negotiable."

"OK, fine. Whatever."

So I began, "One: What did you have for lunch?"

"Nothing."

"Really, nothing?" They served a hot lunch at her school, and she used to love it. This was often the one question with an enthusiastic and detailed answer.

"Is that another one of the five questions?"

I thought about that and said, "No, forget that one. Two: What was the best thing that happened today?"

She looked bored. "I left school and walked home."

"That's not good, Haze."

She just looked at me. Another shrug. "Please hurry up with the rest. I have homework."

"OK, three: Which math class are you in?"

"Mr. Small, geometry, Level B." Down from Level A last year.

"Four: When do field hockey practices start?"

"Next week, I think. Not sure."

"Five: What made you laugh today?"

She looked down at the carpet in the front hall. The sun was bright, and there was an early fall breeze, which I could hear moving through the leafy maple trees on the street. It rattled the glass panes in the front door. "Nothing." She leaned over to pick up her backpack, put it on her back, straightened up, and went up the fifteen stairs.

I stared at the place where she had been standing. Her last reply hung thickly in the air. I yelled after her, "Can I make you something to eat?"

"No more questions, Mom." I heard the door close to her room.

I looked out the window to see a young family walking down Marlborough Street, a mother holding her daughter's tiny hand, and a little sister sleeping in a reclined stroller. Two little girls in pretty matching pale-green dresses, enjoying the lovely fall afternoon. The little girl pointed at something, and the mother laughed. She leaned down to brush a strand of hair out of her eyes, and then paused to kiss her daughter on the top of her head.

I used to love taking Hazel out for the late afternoon stroll, after her nap, when the shadows were long but the sun was still warm. We would walk and talk and look at the people and play "I spy with my little eye..." When she was older, once prompted by the five-questions game, she would share, with great detail, the stories of her school day. I dearly missed those simple, happy times with her.

I turned back to my laptop, staring blankly at the open word document named "Agnes Williams Black." The cursor was blinking on and off at the top of the current page. I watched the clock go from 4:18 to 4:57. Minute by slow, blinking minute. I closed the laptop quickly and moved into the kitchen, turning on the television for the early news. I used to wait until six thirty and watch just one half hour of the nightly news, but over the summer, I had started turning on the television earlier and earlier. I took a glass from the upper cabinet, filled it with ice, added a double jigger of vodka, and then filled it with seltzer water. I looked in the refrigerator for a lemon but remembered we had none. White wine, a blackened lime, a beer, possibly skunked, old condiments, nothing fresh. The refrigerator smelled like old meat.

I heard William's key in the door. My stomach clenched at the sound. I had meant to think through my conversation about Penny. I had indeed made up my mind, but I wanted to express my thoughts clearly, to have with some cogent thoughts about my sister coming here. I was just going to have to wing it. William came in and dropped his briefcase next to the front hall table and began to sort through the pile of mail I had saved for him to go through. Regardless of the day, the age or swirling activity of Hazel and her friends, the weather, the time, regardless of anything, this had been William's routine, and now, even as a current nonresident of this home, he dropped his briefcase at that particular spot and rifled through the pile of bills, letters, and junk mail. I think, even with a raging house fire licking at his heels, he would have methodically checked the mail upon his arrival in the front hall of 30 Marlborough Street.

"Hi. Thanks for swinging by." I was going to be polite. I was going to be decent. I was going to table my lingering resentment and anger, because I didn't want a negative reaction from him about Penny. I stood at the hallway from the kitchen door opening.

"Oh yeah, hi." He turned to face me. He was working very hard on being polite too. I think he was consumed by guilt and shame. "Good day?" He turned back to the mail on the front hall table.

"Crazy."

"Crazy how?" he asked, his eyes still glued to the pile of letters.

"I'll tell you after you have a glass of wine. Can you stay for a glass?" Boy, was I being hospitable.

"Yep. Uh oh, it's wine worthy?"

"Yes, maybe two glasses might be better."

"Hmm. OK. Is Hazel home?"

"Yep, she's upstairs doing homework."

"OK, I'll go up and see her after we talk. We're gonna make dinner plans for one night next week. I'll just go through the mail, and I'll be in the kitchen in a sec."

I turned back into the kitchen to look through take-out menus for dinner. I used to make time to cook when William and I were first married and when Hazel was little, buying fresh ingredients every day and planning delicious meals, something from a new cookbook, maybe even something adventurous like seafood lasagna or raspberry chicken, and always a freshly baked pie or cake or cookies, but over time I had slowly lost my interest in cooking; I just didn't have the energy to gear up in the evening and cook and clean. The days wore me out and by late afternoon, I didn't have the energy to do much else. I opened the refrigerator and closed it again. I kept forgetting we had no food. I was craving Italian. I texted Hazel:

Fez525: *No food here. Wings from Gianinos?*
Hazmat666: *No thx*
Fez525: *Pizza?*
Hazmat666: *No thx not hungry*
Fez525: *Sure?*
Hazmat666: *Ya*
Fez525: *Dad's here.*
Hazmat666: *Be down l8r*

William came back into the kitchen with a pile of mail in his hand.

"OK," I said. "I have no food yet, so I can't offer you anything."

"It's OK. I'm eating in Wellesley with Eddie and Suz anyway," he said.

"Wine?" I asked, already reaching into the fridge for the bottle of sauvignon blanc.

"Sounds good. Thanks," he said. "So what's so earth-shattering that I need not one but *two* glasses of wine before I hear it?"

"Please sit down."

And I told him. I recapped my conversation with Richard, everything about how my parents had a child that they kept as a secret from me, how she lived in institutions all of her life, how her longtime roommate and best friend Dottie had just passed away. He sat quietly as I spoke, periodically taking sips of wine.

"Jesus," he said. "What the hell?"

"I know, it's crazy. Totally, totally crazy," I said.

"I'll say. So wait, what happens next? Are you going to meet her? Or is this still a big secret or what?"

"Well, here's the thing. She and Dottie live—lived—in an apartment, and Dottie, despite her low IQ like Penelope, or Penny, I guess, took care of her. Not just the chores and stuff, but Dottie helped comfort her, I think, emotionally. She was all that Penny ever really knew: her roommate, best friend, caretaker, sister. Everything."

"Sad," said William.

"So sad," I agreed. "And Richard feels very strongly that she shouldn't be alone in the apartment. Dottie took care of Penny and kept her company, and Richard says he cannot imagine Penny being alone."

William looked at me long and hard. His gaze had changed from gentle concern to a shadowy, darker unease. "You're not about to say that she should come live here with you, are you? Please tell me, Fez, that that is not the next thing you are going to say."

I looked down. The floor was covered in crumbs, old crumbs from the spring, and the early evening sun was capturing them in a rich golden light. "Well, I don't know exactly what I was going to say. When Richard told me he thought Penny should come live with us, with me, my immediate reaction was, 'Absolutely not.' I was in total shock in his office this morning...But then I...well, I started thinking about it and about how everybody left her, *abandoned her*, really, and then I kinda made up my mind."

William looked deeply concerned. "With everything we are going through right now and our finances and...Jesus, we're not even living together. I guess I don't know what this means for *us*." He stared at the wooden counter, scraping something off with his fingernail.

"I know. Believe me I know. It is the *very* last thing we...I...need to be taking on right now. *The last.* But it doesn't really mean anything for *us*. It has nothing to do with *us*. The simple truth is that if I don't take her in, she will go back into some sort of institutional living, and evidently that didn't go so well the last time she was there alone, a while back."

William looked older. I noticed his gray hairs coming in, the oyster-gray hue and thinness of his skin, the pull of translucent flesh over his cheekbones. We sat quietly looking at our hands resting on the kitchen island. "Well, then, she should move in, of course. It's absolutely the right thing to do." At first I thought he might have been being sarcastic, but he wasn't. He was sincere. It seemed to take an effort for him to say those words, and then he sunk deeper into himself, a subtle, internal collapse. He kept his head down, surveying the gritty and dirty floor, and then took a deep breath. He stopped himself from saying anything else.

I couldn't believe that was his reply. There was no anger, no vexation, no defiance. He was placating and calm.

"OK, well, that's good because that's what I had decided too." I crossed my arms in front of my chest. In the past, when used to fight, the really loud, hot fighting last spring, I would feel myself pulling away as if I were surrounded by heavy velvet curtains, muffling the loud silence. I used to watch his tiny spittle flying through the air, backlit from the south-facing kitchen window, beautiful little saliva droplets gold and shimmery in the kitchen's orange light. I would sit there on the kitchen stool floating, escaping, blanketed by my departure, and yet hyperfocused. It gave me something in which to lose myself. Today, he was quiet, and I wasn't quite sure what to do with it.

Then, in the calm of this evening, loneliness washed over me. I took a long sip of my drink, tipping the glass up so the liquor could weave its way through the ice cubes and land on my tongue, icy cold and medicinal. I wanted him to be angry, irrational, mean; he wasn't. He couldn't be, I guess. He said what he said and gathered his mail pile, filing it into the outside pocket of his briefcase.

He went upstairs but came back down right away. "She's totally asleep. She must be spent." He left the house, looking defeated, latching the front door quietly as he left.

Throughout the short evening, Hazel never came downstairs. She stayed up in her room, totally, absolutely asleep. Although, deep in the night, in my thick fog of sleep and dreams, I could have sworn I heard the front door unlatch and the click of the bolt.

⋈

The next morning, I awoke extremely early, unrested but determined and strangely empowered by my resolve. I felt ready to bear the burden of whatever this Penny situation was going to mean for us. She was family. *My* family.

I called Richard. What did I need to know? What was the address? Would she be expecting me? Did she understand what was happening? I had more questions than could be properly answered, but at the end of the long phone call, I thought I had gotten what I needed. Richard would tell her I was coming on Wednesday, *tomorrow*, and that she would be moving in with a sister she never knew she had, a sister thirteen years younger and a sixteen-year-old niece. Since this whole situation was unreal and complicated and unfathomable for *me*, I could not even begin to imagine how this was going to be for Penny, a woman of sixty-five years, with an IQ somewhere in the midsixties.

Richard reminded me that Dottie's service was Wednesday morning at the hospital chapel where Penny worked, but where she would work no more, and that Paul would help her pack her few things. She could be ready as early as noon or one o'clock.

I made lists of all the things I had to do to prepare for Penny's arrival: the Penny's-room preparation list, the grocery list, the drugstore supply list, the general housecleaning list, and this group of lists begat another group of lists including the book work list, the Crow's Nest list, the Hazel list, the William list. I looked at the pile of lists, turned it over, buried it in another pile, and called Ellie.

She answered right away, as usual. "Hi!"

"Hi, El. I got your message. Sorry I didn't call back. William came over, and it's been nuts."

"I figured something like that happened. No prob. Anything good to report?"

"Well..." And so I told her the whole Penny story too.

"Whoa."

"Yeah, I know."

"Well, that's nice William was kind of supportive. I can't say I blame him for being a little reluctant."

"I know. I guess I can't, either. He doesn't really have a choice in the matter. But now I have to talk to Hazel, and I am kind of a wreck."

Ellie started to launch into her classic, supportive "do it with love and kindness" speech, but I had to cut her short when I heard Hazel's footsteps on the creaky stairs. We hung up.

She padded slowly into the kitchen, looking wan and sleepy. She had shadowy circles under her eyes.

"Hi, sweetness," I said, pouring milk into my coffee.

"Hey," she said.

I didn't have any idea how to start the conversation so I began a quick jumble of words, "Hazel, I have been meaning to tell you something…I wasn't quite sure how to bring it up and I wanted to be sure about our next steps and how this was all going to work—"

"Spit it out, Mom. Are you and Dad gonna get a divorce?"

It took me a moment to realize what she was asking. "No, Hazel. No. *Not at all.*"

"Well, I just figured since you're separated, that would be the next logical step."

She had her back to me, facing the coffeemaker. I realized, suddenly, that I *had* thought about divorce, I *had* flirted with the idea of divorce, but I hadn't consulted with an attorney and had no real intention of doing that any time soon. The idea of that finality scared me.

"No, Haze, that's not a next step. We're not even talking about that. OK?"

"Whatever."

"Anyway, remember I told you I met with Richard earlier this week? Well, Richard told me the most incredible thing…I have a sister. A sister. An older sister. You have an aunt."

She turned to face me. "What? Really?"

I gave Hazel the synopsis and told her I would be bringing Penny home *tomorrow* and she was going to stay with us for a while, maybe forever, and she was slow and I didn't really know that much but I was doing what I thought was right.

"That's pretty messed up," she said directly.

"What?"

"The whole thing, Mom. The secret, the situation, that she's coming here. All of it. Not really the greatest timing."

"I know," I said quietly. "I'm just not sure what else I'm supposed to do."

"Yeah, I guess," she said, and she poured coffee into a stainless-steel travel mug, added a long pour of sugar from the diner-style sugar dispenser and screwed on the lid. "Good luck with that," she said sarcastically. "So I'll meet her tomorrow?"

"Yeah, I guess so. Plan to be home right after school tomorrow and for a nice dinner. We'll have a 'Welcome, Penny' thing. Or something."

Hazel headed toward the front of the brownstone, and as she reached the front door, she turned back. "Oh, Mom, my math teacher wants you and/or Dad to come in for a conference. I was supposed to tell you before."

"Why? What happened? You've only had one day of school. Is everything OK?" I waited for something to assuage the surging dread, but she just shrugged.

"Probably not, I'm guessing."

I decided to walk with her to school, to try to get more information from her and hopefully ease my burgeoning worry, but the walk and conversation left me more uneasy; Hazel was distant, distracted and said very little. I started to worry that she was ill; so many kids her age seemed to be getting Mono. I made a mental note to schedule an appointment with her doctor.

When I returned from my walk and subsequent errands, I saw a text from William: *What did you decide?*

I looked down at the tired, scratched oak floors. I stared at the deepest marks made from Hazel's cleats, perfect little circular depressions in the dry wood. I started to text this reply: *I'm getting Penny. Tomorrow. I thought about it all yesterday and all last night, and I don't think there's any other choice...*but I couldn't press Send. I deleted it and turned my phone over, the screen facing down. I didn't want to see his reply, good, bad, or indifferent.

Wednesday morning in the empty brownstone, I went up to check the guest room, soon to be Penny's room, a small room on the third floor, with a double bed made up already with fresh white cotton sheets and duvet, a bedside table, a dresser, and two lamps. The light bulbs were in but not working. The room was plain but adequate. The exercise bike I had bought three years ago sat in the corner, the instruction manual balanced on the plastic-wrapped seat. I meant to use it, to get in shape, but I never had. Boxes of papers lined the floors along the back wall: papers from my high school and college; papers, drawings, and tests from the Hazel's schools; William's papers; bills, tax returns, records, birth certificates, one marriage license, all of my mother's papers. Every single piece of paper in scattered piles, not organized in any way, not labeled on any box, all thrown together in various, packed boxes. Years of curling photos in plastic photo boxes sat on top of the boxes of paper. The room was not at all ready for Penny. Maybe I could pick up flowers.

But flowers were not going to fix this mess. I had to gear up and do something. Anything. I had to ready this room now, so after years of doing nothing, I rapidly cleaned and organized it for

Penny's arrival. I took all the cardboard and plastic boxes to the crawl space storage off of William's office down the hall. I would deal with them later. I lugged the awkward and heavy exercise bike down the stairs and into my bedroom, banging and marking the paint on the walls. Maybe I'd use the bike if I saw it every day. I vacuumed the floor and dusted the surfaces. I replaced all the nonworking light bulbs. I fluffed the duvet and pillows. Luckily the bedding was clean. I went to the grocery store for dinner ingredients. I thought lasagna and salad might be good, but I had no idea what she ate or didn't eat, if she had food allergies or aversions. Also, Hazel loved my lasagna and maybe a nice, warm delicious dinner around the island would be good for all of us. It had been a very long time since we had had that sort of sit-down dinner.

I went to the drug store and bought supplies for Penny's bathroom. I stopped at the florist and bought pink roses and put them in a small crystal vase on her dresser. By the time I finished, I was covered in a film of sweat, dust, and dirt. I was already running late and had to shower and dress in ten minutes. I was still putting on my shoes as I headed out the front door.

I got into the car and began the drive to Penny's; the traffic was thick in the city but thinned as soon as I merged onto Route 93 toward Marion. The day was crystal clear with a very slight cool feel to the air, and even the midday sun couldn't bleach out the cobalt blue of the sky.

Marion was a pretty beachfront New England town with scrub pines and hydrangeas landscaping the gray-shingled capes and colonials. It was a town on the way to Chatham; we drove by the exit every year on our annual summer drive to the Cape, but had never stopped. It was strange thinking about all of those years of driving right by my sister's exit. The roads wound around little neighborhoods and harbor-front communities, marinas, boat yards, and little ice cream stands. I followed Richard's directions to Penelope's apartment building, past a strip mall, and a right down a road that led me to a plain-looking white-brick building, four stories tall, with a simple wooden sign reading "Marion Cloisters Apts." My sister was in that building right now, waiting for me, a stranger, to pick her up and bring her home. I was nervous, my stomach unsettled, my heart in my throat, my hands clammy and damp. I thought about William's reservations and then reluctant support and Hazel's indifference; I really was doing this alone. I was so uncertain about so much in my life; to be taking this on felt like one too many things. It was scary. The only comfort to me was that I simply *had* to bring Penny in. I had no choice. What else could I do?

I parked the car, almost locked my keys inside, took a deep breath, and whispered, "Get your shit together, Fez." A passerby overheard me talking to myself and stared. I stared back defiantly and put the keys securely in my bag. I walked into the foyer of the building, wiping my sweaty hands onto my jeans. On the wall were the names of the residents, including Penny's apartment: 3C—SPENCER/WRIGHT. I pressed their buzzer. The inner door clicked, and I opened the door and walked up the stairs.

When I got to the third floor, I knew immediately which door was Penny's. The door had a white board and a marker like kids have on their college freshman dorm doors, with Fourth of July decorations, flags, stickers, and decals. On the white board, a note said, "Penny, I am so sorry about Dottie. Come by when you can, Peg."

I knocked on the door and almost instantly a man answered, about my age, tan, handsome, weather-beaten a bit, blue-eyed, sandy-blond hair, wearing jeans and a blue T-shirt. "You must be Fessenden," he said warmly.

"I am, hi, and are you Paul? So sorry, I wasn't sure who would be here."

"Hi, yes I'm Paul Reynolds. I'm the one who ran the program in the facility in Plymouth before she and Dottie came here to live on their own. Come on in, we're just finishing up a couple of things. Penny doesn't have too much stuff. She's in her bedroom. Let me get her, so you two can finally meet."

"OK, thanks." And then I leaned in and whispered, "Is she going to be OK with all of this? With me?"

He leaned in to me and said, "I don't know. I think so. I hope so."

He went from the front hall into a living area and back to what must have been Penny's bedroom. I looked around. The living room contained a yellow sofa and a yellow chair. The walls were painted a bright, buttery yellow. The carpet was thick, yellow shag. All over the walls were hundreds, no *thousands*, of stickers and Scotch-taped pictures of people and postcards and a poster of a cat hanging from a limb, which read, "Hang on, Kitty," and a poster of a baby with spaghetti on his head, which read, "Tomorrow's another day," and a large poster of Dolly Parton and another poster of the *Beauty and the Beast* characters. The tiny bits of art and decoration covered every surface of every wall. There were dozens of small wooden crucifixes with tiny wooden Jesuses. There were many plaques with inspirational messages, some campy and funny, others serious and pious. Everywhere. On every inch of every wall.

What was I getting into? Who were these two women? Who was my sister? Was she crazy? Insane? Deeply religious? Was she a hoarder? Since my conversation with Richard, I had only thought about Penny as a resident of my house. I hadn't thought of what sort of person she was or what she liked or loved or believed in. I hadn't imagined her as a person with hobbies or beliefs or passions or fears or joys or desires. She was one-dimensional to me before now. These Jesus figures, hanging dead, their tiny feet and hands bloodied on the crosses, made me dizzy. The clutter and juxtaposition of Christ figures and meowing kitties and neon Disney characters was the collection of an insane person. I worried I was in way, *way* over my head. If I could leave right now, go out to my nice, clean car, back away slowly, and never, ever come back. If only I could just go. Quietly. Please let me go.

I leaned in to look at a small square photo on the wall over by the window. It was a picture of a pretty, young, blond woman and my mother, when my mother was in her midforties. The women were sitting side by side in two plastic chairs, their hands on their laps, looking straight at the camera, taken in a hospital or school cafeteria. Mom was smiling a little lopsided smile, which I had seen before. The younger lady was serious. I leaned in closer to try to read the handwriting on the bottom of the picture. As I was leaning in, Paul came out from the back hall, and behind him was Penny. The young lady in the picture.

She was tall, maybe five feet eleven, with very short, very yellow hair. Not even blond. Yellow. She had our father's skin: luminous and poreless. She and I had the same-shaped eyes: big and round, but mine were mossy green like Mom's and hers were the most beautiful clean sky blue, like Dad's. She was wearing frosted pink lipstick and shimmering light-blue eye shadow and had on a springy floral dress.

Paul broke the silence. "Penny, this is your sister Fez...Fez, this is Penny."

Penny was looking down at her fingers. "Hi," I said carefully.

"Hello, Fuzzy. Richard told me you used to be called Fuzzy. When you was a baby girl." I hadn't heard that nickname since I was eight or nine. It made me smile. Penny turned to Paul. "Am I aposta go now, Paul? Or can we have the sammies I made?"

Paul said, "I think lunch is an excellent idea, Pen. Why don't you put out those sandwiches and drinks you made and we'll all sit down? It's been a long morning." I watched how sweet Paul was with her, speaking softly, slowly, patiently.

I stood back from the kitchen area, sat on the yellow couch, and watched my sister. We shared genes. We were family. I saw the features of both of my parents in her and even myself. I saw how she walked, the steps she took, the way she put her feet on the ground, and it could have been my gait, my steps, but much, much slower. As she bent over to open the refrigerator, I saw her hand on the door; it was Mom's hand. My hand. The same nailbeds, the same knuckles, the same skinny, bony fingers. Penny looked over at me. Our eyes met, and I looked away. I feigned interest in the collection of coloring books on the table: flowers, kittens, puppies, fairy tales. All elaborately and meticulously colored. All completed. "Those is my books, Fuzzy. Careful."

"Oh, they're nice," I said looking through them, holding them more gingerly. They actually were nice. "You're good at this."

"I know. Paul tells me all the time. Right, Paul?" He nodded at her and then smiled at me. "Fuzzy, what's your birthday?"

"May twenty-fifth. When's yours?"

Penny looked like she had seen a ghost. "*What's* your birthday?"

I repeated it. "May twenty-fifth."

Penny looked at Paul and then me again. "Me too, Fuzzy. My birthday's May twenty-fifth too!"

"Really, Penny? Really? That's incredible!" She explained to me how she changed her birthday from December 25, when she was little, before I was born. Penny was really excited about the birthday thing. It was pretty unbelievable, actually.

"That's so essiting, Fuzzy, that we gots the same birthday!"

I agreed.

Penny moved around the kitchen area, busy and focused, and took three sandwiches from the refrigerator and set them out on three white paper napkins on the small, round table. She took three lemonade juice boxes and set them down to the right rear corner of each napkin. She was leaning over very close to the table surface as she did this. She adjusted the napkins again, and the sandwiches on them and the precise location of the juice boxes. And when she was finished she stood up very tall and straight and said, "Lunch is served."

"Fantastic, Pen, let's eat." Paul beamed at Penny, and we sat down and wordlessly began eating our sandwiches: a spongy, pink meat with embedded sliced olives and red peppers and orange American cheese on white, pore-less bread.

Penny looked at me and said, "Look, I's really good at this too." She took the tiny pink straw off of my yellow juice box and removed it from its cellophane wrapper and very, very slowly stuck the foil opening with the pointy straw end until it popped and slid into the box. "Now you can have your drink." I thanked her, and we drank our pink lemonade juice boxes from tiny pink straws.

"Dottie is dead," she said to me suddenly. "And she ain't comin back no more."

I looked at Paul, and he nodded at me, and I replied, "I know, Penny, and I am so sorry about that."

"Why you sorry? You didn't die her."

Paul reached over and rested his hand on Penny's. "Fez wants you to know she's sad that you're sad."

"OK," Penny said with a mouth full of sticky bread.

When lunch was done, Paul said he was going to start bringing Penny's few boxes down to the car. He asked Penny if she wanted to give me the "Million Sticker Tour," to which Penny snorted with laughter and said, "There ain't no million stickas, Paul." I heard her New England accent, completely unlike my own, non-Boston accent. My sister, my blood, but a stranger, raised in another place; so much connected us and yet so much had separated us.

Penny showed me the bedroom, where she sat on the bed, bouncing up and down like a little girl at camp. "This is my bed. But I ain't gonna sleep here no more."

I nodded. "I know. I'm really sorry about that too." I was standing awkwardly by the door and a dark shadow fell over us; suddenly, my heart ached for her and the simple world she was losing. I was taking this stranger home to live with me forever. I did not know her; she did not know me.

Maybe Penny saw the shadow too or maybe she saw my face fall, or maybe not, but she patted the bed and said, "Sit on my bed too." I did. It was like a dormitory twin bed with terrible, soft springs and a weirdly firm, crunchy mattress. The weight of our two seated bodies rolled us together, pressing our shoulders together. "That's my window and that's my desk and my desk chair and my roll-y shade. Paul putted all my stuff into boxes."

"Well, Penny, you certainly have a nice room."

"Yep," she said. "I do." She bounced up and down a few more times.

We got up from her soft, springy bed and toured Dottie's bedroom and the bathroom with pink swirling tiles, and back out into the yellow living room. Paul explained that the apartment came furnished, and Dottie's mother had taken Dottie's things, so the only items for us to take were four boxes of Penny's. I asked Paul if the wall art should come, and he said, no, that was going to stay and maybe Penny could start a new collection at her new house.

I said, "That sounds great."

Penny agreed. "Except I's bringing Jesus. And my pictures of Mommy and Dottie and the ladies at the hostipal."

"Oh! Of course! How could we forget?" Paul asked, unhooking the tiny crucifixes from the wall and handing them to Penny to put in the last open box. He then carefully untaped the photographs and piled them neatly in the same box. She held the tiniest crucifix, smiled, and started to run her thumb up and down the length of the cross, rhythmically. Paul said, "Are you ready now, Penny?"

She looked down at Jesus. She shook her head. "I ain't ready, Paul. I wanna stay with Dottie."

"Oh, sweetie, I know. I know." He rubbed her back while she stood stiffly, stroking her crucifix. "But you need to be with your family now, and I'm sure you and Fez will have a nice time getting to know each other." Penny looked down and nodded and started slowly walking to the door.

Paul, Penny, and I went down the stairs and out the glass door to the parking lot. I opened up the passenger side door of the car.

Penny stopped and shook her head fast. "I ain't gonna go with Fuzzy. I ain't."

I looked at Paul.

"Penny, honey, here's a thought: why don't you try Fez's house for *one week* and then we can see how you feel. You remember how quickly you adjust to things?"

"I dunno. What else? What other things can I do? Where else can I live?" Penny was looking back and forth at Paul and me: her two home base options, her two connections. She didn't want to come home with me, and she didn't want to stay there. I tried to think of something to say to comfort her and make her feel better about the decision to come home with me. I couldn't think of anything. All I could repeat was some convoluted litany of sounds.

"Well, um, Penny, hmm, you, why don't, uh," I said as I watched this scene unfold. It was hard enough deciding to bring her home. I hadn't realized how hard it was going to be to see her pulling back in fear. She was stroking the crucifix fast and hard.

"Well, you can go back to the center, but you said you didn't want to go there without Dottie, right?" Paul was trying to formulate something.

Penny shook her head. "OK. One week with Fuzzy, and then maybe I's moving. But I's the boss to *me.*" Penny marched over to the car, sat down in the passenger seat, and strapped in. I exchanged contact information with Paul, thanked him profusely, and told him I would stay in touch. Penny didn't look out the windows or wave goodbye or say anything else to Paul as we backed up and pulled away. She stared at her bubble gum–pink nails, and then she started rocking back and forth and back and forth in her seat. Front to back, as if she were in an invisible rocking chair.

Once we had driven for a while, about twenty minutes, I tried conversation. "How was Dottie's service today?" Penny stopped rocking and looked out the window.

I tried again. "What should we do when we get home?" Again, no response. Penny rested her head against the window.

"I hope you like your new room." Penny closed her eyes.

"Is lasagna OK for dinner?" No reply.

"You're going to meet Hazel when we get home." Nothing.

"Boston is a beautiful place. I hope you—"

She sat up straight, turned toward me, and interrupted, "We's goin a Boston?"

I was so surprised at the sound of her voice after such a long silence. "Yes, Penny. Have you ever been?"

"Nope," she said. "But I was gonna go with Dottie. For a surprise visit. For her birthday. It's *BeautifulBoston.*"

"Yes, it is. I'm so glad you like it." Big victory. But as I looked over at her, she turned back to look out the window, lost in something and started rocking again. Back and forth and back and forth and back and forth.

# CHAPTER 7

# PENELOPE

I gots a sister. A real sister. Not like Dottie, who feels like a sister, but a *sister* sister. After the worstest day ever when Dottie died and wasn't ever, *ever* going to wake up, Richard called me to talk about Dottie and how sad he was and how sad I was and how I couldn't live alone anymore. I got real, real scared on the phone. Plus, I was still so, so mad at Richard about not letting me go to *BeautifulBoston*. Real mad.

*Richard,* I said, *I ain't goin back to that other place alone. I ain't. It was good with Dottie, but I don't wants to go back alone.*

*I know, Penny,* he said. *I agree, you shouldn't.* Then he started talking real slow and said something crazy about my mommy and daddy having a baby sister for me when I was twelve years old.

*Whatchu sayin? I gots a sister, Richard?*

*Yes, Penny, and I know this is very confusing and it's a lot to digest,* he said, but I just kept thinking about Dottie having to go sleeping in that hole in the ground and how dark and scary and cold she must have felt, and it made me so sad and scared. I got to rocking pretty good.

*Penny? You OK, sweetie? I can hear you rocking,* Richard said.

*I's OK, Richard,* I said, but I didn't think I was OK. His soft voice and all his words were making me feel rumbly tumbly in my tummy, and everything was kinda swirly and jiggly. *Where's I gonna go?* I finally asked.

*Well, your sister would like for you to come live with her.*

*My baby sister wants me to come live with her?*

*Yes, Penny,* he continued slowly. *She has a lovely place and a husband and a daughter—*

*My baby sister has a husband and a girl? Is the girl a baby? I likes babies,* I said. Cuz I do. I likes babies. They smell good. They gots tiny fingers.

*Yes, she has a family, but their daughter's not a baby anymore.*

*Wait, Richard, what's my baby sister's name?*

*Fessenden, but everyone just calls her Fez. She was called Fuzzy when she was little.*

*Hmm, Fuzzy…I likes Fuzzy. Like I'm Penelope and everyone calls me Penny.*

*That's right, Penny. Fez's husband is William, and he is living in a different house right now, and there's Hazel, who is sixteen, and she's going to high school near their house.*

*What's their birthdays, Richard?*

*Um, I'm not sure, Penny, but I know you love birthdays. Fez can tell you all that when she picks you up, if that's OK with you.*

*Why Willum's not living in Fuzzy's house? Isn't they friends?*

*I don't really know about the details, but I'm sure Fez will explain everything to you when you guys meet.*

*OK, Richard. So I's not living here at the apartment no more, and I's not going to the Center without Dottie, so I's gonna live with my sister, Fuzzy? How far is Fuzzy's house?*

*I think it's about sixty miles, about an hour's drive. And yes, I think that's the plan. How do you feel about that?* Richard always asked me that question.

*Good, I guess.* But I just felt kinda wiggly again. *What about workin at the hostipal? They needs me bad at the hostipal, Richard.*

*Well, Penny, I think it's best if you don't work at the hospital. Your new home is about an hour away, and it's too far to commute.*

I was thinking about being an hour away and not going to the hostipal no more and not taking the P-97 bus with Dottie no more, and I started to feel kinda sick to my tummy. Richard was talking and talking, but it sounded like he was far away in a tin can, and I stopped listenin so good.

Then I heard him say, *So remember, I'll take you to Dottie's service today, and then Paul is going to help you pack up your things so you can bring them with you to Fez's house. Does that sound OK?*

*OK,* I said, but nothing sounded OK. I just wanted everything to be just the way it was before. I liked before.

*I should be there in about an hour, and I'll buzz your buzzer as soon as I get there. Can you be ready for the service in an hour?*

*What's the service, Richard?*

*Well, it's kind of a goodbye party, but it's sad. Remember the chaplain Father Michael? He comes to the hospital sometimes? He's going to say some nice things about Dottie, and I think Dottie's mom should be there, and Paul and some people who worked with Dottie at the factory.*

*Dottie didn't like her mom so good, Richard. Her mama thought Dottie was an ashtray.*

Richard paused and then let out a lot of air. *Yes, honey, those awful burns. Awful. Dottie's mother had some serious problems. She's a terribly mean and troubled person, but I guess she wants to say goodbye to Dottie too.*

*I don't like Dottie's mama.*

*Me neither,* Richard agreed after a little pause.

After Richard and I hunged up our phones, I decided to put on Dottie's favorite dress of mine, with the pink, pink roses and the bright-green leaves. It matched the theme for my nails that week, which was petal pink. This was the theme after red, white, and blue. The last theme ever from Dottie.

When Richard pushed the buzzer—*bzz bzz bzz*—I didn't let him in but went downstairs to get into his big black, shiny, clean car. Even though he was kinda the boss to me and didn't let me go to *BeautifulBoston* with Dottie, who was never, ever going to wake up, I liked Richard. He was nice and took care of me after my mommy and daddy was gone. We drove kinda quiet to the church near our apartment. It was a white building with big windows that had colored glass and pictures of angels and pretty ladies.

Richard and I walked inside, and it smelled like dust and lemons. Nobody was there yet, so we just satted down in one of the shiny wooden benches and waited for the party to start. I just membered to sit quiet cuz you's aposta be quiet in churches.

The service was bad. It wasn't like a party *at all*. Dottie was in a wooden box, all shiny and painted, and I knew she wasn't happy in there, and I wanted to rip it open and say, *Dottie, Dottie, get outta there*, but I didn't say it. I just sat real quiet next to Richard, and Father Michael said some things from the Bible and some things about Dottie being all nice and how life was hard but the glory of life was everlasting or something. It felt kinda dumb cuz there wasn't no glory. Just a box with my best friend, Dottie, in it, and she ain't ever, ever gonna wake up.

Dottie's meanypants mama was there, but she looked kinda bored or sleepy in her little black dress and tiny black purse and dark-red lips and mean, mean pin eyes, so tiny and black. That lady was so mean to my Dottie and made lots of little round scars on her, and it made Dottie real, real sad, and I didn't even want to see her, so I scrunched up my eyes real tight so alls I could see was tiny orange dots sparkling all around, and that was nice and made me feel happier. Maybe Dottie could see those dots too. *Scrunch up your eyes, Dottie*, I thought. *It's pretty.*

The only other people in the little wooden chapel room were three peoples from Dottie's job at the factery and three peoples from the old place where we used to live before the apartment, who I remembered from group sessions. They was looking down and kinda quiet. Playing with their fingers. Poking at their fingernails. When the church talking stopped and the piano song was done, Richard took me by the elbow, and we all walked real slow out of the church. Everyone's eyes was down looking at the tiny shiny red floor tiles, so I looked at the tiny floor tiles too. Richard said it was time for putting Dottie's box in the ground now.

Richard drove me to the cemetery in Plymouth where they was going to put Dottie's box, and then it was just Father Michael and Dottie's mama and us. But when I saw the big dark, black hole and the green, green grass and Dottie's mama with her pinched-up face, I had to scrunch up my face again.

Richard whispered, *Penny, would you like to put a flower on the casket before they cover it?*

I nodded, and Richard took my hand, and we took two white roses from Father Michael's soft hands, and we put them real quiet on top of Dottie's box. Seeing that box all shiny and cold with the pretty flowers sitting on top made me feel so sad and mad that Dottie was in there and wasn't ever, ever coming out. But I didn't say nothin. Richard and I just sat back down on our folding metal chairs on the grass. I was too tired to even rock, so I just sat kinda slumpy and looked at the grass and my pretty white shoes.

The only other person I member dying was my mommy. And we didn't do no *service* in a church. After she died of the cancer in her froat, Richard told me they just burned her in an oven and throwed her ashes and little bitty bones all over the ocean and up on a hill. I didn't say goodbye to her so goodly. One day she was visiting me with her red-and-black-checked thermos, and then she didn't come around no more.

After the Dottie cemetery part, Richard dropped me off at my apartment building and made sure that Paul was already at my place to help me pack, and then Richard pulled away in his big black, shiny new car, and said he would visit me very soon at my new house with my baby sister, Fuzzy. *Bye-bye, Richard,* I said. *See you soon.*

After Paul and I packed up my things, my clothes, my shoes, my bathroom stuff, my pictures, my fake flowers, I heard the *buzz buzz,* and I asked Paul if that was Fuzzy, and he said, *Yep, I guess your sister is here!* He seemed pretty essited about it.

I felt kinda funny inside, like I used to feel when Dottie got off the bus at her stop for work at the factory. Like I had a big chunk of ham in my throat from a big bite of sandwich. But I hadn't had ham for a long, long time. And then while I was looking deep in the back of my crayon drawer, I heard her voice. Then Paul came back and said, *Come on out and meet your sister, Penny.*

Fuzzy was real tall, like me. Long straight hair, but not yellow like mine, kind of the color of sand or old wood. Her eyes were big and round just like my eyes, but they weren't pretty blue like mine. Kinda green like the top of a pond or olives or moss like we had growing all over the apartment building backyard. She wasn't dressed so good. There wasn't no theme at all. Her fingernails had no polish on them. Not even clear. She had tiny silver hoops at her ears. Her ears were tiny like mine. Dottie always asked me if I could hear good because my ears were so teeny. Now my sister had the same teeny ears. I guess she looked kinda like me except for the old clothes. I felt kinda good to be so pretty and matching in my petal-pink outfit.

She said, *Hi,* real careful like she might break me if she spoke any louder.

*Hi, Fuzzy,* I said, and it was kinda scary and new, but then we got to eat, which was good because I was really hungry and I had made the sammitches a long time ago and wanted to eat them even then.

The sammitches was real good and everyone ate them, but Fuzzy never, ever heard of pimiento loaf. I laughed so hard when she asked about the meat. I laughed and laughed. Who doesn't know pimiento loaf? Jeez.

Paul brought the boxes down to Fuzzy's car. I didn't want to go. At all. I was thinking I's gonna throwed up, but Paul told me just to try living with my baby sister, Fuzzy, so I's not so scared. My baby sister, Fuzzy, wasn't such a baby. My baby sister, Fuzzy, can drived a car, and she has her very own car, which was gray like a pencil and fancy and shiny and smelled good inside. I wasn't so sad to say goodbye to my friend Paul cuz we said we'd do lots of visits and nothing was ever going to change our being good friends, so I wasn't feeling rumbly so much.

*Paul,* I asked, *I's not working at the hostipal no more, right?*

Paul looked at Fuzzy and then at me. *No, Pen, no more hostipal.*

*OK,* I said, *but I didn't say bye-bye to my hostipal peoples.*

*I know, Penny. Let's have you come back another time, and we'll go visit and say goodbye then. Is that OK?*

*OK, Paul,* I said thinking about me no more working at the hostipal.

We got in the car, Fuzzy and I, and then we drove. She was asking a lot of questions, and then she stopped. She got real quiet. So I was real quiet then too. Until she told me we was going to *BeautifulBoston.* I almost esploded with essitedment when she told me that. Fuzzy lives in *BeautifulBoston*! I just couldn't believe it. The place with the boats like big white birds and shiny buildings and grassy parks! And then I was looking out the window at the dark-green, scraggly trees going by so fast, and the road all gray and smeared and the yellow lines going by so, so fast and the sun coming down so hot and bright in patches on my body, and I started to think about Dottie in that cold, shiny box and the sun not shining hot and bright on her lap and her not ever, ever waking up and that I was going to *BeautifulBoston* but Dottie wasn't coming. All of a sudden, I got gooey inside with lumps of ham stuck, and I started rocking. I had to.

I think I rocked most of the way home, until I musta falled asleep with the warm sun all over me in the shiny car. When we got home, Fuzzy gently touched my shoulder and said, *Penny, we're home.*

I woked up and looked at the pretty street with the big trees and the brown houses all right next to each other. They was made of rocks. Big square rocks and big windows and all bumped up to each other.

*They's all the same,* I said still kinda sleepy.

*Oh, the brownstones? Yeah, I guess they are.* She looked at the houses like she'd never seen them before and then turned back at me. *Come on in. I'll show you around, and then we can get your stuff later.*

*OK,* I said and got out of the car.

*Let's go straight to your room, and then we can see the rest after.*

*OK.*

We walked through the big door, which Fuzzy needed three keys to open, and then through a teeny little area, big enough for only the two of us, and then through another door, and we were looking at a big brown staircase and a big hallway going straight back and a little room on the right with a small sofa and two chairs and a small TV. Nothing was yellow. *Nothing.* We went right up the stairs, Fuzzy walking ahead of me kinda bony and slow.

*You're on the third floor, along with William's office and a bath, which will be just for you.*

*OK.*

When we got to my new room, Fuzzy went in and turned on the bedside light and said, *I hope this is OK, Penny. This is your new room.*

Everything was white: walls, bed, sheets, puffy quilt, bedside tables, lamps, dresser. The wooden floor was brown. No carpet. *I like yellow,* I said.

*Oh,* she said all weird. *OK, well we can work on that.* She looked strange and like her pants were too tight, but they were not. She just looked like she couldn't figure out which leg to stand on. So we just stood there, and she was kind of patting the puffy quilt and looking around.

*Why don't we get your things and you can start settling in a little?* she finally said. I just nodded and waited for her to lead the way out of the very white room. What kind of peoples has white rooms? It looked a lot like the hostipal rooms I used to make up every day in my old job at the hostipal. It didn't smell like the hostipal, which was a very good thing, cuz that's a gross smell. That was the smell of pee and bowel movements and blood and throw-up and medicines and old ladies' powder and perfume. Even the plastic of those IV bags had a smell. This room at Fuzzy's house smelled like nothing at all.

Fuzzy and I carried up the four boxes to my white, white room, and Fuzzy asked me if I wanted help unpacking, and I just said no, cuz I didn't want to be with Fuzzy no more. I just wanted to be with Dottie, and I started to feel real sad, and the light coming in the windows started to get kinda orange, and that made me feel real sad too.

*I'll just start putting dinner together then,* said Fuzzy. *Let me know if you want help or need anything, OK?* And she left, and I heard her boots going down the two flights of stairs. *Clunk, clunk, clunk.*

When I opened up the first box, the first thing I seen was my photo of Dottie and me at the amusement park from this summer. Paul had tooked us cuz he said we needed a *fun getaway,* and so he drove us to a water park on Cape Cod over the tall bridge. The place was so much fun and had lots of colors and music playing everywhere, and Dottie and I gots corn dogs and root beers and soft ice creams in swirly chocolate and vanilla. I think Dottie might of just got vanilla axually. We stayed on the kiddy side cuz Dottie and I was too scared to go on the tall rolly-coaster cuz alls we heard was screaming and hollerin, and Dottie said, *No, thank you,* to that. I guess she figgered if peoples was so scared they was screaming, it wouldn't be too good for us. We sometimes got ascared of stuff. We did go on a little water park ride that went up and down on a log, and we got splashed, and Dottie said, *My heart's beating outta my chest!* I sure hope that's not what killed my Dottie, that stupid log ride. Maybe it made her heart hurted so it breaked later.

Seeing Dottie and me in that picture, smiling with melty ice cream cones in our hands and the drips running down our fingers, I started feeling pretty bad. And so I sat down on my new white bed in my new white room and just started rocking. Back and forth and back and forth, until the light faded in the room, and then the orange sunlight stripes was brown, and the brown boxes disappeared, and the white things turned gray, and my head was tired and heavy.

# CHAPTER 8

# HAZEL

I woke up, facedown, smushed into my pillow, rolled over onto my back, and immediately felt shitty. Sick to my stomach. Wicked headache. Dry cotton in my mouth. I looked at my phone. Wednesday, 6:47 a.m. Fuckin school day. This year was gonna suck. I already hated junior year, two days in. I hated sitting in those stupid classrooms listening to monotone teachers' voices about bullshit info I'm never, ever gonna use.

I started looking at my phone from the night before, trying to piece shit together. Ty and Bex never answered my texts. So fucking rude. I couldn't figure out if they were together or not. I kinda got an uneasy and weird feeling when I was with them together, like she was pissed at me, or was just always trying to ditch me. Ty, by himself, was always totally chill, but maybe kinda backing off too. Maybe I was gonna give them a little breathing room. Gina was doing nothing, I guess. She wasn't texting me back, either. At about nine, I didn't really have anyone else to text or call, and I sure as shit wasn't gonna do school work, so I took a couple of Xanax out of pure boredom and cuz I wanted to, I guess, and just listened to music in my room. I had earphones in, just listening to

Lil Wayne, and his cool, high, tinny voice, until I fell into a deep, deep black and dreamless sleep.

I remembered Mom was going to pick up her special needs sister today. Not exactly what we needed. And I was gonna have to take part in some family dinner tonight. Might have to pregame for that one, at least enough to make it decent.

The early morning sun was coming in so bright it made my forehead hurt, pinching a little spot between my eyes. I sat up slow, felt a little dizzy, waited for the lightheaded feeling to stop, and then stood up and tiptoed into the bathroom. I closed the door, locked it, got my stash from out of the cabinet and vaped. With the door locked, the exhaust on, and the super clean vape, I could sit there, with my mother practically in the next fucking room, and get high. She was totally clueless. I'd been doing it for a while now. She must have thought I was constipated all the time or something. LOL. I'm pretty sure she didn't think about it at all. I don't know if I felt good about doing it right under her nose or really, really bad. But I did it all the same.

She must've heard me walking around. "Haze? You up?" she yelled up the stairs.

I exhaled up toward the exhaust fan and yelled through the thick wooden door, "Yeah."

"Ready for school?" She sounded so optimistic.

"Yeah, almost," I yelled.

I took a hot shower, letting the water and the soap wash down me in clean, hot sheets, inhaling the smell of the creamy coconut shampoo, deep breathing the hot steam, trying to get squeaky, actually feeling the squeakiness of my skin with my fingers. Noticing the sharpness of my hipbones and kneecaps. After, in my towel, I wiped the steam off the mirror, leaving a little circle of clear mirror. I squeezed Visine into my eyes, brushed my teeth, gargled with Scope, put on concealer under my eyes, which had weirdly gotten sorta dark, and got dressed.

I didn't fuckin want to go to school. I was tired, really tired, and I just wanted to stay in bed all day, listening to music, texting, napping. I didn't really want to do shit.

Mom decided to walk me part of the way to school so she could pick up some stuff for Penny, my new aunt. So lame, walking with my mom, but whatever. On the way, there was an elementary school with a playground where kids were hanging out and playing before their day started. The young moms were all standing on the side of the playground with stainless steel to-go cups of coffee. They were chatting and laughing, giddy, hair pulled back in ponytails, dressed in yoga pants and running shoes and expensive-looking exercise gear. I stopped to watch a bunch of kids screaming and going around and around on one of those round things you have to push and jump onto. Their hair was flying all around in the morning breeze and because of the speed of the ride. Their new, thin fall jackets and sweaters were bright, almost neon colors: lime and tangerine and magenta.

Mom said, "Haze. What're you looking at?" She had walked ahead and was coming back to see what I was seeing. "You OK? You seem really tired." She stared deep into my eyes.

I *was* tired. I was also high to fucking bejesus. I couldn't stop staring at the colors going around and around and around the roll-y thing. "I am tired. I didn't sleep so well last night," I lied.

Mom rubbed my back through my thin black sweater and said, "Are you sure you're not coming down with something?" She looked at me with concern. "I want to take you to the doctor and test you for mono."

I pulled my gaze away from the swirling colors. "I'm fine. I don't have mono. I'm just not sleeping that well, I guess." I wasn't gonna go to any fucking doctor. No way.

"I still think we should test you to be sure. It's going around." She put her hand on my shoulder. "Are you nervous about junior year? I know it's a very stressful time."

"Yeah," I lied again. "That's probably it. I guess I'm a little anxious about school." I spoke slowly, careful to articulate each word. It was so easy for the words to slur all together. Mom rubbed the back of my neck, and we kept walking, away from the kids and the colors and the high-pitched, happy voices. Seeing them made me feel like I was a million miles from anything good. I just got real lonely. I'm not sure why. All those kids smiling and laughing and my mom so fucking clueless and me feeling kinda shitty and high at the same time. All of a sudden, I couldn't figure out what the point was. I couldn't remember what mattered.

# CHAPTER 9
# FESSENDEN

I smelled smoke. I ran into the kitchen and realized that the oven, preheating for the lasagna, was so greasy from whatever was last cooked in it, was now black with smoke and emanating out into the kitchen. I turned off the oven, opened the oven door, opened the windows and the back door, and started fanning the air with the placemat I found on the table. The smoke detector did not go off, which was a relief and a concern, simultaneously. I would have to clean the oven after it cooled down, and start this dinner process over again.

It was six o'clock. I hadn't heard from Hazel. She was usually home by now, even if she had a project or stayed at school for study groups. She was usually good about texting her whereabouts. I checked my phone. Nothing. Nothing from William, either, which bothered me; he promised he would be here for dinner.

I texted Hazel: *Penny's here. Don't forget family dinner. Lasagna!*

I texted William: *Lasagna at 7:30 or 8:00 if you want to come by to see Hazel. Penny is here.*

I scraped out and scrubbed the crusty insides of the oven, dried it, and turned it back on. I set the island for dinner using our linen placemats and napkins. I set out our fine china and silverware as well as our light blue glass goblets. The island looked nice. I was on a roll, so I decided to go all out and get out candlesticks and candles. I put together a green salad and assembled the lasagna and placed it in the oven. The nightly news was over. I checked my kitchen clock: 7:03 p.m. I checked my phone—nothing. I called Hazel, and the call went straight to voice mail.

"Where are you?" I asked.

I made myself a drink and looked into the oven. Not bubbling or ready yet. I turned to watch the television and got lost in a program on shark attacks. An increasing number of Great Whites had been drawn into the Chatham beaches and the footage of the large creatures was dramatic and disturbing. I watched the entire show, rapt and slightly aghast. Those beaches mentioned in the show were the same ones we brought Hazel swimming when we wanted big waves; our Crow's Pond was a lovely place to take a dip or a long swim, but there were never any real waves. I remember making picnic lunches of tuna fish sandwiches and pickles and lemonade, packing up the car with beach towels and foldable beach chairs, and making the short drive from the Crow's Nest to Nauset, the beautiful National Seashore beach. When Hazel was nine or ten, she went into the water with William, and we lost her in an especially big wave. I was watching carefully, my eyes trained on Hazel, and William was swimming right next to her, but Hazel got caught up in a powerful cresting wave that rolled her around and then spat her out crashing and coughing on the sand. She was disoriented, waterlogged, and terrified when she came out of the water, sputtering and then sobbing. William immediately got out of the water and knelt down, hugging Hazel, consoling and calming her. William asked her if she wanted to try it again, maybe "get back on the horse," but Hazel was terrified and shook her head. She walked up to me, shaken and defeated. William went back in the water, and Hazel sat next to me, her head resting on my shoulder, and didn't speak. She watched William swimming for a while, then fell asleep wrapped in her towel, curled up in the fetal position.

The lasagna was bubbling and ready, ready to be taken out of the oven. I couldn't believe Hazel hadn't responded to my texts and calls. I wasn't sure that William would, so his silence wasn't unexpected. I was starting to feel a rising and tingling panic about Hazel though. Where could she be? What was she doing? Was she still at school? At a long field hockey practice? Maybe working on a project? Maybe I didn't hear her say she was going to be late. Or was she hanging out with friends? Another glance at the phone. Nothing. I called Hazel again and the phone went immediately to voice mail, meaning her phone had died or she had turned it off.

"Hazel, it's me. Please check in. Dinner is ready and tonight is important. Come home. Please."

I thought I would see how Penny was doing and see if she was going to be hungry soon. At least *someone* would eat with me. I walked up the stairs and rapped gently on Penny's door. "Are you ready for dinner, Penny?"

She was slow to respond, but then I heard her say quietly and far away, "I's not hungry, Fuzzy."

"Oh OK, Penny. Are you sure? I've got a nice lasagna dinner all ready downstairs."

She replied, "I's jus gonna sleep now."

"Are you sure?" I asked.

I stared at the closed door for a moment, hoping for a different response, but heard nothing. I left her doorway and headed quietly down the stairs, wondering about the wide array of feelings she must be having. She must be lonely, I thought, and scared and unsure about how her life was supposed to be going. Did she understand, really understand that Dottie was gone? Did she understand her work life was over and that her life in Marion was something of the past? I knew how hard it was for me to understand a major life change, especially death and the grieving associated with it, but how was Penny going to do that? Had she mourned our mother? How and when did she know *she* had died? Had Richard been the one to call or visit Penny and give her the news? I had an endless reel of questions.

When I got back to the kitchen, I was met by the warm, rich, and sweet smells of tomatoes and meat and onions and garlic and basil.

I ate in the quiet of my white kitchen, surrounded by marble and butcher block, all alone, with the blue light of the television and the dimmed pendants over the island. I called Ellie.

"Hi! How is Penny? How are *you*?" she asked quickly.

"She's OK," I replied. "I think she's freaking out right now. She's in her room and didn't want dinner."

"Why don't you bring a plate up to her room? Maybe she's just feeling weird."

"Maybe. Yeah, that's a good idea. She probably is. I'm sure she is."

"What did William and Hazel say? How was all that?"

"Well, William had his reservations but was OK, and Hazel was just flat and kind of annoyed. But she's just hard to read right now. Anyway, Hazel never came home for dinner. And I had made a point this morning of saying I really wanted her here for this dinner. She *knew* Penny was going to be here."

"Really? That's not good." Ellie always reacted exactly the way I wanted her to, validating my feelings, and right now I needed her to be outraged. She was. "What's going on?"

Ellie was the best listener I had ever met. She *genuinely* listened. She really heard. She knew what to say. She was frank and told me exactly how she felt, even if it meant I might feel hurt or offended. When I met her during our freshman year at college, we became friends immediately. I was dating someone at Georgetown at the time, and she was from Bethesda, Maryland, so we cemented our friendship on long road trips to the DC area during that school year. We had many long, deep, and honest conversations on those five-hour car rides. Her excellent communications skills led her straight to graduate school where she got her masters in social work and then to her current job.

She worked at Edgehill, a psychiatric hospital based in Belmont, Massachusetts, that specialized in inpatient care for patients with extreme depression, anxiety, personality disorders, schizophrenia. The hospital also had excellent outpatient care for those with both alcohol- and drug-dependence and for those working through depression and anxiety issues who didn't need to or want to do the inpatient thing. Ellie was an administrator there and a counselor, and from what I could imagine, she was amazing with the patients, handling intakes with gentleness, kindness, and extreme sensitivity. I'm sure her humor and frank approach was useful as well: listening to them, hearing their stories at their lowest moments, helping their families and loved ones let the patient go to be under Edgehill's excellent care. She loved her job there, but I couldn't imagine what she dealt with every day. Somehow, she kept her upbeat attitude and never seemed to let the job bring her down.

"What's going on?" Ellie asked, the concern clear in her voice.

"Well, you know I told you her grades dipped a bit…"

"Yes, you did, but I didn't think it was such a big deal…I thought you and William figured the Bs made sense given her course load."

"Yeah, we did, but then this summer, it just felt like she was drifting away. She had her camp job, which was fine, but she was hanging out with a new group of friends, and out a lot of nights and definitely drinking. She said she's not drinking much, but I'm not so sure. Also, I'm not positive, but I'm pretty sure she was smoking too. *And* she just seemed to be sleeping a lot. It probably sounds paranoid and disjointed."

"No, it doesn't. I mean, there could be plausible explanations for everything, like, kids drink at that age and kids smoke at that age."

"That's exactly what William says; it's all perfectly normal, but my gut is telling me she's changing and it's not just 'normal.'"

"Hmmm," said Ellie very carefully, "gut feelings are important, and if you're feeling something, it's real enough to deal with. Maybe it is something." I heard her ice tinkling in her glass. She continued. "How was it for her without William there this summer?"

"Tough, I think. They're so close. They used to have really nice evening outings for ice cream and sunset boat rides, and we didn't do any of that." I hated that she didn't get that time with him.

"Well, part of that could be her age…I never hung out with my parents in the evenings in high school. Why didn't you take her for that stuff? Was she never around?"

"Sometimes she was, but evenings turned out to be my best time to crank on the book…God, I think I totally blew it as a parent this summer."

"No, no, no, stop. You're not going to feel guilty, OK? We're all just doing the best we can. And I know right now is a really hard and crazy time for you with everything going on. So here's what I'm going to do. I'm going to come over and meet Penny, whenever you say. I'm going to tell you to just let your anger at William go, for the moment. I know you're angry with him, and you have every right, but I think you're being a bit punitive, both to him and to yourself. And as for Haze, you know I don't want to scare you, or overreact, but this is what I look at in my work, and I am a worrier. She's young. I know kids party earlier these days, but I do think about your mother and family history."

"I know," I agreed. "I'm thinking of that too."

"So when can I come over?" she asked.

"I'm not sure," I replied. "Let me get Penny settled here, and then you can come over for dinner soon. Thank you for listening and for your sage advice. Really."

"Always," she said. "I'm coming over *very* soon, OK? Do *not* keep me waiting. Love you." Her unwavering support and loyalty made me smile.

I went upstairs and sat on my bed with my cell phone and left a message for William. "Hazel isn't home yet. She's not with you, is she? Can you please call when you get this?" I didn't want to start calling parents of Hazel's new friends. I didn't know these people, and I knew my calling would be an indication of my lack of control, an admission that I had really lost Hazel; I was the mom who had *no* idea where her child was. I opened up the school directory. What was Gina's last name? Tyler's? Bex was short for Becker something, I thought. I tried to remember. I didn't know these people.

As I was flipping through the directory, I heard the front door open. It was nine thirty. I heard Hazel drop her heavy backpack. I ran out of the bedroom and over to the top of the stairs. "Hazel?" I looked down the stairs. Hazel was standing at the bottom of the stairs, holding the newel post. Her knuckles were white as she struggled to stay upright. She wavered.

"Hey, Ma," she slurred. She sounded exactly like my mother. Drunk or stoned on something. She was a mess.

"Jesus, Hazel. Where have you been? My God, I have been worried sick!" My panic of a few minutes ago quickly surged into hot, fiery rage. Hazel looked up at me with heavy lids. It didn't even seem like she was just drunk. It was something else, or a combination of things.

"Out. I wuzz out." She smiled at her own clever answer, her indifference evident.

"Jesus Christ, Hazel. What the fuck? You missed dinner, and Penny is here, and oh my god, you are a mess! It's a school night and where have you been? Who was with you? What's—" I couldn't even finish because I knew it didn't matter. She was too out of it to hear me or to care. So I stopped. "Just go to bed," I said quietly.

I remembered how my mother used to act when she was drunk, all wavy and slurry, soft and limp. As a little girl, and as a young teenager, I used to feel I could affect a change in her, that my words would make a difference, even when she was drunk, but I learned from years of righteous confrontations and my mother's laconic stares that nothing ever came from those fights. No change. No inspiration. No improvement. So I simply stopped trying.

Hazel held on hard to the railing and very, very slowly walked upstairs. It was as if every step took a great deal of effort. Her bony body rattled. She passed me, the smell of alcohol strong on her.

"Nigh nigh," she slurred, and she went into her bedroom and closed the door. She fell heavily onto her bed.

I put my cell phone into the charger next to my bed and checked to see if William had called. He hadn't and still no text. I called and left him another message, this time frantic and angry. Why the fuck wasn't he calling me back? I had to speak with him. Every time I told him I was worried about Hazel, he'd reiterate his "kids will be kids" line and remind me how we used to be, make me feel paranoid and confused. But it wasn't OK. I needed him to understand that it wasn't OK. It was very much *not* OK.

I climbed into bed, my phone next to me on the sheets, waiting for his call. I'm not sure how I managed to fall asleep except that I guess I was wrung out. A few hours later, still in the dark of night, I awoke to a sound, a rhythmic banging sound. Not loud but persistent. I got out of bed and went down the short hall to check Hazel's room, where she slept silently and unmoved, still dressed.

I followed the banging sound up to the third floor and realized, with alarm, that it was coming from Penny's room. I knocked. "Penny, are you OK?"

The banging stopped. "Yes, Fuzzy," she said after a pause.

"May I come in?" I asked carefully.

"OK, Fuzzy," she said quietly. She was sitting up in bed, her arms crossed in front of her, and her eyes looking down at her lap. Then she looked right up at me, and then began her rocking again, banging the white iron headboard against the wall over and over.

"I wanna go see Dottie."

I sat down on the bed beside her. "What?"

"I wanna go see Dottie. I wanna go see Dottie. I miss my Dottie. And she's never, ever waking up, but I wanna go see Dottie. And I don't like it here, and it's too white, and there's no yellow, and I's not even unpacking cuz there ain't no Dottie here, and you's not my sister cuz I don't even knows you."

I didn't know how to respond. I couldn't bear her sadness. With everything feeling unsettled, broken, and splintered in our household, I just needed Penny to be OK here, with me, in this house. I reached over to take her hand, but she pulled it away. She was just looking down and rocking. Back and forth, back and forth.

"Wait one second," I said, and I went down the hall to the bathroom. I grabbed the bath mat off the floor and brought it back into Penny's room. "May I put this over the headboard?" I asked her, holding the mat up in the air. I had to solve *some*thing.

"Why's you doon that?"

"I just thought if you're going to be rocking like that, this might be more quiet."

"OK." Penny leaned forward so I could hang the mat over the headboard.

"Let's see if that works." Penny started rocking back and forth again and this time the headboard made quieter padded noises as it hit the wall. Penny looked up at me and smiled a slow smile. "It worked, Fuzzy."

"OK, great. Now about Dottie," I said, looking at her carefully. "We can definitely, *definitely* go visit Dottie's gravesite in a little while, but right now, how about we get you settled here? I need to get some things organized, and I just can't take you there right away. But soon, OK?"

"I want to go see Dottie *now*," she said more forcefully. "And I don't get why you's my baby *baby* sister and you's driving a car and has a husband and a baby, not a little baby but a big girl now. I don't likes it. I's the big sister, and you's my baby sister." She looked down at her short pink nails. "I don't likes it at all."

I looked at her as I tried to think of what to say. "I don't know, Penny. I don't know what to say. I *am* your baby sister, and we don't know each other very well right now, and we're different, and we have learned different things, and I know it doesn't seem fair."

"It *isn't* fair. You's my baby sister. But now you's the boss to me."

"I will never be the boss of you, Penny. Just right now I'm taking care of you, and you just got here, and we will go see Dottie at the cemetery, but we can't do it right now. It's complicated but…" I couldn't go to Marion tomorrow. After what I had just seen, I wasn't going to leave Hazel anywhere alone, and I couldn't imagine bringing Hazel with us, either.

"I hates complicated."

I smiled at her. "Me too. Now, there is something we can share." Penny looked up at me and smiled a quick tic of a smile. I stood up to lower the roller shades on the windows. As I came around the bed, I saw golden candy wrappers, dozens and dozens of candy wrappers.

Penny saw me looking at the yellow cellophane wrappers. "Also, tomorrow I'm gonna need some more Werther's Original Butterscotch Candies, the Ones Grandma Used to Make. *Please.* Sometimes I forgets to say 'Please.'"

"Sure. OK, we can get those." In the silence that followed, I heard Hazel walking unevenly in the hallway downstairs, the creak of the bathroom door, and the unmistakable sound of vomiting. Oh God, I thought. Penny looked at me, her eyes wide with alarm. I stood up to go downstairs, and Penny started to get up from the bed too.

"Penny, I'll be right back up. I just need to check on Hazel. You stay here."

"No, Fuzzy, I's coming too." I didn't even know how to respond or to push back, so I acquiesced and let her follow me. We walked down the third-floor stairs, and I stood in the doorway outside the hall bathroom. Hazel was sitting on the bathroom floor, her head on her hands resting on the toilet seat.

"Hazel. What the—"

"Hey," she said thickly.

Penny poked her head around, so she was looking into the bathroom too. "Hi, Hazel." Having Penny participating in this scene was unspeakably weird.

I formally introduced my sister to my daughter in the vomit-covered bathroom. "Yes, well, Penny, this is Hazel, your niece... Hazel, this is Penny."

"Hey," Hazel said again. She looked awful. The vomit smell was strong and acrid. "Sorry. I'm *really* sorry. I feel awful, and I know I fucked"—she looked at Penny—"sorry, messed up. I guessed I kinda missed the toilet...It's all over my bed too..."

I looked at her with a mixture of horror and pity. "OK, OK. Jesus. Are you done? Do you need to be sick more?"

Hazel looked really old all of a sudden. "No, I think it's all out." She looked at Penny, embarrassed or spent and said, "Sorry, Penny."

Penny looked squarely at Hazel and said, "It's OK, Hazel. I barfs all the time."

I hadn't seen Hazel smile a real smile in so long, it took me a few seconds to register her reaction. "OK, uh, Penny, thanks. That actually makes me feel better." Penny smiled back at Hazel.

I said, "Penny, I'm going to get Hazel cleaned up. Can I help you get ready for bed?"

"No, I's gonna go night-times myself. I's tired now. I's ready for beds. Tomorrow I's gonna go see Dottie. She's not liking her new box she's sleepin in."

"We'll talk about that tomorrow. Night, Penny."

Penny started to walk back upstairs to her third-floor bedroom but turned around to say, "Nigh nigh, Fuzzy. Nigh nigh, Hazel." Penny sounded exhausted, and she must have been. I didn't hear the banging anymore that night.

# CHAPTER 10

# PENELOPE

I knew I was gonna see Dottie, so I woked up real early and made sure I had all my important things in my Hello Kitty backpack. My shiny pink Hello Kitty wallet was there, and it was filled with moneys from Richard, who said, *Have your new sister take you out shopping.* But I wasn't gonna go shopping. I was gonna go see Dottie.

So I made sure I had my Maybelline Superfrost Pouty Pink lipstick. Yes, Dottie always told me, *Have hand creams,* cuz my hands gotted so dry, so I made sure the strawberry hand cream was there in the pretty tube with the strawberries and leaves on it. My apartment keys wasn't there cuz I don't live there no more. So that was a no. Hairbrush. Yes. Comb. Yes. Gum. Yes. I was gonna wear my big pink sweater cuz sometimes it gets chilly and you gots to be ready. I was still in petal-pink theme, so I put on my pink stretchy pants and the same white shoes as yesterday. It doesn't matter about my underpants and my bruzeer cuz no one sees those. They's all white anyways.

I looked in the mirror over the white dresser and put on my pale-blue eyeshadow with the tiny white, spongy brush. It made my eyes bluer; that's what Dottie said. I put on my frosty, pretty lipstick. I made my cheeks pinker with my Maybelline rouge. I's pretty.

I tiptoed down the stairs. I's pretty sure Fuzzy wasn't gonna take me to see Dottie, so I was gonna go by my own self. I went with no squeaking cuz of my white shoes being so rubbery and quiet. Fuzzy's boots was loud. She wouldn't be allowed to wear those if she was at the hostipal. You had to wear quiet shoes if you worked at the hostipal. It made me so, so sad that I was living far, far away and I's not working at the hostipal no more. I's real good at my job there, and now I's aposta be here now with Fuzzy, and it's too far to go to work there. I didn't like that one bit.

It was so early, and the sun wasn't even shining in the windows yet. It was a little bit dark out. When I got to the bottom of the stairs, I looked down and realized my shoelace had come untied, so I walked over to the living room sofa to sit and tie my shoes. You gots to tie your shoes, or you could falls down and smart yourself. I sat down and was leaning over to tie my shoes when I saw it: my doll Dolly. She was sitting on a little teeny rocking chair near the fireplace. My old doll I used to carry around all the times. *My* doll. Why did Fuzzy has *my doll?* I lost it when I seventeen years old. May of 1967. I member real good. My mommy gave me that dolly in that pink dress when I was little, and then it went away. When my mommy would visit me, I would hold that doll named Dolly, and sometimes my mommy would hold that doll named Dolly. My mommy would come sometimes before she died and gots burned up in the oven and was thrown in the woods and the water, and she would visit me. It was always in the afternoon and when the light was starting to get darker for the nighttime. She would come and stay for a little while. She would have her special drink in the red-and-black-checked thermos that she broughts herself. She would say, *I don't want to trouble you, Penny, so I brought my own drinks.* Mommy would come inside my room and sit and visit with me and Dottie and sip her special drinks, and I'd get out a box of Keebler Pecan Sandies cookies that elves make for the three of us, and Momma would tell us stories about herself and her sister, Bunny. Really, her name was Bunny, like a rabbit, but it was a real lady, not a rabbit, and my mommy and Bunny used to have a lot of adventures when they was little girls, and they even went to school together at Smiff College, and I asked Mommy, *Are you still bestest friends with your sister, Bunny?*

And Mommy just looked down at her plastic cup with her special drink and said, *Bunny is very busy now,* and kinda swirled the juice in her glass around. When she was holding Dolly, my mommy would stroke her hair real soft.

Seeing my doll Dolly just sitting in that chair gots me real confused, and it gots me thinking about my mommy. But she's dead now. And she's not ever waking up either. Just like Dottie.

I was ready to go find the bus to Dottie all by myself. I was facing that big wooden door. I looked at my Dora watch: 6:27 a.m. Thursday. I opened the big door and it was so heavy, and then I was in the tiny room between the two doors, and I opened the second big door with all the keyholes, and then I went outside. I made sure the door clicked closed like Paul taught me. *The door is closed tight when you hear a click,* he said. I heard a click. I walked down the seven steps, and then I was on the sidewalk where all the trees were. I didn't know which way to go, but I remembered that you just gots to ask people questions if you need help. So I went to the left side and walked on the sidewalk, and I read the street signs, and I saw Marlborough, and I walked eighty-seven steps and I saw Berkeley, and then I walked 247 steps and I saw Clarendon, and I didn't see no peoples yet. Then I walked 253 steps and I saw Dartmouth, and I saw a lady, and she was running in black tights and white sneakers and a green jacket and nothing matched, and I asked her, *Where's the bus?* and she had wires in her ears and couldn't hear me and shook her head and never stopped her running. So I walked 238 more steps and I saw Exeter, and then I saw a man wearing a lot of gray and a red necktie with a big brown briefcase, and he had wires in his ears too, and I asked him, *Where's the bus?*

He stopped and said, *What?* He looked mad to me.

I said, *Where's the bus?* Then I remembered: *Please.*

He looked at me funny and said, *I'm not sure. The train is down Dartmouth Street, if that's what you mean.* Then he kept walking. He was talking kinda funny with those wires in his ears. Really loud. But I didn't mean the train station. I meaned the bus.

The bus is really easy in Marion, Massachusetts, where I live. Or where I used to live, I guess. The bus was right in front of my apartment, my *before* apartment, and I rode the P-97, not any other number, to the stop where the hostipal was. I could see the hostipal in the windows of the bus, so I didn't have to count stops. Plus, the driver usually knew me and said, *Hi, Penny, have a nice day,* and things like that, and she knew where the hostipal was.

So I turned around cuz I remembered Dartmouth from the other sign, and I walked to Dartmouth Street, and I wasn't sure which way to go, so I went right. Maybe the buses were right next to the trains.

But then I kinda got confused cuz the roads was all busy all of a sudden, and there was more and more peoples, and they was so buzzing and fast, fast walking with bags and ear wires and talking loud into the air and sometimes yelling, and there was horns honking and fast cars, and so I decided to get off of that scary place and take a left on Newbury, where it was pretty stores just like in Marion, but more and tighter together and huge glass windows and fancy gold letters. There was restaurants with coffee smells and peoples walking, but not so fast. Starbucks, Blue Mercury, Jennifer's Nail Salon and Skin Salon, Tommy Bahama, and then I saw Clarendon, and I turned left onto Clarendon until I saw a pretty road called Commonwealth that had lots of peoples made of stone. There was a grassy center part and lots of benches and trashcans. I had to sit on every bench. That's what Dottie and I always did. It's good luck to sit on benches, so we always sat on them. But there was about a hundred benches up this pretty road. So I crisscrossed back and forth and back and forth to sit on every one of the benches. I counted. I sat on twenty-seven benches. There was a big metal fireman's hat on a big stone thingy with words all over it, but I didn't read them. Every time I got to a new street, I saw more stone and metal peoples. Not real people. Like artwork peoples. First I saw a man in boots and a cape. He had spiderwebs between his legs. Then on another block, I saw a stone man in long robes, and there was a stone lady in robes holding some leaves high in the air. The artwork peoples were so pretty, I forgot all about the bus station. Then the pretty road ended, and I was looking across the street to a park, and I saw Arlington and a *huge* horsie across the street! Not a real, live horsie but like a art statue horsie. *Huge!* So I crossed the street when the white-person-walking picture came on, not the red hand on the big sign, and I went to go see the horsie, and it said George Washington right at the bottom of the metal man and horsie. Then I looked past the horsie, and I saw the bestest thing in the whole world. I really did. The bestest thing ever.

I saw a huge green grass park, and I saw a beautiful big, big pond, and I saw the *big white boats that looked like birds*! The ones Dottie and I loved! The ones I saw in the TV for *BeautifulBoston*, and there they was. I was so, so essited.

I sat on a green bench right next to the big blue pond with my backpack on my lap, and I watched. I looked at Dora, and she said it was 9:53 a.m. This place was just like the pictures on the TV. The green, green grass, and all around the big green park were big, big tall buildings. *Way* taller than any buildings in Marion. And the tall buildings made me feel kinda essited and kinda scared. And there were big tall buildings behind the tall buildings, and I saw a man way up high in the air working on a window, and I sure hoped he wasn't gonna smart his self. And then I watched those beautiful white bird boats. Peoples was sitting in those boats and riding around in the water all happy, and there was kids with lollipops. The mommies and the childrens were smiling and happy and so essited to be in those boats. And the sun was out, and the sky was pretty blue like my eyes, and the wind was blowing my hair.

I watched a squirrel bury a nut, and it was so funny because he worked so fast and his teeny tiny hands were digging and digging, and then he put the nut in the ground, and then he was putting dirt on the nut and patting, patting more dirt. It was so, so funny. I started laughing real hards. Then after all his fast, fast patting, patting, he put a leaf right on the tiny dirt pile. Maybe to member where he put that nut. I was laughing so hard at his tiny, fast hands, and there was peoples looking at me funny when I was laughing, so I stopped laughing. I don't know why. I just did.

So I sat and sat, thinking about getting on those boats for a ride, but I decided I was a little scared about those boats. Those boats was kinda big looking. I sure wished Dottie was here to come with on the boats cuz she'd know what to do and how to gets on those boats. I heard a little girl yelling to her mommy, *Look at me, Mommy!* and she was riding all by herself on that big boat. It just made me feel rumbly all of a sudden. I started rocking on the green bench on the green grass and let the sunshine warm on my pink sweater and watched the boats go back and forth and round and round.

Seeing that girl yelling at her mommy on that boat reminded me of my mommy, who is dead and is never, ever coming back, and about Dottie, who ain't never, ever coming back, and how I's gotta live with my baby sister, Fuzzy, who's just a baby and who's tryin to be the boss to me, and it started to make my tummy feel funny and my head feel mad inside. My baby sister does *not* getta be the boss to me. *I* is the boss to me, and I's a big growed-up lady. She doesn't tell me if I gets to see Dottie or tell me nothing, and why did she have my doll Dolly? *Why?* I was getting really, really mad thinking about Fuzzy and Mommy and Dottie, but then I smelled frankfurtas, and I saw a man with a yellow cart selling frankfurtas right next to the bird boats tickets place. So I got up off the bench with my bag, and I said to the very, very fat man, *I'm Penny. I's like a frankfurta. Please.*

And he looked at me and smiled a funny smile and said, *Sure, lady. Five dollars.* I reached into my bag and got out my Hello Kitty wallet and handed him one five-dollar bill.

His cart said Dem Dawgs, which didn't make no sense to me, but he was making frankfurtas for sure, and he said, *Whaddya want on it?*

And I said, *Ketchup and yellow mustard and sweet relish.*

He smiled a little smile with his scratchy face and got to putting my frankfurta in a bun with big silver tweezers and adding all the stuff from big squeezy tubes with no letters on them. Just plain plastic bottles. I didn't like that. But I didn't say nothing. He handed me my frankfurta, and he looked at me for a long time, and I looked back at the scratchy man, and then he said, *See the tip jar?*

And I did see a big old mayonnaise jar, and it said Tips in red marker, and I said, *Yeah.*

And he said, real, real slow, *It's cust-o-mary to put something in the tip jar.*

So I looked at the tip jar, and I reached into my bag and got a piece of paper with Richard's phone number on it, which I never needed, and put it in the jar. *There,* I said. *There's somethin.* I was proud to myself, but he didn't look so proud to me.

I just took my Dem Dawg frankfurta and went back to the bench.

I sat on that bench for a long, long time watching the boats and the people and the window men and the beige childrens with brown mommas and peoples buying Dem Dawgs until I gots sleepy and laid myself down on the bench to nap. I figgered I was gonna find the bus station just as soon as I sleeped. I hadn't sleeped so good at Fuzzy's on accounta that room being so white and new and all the strange new noises like cracking and popping and buzzing from the old white walls. Plus the cars were so close to the house so I could hear every single one driving by, their wheels crunching the road like it was right in my ears. And one more thing: I was mad to Fuzzy for being the boss to me now, even though she was my baby sister and didn't know nothin bout me or Dottie or nothin. All that stuff made me sleep all funny. Dottie used to call it sleepin in *fits n stahts*.

When I woked up, it was so scary. I opened my eyes to see three police mens standing right over me looking real serious and kinda mad. They blocked the sunshine, and that's what woked me up. The sun was getting lower in the sky, and one man with a lot of rattly heavy things on his big black belt said, *Ma'am, do you have some identification?*

But I was so sleepy and confused, I didn't know what he meant. *Huh?* I said.

*Please show us some ID.*

*I gots Hello Kitty*, I said. I didn't know what ID meant. And those two guys looked at me like they'd never heard of Hello Kitty before. I sat up straight on the bench.

*Excuse me, do you have a driver's license?* the big one asked. He was nicer.

*Nope*, I said all growed up like. *I not aposta drive a car.*

*OK, can you tell us your name, ma'am?*

*Yes. I's Penelope Wright.*

The two guys looked at each other and nodded, and one of them got onto the little tiny black phone and said, *Tell Mrs. Bradlee we found her sister.*

# CHAPTER 11

# FESSENDEN

I reached for my phone as soon as I opened my eyes. There was still no response from William. Fury fueled me out of bed. Even during this now five-month separation, this was a first in our twenty-five-year marriage. I sent him a text: *PLEASE CHECK IN. I KNOW YOU'RE UPSET, BUT NOW I'M WORRIED.* I went upstairs to check on Penny. Her door was shut, so I decided to let her sleep in. Last night's discussion had made me realize the reality of her unhappiness to be here, her resentment toward me, and her generally high level of anxiety. I needed to reach out to Paul today to talk about what I could be doing to make her feel more comfortable and "at home." This was going to be a long and bumpy road.

I went back to the second floor and opened Hazel's door. She was asleep, on her stomach with her head turned away from me, her head resting on the crook of her elbow. Her hair fanned out on the pillow. The smell of vomit still pungent, though milder after last night's cleaning of her floor and sheets. I sat on the side of her bed to awaken her.

"Honey," I said gently. "Time for school."

She moaned and turned her head toward me. "Ugh. What day is it?"

"Thursday, and I know you probably feel awful, but you have to go and we need to talk after school."

"I don't want to talk. I already told you last night. I fucked up, and I'm sorry."

"Dad and I are really starting to worry about you."

"Mom, stop." She said, brushing the hair off of her face and looking at me, sleepy and annoyed. "It's nothing. That was just a stupid mistake. I'm not doing that anymore. Seriously."

"Still," I continued. "Dad and I want to talk with you, OK?"

"OK, OK." She sighed. "Don't forget to call the math teacher. I was supposed to give you a note he wrote, but I can't find it, and he's going to get mad if you guys don't call him. The number's in the school directory."

"All right, I'll call later."

"If you go meet with Mr. Small, is Dad gonna go too?" she asked. Her eyes were heavy, and she closed them again.

"Definitely." The lie was out of my mouth before I even realized it. I had no idea what he would be coming to or not.

Hazel opened her eyes and looked at me. She raised her eyebrows. "OK, Mom. Whatever."

"Listen, just get in the shower and go to school, and then come straight home afterward. I'll talk to Dad about trying to get home early so we can have that talk." I couldn't believe how much money we spent on tuition. In her current state of mind, this just felt like a huge waste of money.

She slunk down the hall to get in the shower. The door clicked behind her in the bathroom, and I exhaled. I went downstairs in my pajamas and bathrobe and made coffee. I walked out the first front door, through the tiny vestibule, through the locking front door, and outside to the stoop to get my daily *Boston Globe* and *New York Times* newspapers. Another beautiful fall day.

I started the crossword puzzle, waited for the coffee to brew, and then felt the buzz of a new text on my phone, nestled in the pocket of my bathrobe.

William: *Call when you wake up.*

I immediately dialed his cell.

"Hey," he said.

"Where are you? Did you get my texts? And my calls?" I was pissed.

"I'm still at Eddie and Suz's. I'm sorry, my phone died. I just got your messages. Is Hazel OK?" He was driving. I could hear his blinker.

"William, I was really worried. Hazel came home late. Really, really drunk." My voice was louder than I meant it to be.

"What? Shit! I'm so sorry I didn't check in. What did she do?"

"I think she just went to somebody's house after school and drank. She didn't seem to remember. On a Wednesday, a school night!"

"Jesus. Not good. What are we gonna do?"

"I really don't know, but I talked with Ellie and she wants to talk with Haze. Ellie thinks maybe it's not just regular teenage behavior, as you so like to say. I'm worried; I know you probably think I'm overreacting, but I know I'm not. Oh, and on top of all that, Hazel says her math teacher wants to meet with us." My hand holding my coffee mug was shaking. I couldn't make it stop.

"Wait, already? There's a math issue already? After a few days of school? When did he want to meet? I'm going to Chicago today for a few days for work. I can't meet with anyone until next week. Sorry, Fez." He was apologizing a lot these days.

"I'll call him today and set something up. I kinda want to see him soon, and I'm sure he feels the same way, so…I guess I'll let you know what happens." A Chicago trip sounded really nice right now. I know he was desperately trying to build his company back up, but I thought it must be nice not to have to deal with any of this, either.

I heard Hazel's footsteps on the stairs; she was moving slowly, softly, carefully like an older woman who might stumble if she didn't focus on each tread. She was looking down as she came down the hallway toward the kitchen. I watched her. She looked up as she entered the kitchen and nodded hello to me and filled a travel mug with coffee. She had showered; her hair was wet and combed back. She was wearing a gray T-shirt and a long black skirt with black boots. Her arms were so thin that her elbow joints looked too big against her upper arm bones. Her veins popped blue and tubular against the white flesh.

She turned to go, and I said, "Remember to come home straight after school." She took her backpack and left through the front door. The closing of the door sounded hollow. I looked at my shaking hand and put down my coffee mug.

I thought it was time to wake up Penny and see what we could do about making her feel less agitated, more comfortable, less angry toward me. Maybe we could do something today to help her feel more settled.

I climbed the steps to her new third-floor room, and I rapped softly on the door. With no response, I slowly opened her door, but she wasn't there. The bed was made in the neatest, tightest, sharpest way I had ever seen. There were no wrinkles and very tight hospital corners. The pillows were perfectly stacked. Her boxes remained unpacked with the exception of a picture of her and another woman holding dripping ice cream cones at a fair or amusement park. I didn't see the Hello Kitty backpack she had carried so carefully into the house. I didn't see the white nursing shoes, either.

I walked down to the bathroom and carefully opened the door. "Penny?" Nobody there. I went farther down to William's office. "Penny?" Empty. I went back to the second floor, walking more quickly. I checked Hazel's room, the hall bathroom, behind the shower curtain, my bedroom, my bathroom. Under beds, in closets. Nowhere. Back down to the first floor. She wasn't in the living room, the dining room, the kitchen. I panicked. She was in the basement. She had to be. The dank, dark basement. She would be terrified. She must have gotten disoriented when she woke up and headed all the way down there.

I opened the basement door, turned on the light and slowly descended, gripping the handrail tightly. I hated this room and avoided coming here for any reason. It held our water heater and furnace, ductwork and electrical panels and some plastic bins of storage as well as some old, mostly broken, furniture of my mother's. But the smell was of damp old rags, mold, mildew, airlessness, and the shadows seemed to house an array of mice and spiders.

"Penny? Penny? Are you down here?" But she wasn't there or anywhere. My heart was beating fast. Where was she? She had no phone. I had no way to reach her.

Where would she go? Where could she go? Had she actually left to go to Marion to see Dottie's grave? But how could she know where to go? And Boston was so different from her small, sleepy town of Marion, where her life was close and familiar. Anything could happen to her here. This city, like other cities, housed people who fed on the weak, the naive, the young. Penny was a sweet and trusting soul; she was so vulnerable.

I had only been her guardian for fifteen hours, and it seemed I had lost her in that short time. I couldn't tell Richard yet. I couldn't let him down. I couldn't let her down. I had to have more time to find her. I walked outside, thinking that maybe she had locked herself out of the front door. I walked back and forth on the sidewalks on our block calling her name. It was early, and no one was there, no one to ask if they had seen my sister leave.

Futilely, I rechecked every room of the house, called her name, knowing somehow that she would not call back. Fear prickled the back of my neck. I paced back and forth in front of the bay window. Where could she be? I finally called 911 to report her missing, which led to a series of forwarded calls to different departments and finally, I reached a detective who said they couldn't declare her missing until she had been gone at least twenty-four hours. This infuriated me to no end, and I kept insisting that she had special needs and I could not be sure where she would be going and I certainly *could* be certain that in her innocent and simple state, she could get into serious trouble. I used the word "nefarious" in my description of dangerous people Penny might encounter, and I heard the detective emit a subdued snort of some sort. I told him I was going to go find her since the Boston Police Department was so utterly unhelpful and at some point, the despair in my voice touched something in his hardened core, and he said he'd stop by 30 Marlborough to get a recent picture of Penny and get the picture out to his men on the ground.

"We'll keep a look out," he finally said. That was at 8:27 a.m. I had no idea when she had left.

I spent the day searching. My mind went to every headline I had ever read about crimes on the streets of Boston. I saw the crime scene pictures in my head, the pictures of the deceased covered in plastic, their body outlines on the sidewalks, the yellow police tape fencing off the scene. I imagined Penny's confusion and panic as she walked the streets of this city dizzily, trying to find a safe place to go.

I covered every street on Back Bay from Storrow Drive to Boylston and Arlington to Mass Avenue. As I recognized she desperately wanted to see Dottie's grave, I walked to the bus station and both train stations: Back Bay and South Station. Was there even a bus to Marion? There was, but she wasn't on any of them. The ticket agents had seen no one matching her description. I walked into the Boston Public Library. I went up all the flights of stairs and up into the Sargent Gallery hallways. Nothing. I walked into shops near the Prudential Center, coffee shops on Boylston, I walked over to Charles Street and Beacon Hill, thinking she might have followed the yellow bricks of the Freedom Trail somehow. I went to Mass General and checked the emergency room. Then I circled back and hit those spots again. I checked my phone constantly awaiting some news from the police. The school called several times and I let it go to voice mail. I would deal with the math "crisis" later. I called Paul; he was very worried and said he would keep his phone nearby for my calls. I did not call William; I didn't need to remind him that taking in Penny was my mistake. I finally did call Richard, but Darlene had answered and said he was on a plane, unreachable for several hours. She would have him call me the minute he landed. She was officious and smug.

I went back home, blisters on my heels, bone-weary, frightened, and sweaty at three thirty to see if anyone had called the home phone instead of my cell. More messages from the school, which I didn't listen to. Nothing about Penny. Hazel was waiting there, sitting at the kitchen island eating cinnamon toast and drinking milky tea.

"I thought I was supposed to come home and talk to you and Dad." Her voice was tinged with annoyance.

"Penny is missing, and I've spent the last eight hours looking for her all over Boston," I said breathlessly.

"Oh," she said.

"What does 'oh' mean?" I asked sharply.

"Nothing." She was dipping her toast into the tea and eating the soggy pieces.

"Hazel." I sighed. "I don't have time for whatever you're trying to say. I just really want to find Penny."

Hazel said nervously, "The school is going to call you."

"I know, I know, I'm going to call Mr. Small as soon as I find Penny."

"It's not about math," she said. Her voice sounded shaky.

Before I could ask her what she meant, my cell phone rang and Detective Johnston was on the other end to say that Penny was found sleeping on one of the benches in the Public Garden near the Swan Boat ticket sales booth. Two officers were bringing her back right now. Thank God. *Thank God.* The relief fell over me heavy and fast. I couldn't imagine what I would have done if something had happened to her.

Shortly, the doorbell rang, and Penny and the two officers came through the door. Penny was looking down at the floor. I turned my attention to the police officers, thanked them profusely, and watched them as they left the brownstone, their heavy black boots clomping and their belts, laden with keys and sticks and flashlights and guns, clinking heavily as they walked down the stairs of our front stoop.

"Penny!" I yelled as I ran toward her at the door. She looked at me defiantly. "You had me...I mean, *us* so worried." Hazel was standing behind me in the front hall, wiping cinnamon from the corners of her mouth.

Hazel said, "*I* wasn't worried, Penny."

I glared at her before turning back to Penny. "Well, *I* have been going crazy all day with worry. I didn't know where you went. You can't just leave like that. It's very dangerous and anything could have happened." I was speaking quickly, loudly.

Penny looked at me and let out a big breath of air, letting her cheeks blow out. She let her shoulders drop, slouching dramatically. She had little smears of mustard on her pink sweater and on her white pants. She set her plastic backpack on the ground. "I wanted a go see Dottie."

I looked at her. I reached for her hands and held them, sticky and dirty. "OK, Penny, we'll go see Dottie," I finally said. "Can we go tomorrow? Or Saturday? Can you please wait?"

"Nope," Penny said. "I wanna go see Dottie now. I wanna see my Dottie. *Now. Now.*" She stomped her foot hard on the last "now." She looked at me hard, narrowing her eyes and added, "I hates it here."

I stared at her, trying to let go of the tightness and anxiety I had felt all morning, and realized there was only one thing to do. Go see Dottie. *Now.* I moved over to the stairs to sit down. My back hurt. My legs ached. My feet were sore. The blisters had bled through my peds. I could have closed my eyes at that moment and slept for hours. I said the only thing I could say: "*OK.*"

"Hazel," I said, pointing my finger at her. "Penny and I are going to Marion to the cemetery, and then we're coming right back. *Do not* go anywhere. Stay here and do your homework. Please. *Please.* Do you understand?"

Hazel looked at me blankly and said, "Sure." Her blinks were languid, strangely slow. She slowly walked up the stairs and disappeared around the corner into her room.

I looked at Penny and asked her if she was ready, and she nodded. I picked up my handbag from the front hall table, and we went right out the door and down to the car. Upon leaving Back Bay and heading toward Route 93, we immediately hit the daily grind of afternoon rush hour, the thick late-afternoon traffic. I looked over at her as we were stopped, and she was looking out the window. I had to try to reach her.

"Penny," I began. "I'm so sorry you're sad. I'm going to do the best I can to make you feel better."

She just shrugged. "I hates it here. I hates my baby sister. I miss my Dottie." In the setting sun of the car, and the low orange rays of the afternoon, Penny started her rocking. Back and forth and back and forth, and I noticed something else. Another rhythmic tic. Her thumbs moved quickly back and forth across the soft pads of her fingers. From the pinky to the pointer finger. In fast round circles. Around and around and around. Her hands looked like frantic little fleshy puppets. Soft and frenetic. And I got an idea, a beautiful, brilliant idea, which I would bring up with her when we got home. But now, we just had to get to Marion.

As the traffic started to thin out and loosen up, we got to an even, regular speed and the sun washed over us in long golden strips, Penny's rocking started to slow down, and her hand circles stopped. She had crossed her hands in her lap. She was thinking about something. I could see her eyebrows furrow and her eyes squint as if trying to retrieve something deeply buried.

"What are you thinking about, Penny?"

"Why does you has my doll, Dolly?"

I looked at her. "What?"

"That doll in the teeny, tiny rocking chair by the fireplace. Why does you has that?"

"In the living room? That's Baby Nanny. Mom gave me that doll when I turned five. Does it look like a doll you used to have?"

"*No.* It *is* the doll I used to has." Penny now crossed her arms across her chest and looked out the window. "You's got my doll, Dolly."

"Penny, I promise, Mom gave me that doll when I was five. I didn't know it was yours. I promise."

"When was you five?" she asked, staring at me again.

"On my birthday. May of 1967," I answered.

"Well, Fuzzy, that's exactly when my doll, Dolly, went missing. *Exactly.*"

"Penny, I am so sorry. I don't know how that could have happened."

Penny looked out the window, and I could tell she was thinking. "I's not sure. I's gonna keep her now, OK?"

"OK, Penny, that's OK."

Penny smiled a funny smile, like a little kid who just won a game of go fish, and she stared at my profile for a while. Then she said, "Do you knows about the monster?"

"What monster?"

Penny looked serious and like she didn't want to say too much. "Nothin, Fuzzy. It's nothin. Mommy talked about a monster one time when she visited me. I'm not aposta say nothin." Then she put both of her hands on her mouth to stop her own talking.

I turned my head quickly to look at Penny. "Wait, what? Mom used to visit you? Really?" I had assumed Penny's institutionalization marked the beginning of a non-relationship with Mom. How often were these visits? I couldn't picture Mom going anywhere, let alone visiting with Penny and Dottie. It would have meant she had to drive to Marion, actually be sober enough to drive there. I couldn't remember my mother driving anywhere. She was basically agoraphobic. I couldn't see her dressed and in a coat and holding a purse and looking for car keys.

"Yep. Sometimes Mommy visited me."

I tried to imagine it. How did she have enough energy to visit Penny when she couldn't even get out of bed to get dressed or shower or fry me an egg for dinner? Or heat up a can of Campbell's cream of mushroom soup? Or drive me to school or anywhere? But she could go visit Penny? This just made me feel shitty. And what about a monster? I had no recollection of Mom mentioning any monsters. Mom didn't talk about anything, let alone monsters. Maybe Penny had the words and the story mixed up.

As we were well south of the city limits, the view had shifted from buildings and billboards to scrub pines and grassy shoulders. Penny was struggling to say something.

"Mommy would tell me things."

"Like what sorts of things?" I asked.

Penny continued, "Like something bad happened with a monster, and Mommy was scared and sad."

"What? Are you sure?" I asked, confused.

"I don't know, Fuzzy. Just that Mommy talked about a monster and said, 'The nights was hard, Penny. The nights was hard.'" Then she looked like she had said something she wasn't supposed to. "Never mind. I forgotted. Never mind, Fuzzy. It's nothing. It's privacy."

I really couldn't tell if Penny was confusing some story or if Mom had confused the story herself from the fog and confusion of old memories or the haze of vodka and Valium.

"Penny, when did Mom come and visit you?" I wanted to understand the relationship between my sister and my mother.

"Different times. I don't member." She was watching and counting the passing cars.

"Did she eat and drink anything at your house? I mean, did she come for a meal or stay for a while or what?" I was trying to understand if this really happened.

Penny thought about her answer. "Mommy and Dottie and I had Keebler Pecan Sandies, cookies Like the Elves Make, and Mommy brought her special juice in the checkered thermos. I don't know how long she stayed. I don't member. But we hads the bestest times, and I loved my mommy. She was funny and silly. But she's dead now, so she's not funny and silly anymore."

What? Who was she talking about? Who was this woman? Mom was funny and silly? She was the *opposite* of funny and silly. She was absolutely nothing at all. She was stale air. I almost wanted to show Penny a picture of Mom and confirm she was her mother too. But I did remember the black-and-red-plaid thermos always on the counter in the kitchen. Her "travel mug." I imagined Mom sipping her cocktail at Penny's, snacking on the crumbly sweets, rambling on about people, real or not, memories actual or exaggerated, while assuaging her own guilt for sending her now adult daughter away when she was four. Penny, in her innocence, her naïveté, her willingness to let her in, fed her cookies and listened to her nonsense, including stories about monsters.

My cell phone rang, and I recognized the school number. Shit, Mr. Small. I picked up the call and put it on speaker mode, "Hello, Mr. Small, I'm so sorry, I was *just* about to call—"

"Sorry, Mrs. Bradlee," began a deep female's voice. "This is Elizabeth Sanderson." The earnest, intense headmistress of Hazel's school. Completely dedicated to her students and her job.

"Oh, hi, Dr. Sanderson. Sorry, I was thinking you were Mr. Small. Is everything OK?"

"Well, Mrs. Bradlee," she said carefully. "I've been trying to reach you on your home phone. I'm wondering if you might be able to come in tomorrow and meet me in my office."

My stomach lurched. My heart started pounding, and I felt the palms of my hands prickle. "Um, OK. Could you, uh, tell me what this is about?"

"I think it would be better to just talk in person. And if Mr. Bradlee is free, I think he should be there too. Is nine o'clock OK? Please bring Hazel with you."

We hung up. Shit. This was bad. Dr. Sanderson only called meetings when something was very, *very* serious. Something prickled at the back of my head, tiny needles going into my skull. My hands were hot and moist so that the steering wheel felt slick in my grasp.

"How many more minutes?" Penny asked. "I wanna go see my Dottie."

I pointed to the green highway sign for Marion and put on the blinker for the exit. We were nearly there. "Soon, Penny." I barely got the words out. "Soon."

# CHAPTER 12

# PENELOPE

The cemetery was kinda dark, and Dottie's box was under the grass, and I got so sad thinking about Dottie in the box under the grass. I could see the line where they cut the grass pieces to make the hole for Dottie's box. So Fuzzy and I just sat on the ground, and I talked to Dottie about Boston and about my day with the funny squirrel and the boats, and Fuzzy just kinda looked away while I did all my words to Dottie. Then Fuzzy said she had to walk around, so she walked on the cemetery paths while I spent my time with Dottie. I's glad Fuzzy went walking around cuz she was all shaky and funny after she talked to Hazel's school lady. On the way home, Fuzzy let us get McDonald's Happy Meals, which is so happy, and they's got toys in them bags, and I love special treats. So that was good.

Fuzzy called her husband, Willum, from the car. She said, *William, hi, it's me. The school called, and we need to meet with Elizabeth Sanderson. Tomorrow, 9:00 a.m. I know you're in Chicago, but if anything changes…I guess I'm just hoping you can be there too. That's it, I guess. Call when you get this.* I don't think he was there, or else he didn't say nothin on the phone. She did all the talking. She looked real sad when she was talking, and her voice was real low and bumpy.

*Are you sad to Willum?* I asked.

It looked like I had just woken her up with my question. Her eyes was open, but she was kinda asleep too, even though she was driving a car. You's aposta be awake when you's driving. *Um, no. Not sad with him. Just kind of dealing with some big things right now.*

*Like what?* I asked. It's important to share. Dottie and I was always talking about our days and stuff. Everything: good, bad, and in-betweeny.

*Oh, it's kind of complicated, Penny.* Boy, did she look tired. She had big gray things under her eyes. Like her skin used to be baby pink but now it was sad rain-cloudy gray.

*It's easy. You just say it.* How hard was it to say stuff? Jeez, Fuzzy wasn't so good at sayin stuff. I's good at sayin stuff. Maybe she's got her own special needs. I said, *I's waiting, Fuzzy.*

Fuzzy turned to me while driving. She looked like she had a splinter or a blister in her head. *OK, I'll try to explain.* Then she breathed in a lot of air and blew it out like she was blowing out birthday candles on her cake. *I think Hazel is in big trouble at school. I think she might need some help. I'm worried that something is really wrong.*

I nodded knowingly. *Like how she throwed up?* I knowed all about that, Fuzzy. *She's just essited or nervous or sad I think. That's usually why I throwed up.* I nodded big cuz I's her big sister and I's helping.

Fuzzy looked really sad when I said my words, and then I saw big wet tears coming out of her eyes. I reached over and wiped away her tears with my fingers. She didn't say nothin for a long time. Then she said, *Thanks, Penny. I appreciate your nice words. You're right. Let's see if we can make Hazel feel better.*

I asked her again, *Are you sad to Willum?*

She looked at me, and those big circle tears kept on coming down her thin face. I don't think she liked the cryin thing. She kept wiping and wiping and then lookin out the window on her side of the car like I couldn't see her or nothin. Like she wasn't even cryin. She shook her head and said nothin.

*You's aposta talk it out,* I reminded her. *We's always talkin in our groups when Dottie and I was livin in the Center.*

She didn't say nothin for a long time, and the sad tears kept coming down, and I kept on wiping them away. All weird and fast. But I could see the water. There was a lotta water on her face. It kept coming out of her big eyes. Finally she said, *I am sad about William. I guess I'm sad about a lot of stuff.*

That was pretty obvious. *Why you so sad to Willum? Did he smart your feelings?*

Fuzzy smiled a little and looked at me for a second. *Yeah, I guess he did in a way.*

*What way? How did Willum smart your feelings?*

Fuzzy bit the inside of her cheek and scrunched up her nose. It was kinda a weird face, but maybe it helped her think better. *Well, I guess he lost some money at work and then told a lie and then did something so we probably can't keep the Cape Cod house anymore.*

I didn't know what *the Cape Cod house* meant. *Was it on purpose?*

*What, Penny? Was what on purpose?* She said that like she needed a big nap.

*Did he lose the moneys on purpose, or was it an axident?* I kept having to say things over and over. Jeez.

She kept scrunching. *I guess he didn't do it on purpose.* She said the word *purpose* for a long time. Weird talkin.

*So he wasn't being mean? He made an axident?*

She smiled a little. Still looking at the road in front of us. *Yeah, I guess it was just an accident.*

*Fuzzy, we learned at the Center that axidents are OK, and you're aposta say OK when axidents happen cuz they're just axidents. One time I spilled a whole tray of supper on the clean floor, and the clam chowder went everywhere and the glass of milk went everywhere, and so did the bread slices and the little gold butter packets—everywhere.* I showed her with my hands how the spill was *everywhere. I made a big mess and I was so sad, and Paul was there, and he came over and said,* Penny, it's OK. It's just an axident. *And Dottie came over and patted my back. I didn't spill nothin on purpose. It was an axident.*

Fuzzy was smilin a little now.

*So,* I said, *you just say to Willum,* It's just an axident. It's OK, Willum. You didn't mean nothing.

*OK, Penny, maybe I will.*

*That's real good. Real good, Fuzzy. Oh, and Fuzzy, what's the Cape Cod house?*

*It's a house that used to belong to my...our grandparents, and that we started to take care of and stay in during the summers after Mom died.*

*So, it's different than the* BeautifulBoston *house?*

*Yep,* she said fast.

*You gots two houses, Fuzzy—two?*

*Um, yes. Two.* She looked at me again.

I thought for a little while, like I was adding numbers. *So you's sad because Hazel has a tummy ache and Willum made an axident and you might only gots one house?* Boy, was I confused.

*I guess. Kind of.*

I don't really understand my sister, Fuzzy, yet. We both watched the gray road going under the car.

*Fuzzy?*

*Yes?*

*Tell me something nice about Willum.*

*Why, Penny?*

*Just cuz. I likes happy. I don't likes sad.*

*OK, let me think...*She looked up at the ceiling of the car, like that's how she was gonna member. *Well, he makes up silly songs, and he always sings them in the shower.*

*So, now that Willum isn't livin in the house, is the shower times quiet?*

*Yes, Pen, it is kinda quiet in the bathroom now.*

*Fuzzy, do you miss the silly songs? Cuz I miss the way Dottie useda hum when she was coloring.*

*I do miss the songs, actually. It's pretty quiet in the house now.* Fuzzy looked out the window at something.

Then she shook her head and looked funny and stopped crying, so maybe the talkin thing was good. My baby sister had a lot of learnin to do. Good thing I was here. I guess she needed a big sister after all.

# CHAPTER 13

# FESSENDEN

Friday morning, I couldn't leave Penny at home while Hazel and I went to the school. I didn't feel I could leave her at home at all after her running away. At least not today. So despite its inappropriateness, I had to bring Penny to the meeting with Dr. Sanderson. Before we left, Penny had cereal, though she seemed very disappointed by my options. She asked if we could get Lucky Charms at the supermarket one day soon.

"Sure, Penny," I told her. I had coffee and milk while she ate, and when the cereal was gone, she picked up the bowl and drank up the entire bowl of sweetened milk. She wiped her mouth with a paper towel and smiled. "All done." Hazel came downstairs and was quiet. She could not or would not explain why this meeting was happening.

The school was about a fifteen-minute walk from home. The day was nice, sunny, and warm. This early fall had been beautiful so far. I was grateful for that. A cold, rainy day would have been too sad to handle. My phone buzzed in my bag with a text from William: *In Chicago now. Please fill me in on mtg.* He used to sign texts xxx. Not anymore. Was he even worried? I couldn't really tell. Was he feeling the same sickening pit in his stomach that I had this morning? Or once again was I alone in my anxiety and worry about Hazel? Was I crazy? Or was he negligent? I wanted to scream, *I told you!* Something was definitely wrong.

The school was in Back Bay, in the other direction of Boston's central Public Gardens and situated in an old stone mansion, once owned by the illustrious Richardson family. It was a wonderful private high school where I had gone, and yet it was now another expense completely straining our dwindling savings account. Penny and I said little during our walk. She was counting her steps. I was nervous, jittery. Hazel hung back behind us. I put a mint in my mouth. I couldn't remember if I had brushed my teeth this morning. Did I use deodorant? Did I forget that too? I tried to smell my underarms. I think they were OK. I really didn't want to go to the school reeking of stale breath and sweat.

When we approached the school, Penny took my hand in hers and said, "It's OK, Fuzzy." I was grateful for her simple, comforting words. Something had happened in our car ride yesterday. Something nice. Some sort of a little connection between us.

The school was in session at nine o'clock and very quiet. Hazel should have been in Spanish class. We entered the beautiful foyer with its sweeping staircase, its pale-gray carpet, the ornate gold-framed portraits of the past headmasters and board presidents, and turned left to enter the school's administrative offices. The headmistress's assistant walked Hazel into her academic adviser's office and sat Penny and me in two green leather chairs opposite Elizabeth's desk and told us she would be in shortly.

Penny plopped right down in her chair. Her thumbs were moving in circles around the inside of her fingers: rhythmic, steady circles. I sat down slowly and was nauseated. My thighs were sticking to the seat. Why was I here? What was I about to find out? How bad was the shit Hazel was into? Less than a week into school, was she already behind in work? Was she behaving badly? Was she disengaged, as she was at home? I really wanted William to be here to share this angst with me. I wanted him here with me, not so much to comfort me, but to absorb some of this. I thought how nice it must be to travel for business, to lose oneself in the rhythm of hard, linear, thought-consuming work.

Dr. Sanderson entered the room and shook my hand. Normally she was warm and effusive, but today she was abrupt and unsmiling. She looked surprised when she saw Penny.

I jumped in, my words sloppily spilling out of my mouth. "William is traveling. My sister, Penny, has come to live with us, and I needed to bring her. I'm sorry. I didn't really have a choice." I wiped a drop of spit off her desk.

Dr. Sanderson looked warmly at my sister. "Hi, Penny."

"Hi," she said. She started rocking in the green leather chair. The leather crunched rhythmically.

Dr. Sanderson was unfazed by Penny's rocking. She looked at me. "Are you sure you're OK with sharing this information? This is a highly sensitive meeting. I just want to be sure you'd rather not have Penny wait outside."

I looked at Penny, and she looked nervous. Something about this environment made her uncomfortable. Her rocking was dramatic, and her hands were going fast. I turned back to Elizabeth. "I'm not sure I can keep her out of my sight. I think we're all going to stick together for this one." I offered an apologetic smile.

Dr. Sanderson leaned forward on her desk, and opened a manila folder marked HAZEL BRADLEE on its tab. She was holding a gold pen between her hands, all business. "I'm just going to get right to it, Mrs. Bradlee. We know that Hazel is an extremely bright girl. She scored in the top decile of her PSATs. She came to this school two years ago as a freshman and was very appropriately placed in all honors classes. Every single one. Her GPA freshman year was a ninety-eight-point-seven."

I nodded. I knew all this, and I knew where this was going. Elizabeth continued, "She played three sports freshman year. She continued her piano lessons through the school's music program. She took part in the freshman spring play."

"Yes," I said. This was moving in a frightening direction. I knew it. I thought I might be sick. I swallowed. I remembered to breathe through my nose. Slow, methodical breaths. In through the nose and out through the mouth. This student portrait she was painting was not the daughter I had now. I missed that girl and didn't know where she had gone. There was a sharp pinching sensation in my chest. I pressed my hand to my heart.

"Now to sophomore year." Elizabeth opened the file centered on the desk surface and said Hazel's four quarter averages were 97.5, 96.4, 91.3, 84.2. She looked up at me. I knew this. Penny slowed down her rocking, but her hands were still going furiously. It was extremely hard to focus on this conversation with my sister's distracting and loud tics. I looked over at Penny, imploring her with my eyes to slow down all of her movements. She looked straight at me, paused, totally frozen, eyes wide, and then continued her rocking.

"I'm telling you all this because I'm trying to clarify a trend. She has opted out of sports this fall, which, as you know, is allowed, but given the directions her grades are turning, I am not happy about that. Sports have always been an excellent release for all our students, but especially Hazel, and she was showing such promise in field hockey. Coach Gilmore is so disappointed. So am I. Did you support her decision to quit?" Her lips were pinched together, and her eyes narrowed slightly.

I hadn't known she had quit field hockey. Hazel told me they hadn't started practices yet and that there were no pre-season sessions this summer. "I didn't know. Hazel told me the season hadn't started yet. She said she didn't know…" But as I said it, I realized it didn't make sense. Coach Gilmore would have absolutely had pre-season training sessions and practices as of many days ago. How did I miss this?

"Well, she has. And it looks like you signed the sports waiver." Elizabeth looked at her file and pulled out a form with a signature at the bottom, which was not mine. It was an excellent copy of mine. I shook my head and said nothing. Elizabeth continued, "Here's what I really need to talk with you about. I've known you for so long, and I really think the world of Hazel, so this is extremely hard to say."

I was looking over her shoulder, out the window at the neatly trimmed boxwoods, the sunlight making the tiny leaves a glowing, lime green. It was a beautiful and serene day outside. Outside was happy and fresh. Wasn't all this other news, this summary of her failures and slow and steady decline enough? There was something else?

This whole room felt exceedingly hot. Why didn't they have air-conditioning in here? I moved my legs up and down, trying to peel the skin on the backs of my thighs off the sticky seats. Penny was rocking slowly and steadily and looking out the window behind Elizabeth's desk. I couldn't tell if she was listening intently, or lost in some reverie.

"Fez, yesterday after fourth period, Hazel left to get lunch, which was an excused absence. When she returned at one thirty, the front hall security guards smelled marijuana on her as she walked in the front door."

My jaw unclenched. "What?"

"I was summoned. The smell was unmistakable. She must have smoked on her walk back to school from wherever she had lunch. She was with three other students." I knew exactly who they were.

Jesus Christ. Penny had stopped rocking and was staring at Elizabeth.

I couldn't come up with any words. My mouth was open, and I was trying, but they were all stuck in my throat. She continued, "You may know that when we suspect students of misconduct of any kind, we are allowed by the by-laws of this school to check their person and their bags."

No. No. No. Elizabeth pulled a small paper bag up from the floor onto her desk.

"A search of Hazel's backpack Friday revealed a bag of marijuana, a lighter, rolling papers, and this bag with what we believe to be Xanax bars." I had never seen the long, yellow pills before.

"Wait, what? I...don't...even...What are those?"

"They're the street drug version of the prescription drug Xanax. Two-milligram dosing in four half-milligram fractions. I didn't know what they were, either. I had to look them up online. Needless to say, drugs and drug paraphernalia cannot be on campus. She was not the only one with illegal substances in her possession. The other three students have been expelled. They each had previous 'strikes.' This was Hazel's first offense, but as you know, it calls for an immediate suspension.

"Fez, I don't need to tell you how extremely disappointed I was in those students yesterday. The other three students were utterly unfazed by their expulsion. They seemed relieved somehow to leave here, but Hazel shut down. She was completely despondent. After we checked her bag, she said nothing, absolutely nothing. She showed almost no emotion. She seemed and seems extremely listless and depressed, either by drugs or in general."

She did seem low energy or depressed lately. Very, actually.

"Hazel mentioned that her father isn't living at home right now." Dr. Sanderson waited for a reply.

"Yes, that's true. We've been separated since May." I did not meet her gaze but looked at the pens lying parallel on her desk, and the glass Independent School Educators' Award she was using as a paperweight.

"Well, that of course might be a factor, or a trigger. Any change in a child's environment can be difficult and confusing." I was starting to feel entirely and directly responsible for all the changes in Hazel. She continued, "Have you seen any symptoms of depression and/or drug use at home?"

I stammered as I started to speak. "No to the drug use. I would have to say maybe yes to the depression. Sometimes I can't tell if it is depression or some sort of teenage angst. She's never around, or up in her room with the door closed. Or out. Or angry with me." I was awkwardly stumbling though my sentences, throwing out words in a sloppy jumble. My unawareness proved how out of touch I had become. I had missed something huge in my own child. She was using drugs. I had no idea. And I thought she might be depressed, but somehow I told myself she was a normal, typical adolescent pulling away. Was Dr. Sanderson looking at me with disdain or disgust or pity? I felt her eyes burning into me. I looked down and stared at my feet. I had two different shoes on. Jesus, I couldn't even dress myself.

"When she was in my office, we talked at length about the seriousness of her actions, and I decided to delay discussing this with you, as I wanted to have this conversation in person. Needless to say, she is in trouble; she is suspended indefinitely, but she stayed in my office until I sent her home at about three o'clock. I asked her to come into the school with you this morning so that her academic adviser could continue this conversation. She loves Hazel too and wanted to spend some time with her. Anyway, I called you several times yesterday but didn't hear back from you. Your mailbox was full, and I couldn't leave a cell message. You'll probably find my three messages on your home phone." I never checked the home phone messages. "I'm glad I finally reached you." She was judging my unavailability, my ineptitude.

She continued, "Fez, I see in Hazel potential for great success. We're worried, her teachers and me. Her math teacher picked up on something as well. He told me she was a focused and engaged math student until last spring. Then she seemed to stop caring. He said she shows real promise in math. He wanted to talk with you about having to drop her down a level. I believe he reached out to you. I know he did want to share with you that she is at Level B now." I nodded. She raised her eyebrows.

"Anyway, here's what I want to say to you. Forgive me for being blunt. I'm quite concerned that her drug use is serious, and I strongly suggest you take Hazel to an outpatient facility for mood disorder and/or drug abuse just to have her evaluated, simply so you can address the issues early. Xanax is extremely addictive, and I don't know how long she has been using, but we feel that you need to address it immediately."

I completely agreed that her mood and drug use was very serious, but did she need a facility? Didn't that seem a bit aggressive? Premature? We didn't really even know what the real issues were. I started to formulate a response, but before I could, she continued, "I'm suggesting this as a friend and as a school administrator who really cares about your child. I believe she needs help. Take her so she can get treatment. Whatever they think is the appropriate treatment. I'm not trying to be dramatic here; I'm trying to be helpful. If she's taking Xanax, smoking pot, and drinking, and more importantly, showing signs of depression, I want her to get help. I really don't think she should be here at school until I'm sure she is better."

I didn't know what to say. It was as if she was talking about someone else's child. I couldn't wrap my head this. Her words were swirling around in my head in an angry maelstrom. Penny was a statue next to me, quietly staring out the window at the rhododendrons. She wasn't rocking or moving. Her hands were clasped together on her lap.

"So you're telling me to take Hazel to a hospital?"

"Yes, Fez, an *outpatient* facility. Do you know Edgehill? It's close and—"

"Yes, of course. I know Edgehill." I was not feeling well. I was definitely going to throw up. I could taste the bile at the base of my throat. Dr. Elizabeth Sanderson, a highly respected school administrator, thought Hazel needed serious help. "My closest friend, Hazel's godmother, works there." My words were stilted, choppy.

Penny, who had been almost frozen, staring out at the plants and flowers through the paned window, said, "I knows Edgehill."

Elizabeth and I turned our gazes from each other to look at Penny.

I said, "That's great, Penny. We can talk about that later."

"OK, we's talk about it later." She reached into a glass canister on Elizabeth's desk and took a peppermint candy. She slowly unwrapped it and put it in her mouth. She held on to the little cellophane wrapper, smoothing out the wrinkles.

Elizabeth turned back to me. "OK, that's good. Take Hazel home today. She's in her adviser's office. Take her home and consult with Edgehill. It's important. We'll stay in touch."

"I understand. OK." I didn't understand. Nothing was OK.

Penny just stared out the window. The way the light washed over her made her look so young and sweet. Her skin was pale pink and soft, and her yellow hair was both absorbing and reflecting the clean sunshine from the window. She slowly reached into the candy jar and put a handful of peppermints into her purse. Then another handful. And a third. Until the candy jar was empty. She put the glass lid back on the jar, carefully. Elizabeth and I watched her slow but deliberate movements.

Penny looked at Elizabeth and then at me. "Can we go now? I's ready."

# CHAPTER 14

# PENELOPE

Fuzzy didn't look so good. We left the slippery-green-chair room and went into another room where Hazy was sitting. Fuzzy's head was down very low. She looked like the letter *C*. Hazy didn't look so good neither. She was reading a book called *Zen and the Art of Motorcycle Maintenance*. Fuzzy said all hushy and low, *Let's go, Hazel. Let's go.* Hazy didn't say nothin but just picked up her black and gray backpack with the North Face name on it and the picture of the mountains, and she walked all slumpy over to Fuzzy. Fuzzy looked at Hazel, and then Hazel looked up at Fuzzy. They was both so gray and sad. All walking kinda slow and bendy. I didn't say nothin neither cuz everybody was all quiet and frowny. So I just kept my mouth shuts. We walked outta that school past the fancy stairs and the shiny wood floors and the pictures of the old mens in fancy gold frames and the skinny lady in the blue dress and the slippery-chair room and just kept on walkin til we was on the sidewalk and seeing the sunshine, and the shadows from the trees maked pretty sparkedly splashes on the ground.

Nobody was sayin nothing. *Why's you twos not talking?* Nobody answered me, which was kinda rood. Fuzzy was walkin in front, and Hazel was walkin kinda behind her and looking down. I thought of all the times Dottie would hold my hand to make me feel happy, so I reached over to grab Hazel's hand, but she pulled it away. And she looked away with her sad eyes. I tried again, but she wouldn't let me hold her hand. *Why's yous not holdin my hand? I's gonna make you feel more better.* But she just kept walkin and lookin at the sidewalk and all the bricks going crissy crossy. Fuzzy's mouth was all tight like a thin tiny line.

Fuzzy stopped walkin all of a sudden and turned around to look at Hazel. *Hazel, what is going on?*

Hazy shook her head. *Nothin.*

Then Fuzzy said, *Nothin?* Louder now. *Honey, not nothing. Please talk to me.* I didn't like the loud voice so good, so I covered my ears. We all stopped walkin then.

Hazy said, *Yeah, Mom, I don't know. I don't know what to say. Just nothin.* A man walking his tiny, fluffy, white dog was passing us all right then, and he looked at Hazel when she said her loud *nothin* word, and he raised his big eyebrows and looked kinda surprised, and then he walked away real, real fast pulling his poor tiny dog hard on the bright-green leash.

Then they just stood there staring at each other until Fuzzy said, *Well, your* nothin *just got you suspended from school.* Hazy just looked down at her feets and said nothing. *And now,* Fuzzy said, *I don't even know where to begin. I don't really know what to say.* Hazel didn't say nothin. She just kinda kicked her black boots on the place between two crookedy bricks. *Cuz I don't know if you're sad, or mad at the world, or depressed. Are you depressed? Do you feel depressed? I don't know; I guess you are. And the pot and pills and the drinking. I really just don't know what to say.* The way Fuzzy said her words was sad and mean. Her whole face scrunched up. Hazel kept looking down and nodded, and she was kinda smiling in a sad way. She wasn't saying nothin, but her face was getting scrunchy too.

Then Hazel said, *I know.* Really quiet, like we almost couldn't hear it and like she was saying it to her feets.

Fuzzy looked at Hazel and then looked like every bone in her bottom kinda settled down toward the ground. Like Fuzzy's bones used to be all high and tight and crunched together and then, just then, they all got all loose-y and fell down so Fuzzy was slumpier. *Oh, honey,* Fuzzy said. *I'm so, so sorry. I didn't mean sound mad. I'm so sorry. I'm sad that you're sad. Really sad. I just don't know what to do. I'm scared.* She stepped toward Hazy and pulled Hazy into her in a big tight hug. Hazy just stood there looking down all tired, and her hands was hanging limpy at her sides. Jeez, Hazy was a bad, bad hugger. So I pulled Hazy's arms up and wrapped them around Fuzzy's skinny back. Hazy rested her white cheek on Fuzzy's bony shoulder and closed her eyes for a long time. Then, she opened her big eyes and looked at me and made the tiniest smile. Just a little one. I think it was, anyway. She clasped her hands together at Fuzzy's back. Nobody said nothin. Fuzzy was squeezing her pretty good. I thought I could hear bones crunching, but it mighta been the sounds of cars drivin on the streets. The peoples on the sidewalk walked around us and just acted like nobody was hugging in the middle of the sidewalk. The peoples just walked a big circle around Fuzzy and Hazel, who was hugging for a long times.

Fuzzy pulled away and said, *Let's go home and call Ellie and figure out this whole Edgehill thing, OK?* Hazel just nodded, and then we was all walking again. Going back home to call Ellie. Fuzzy started walking faster and faster. I think she really wanted to get home.

*I knows about Edgehill,* I said again.

Fuzzy stopped marching and turned around to face me. *Penny, this might be a different Edgehill than you know.*

*I knows about Edgehill,* I said again.

Fuzzy looked really confused now and a little bit mad, like she was trying to be patient with me. *OK, Penny. What, exactly, do you know about Edgehill?*

I looked right at her. I wasn't afraid of her kinda mean voice. *Mommy went there one time.*

Fuzzy looked like she seen a scary aminal or something. *What?*

Boy, she really didn't hear so good. She was always asking *What?* and things like that. *Our mommy went to Edgehill.* I said that real slow so she wouldn't say *What?* no more. *She told me all about it. The hostipal in Belmont, Massachusetts. She went there in December 1953.* I was real good at membering numbers and days.

Fuzzy stared at me with her mouth really open. *What? Are you sure? Mom? Why?* Fuzzy asked.

*She gots sick and she hadda go to the hostipal to gets better.* I was talking real, real careful. *Yes, I's sure.*

*Right,* said Fuzzy. *Did she ever tell you about it? Like what made her sick?*

*No, no, cuz it's privacy.* Mommy said some things was privacy. I wasn't aposta to say some things, so I wasn't gonna.

Well, then Fuzzy looked like she had too much stuff squiggling in her head, and she turned around and walked normal. Hazel was walkin next to me. I reached for her hand again, and this time she let me take it. It was real cold and thin, like a little birdy's. I could feel the bones and the little veins and everything. I could roll those little tiny veins back and forth with my thumb. I held her little tiny hand all the way to 30 Marlborough Street, Boston, Massachusetts, 02116.

Fuzzy forgotted to hold the door for us when we got home. She walked way ahead so, so fast, and she marched right into the house and was already talking to her bestest friend, Ellie, on the phone when we was walkin in.

*…and they are recommending an evaluation…Yes…I know, I mean… I don't know…I…Well, yes, OK…I never would have thought…I know. I know…What? Oh, she said an indefinite suspension pending Edgehill's evaluation of her. Now? Yes, definitely, can we? OK, thanks so much, El.*

Fuzzy hunged up the phone and said, *Ellie wants us to come out to Edgehill now. She's moving around a couple of appointments so we can talk with her.*

Hazy shrugged her shoulders and said, *OK.*

*I's coming too,* I said.

Fuzzy just looked at me like she didn't know what to say. *Of course you are. Of course, we'll all go. We'll figure this out as we go, I guess.*

I didn't know what that meant, but I was essited for a car ride, and I kinda wanted to see the Edgehill place where Mommy went to gets all better. Plus, Fuzzy's car was shiny and nice.

*I have to call William, and then we'll go.* Fuzzy left a message for William, and it was really short. *It's Fez. Call me back as soon as you can. It's about Hazel.* She hung up real fast, and then we was all heading for the door. She was clomping her feets pretty loud.

We locked up the house with three different locks and walked down the crookedy brick sidewalk to get into the shiny, nice car, and Fuzzy sat in the seat with the wheel, and Hazy sat in the seat next to her, and I sat in the back, and we all strapped into our seats with the seatbelts, and they clicked into the orange parts, and when I heard the three clicks, I knew we was safe for goin. I asked about the trip. Fuzzy looked at her phone and the map picture was there, and she told me the drive was 7.9 miles and nineteen minutes of driving cuz that's what her phone told her. I checked my *Dora Espplora* watch. It was 12:19. We was gonna get there at 12:38.

The drive axually took twenty-three minutes cuz of *lunchtime backups,* whatever that was, and Fuzzy bitted her nails and said nothing, and Hazy putted her feet up on the shelf in the car above the little cabinet with her boots really close to the glass.

*Careful not to break the glass with your big boots, Hazy,* I reminded her. Glass was breakable, and it made a big loud noise when it broked. I knew that real goodly.

Hazy didn't even turn around to look at me but just took her boots off the shelf and slid down in her seat and closed her eyes and kinda went sleepynights. That's how the twenty-three minutes was. No talking, just nail biting for Fuzzy with one hand on the driving wheel and one hand in her mouth and quiet time for Hazy, and I just looked out the window at the cars driving by and the sunshine spots and the trees when the trees came back after the fast, fast road. We was driving next to a pretty and curvy river for most of the trip. There was peoples rowing all together at the same time in a long, skinny boat. Eight peoples rowing really hard and one little person yelling at them with earphones and wires and a tiny microphone near her mouth. She was making those peoples row faster and faster and harder and harder. She was kinda cranky. *BeautifulBoston* sure had a lotta different kinds of peoples.

Edgehill was a big scary, scary building way up on top of a tall hill. All bricks and pointy roofs and a round tower thing like in the Rapunzel story and black windows, and right when we pulled in, there were all these black birds eating something in the grass. They was squawkin and making scratchy noises with their birdy throats. I didn't like them birds so good. They was mean. Hazy woked up just as we was getting near the Edgehill parking lot. She pulled her hood onto her head from her sweatshirt, and she started clickin the buttons pretty good on her phone. Real, real fast—*clk, clk, clk, clk, clk.* Fuzzy and Hazy still didn't say nothin. I just looked out the windows and did my rockin.

When we got outta the car, Hazy said real quiet, *I don't wanna do this.*

Fuzzy didn't look at Hazy. *I know, sweetie, but we have to, Hazel. We just have to.*

Hazy musta gotted it, I guess, cuz she didn't say nothing else.

We waited in the front part of the building, and I didn't like it. I was kinda scared. I don't know why. It was dark and smelled like a hostipal but worse. It smelled sad. And mad. Those scary birds were sitting picking at that grass. I counted and there was seven. Seven black birds picking at something chewy. *What's those black birds, Fuzzy?*

Fuzzy looked up at me like she forgotted I was with her. *Uh, what?*

*What's those big black birds, Fuzzy?*

She followed my finger with her eyes to where I was pointing. *Oh, those are crows.*

*They's seven crows, Fuzzy. I counted.*

Fuzzy just stared out at the crows like she was dreaming. She said, *Mom used to tell me a nursery rhyme when I was a little girl about counting crows.*

*We useda have Rhyme-Time at the Center. I loves rhymes. Do you member it? The rhyme abut counting crows?*

Fuzzy looked up at the ceiling like the rhyme was up there someplace in the dirty ceiling tiles. *Uh, yeah, I think I do...Let me think...Oh yeah. One for sorrow, two for joy...three for girls and four for boys...Um, what's the next line...Oh yeah...Five for silver, six for gold, and...seven for a secret never to be told. More verses maybe, but I can't remember. I think that's it.*

I looked out at the seven crows pickin and scratchin and pullin at some stuff in the grass, and I counted them again to be sure, and sure enough, they was seven. *Seven. Seven crows.* And I got a big shiver like I was freezing cold, but I wasn't. I wasn't cold at all.

A lady came out through a glass door with a big smile. She reminded me of Fuzzy. She was tall and skinny and had on black pants and boots and a pretty blue soft sweater and a name tag on her gray jacket: Ellie Logan. She went right up to Hazy and gave her the biggest, biggest snuggly bear hug. Hazy was hugging her OK, but the Ellie lady was hugging her hard. And two times Hazy dropped her arms to stop hugging, and the lady Ellie kept on squeezing. Jeez. Then Ellie hugged Fuzzy fast, and then she looked at me. *You must be Penny.* Of course I was Penny. You don't gots to tell me who I must be. I just nodded, and she took my hand and shook it up and down. My arm was all floppy.

*OK, I'm going to take Hazel and Fez in. Penny, you come in, and you can sit just outside my office. We have a TV and activities and stuff to do while you're waiting. Is that OK? You'll be able to see us through the glass.*

162

I looked at Fuzzy, and she nodded like it's OK. We all walked through the glass doors, and there was a nice room with a yellow sofa and yellow-and-green-flowered pillows and a TV and a basket of toys for childrens and a table with big picture books and paper and a basket with pens, and I said, *This is nice.*

Ellie said, *Great. Make yourself comfortable.* I did make myself comfortable. I sat down on the comfy sofa, and I was sure comfortable, and there was a big pad of paper and a box of markers on the table, so I colored pictures, and the TV said a message over and over again with words, not outloud: *Welcome to Edgehill. Welcome to Edgehill. Welcome to Edgehill.*

Fuzzy and Hazy went into the glass office right next to me, and I could see them talkin, and first their heads was down low, and then I saw Fuzzy's head was pink and Hazy's head was down and gray, and then Hazy lifted her head, and then they was all talkin, and then Ellie looked at me and did like a thumbs-up thing, like asking me if I was OK, and I did like a thumbs-up thing and shouted, *I's good, Ellie.* That turned outta be kinda loud in the quiet, quiet room. They kept talkin for a long, long time, and Ellie kept reaching across her desk to Hazy and touching her hand, and then Ellie was smiling a little, and Fuzzy's shoulders came down a little, and then they was all standing and smiling a little, and Ellie was handing Fuzzy a tissue, and Fuzzy hugged her, and Ellie hugged Hazy. They was in there for fifty-seven minutes. *Dora the Essplora* told me.

We all got into the car and said our bye-byes to Ellie, who smelled really good like tangerines. She was nice, the lady Ellie. She made Fuzzy smile and Hazy smile and their shoulders come down, and maybe now Hazy was going to get better at the hostipal where my mommy went in December of 1953. Fuzzy said Hazy wasn't gonna sleep there. But my mommy slept there. She told me. My mommy also told me a big secret, which I wasn't never gonna tell no one. Never, ever. She told me this secret in November of

1979, when she was a little bit sick in her throat. My mommy finished her thermos of happy juice, and she was all wavy in her chair. She musta been so, so tired cuz her voice was kinda slippery and slidy, and she couldn't really sit up straight, so she rested her head on her skinny arms on the table. Right then, my mommy told me she went to Edgehill Hostipal in Belmont, Massachusetts, for *two reasons.* She lifted her head and held up her two bumpy, purple fingers when she told me this. *One,* she said, *because you, my sweet Penelope, went far away when you were a teeny tiny girl, and two,* she added, and her eyes gotted wet, *because a horrible monster destroyed me and changed my life forever.* I was trying to picture the monsters like in the cartoons, but I couldn't do it. Plus, Mommy's face went all weird when she said it, and it gave me prickly shivers on my head. Mommy told me, and I promised I ain't never gonna tell no one my mommy's secret.

# CHAPTER 15

# FESSENDEN

As we left Edgehill, the crows, still on the small knoll, under a copse of sickly-looking cedar trees, got spooked and flew away with heavy, lethargic wings. When we walked toward our car, we saw an older couple and two young adults. The man was maybe in his mid-fifties, with a bald, pink, shiny head, and in a pale-blue-checked button-down shirt and khaki pants. Boat shoes. He was out of the car and opening the passenger side door. The woman, his wife, I guessed, was sitting in the car seat, crying. Hard. She was having a hard time catching her breath. The two young adults, maybe in their twenties, maybe their children, were standing behind their father, leaning around him, comforting her. "Mom, it's OK. It's OK. It's going to be OK." They were rubbing her back and her right shoulder. But she was crying so hard and now she was choking, on her own tears, gasping, fighting back.

"No, no, no," she was saying. "Please don't make me go." The words came out between choking sobs. Her skin was purple-red, a beet freshly steamed. She was very thin. She reminded me of my mother. Her bony figure, her stooped posture, her flaking skin, her thin hair revealing her milky-white scalp beneath: this was my mother. "No, no, no," she cried. Then in the midst of crying and choking and sobbing and wailing, she started to gag, and then she threw up a thin, viscous yellow liquid all over her brown pants, and the car's beige carpet floor mats.

Her husband said, "Oh dear. Oh, Joan." He reached for his handkerchief and started to mop at her pants. The adult children stepped back, covering their mouths, talking quietly to each other. In that moment, one of Edgehill's administrators came out to assist, and we—Penny, Hazel, and I, who had been transfixed, watching this awful scene play out—continued walking to our car.

I reached over and took Hazel's hand in mine. It was thin and cool. It weighed nothing at all. The hand of a bird. She let it be limp in mine. "Honey, I am so sorry."

"Whaddya mean?" She was exhausted.

"I'm just so sorry you're sad."

Hazel looked out the window, her face warm and yellow in the light. She let her head fall back against the headrest. She paused and then said, "Yeah, me too." I watched her little face, young and small still; her three words hung heavy and thick in the air. She never turned to face me. She just kept looking out the window, at the passing cars, the filtered light, the telephone poles, a jogger running with headphones.

"So how'd you feel about what Ellie said?"

"About the program?"

"Yeah…the program, and you."

"Mom, it just seems like a lot. I understand about the depression, and the treatment. I get that. But all the drug testing, group meetings, social worker meetings, the psychiatrist…It just seems like way too much."

"I know, maybe, but maybe not. I think we just have to follow the protocol. We'll see how you do. This is new for all of us. It's four weeks, and you'll be living at home, and we'll use the time to get you feeling better. We'll address the depression first and foremost." I smiled at her, but she continued to look away.

Hazel slumped farther down, still staring out the window. Her eyes were heavy, but she kept them open, staring vacuously at the passing shadows. Her hands rested quietly in her lap, her chipped black nail polish almost gone. She was watching the trees go by, black and brown and gray and green, going by in a whir. Seeing her small and so vulnerable and realizing how sad she really was, how truly depressed she was, brought hot tears to my eyes. I thought about all that she had seen in the last year: the loud, long evening fights with William, the fights over money and my anger over the certain loss of the Crow's Nest, his moving out in the spring, my preoccupation with my book. And all the while, she was settling into something sad and scary, all alone.

I wiped my cheeks and looked in the rearview mirror. Penny was in the center of the back seat, her fingers and hands going again, her thumbs circling over the pads of her other fingers. I remembered what I wanted to do for her, my bright idea, which had come to me on our drive to visit Dottie's gravesite in Marion.

"Penny, have you ever knit before?" I asked, seeing her through the rearview mirror.

She looked at my eyes in the mirror. "No, Fuzzy, I ain't never knit before. Dottie did some crochay-ing and made some aftgans, but I ain't never learned nuthin but weaving those pretty pot holders."

"Well, do you think you might like to learn? I could teach you." I raised my eyebrows in optimism.

She thought for a second, scrunching up her face a little. "OK, Fuzzy. I's essited to learn to knit. Paul sez I's a quick learner."

"That's great, Penny. We can stop at an art store on the way home and get you some yarn. We can start with a scarf. That's the first thing I learned to make."

"Is it easy cuz it's straight?"

"Exactly. Straight knitting is the easiest. Then when you get the hang of the basic stitches, I can teach you different stitches and how to make hats and mittens and sweaters and whatever you want. Sound good?"

"Sounds good, Fuzzy. Oh, and Fuzzy?"

"Yes?"

"I wants yellow yarn, OK? Just yellow."

"Yellow it is."

"Fuzzy?"

"Yes, Penny?"

"What did Ellie say in her glass office?"

"Well, we talked about how to make Hazel feel better. Hazel's really, really sad, and Ellie says maybe Edgehill can help her feel less sad."

I had wanted to ask Ellie about my mother's stay there, if that was the case, but I hadn't wanted to ask her during our meeting with Hazel. I would call her later and bring that up with her.

I also knew I had to call William and talk about the expenses of Hazel's stay at Edgehill. He had the insurance policy through his work. Until right this minute, I hadn't even thought about the costs; they would be outrageous. Was this course of treatment eligible for coverage? I was going to have to hope that Hazel's care at Edgehill wasn't considered elective. But even as I thought that, I realized that of course it was elective. *Of course* it was. How could it not be? Hot panic was overtaking my thoughts. We were running out of money. All of our bank accounts were getting low. Talking with William about this was going to be difficult. He would be as scared as I was starting to feel, maybe more so. The thought of having another exhausting fight about money with William was something I didn't want to think about right now. Maybe a quick sale of the Crow's Nest would allow us to catch up on bills, including these pending ones. I would have to call Janet soon to instigate the listing process.

Penny leaned forward, almost all the way through the middle of the two front seats, pulling her seatbelt to its maximum give. She was inches away from Hazel's face. She reached up and stroked the peachy hair on the side of Hazel's cheek, golden in the light.

Hazel turned her head toward Penny.

"She's like Mommy," Penny said while running her index finger up and down her cheek.

"I know what you mean. Same big eyes. Same lips, I think."

"No, not like Mommy that way. Or maybe that way too. But I mean she's like Mommy's sad face."

I looked at Penny looking at Hazel, who was lost in thought. "What do you mean, Penny? Mommy's sad face?"

"When Mommy'd come to visit me and Dottie, her mouth always went down. And even her happy juice couldn't make her smile look right. Dottie called her 'sad Mommy.' Hazel looks like 'sad Mommy' when she's quiet and not all mad to you. She's usually mad to you a lot. Then her face is scrunchy."

Penny was right. Hazel had that weary, sad, blank-eyed stare that Mother used to have. I always assumed that was just booze or pills or hangover with Mother, and it was. But maybe it was more, like sadness or heartbreak, or some sooty blackness, which filled her soul.

Hazel leaned back so she was leaning against the passenger window, facing me. "Mom, why don't you ever talk about your mother?"

"I don't know, Haze. Not a lot to tell."

"Were you guys close at all?"

"No, not really." I put the blinker on for our exit, hoping to end this conversation quickly.

"There must be some good stories, right? You hardly ever mention her." Hazel was squinting at me in the bright light.

"There are definitely stories, but not too many good ones. Trust me; you don't want to hear them."

"I do, actually." Hazel was not letting this go.

"Another time then, OK?" We pulled into the parking lot at Stitch by Stitch, the store in Cambridge where I bought my wool for knitting and my canvases and wool for needlepoint. My grandmother had taught me my love for handiwork. Mimi felt very strongly that a lady should always have some needlework in her hands.

"Idle hands are the devil's workshop," she used to say, pointing her tanned age-spotted finger at me. Mimi knit all of my mittens, hats, and scarves and had made needlepoint pillows for my room and had crocheted beautiful blankets and throws for my bed. We would sit together in the evenings at the Crow's Nest knitting and stitching quietly while Grandpa watched his television. Mimi was always there, sitting in the same room. I guess she just didn't want to be away from her beloved husband; they were inseparable.

I put my hand on Hazel's shoulder. "You want to come in? Or do you want to stay in the car?" Hazel's eyes were puffy. She looked young. I was expecting her to say she would nap in the car while we went in.

"I'll come in, I guess."

I smiled and patted her bony knee.

We all went in, and I greeted Kate, the owner. The yarns were all organized by color in white shelves and cubbies on the walls. Penny walked right up to the yellow section. "I's liking this one." Penny was holding a skein of bright-yellow yarn.

"OK, Penny, that looks good. Take three of those."

Hazel was near the door, standing awkwardly, picking at her nail polish. Penny walked over to her with her yarn. "What's you gonna get, Hazy?"

Hazel looked at Penny, slowly, heavily. "Nothin'. I don't do that stuff."

Penny said, "Me neither. I's learnin today cuz Fez sez I's gonna likes it. You gots to learn today too!"

"Nah, Penny. Thanks, though. I'm good."

Penny looked down, disappointed and said, "I thinks you should learn too. It's gonna be fun." She was rolling the yarn skeins around in her hands. Staring at Hazel.

Hazel just stared back at her for a second. Then she started fiddling with a basket of knitting needles on the table by the door, feeling the smooth, beautiful bamboo sticks with her fingers. "OK."

Penny stood up straight, and her face went round and full with her smile. "Really, Hazy? Yeah? You's gonna learn with me?"

"Yeah, sure. Why not?" She shrugged. "What the hell."

I watched Hazel and Penny walk back to the shelves of yarn. Hazel picked out charcoal-gray wool. Penny pointed to the shelf. I saw her put three fingers up, and Hazel took two more skeins. They walked up to Kate and me at the register, the yarn in their hands.

"Hazy and me's gonna learn together. OK, Fuzzy?" Penny said.

"Really?" I said. "I think that's great." Hazel shrugged, but I saw something there. A faint smile. A little something pink and warm and pretty. Just for a second, and then it was gone, but I held on to it like it was real.

Penny said she was hungry and wanted pizza. We drove back to Back Bay, parked at the brownstone, and walked to Gianino's on Dartmouth Street for their delicious, cheesy thin-crust pizza. Hazel and I ordered a large plate of chicken wings to split, and Penny ordered a full cheese pizza.

Growing up, before Dad left us for Rosie, Tuesdays were pizza night. My father and I would drive to the next town to pick up a large pepperoni pizza and three cold bottles of Coca-Cola. On the drive back, I'd sit with the hot cardboard box on my lap, smelling the hot cheese and doughy crust, the box almost too hot to hold. When we got home, Dad would put a single slice on a small plate with an opened bottle of Coke on Mother's bedside table.

He and I would sit at the small gateleg table in the kitchen and eat our dinner quietly. Dad was tired from work, and he didn't have much to say. I'd talk about something that had happened at school or what my friends were talking about at recess or how my sports were going, but my attempts at conversation died quickly, and I would give up, focusing instead on my dinner. Every Wednesday morning, Dad brought down the uneaten, hard, coagulated pizza slice and threw it in the trash. Mother always managed to finish the cold, sweet soda.

Penny leaned in hungrily to eat her slice of cheese pizza. She made loud noises of satisfaction as she chewed. "So, so good, Fuzzy." The cheese was dribbling down her chin. Hazel reached over with a thin paper napkin to wipe it off. "Thanks, Hazy. I's like callin you 'Hazy' cuz I likes the *eeeeee* sound at the ends of names like Dottie and Fuzzy and Penny and Hazy. K? K, Hazy?"

"Sure, Penny. That's cool." Hazel wasn't eating. She was drinking her water and stirring the ice with her straw.

"Not hungry, Haze?" I asked her. "Why don't you just try a bite of something? You haven't eaten all day."

"Nah." She was watching a group of teenagers laughing at a different table. She looked away.

We sat in silence, eating and stirring ice water until Penny said with a full mouth of pizza, "Fuzzy, now you gots to tell us a Mommy story. A happy one."

Hazel looked up at me then. "Yeah. Let's hear it."

"Not right now." I said, digging into a spicy buffalo wing. "Maybe later."

"Now's good," said Penny. "We needs a happy story cuz Hazy's real sad. Right, Hazy?"

"Yeah." Hazel looked at me. "Sure."

"OK. OK. Let me think." I wiped my fingers on the napkin. The buffalo sauce was stinging a little spot next to my thumbnail, a torn piece of cuticle. I couldn't think of anything. Hazel and Penny were looking at me, imploring me to tell them something and something *happy*, and nothing was coming to me. That said it all; I was unable to come up with a happy thought about my mother. "Um, I'm still thinking..."

"C'mon, Fuzzy." Penny's mouth was full. "We're *waiting*."

I put down the tiny bone from my eaten chicken wing, wiped my fingers, and then I remembered something. A dim memory rose up through the fog. "OK, here goes. I remember, one day at the Crow's Nest making a picnic with Mom on the beach. I think I was five or six. We packed up ham sandwiches and green grapes and cookies and lemonades, I think, and we brought down a blue-and-white quilt from the house and set it on the beach, and we stayed there all day. I mean *all day.*"

Hazel asked, "What did you do after you ate your picnic?"

"That was kind of the best part," I said. "We just were together all day. I remember holding hands and going into the water, swimming together, and then putting little hermit crabs into a bucket and then letting them all go. They scattered everywhere really fast with their curved white legs, and we laughed. Mom was in her green Lilly Pulitzer cotton bathing suit. It had little straps, and I can remember her skinny, skinny legs. She was sitting cross-legged in the sand. My bathing suit was all tiny orange gingham with a smiling big sun on the front. You know, with the sunshine rays sticking out? I haven't thought about that suit for ages. We dug holes with little plastic shovels and made little sand castles. Just piles of sand, really. I remember the smell of the Bain de Soleil orange gel sunscreen. I remember the smell of that on Mom's warm skin. And I can see her laughing, her head back. Making a funny face when she sipped the tart lemonade."

Penny and Hazel were staring at me. Penny had stopped chewing, and Hazel was just listening and looking. Hazel said, "Mom. I've never heard you say that much about your mom. Never."

Penny added, "I likes a happy story. That's such a happy story. I loves pink-nicks so much. Fuzzy, was the sunshine-y on your baby suit yellow?"

I smiled at Penny. "Yes, actually it was yellow, I think."

"That's the bestest part of the story," said Penny, reaching for another slice. "Yellow makes everythings better."

When we were finished and Penny had eaten the entire pizza, we walked back home from the restaurant with slow, plodding steps. It had been a long day. The light was beautiful and golden and low, casting long shadows, which Penny stepped around. She was focused on counting her steps the entire way.

When we got inside the house, Penny announced that she was going to unpack and get settled in her room. "Do you need help?" I asked, but she said she was going to do it all by herself.

I checked my phone. William had texted: *I'm back in town. I left early. Got your messages. Can I come over? I want to see Hazel.*

I replied: *Sure, we're just back. Come by whenever.*

Hazel and I went upstairs. She was quiet. "OK, Haze, wanna talk?"

Hazel moved a pile of clothes from her armchair to the floor and fell into the chair. "I don't know."

I sat on the bed. I tried to sound upbeat, organized. "It's gonna go fast, honey. It really sounds like a great program."

"I don't want to do this, Mom."

"I know, Haze. I know."

"I mean, I *really* don't want to do this."

I looked at her. I stared at her. She was so frail. Even sitting seemed too much for her. She slumped down farther in the chair and rested her head against the back. The chair was old, threadbare, and needed to be reupholstered. Hazel closed her eyes.

"Haze, how long have you felt like this? This sadness."

She kept her eyes closed. "I don't even know. I don't even think I knew I was sad. I just feel tired. Really tired."

"This summer, I didn't feel like I even saw you. Do you think this started this summer?"

She opened her eyes. "Maybe. This summer was a bummer. I really missed Dad."

I continued, afraid of her answer even as I asked it. "Was I not there for you?"

Hazel looked at me. "It's not your fault I'm depressed, Mom." Her expression was flat. "I mean you were working a lot this summer, but I'm not blaming you for anything. I'm just saying you seemed kinda lost in your writing. You were busy."

I thought back on this past summer, my days at my desk overlooking Crow's Pond. My piles and piles of papers spread all over. Hours lost on the Internet, researching Agnes's life and trying, but not succeeding, to meet deadlines. As I thought about those three months, I couldn't recall any meaningful moments with Hazel, any conversations or meals or time together. I could only see the papers.

"Hazel, I am so sorry. I really blew it."

"Mom, it's OK. I don't want to talk about it. Is it OK if I take a little nap, and then we can talk later? Dad's coming over, right?"

"Yeah, he is."

She smiled.

"Go to sleep, honey, and I'll wake you up when your dad gets here." Hazel climbed into her bed, fully dressed, boots on, and I pulled the covers up to her chin. She closed her eyes, and I kissed her on the forehead. I think she was asleep before I left the room.

As much as I hated thinking about my mother, I really wanted to get to the bottom of whether my mother stayed at Edgehill or whether Penny was mixing up her facts. I was curious if something was really wrong with Mom and what demons or "monsters" she battled. If she was there, at Edgehill, if she battled some disorder, there was something to be learned from the medical records, maybe information that would be of use to me, and of course Hazel and Penny. Also, with Penny living with our family now, and feeling so happy that the secret of her existence had been unveiled, I think maybe I was just enjoying this unveiling process. I dialed Ellie's cell as I walked down the hall. I sat down on the upstairs window seat as soon as she answered. I knew Ellie could tell me right away.

"Thanks for your time today, Ellie. I know it made Hazel feel better to be with you, and it helped me too."

"You are most welcome, my dear friend. So tomorrow, she'll start at nine o'clock. First she'll come to my office, and then I'll shepherd her to Dr. Bowman to discuss antidepressants."

"Yes, absolutely. El, just one other question I didn't want to add to our meeting...Penny seems to think my mother stayed at Edgehill in the fifties."

Penny yelled down from the third floor, where, evidently she could hear me. "In 1953. *Not* the fifties." I looked up at her standing at the top of the stairs with a box. She shook her head like I was a terrible listener. "*December* 1953. I don't remember the dates. She didn't tell me no dates."

"OK. December 1953. Thanks, Penny. El, can you confirm that? I'm trying to understand *if* she really stayed there and why."

Ellie paused and shifted in her seat or something. I heard the sound of vinyl. "Oh wow. Huh. Well, Fez, I'm not allowed to confirm that..."

I laughed. "What? What do you mean?"

"I can't. Patient confidentiality. I can't ever confirm or deny her stay here." She stopped talking abruptly.

"Ellie, you and I are practically *family*. Of course you can tell me."

"No, I really can't. I'm sorry. My hands are tied."

"Seriously?" I asked.

"Seriously, Fez. I'm really sorry. Isn't Richard the executor of your mom's estate? He can do the paperwork."

"Yeah, I get it. I'll call Richard tomorrow. Sorry to even ask."

"No worries. I'm so sorry. Just have Richard send the stuff and we'll see you tomorrow. One more thing: Can you come in after you bring in Hazel tomorrow to talk about insurance eligibility and payment? We can talk about all the treatment expenses and your options for payment. OK?"

"OK, El." Shit, shit, shit, payment stuff. As I hung up, I could hear William coming in the front door. I walked down the stairs to meet him. "Hey," I said. For the first time in months, I was genuinely happy to see him.

"Hi." He stood like a guest in the foyer, a small wrapped present in his hand. "I brought you something." He smiled.

"Wow. What is it?"

"I think you're supposed to open it to find out." He smirked and handed me the small present. We walked into the living room and sat side by side on the small sofa. I untied the ribbon and tore open the paper. It was a small, framed picture of us, taken right after we met, in the bleachers at Fenway Park.

"Oh, I remember this date. That was fun."

"Yeah, it was. Remember the score?"

"No, but I do remember the Red Sox beat the Yankees."

"Yep, five–three. I'll never forget that date. Eddie and Suz had this picture in their TV room, and I asked if maybe I could have it. Anyway. For you."

"Thanks, William. It's sweet. What's the occasion?"

He put both hands on his heart, mocking the pain of heartache. "Today marks the day I met you at Joe's."

I was stunned. He never used to be sentimental. "Oh yeah, the famous coffee shop meeting. I can't believe you remembered."

"I'll never forget. Most important and most fortuitous encounter of my life." His eyes were wet. "Anyway..." He leaned over and hugged me.

"Thanks so much, William. That's really sweet." We got up and headed back to the kitchen.

"Want a glass of wine?" I asked.

"Uh, sure. Where's Haze?"

"She just wanted to take a little nap. She's exhausted. I thought maybe we could spend some time together when she wakes up. She really wants to see you."

"Sure."

I poured him a glass of wine and myself a cocktail. "We already ate, but I have leftover lasagna if you'd like some." He started to shake his head no but changed his mind and agreed to a plate. I put a slice into the microwave. While he sat at the island, I told him everything that had happened in Dr. Sanderson's office and everything that had happened in Ellie's office.

"My heart is breaking for Haze." He looked older. His suit hung on him differently. His collar looked too big.

"Mine too." We sat there at the kitchen island, waiting for the timer to beep, our hands cupped around our glasses, as the light shifted and faded.

"Hazel's glad you're here," I offered.

"Good. That's good," he said, looking down at his glass. "How about you? Are you glad I'm here?"

"I am, actually." I meant it. We needed to pull together for Hazel now.

"I need to tell you why I was in Chicago."

"OK..." I said warily.

He began, "Well, you know how you've asked me a thousand times to finally dump my dying company and get a job with an established agency?"

"Uh, yeah? But you have persisted in saying you could save—"

"I know. I know," he interrupted. "I have tried desperately for months and months now to save my company, and I just wasn't ready to let it die. I couldn't admit that you were right and that I needed to do this, but I can't do it anymore. And I hear you, and I am finally acquiescing. I was interviewing in Chicago with the parent company of a big firm with a Boston office. They need an account manager, and I guess maybe I'm their guy. It's a big step-down in terms of responsibilities, and of course it's not my own place, but you're right, and it's time."

I knew it took a great deal of humility for him to even think about closing his eponymous office and for him to reenter another person's firm. I was moved. I knew he probably had to; he had no choice, and his and our fiscal situation demanded it, but I knew how hard this must have been for him, especially the saying "you're right" piece.

"William, wow. I don't know what to say. It's great, I guess and congratulations and I'm sorry and—" I had so much more to say, but I heard Penny's footsteps coming down the stairs, and she came around the corner holding an empty box.

William stood up, pushing his stool back. He looked like he had forgotten she was here. "Hi. You must be Penny." He put out his hand. She set the empty box on the island.

"I must be Penny, and you's must be Willum. Right, Willum?" She gave him a limp handshake.

"Yes, I am," he said with an amused look on his face. "How are you?"

"Well, I's not so good, Willum. First, my bestest friend Dottie died, and now I's here, which is hard, and then we's sad cuz Hazy's sad, and Fuzzy's sad and bendy, and you's not here so much, and I's learnin how to knits."

William took this all in, staring closely at Penny and her mannerisms and her way of speaking. He looked squarely at Penny and then looked at me and smiled, a big broad beaming smile. "Well, Penny, you sure said it."

"Why don't you two get to know each other a little?" I said. William shot me an uncertain look. "I'm going to check on Haze and see how she's doing." William sat down slowly, and Penny sat next to him at the island.

I headed up the stairs, trying to imagine what Hazel must be feeling. For me, things had escalated remarkably quickly from "bad summer" to depression and possible addiction, and I was wondering if she was aware of the transitions or if she was just getting through each day. I came around the corner of the stairs and saw her bedroom door was opened. The hall bathroom door was closed, and the light was on. I rapped on the door.

"Haze?"

There was no reply. I heard a shifting sound. "Haze? You OK?" No reply again. "I'm opening the door, OK?" I pushed open the door and saw the towels first. Several towels on the floor soaked in water and blood.

"Hazel! What happened? Oh my God!" She sat on the side of the tub staring at me quietly, ghost white. She was pressing another towel onto her right thigh.

"I went too far," she said weakly. "I didn't mean to go so far."

I pulled back the towel, and she let me. She just let her hands go limp. There was a deep, deep cut in her thigh, bleeding heavily, pulsing out. But there was more. All around the new cut were dozens and dozens of scars. Some raw and red, some pink and healing, some already silver and fine. Too many to count. I pressed the towel back down, hard.

"My God, Hazel!"

"I'm sorry, Mom. I'm sorry. I wasn't trying to…"

As she closed her eyes, the sounds of my screams for William echoed around the cold, white bathroom.

# CHAPTER 16

# PENELOPE

Well, this nighttime started out real nice, but things went scary and bleedy real fast. The nighttime was so, so bad.

When we gotted home and parked the car on the street under the big trees and next to the crookedy brick sidewalk, we walked 763 steps to a yummy pizza place called Jeeneenos, and we all told stories, but Hazy didn't tell no stories, and she didn't eat nothin on accounta her being all sad and stuff. When we gots home, we gots our bags outta the car, and Fuzzy and Hazy and me went inside with our bags and our knitting stuff. Hazy and me each gotted our very own Stitch by Stitch plastic bag.

Hazy went upstairs to her room, and I went up, up upstairs to my room up thirty stair steps cuz I figured it was time to start un-packin and getting cozy in my new room. I wasn't gonna run away no more cuz of they needin me so much here. That was pretty obvious. Fuzzy and Hazy was talking all hushy and sad, so I went upstairs and started doon my boxes all by myself. I didn't need no helps. I heard Fuzzy talking on the phone to Ellie about Mommy's time at the hostipal. Fuzzy was sure curious about Mommy's stay at the Edgehill Hostipal. I's not sure what the big deal was. Mommy was sick and my mommy's dead now.

I took out all the underpants out of the box, and I putted them in the top drawer in the white dresser in my new room. Then I putted the bruzeers in that same drawer, then my socks, and then that drawer was fulled. I did that with alls my shirts and pants, and I membered what Dottie said about makin my clothes all neat in the drawers. So I tooked out the underpants and the bruzeers and the socks, and I folded them real nice like Dottie used to do. I membered too about how the clothing had a theme, so I sat on my bed and tried to member really hard about the different themes. Dottie made really happy names for the themes: there was Penny pinky, and baby blue, and flaggy—that was red, white, and blue. And there was flower power—that was my flower stuff—and I tried to member all the themes, but it made my head smart, so I just did what I membered, and I put all those clothes away in the themes. That way when I got dressed, I'd take out a pants and a blouz that matcheded.

When I came downstairs to ask Fuzzy about the empty boxes, I saw Willum! He was real nice and smiled a big smile. His hairs was gray. His work suit was kinda baggy and gray. His eyes was kinda baggy and gray too. Fuzzy says he don't live there no more on accounta they's not such good friends right now. Seems kinda dumb cuz he seems kinda nice. Jeez, these peoples gots problems.

That's when things gots real bad. Willum and I was talking and *getting to know each other*, which Fuzzy had said we was aposta do, and Fuzzy went upstairs to check on Hazy, and then a little bit later, Fuzzy was screamin, *Willium! Willum! Willum!* The loudest screams ever.

Willum went racin up the stairs, and I was behind him, and then he was kneelin in the bathroom, and he and Fuzzy was pushin the towel on Hazy's leg, and then Willum reached into his phone and called 911. Then Fuzzy was cryin real hard and scared lookin, and Hazy was real quiet and her skin was white, white like paper, and her eyes was open but slow, slow blinkin, and I just stood in the hallway starin and starin real quiet.

In the hostipal where I used to work, sometimes there was mergencies in the rooms, and if I was in there cleanin or changin the linens, I'd jus stand back and look real quiet. I wasn't aposta to say nothing. So I didn't say nothin now. Jus watched real quiet. Then when the big front door had long loud knockin, Fuzzy asked me to go open it for the peoples. So I done that and was a big help. They was two big guys and a lady too, and they was rollin a big rolly bed thing, and they had lots of clunky clothes on and rattly things, and one man and one lady went into the bathroom, and so Willum and Fuzzy came out with me, and we just watched while the man and the lady did their things.

That was when I membered the peoples coming to see Dottie after she was sleepin in her room, when she wasn't really sleepin but dead, and then I started to feel real bad again, and I stepped away from the bathroom, and I walked down the hall, and I throwed up. The mess went onto the carpet on the hallway, right on a blue part. I didn't meana do it. It just came out, and I said, *I sorry. It's a axident,* and Fuzzy and Willum jus looked at me like they didn't even know what to do.

I walked back toward the bathroom then, and the clunky peoples was tyin something on Hazy's leg like a rubber band, and then they putted her on the rolly bed thing and strapped her down kinda so she wouldn't slip out, and then they said to Fuzzy and Willum, *She's gonna be OK. She didn't get anartery, but she'll need stitches. Meet us at the Mass General ER.*

I didn't know what *anartery* was. I guess it was good she didn't get it, cuz Fuzzy's shoulders went down, and then she putted her head on Willum's soldier, and she cried so hard. She was crying and making snots go on Willum's nice blue shirt. Willum looked kinda sick and sad, and he was rubbin Fuzzy's soldiers, and then we all hadda go to the hostipal. Not the Edgehill Hostipal but the stitches hostipal. They's two different places. Fuzzy went in the white-and-red truck with the doctor peoples and Hazy, and Willum and I went in Fuzzy's car.

We didn't say nothin in the car. I knows it's because when peoples get sad or scared, they sometimes say nothin. So I says nothin too. I thought that would be the bestest thing to do. Willum sat way forward in the car like he wanted to see out the windshield better or get there faster or somethin. He was breathin heavy.

We gotted to the hostipal fast cuz the hostipal was practickly right next door, like it was seven minutes, and I know that cuz I counted to 420. Willum parked the car really bad, not even between the lines, and then we ran real fast in the doors and founded the ER place and then said something to the cranky lady with the black hairs at the desk, and then we was walkin back to a room with curtains all around it, and Fuzzy was there holdin Hazy's hand and resting her head on the bed next to Hazy's tummy. Hazy was still like Casper the friendly ghost but not so friendly, jus sleepy.

Fuzzy lifted her head and said, *She needs stitches, but she's going to be OK.*

Willum smiled at Fuzzy. *That's good.*

Hazy looked at Willum. She was sure tired. *I'm sorry, Dad. I'm really...*

Willum stood right next to her and was stroking her arm and sayin, *No, no, honey. Don't be sorry. I'm so sorry.*

I'm not sure why everyone was so sorry, but it was real quiet, and then the doctor came to clean up the axident and make stitches. I membered all the doctors at the hostipals where I used to work. They always said the same things.

*Hazy,* I said. *Iz gonna be OK. K?*

Hazy looked right at me and smiled a teeny tiny smile. *OK, Penny.*

I added, *There's just gonna be a tiny pinch, and then you's gonna be all better.* I membered about shots.

Hazy smiled a tired smile. *Thanks, Penny.*

Willum and Fuzzy stayed with Hazy for the stitches part, and I was aposta go sit in the room with the *Highlights* magazines. And there was a TV there and it was on, and so I jus watched TV till I don't member cuz I think I falled asleep.

When I woked up, Willum and Fuzzy and Hazy was all standing there, and Hazy was wearing shorts like hostipal-gown material but shorts, and she had a big, big Band-Aid on her leg. We didn't say nothin. We just walked out to the car real quiet and headed back to 30 Marlborough Street.

It looked like Willum and Fuzzy had lots of growed-up privacy stuff to talk about cuz of Hazy being sad and her goin to the stitches hostipal and then the Edgehill Hostipal, so I went upstairs to keep unpackin and to keep knittin. I putted on my pajamas, the yellow flowery ones, and I brushed my teeths, and I washed up my face and hands with the white soap in the bathroom, and I climbed into my bed and I knitted for a long, long time, and my bed was comfy and fluffy, still all white like snow with no yellow, but I was getting useda it, and I axually went sleepynights. The next thing I knew, it was morning time, and the sunshine was coming inside my room. Kinda white and yellow mixed.

I putted on my bathrobe, and when I passed by Willum's office, the door was open, and I seen a blankie and pillow on Willum's sofa, so I thought maybe he had sleeped over. I went downstairs real quiet like cuz I didn't member what times Fuzzy and Hazy woked up, and I member you's not aposta waked peoples up in the morning times. Especially after stitches.

But Fuzzy and Hazy was in the kitchen already awakes.

*Morning, Penny,* Fuzzy said. She was talkin real quiet. She was wearing the same clothes as yesterday.

*Morning time, Fuzzy and Hazy.* Everybody was bein so quiets. Like whisperin. *Did Willum sleepynights in his office?*

Fuzzy nodded. *Yes, he did. We're all going to Edgehill together later this morning.*

*Hazy, you better from your axident?*

She kinda nodded.

*Does it smart?*

*Yeah, kinda.* She was wearing the same thing as last night. Maybe she didn't go sleepynights at all. Hazel was sitting on the window seat in the kitchen knitting. The sun was comin in all around her like caramel from ice cream sundays. *Mom, I think I messed up. What happened here? It looks funny.* Fuzzy walked over to Hazel and sat next to her.

*Let me see. Oh, I think you might have dropped a stitch. Happens all the time. It's easy to do…Sometimes if you're not paying attention, your mind wanders, and you can kind of forget what you're doing. It's easy to drop a stitch or even knit two together. Here, let's go back and pick it up. I'll show you how to fix it.*

Fuzzy took Hazel's knitting and took out a few stitches and started back up again. Fuzzy's hands was really, really fast. But then she slowed down and held the knitting up for Hazel. *See? You just have to go back to the drop and pick up that loose stitch like this. If you miss it until you've knit a whole way past it, it's still OK, but you get a kind of hole where the stitch was dropped.* Hazel and Fuzzy's heads was really close together, and Hazel was watching Fuzzy do her knitting. Then Fuzzy handed the fixed knitting back to Hazel.

*Thanks,* Hazel said and put her head back down and started knitting again real slow. Her hands made big loops with the yarn. She was making her forehead kinda wrinkly cuz she was thinking so hard. I sat down at the table too and started workin on my scarf again. I liked knitting so much already. I was gonna be the bestest knitter ever. I was gonna be proud to my new yellow scarf.

We all just stayed kinda quiet doon our knitting for a while, and Fuzzy was kinda puttering around the kitchen getting stuff ready for breakfuss. She kinda made a lot of noises banging pans and stuff.

Fuzzy was talking to Hazy about packin for Edgehill cuz now Hazy was gonna sleep there on accounta her cutting her leg real bad. Hazy put her knitting down and just stared at the floor. She looked like she was scared or homesick or jus regular sick. Her lips were the same color as her face. I sat down on the window seat next to her. *Hazy, you ascared a go to the Edgehill Hostipal?*

She stared at me like she hadn't heard me. *I dunno,* she finally said.

*You kinda look ascared to me,* I said.

*Yeah, I guess,* she said quietly.

Fuzzy stopped her kitchen banging and sat down on one of the stools, looking at us.

*Well, Hazy, I know whats you going through. I went to live in a special place when I was a little girl. I was four.*

Hazy looked like she didn't get it. *Really? You did? You were only four?*

*Yup,* I said. I was nodding my head. *I was a little girl, but my daddy and mommy said I had special needs, and I hadda go to a special place, and it was aposta be like a school, but it was kinda more like a hostipal.*

Hazy was listening real good and then asked, *What was it like?*

*Well, I went to different places, and some of the places wasn't so good, but the Center place was really good, and that's where I meeted my bestest friend, Dottie. If I hadn't gone to the special place, I never would have meeted my bestest friend, Dottie.*

Hazel said, *That's good then, I guess.*

*Yep. Real good. And Dottie teached me things I never knewed before. And she tooked real good care to me. Real good.*

*Dottie sounds great.*

*Yep, Dottie was the bestest, but she's dead now, and she ain't never comin back.*

Hazel looked right at me. *That's really sad.*

*I's sad too, Hazy. But guess what?* I patted her hand, and then I held it.

*What, Penny?*

*I meeted you. And Fuzzy and Willum. And I ain't never gonna meets you with Dottie with me. So that's good, right?*

*Right. That is good. I'm glad you're here.*

*I's glad too. Now, here's something so important I gots to tell you,* I told Hazy. I sat up real straight and made sure Hazy was listening real good.

*What?* she asked.

*When you go to the hostipals and you go to the foods room, do not, do not,* do not *eat the creamed corn or the chicken croke-etts or roasted beast oh jew, or the chippy beef. Those things are asgusting and will make yous barf more than you already do.*

Hazel made a funny smile. *Penny, thank you. That's good advice.*

Fuzzy was smiling a little too, and she came up behind me and said, *Thank you, Penny. You are so helpful. I don't know what we'd do without you.*

That's pretty obvious. I don't know neither.

# CHAPTER 17

# FESSENDEN.

Our drive to Edgehill was quiet. William drove, for which I was grateful. I was shaky and nervous. Hazel sat in the back, quiet. She was looking out the window, biting her fingernails. Then texting on her phone. Then pulling the skin at her cuticles. Then looking out the window again, resting her forehead against the glass.

Penny sat next to Hazel. Of course I couldn't leave her behind, so she was going to have to be here with us for this awful day. I texted Ellie: *El, we're on our way. Can I have Penny use that waiting room while we check Hazel in?*

She texted right back: *Yes, absolutely.*

We parked the car in the inpatient visitors' lot and walked into the building. Penny was holding her knitting bag in her right hand, and Hazel's hand with her left. Hazel was looking down, walking stiffly from her stitches. Penny was looking at Hazel. "It's gonna be OK. K, Hazy?"

Hazel just shook her head and said nothing. My heart hurt. I looked at William, and I could see he was in pain, and selfishly, I found it difficult to see him this way. He was our rock, our anchor. He rarely emoted. To see him clenched and suffering was both rare and unsettling. We sat in the sterile lobby on black leather Eames chairs, with outdated *Time, Newsweek, Psychology Today,* and *Consumer Reports* magazines fanned on glass and chrome coffee tables. We waited for Ellie to check Hazel in.

When she came, she hugged Hazel first, then Penny, then nodded at William and me. We stood in a circle. "OK. I know this is a really, really tough day." We nodded at her. Hazel was shaking a little. She put her hands at her sides. "We're going to go into my office, just to do all the paperwork stuff, and then we can talk about how this is all going to go. OK?"

I said, "OK."

Ellie looked at Hazel. "OK, Haze?"

Hazel looked up and nodded. She was terrified. Her skin didn't look right. It was gray, almost a pale green. Her slight tremor had become a true shiver. I took her in my arms. She was a quaking leaf. Rattling bones in my arms, frail and terrified. I looked up at William, and he stared right at me, his face pink with emotion, and he put his hand up to his mouth and began to sob. Deep, silent heaving and tears spilling out of his beautiful pale-blue eyes; I hadn't seen William cry in years. He joined us in a circle and wrapped his arms around both of us. Feeling his arms around us calmed Hazel, and then I started crying, the kind of crying that comes from the toes and moves its way up the entire body, though the chest and out a tight, constricted throat. Penny stood back, still and quiet, watching us all.

Ellie respectfully waited for us to stop crying, and when we disbanded, she moved us all down the hall into her office. She set up Penny in the waiting room where she had sat once before. She sat us down and told us how the next several weeks would go: Hazel's schedule, her therapies, the family visiting dates, the family therapy session dates. She was efficient and kind. Her manner of speaking was soothing, and Hazel began to unclench her grip on the arms of her chair. William and I listened intently, leaning forward in our seats, and Ellie gave us the paperwork with Hazel's schedule and dates and times for our involvement.

It was surreal. It was like one of my flying dreams. It seemed as if this was happening somewhere below me. Like I was floating above that office and watching those four people from above and hearing their voices but tinny and far away. I was flying far, far above, drifting up higher and higher.

Ellie said, "OK, Haze, you come with me now, and I'll show you where you'll be staying." Hazel's eyes opened wide. "It's going to be OK. I promise. I am here almost every day too." Hazel swallowed. "Fez, William, this is where you'll say bye for now. You'll be back soon enough."

I couldn't think of what I was supposed to say. The words were stuck in my throat. All I wanted was to go with her. To follow her into her room and curl up on the bed and hold her and never let her go. I pulled her into my arms and hugged her into me tightly, fully enveloping her. I smelled her hair, the cool pale scalp visible beneath her fine hair, her thin skin on her forehead, and I kissed her. She was my little girl, my baby. The sweet little girl who was scared of big waves and firecrackers and thunderstorms. The girl who played with LEGOs and Barbie dolls and wooden blocks and Colorforms. The girl who sharpened her crayons on the back of the box and colored pictures of birds and zoo animals and princesses and castles and rainbows. The girl who sat with me on rainy days in the Crow's Nest and played crazy eights and war and actually finished jigsaw puzzles with me in the fading light of a long summer day. The little girl who wanted to be a doctor when she grew up. My baby.

I whispered, "OK."

William hugged her and choked out the words, "OK, Haze." We all walked out of Ellie's office. We stood and watched her walk away, her walk slow and uneven, her back a little stooped, her bony spine visible through her thin, gray T-shirt. Ellie held her small duffel bag in her right hand, and placed her left hand on Hazel's shoulder until they had both disappeared down the long straight hallway. Neither looked back.

# CHAPTER 18

# HAZEL

Ellie walked me to my room, which was gray and white, pretty much. Light-gray linoleum tile floor, shiny and waxed like in the bathrooms at school, and white walls with nothing on them. The windows had that honeycomb opaque kind of glass in them. I was guessing they didn't open. No art, no posters, no motivational shit like in all the teachers' offices at school. I was so fucking sick of the "you can do it" bullshit at school. And at home too. *No, I can't do it*, I guess. Anyway, I was thinking that the Edgehill people figured, if anyone was sad enough or fucked up enough to be staying here, they could find a way to kill themselves with a thumbtack or picture-hanging nail or the sharp edges of a fucking paper poster.

The beds were just single beds. They looked even smaller, like camp beds, with stiff white sheets and a single white pillow. There was a dresser and the only lights were ugly, bright fluorescent lights embedded in the spongy-looking ceiling tiles.

I had a roommate. She was sitting on the other bed in the room. She was just sitting and looking at the floor. Her hair was cobalt blue and stiff looking.

"Hey," I said.

She looked up. "Hey, I'm Sylvie."

Ellie told us to get to know each other, and then I was gonna meet with a social worker in about forty-five minutes and then a guy named Dr. Bowman a couple of hours after that. "OK, Ellie." I said. "Thanks."

"Welcome, Haze," and she hugged me again. "Remember, I'm right down the hall."

When she left, Sylvie asked me, "Why're you here?" She was wicked direct.

"Uh, depression, anxiety…and…cutting."

"No drugs?"

"Yeah, some."

"Yeah? Which ones?" She was picking at an acne scar on her face. Her nails were bitten down to nothing.

"Xanax, pot, booze. How about you?"

"I'm here for blues and wicked anxiety, OCD, shit like that."

"Shit." Ty was looking for blues one night. I remember someone saying it was, like, the last thing you did before heroin.

"Yeah, it wasn't good. I got pretty fucked up."

"How long have you been here?" I asked.

"Three weeks. It totally sucks. I thought I felt bad before I came. I feel fuckin worse now." She added, "Oh, welcome, by the way."

"Yeah, thanks." This couldn't be the right place. This wasn't me. I was beginning to panic, and I sunk into a horrible falling feeling, like I was dropping down really fast from a building and going straight into a deep black hole with no way out. The sinking feeling was real, physical. I was dizzy, like I had vertigo or something. I dumped my duffel bag into two bottom drawers of the dresser and stowed my empty bag under the bed. Fuck, I felt bad.

"How long you been using?" she asked.

"Too long, I guess. I started drinking and smoking about a year ago, and then I tried Xanax early this past summer. Kinda loved it right away." I hadn't taken them for that long, in comparison to some addicts' stories, but Xanax felt amazing. The whole "takes the edge off" idea made sense. Tyler always had bars, and not even that expensive. Crazy how easy it was. And all I had to do was ask my mom for a little money for lunch or coffee or I'd just keep the change from money she gave me to run errands. She was so busy on her book, she never kept track of her cash. It was crazy easy.

"Do you have to do the whole detox thing or no?" Fuck, she was nosy.

"I don't know. Why?"

"Cuz it totally sucks, that's why." She looked at me like I was an idiot. "You feel worse than you normally do. And that's sayin' something."

She laid down flat on her bed, biting her stubby little nails, picking at her face. Talking about her drunk mother, her dead dad, her brother in juvie. Her shitty little row house in Lowell. I lay down on my bed too, curling up into a ball, and facing the cement wall.

I think, if I really wanted to, I could have killed myself with a fucking thumbtack. Right then and there.

# CHAPTER 19

# PENELOPE

When we dropped off Hazy, it was such a sad, sad day. Willum and Fuzzy droved home with no words at all, and I jus sat in the back seat cuz I don't think I was aposta say nothing. So I didn't. Willum drove us back to 30 Marlborough Street and parked the car, and we all got out and he walked to work somewheres. Fuzzy and me went home. I gotted my knitting and sat in the kitchen, and Fuzzy started cleaning.

I ain't never seen someone clean like Fuzzy was cleanin on this day. She tooked all of the dishes and cups outta the cabinets, and then she scrubbed those with a blue cloth and bleachy stuff, and then she putted water on the cloth, and then she'd squeeze out the bleachy water, and then she dried the shelves with a paper towel, and then she'd put the dishes and the cups back in the shelves, but neater and straighter than before. She did that with *all* the cabinets and *all* the drawers in the whole entire kitchen.

Then she tooked off her sweater and rolled up her sleeves, and she vaccumed the kitchen floor and the whole first floor, and she was sweatin pretty good now, and I said, *Fuzzy, can I heps you?*

She jus said, *No, thank you, Penny. I got this,* and she gots it all right cuz she did that all day. I didn't even ask her for a sammie at lunchtimes cuz she was all sweatin and busy and stuff. I maked my own peanut butter sammy and ate it right there with her runnin all around scrubbin and cleanin.

Then she was dustin and even vacuumin the curtains and the high shelves, and then she started throwin stuff into the empty boxes I had brought down from my room. I was still knittin, and I said, *Fuzzy, what yous putting in those empty boxes?*

And she said, *I'm just clearing out old stuff.*

She was clearing out all that stuff so fast, like the cartoons on TV when the devil is all twisty. I forgets his name. She was sweatin hard. She's one crazy cleaner.

She threw herself down like a rag doll on the window seat in the kitchen and said, *I think it's time for tea. Want some tea, Penny?*

I said, *I'd like to drink the tea like Dottie liked it, all full of sugar and milk.*

And Fuzzy looked at me kinda frowny and said, *Yeah, let's do that.*

I said, *I hope Hazy's doon OK in her new place.*

*Me too,* said Fuzzy. *Ellie's coming over in a bit to tell us how she's doing.*

*That's good,* I said. I liked Ellie.

And then sitting there in the afternoon time with the light all orange-y kinda made me sad. It was the sad time of day when everything kinda gotted lonely and empty cuz the day was ending, and endings was tough. The light wasn't so yellow-y white-y like in the morning when everything was new and breakfuss was coming up. It gotted me thinking about my Dottie.

I sure missed my Dottie. I thoughted about her all the times and missed all the silly things we used to do together. She used to laugh this snorty, grunty kinda laugh, and it felt like everything I said made her make her snort like a piggy when she was laughin. I missed the hostipal peoples too and my job there makin the beds all tight and right and everybody sayin hi and everything. I liked havin my clipboard with all the things I had to do there. I's not even really sure how they's getting along without me. I was a very important person there, and they always tolds me that. *Wow, Penny, you sure are doon a great job,* and *Penny, what would we do without you?* and *Penny, gee, nobody makes a bed like you!* and stuff like that. But my baby sister, Fuzzy, gots so much water comin out of her big green eyes, and Hazy's got a sickness like my mommy, but not the kind like in the froat, but another kind of sad sickness, and it's so lucky that I's here too. They needs me real bad: Fuzzy's talkin and not sayin nothin all the times, I's huggin Hazy and teachin her about the hostipal, I's teaching these peoples lots of stuff about lots of stuff. But I gots lots still to do. For one thing, Fuzzy doesn't wear no makeups at all. Nuthin. So I's thinking real soon I's gonna teach her about macscary and eye powders and rooj and licksticks. It's what ladies do. I don't think Fuzzy does nuthin but chackstick. Jeez. And I's making a prezzie for Hazy right now, and I's gonna give it to her later when I visit her cuz it's gonna make her feel better. So I's real, real bizzy.

Right when I was thinking about my plans, Ellie walked in. No bells or knocks or nothing. She jus walked right into the house. I was sittin with the long scarf I was makin, and Ellie came right over to me and sat right next to me.

*Hi, Penny,* she said all loud and bouncy.

*Hi, Ellie.* I sure liked Ellie. She was nice. I didn't have to change her name to an *eeeee* ending name cuz she already gots that.

Ellie looked up at Fuzzy, who was drinking her tea at the island. *Hey, Fez. How're you doing?*

*OK. No, shitty. Today was really awful.*

*I know,* Ellie said. *Awful. I'm so sorry.*

*Tea, El?*

*I'll have grape tea instead.* She smiled at Fuzzy like they hads a private joke about grape tea, which I never knew about, and Fuzzy got up and opened the refrigerator and got out a bottle of yellow juice with the corky top. She poured herself the juice into a fancy growned-up glass and sat at the island next to Fuzzy.

*So, I wanted to tell you how today went for Haze.* She was looking right at Fuzzy, real hard.

*OK, I'm ready,* and Fuzzy sat down, her blue cleaning rag still in her hand.

*It actually went pretty well. The worst part is sometimes that first good-bye, and I know how tough that was for all of you.*

Fuzzy nodded.

*We got her settled in her room, which is pretty spare, but bright and sunny. Then she met with one of our social workers to talk about the details of the program. Then she had an hour session with our chief psychiatrist, Dr. Bowman, who can start to get to know her and start to put together a comprehensive treatment plan, both in talk therapy and in medications.*

Fuzzy was listening really goodly. *OK, what kind of meds?*

*I'm not sure yet. I'm guessing they'll start her on Wellbutrin, which is an antidepressant, which also has a little energy boost to it. They may prescribe others later, but they'll need to start with something like that for now.*

*OK,* Fuzzy said.

Ellie talked more. *They did blood work and urine testing and found THC and Benzos; that's the Xanax. No other drugs. When you and William come in next week, you guys will discuss with Hazel's team what specifics they're working on with her. As we discussed before, they'll be treating the depression, the cutting as an expression of that, and the alcohol and drug use, maybe her own forms of self-medication.*

Fuzzy was quiet and staring at Ellie like she was confused. *In retrospect, everything seems so obvious.*

Ellie reached over and held her hand all nice. *It's OK, Fez. It's hard to see it sometimes. It gets confused with what I call the whole tunnel of adolescence. A* healthy *teenager can exhibit a lot of these symptoms: the drinking and smoking and defiance and surliness.*

*But not the cutting,* Fuzzy said real quiet into her mug.

*No, the cutting is a real symptom of depression, a way for a person to feel something tangible, a way to make that nebulous pain of depression something real, concrete. It's hard to explain. You'll talk about it more during your visits. And of course, the cutting was completely hidden from you. There would be no reason, no way for you to have seen that she was doing that, or that her upper thigh was scarred. She hid that on purpose. That was hers. Her secret.*

Fuzzy did no talkin. She got up and put ice into a glass from the cleaned-up cupboards and then poured the bottle called Titos into the glass and then gotted a lemon from the refrigerator and cut it into a slice and put that in the glass and then poured bubble water on top. She sat back down and took a big long sip.

*My mommy drank that same growned-up juice, but it was in a thermos. It looks like it.* I was kinda tired of their sad talkin.

*Great,* said Fuzzy, but like it wasn't great. *Now I'm just like Mother.*

*You's not at all like Mommy, Fuzzy. You's so, so different.*

Ellie smiled at Fuzzy and asked me, *How is Fez different than your mommy, Penny?*

*Well,* I said, *for one thing, Fuzzy's got long hairs. Mommy had short hairs. Fuzzy's skin is pink, but Mommy's skin was purple. And Mommy had legs kinda like a spider. Skinny, skinny like sticks. Fuzzy's legs is normal.*

Ellie said, *What else?*

I thought and then added, *Well, my mommy goed to the Edgehill Hostipal, and Fuzzy never goed there. Right, Fuzzy?*

*Right, I never went there. Penny, do you know why Mommy went to Edgehill?*

I do know why, but I's not aposta tell. It's cuz of the monsters. I almost told the secret by mistake once, in the car. I wasn't gonna do that again.

*I's not aposta tell. Mommy told me never to tell, and I's a good secret keeper.*

Fuzzy looked at Ellie and turned her head crookedy. *See, Ellie? A big family mystery, and* you *won't help me figure it out!*

*Fez, stop,* Ellie said. *I told you I can't. Did you reach out to Richard?*

*Yeah, yeah, I did. He wasn't very forthcoming. He doesn't seem to re-member Mother going there, and he didn't seem to think* digging around *was going to serve any purpose. He asked me why I wanted to know all this* old history, *and I just said,* I just do, Richard. *He's submitting the necessary paperwork to Edgehill, but it could take a while, and I'm more than a little curious about this.* No one in the family has discussed this. It's ridiculous. First, a secret sister, and then some secret about Mother's mental health? I'm really tired of all of these secrets...

*I'm sure.* Ellie stood up to get more yellow juice.

*Ellie,* I said. *Can I go visit Hazy all by myself someday? I's got a prezzie to give her, and it'll be done soon.*

*Well, yeah, I think you could probably come in one day next week. Would that be OK?*

*Oh, OK. But I wants to see her now. Today.*

*Not today, Penny, but—*

*What's the* earliest *day I could go?*

*I'll find out. But probably Monday...What do you want to give her?*

I took Ellie by the hand and walked her over to the window seat where I was knitting my yellow scarf. It was really pretty, and I was so proud to me. *I wants to give her this cozy so it makes her all cozy if she's sad.*

Ellie felt the scarf in her hands, being careful not to lose any stitches on the needles. *Penny, this is absolutely beautiful.*

*I just learned,* I said with my hands on my hips.

*Wow. That's amazing. You really do have a talent.* Then, as she was feeling my beautiful yellow scarf, she got this big, big smile on her face. *Penny, I have a proposal for you.*

I didn't know what a proposal was, so I just waited for her to make sense with her words.

*How would you like to knit cozies for the people at Edgehill? It could be a really nice thing for people to have to make them feel a little better. And the color is so happy.*

I thought about how much I was missing being at the hostipal and bein so busy doon things for all of the peoples, and then I gots a big, big smile on my face just like Ellie. *I'd like it real good, Ellie. I's gonna make cozies for the peoples at Edgehill Hostipal!*

*Awesome,* Ellie said. *That's perfect. Thanks for agreeing to do these. We really need you, Penny.*

*I know, Ellie,* I said. I knew that real goodly.

# CHAPTER 20

# FESSENDEN

It was a crisp October day. The leaves were at their autumnal peak, ranging in hue from a yellow tangerine to an almost neon orange, and all of that brightness melted into our house. The leaves glowed and somehow those reflections glimmered and leaked and dribbled around our house. The cool fall air moved through the trees and the leaves, though still soft, were starting to dry a little, causing a pleasant rustling. We had the windows open, and the papers on my desk in the living room were starting to blow off the surface.

Hazel had been at Edgehill for just over three weeks and I was starting to notice subtle changes in her. Her coloring was a little better. She had a peachy color to her soft skin that I hadn't seen in months. She seemed to have gained a few pounds so her clothes weren't completely hanging off of her bones. She made a new friend there named Sylvie. We had a family-visit therapy today, and Penny and I were heading to Belmont and would meet William there. But I was worried that our family sessions had felt somewhat unproductive thus far. Hazel had been very quiet, offering only a few thoughts in an hour's meeting, and I was waiting for a time when she would be able to be more open and share more with us.

Dr. Bowman reminded us that it might take a while for Hazel to open up.

Penny came downstairs as I was picking up the first quarter of my Agnes book off of the floor. "Is that Aggie blowin around?" Penny asked as she helped me collect the sheets.

"Oh, thanks, Penny. Yeah, I'm loving this cool air, but it might be blowing a little too hard to keep the windows open."

Penny took an empty glass vase from the shelf and put it on the pile of papers on my desk. "There," she said, her hands on her hips. "That should stop Aggie from blowin."

"Perfect. Thanks."

"You's doon the *book* book now, right? Not just the notes part?" Penny and I had been discussing my frustrations in organizing my research.

"Yes, finally. Finally, I feel like I'm getting somewhere. It feels great."

Penny nodded. "So Fuzzy, I don't wants to be late for my important job at the Edgehill Hostipal. Dora the Essplora says we's gonna be late if we don't leaves now." Penny looked at her watch and pointed to the face.

Ellie had given Penny an "office" at Edgehill. It was an old storage closet next to Ellie's office and she had a nameplate made for the door: *Penelope Wright, Staff Assistant.* The first time Penny saw the sign on the door, she jumped up and down and hugged Ellie so hard, Ellie almost fell over backward. Penny went in with me twice a week when I went in to see Hazel, and she would knit in her office. She also did simple jobs for Ellie around the hospital, like delivering interoffice mail, emptying office trash cans, shredding papers, and keeping the administrative break room tidy. One of her favorite jobs, besides knitting, was fanning the magazines on the foyer coffee tables. She would sit down and organize the magazines by issue date and then make an elaborate show of fanning the magazines in perfect semicircular patterns. Delivering the bright yellow cozies to the patients was her very favorite task, though. She and Ellie would deliver each one together at the frequency of about two per week. The speed with which she made them was incredible. I was stunned at how quickly she had both learned and mastered the craft of knitting. Ellie told me the patients not only loved the cozies, but also loved Penny's optimism and her fun, quirky personality.

We got to Edgehill at 9:45 a.m. with plenty of time for Penny to get to her office by 10:00 a.m. and start her regimented routine. I walked Penny in and then dropped by Ellie's office.

"Hey, Fez!"

"Hey, El. What's going on?"

"I was *just* on the phone with the medical records department. They received Richard's formal request three weeks ago about your mother's stay here, and I'm not sure what's holding them up. I've been calling them every single day; I think Gladys is really sick of me by now. I was hoping to have them to give to you today. I'll keep pushing."

"Thanks. It does seem weird for it to be such a big deal. Isn't it just scanning or copying documents?" I was getting tired of the waiting.

"Yep, that's it. But I think those ladies down there like to empower themselves with making everybody wait. You should hear their 'tude when I call."

"So at least we know for sure that she was here."

"Yeah, I figured...if she hadn't been here, I certainly hope they would have showed 'no admission' or something."

"Yes, I think that's true. I guess Penny was right. You should never doubt her." Ellie smiled.

"I won't. She seems to be right about a lot of stuff." I looked at my watch. "I've got to go. Time for our session."

"I'll let you know if I hear anything more about that file. Oh, and by the way, I'm loving Penny's company."

"Thanks so much, El."

When I passed by Penny's office, her head was down, and she was knitting furiously. She didn't even notice me as I walked by.

Hazel was already in Dr. Bowman's office when I came down the hall at 9:55. I came in and hugged her, long and hard.

I extended my hand. "Hello, Dr. Bowman."

"Hello, Mrs. Bradlee. Have a seat. Will Mr. Bradlee be joining you today?" He was just starting to sit back down when William entered the room.

"Sorry, I'm late," he said breathlessly. It looked as if he had run down the hall.

Dr. Bowman replied, "You're not late at all. I'm so glad you're both here. I know how hard it can be to get here, with work and traffic and life. It's great to see this commitment from both of you.

"So, Hazel, why don't you start with how you think this last week has been for you?"

She was sitting forward in her chair, her thin fingers playing with the brass nailheads on the arms of the chair. "Um, pretty good, I think."

"Like, how, pretty good?" he said warmly, taking a sip of his tea.

"Like, I didn't hate it this week. I'm not saying I'm loving it, but it's not the worst thing ever, either."

"I think that's great. I always want our patients not to *hate* it." Dr. Bowman smiled at Hazel, and she smiled a little at him. "Do you think you'd be comfortable talking about what we talked about in our one-on-one this week?"

Hazel scrunched up her nose. "I guess."

"You don't have to if you don't want to, Hazel. But when you are ready, I think it will be really helpful for your parents to hear some of your insights."

"Um, OK, I guess. It's kinda hard."

"Yes, it is," Dr. Bowman agreed.

William and I were looking at Hazel, and she was looking at the floor, at her black boots. I was picking at a loose piece of skin next to my thumbnail. I stopped and crossed my hands in my lap. William was jiggling his legs. I desperately wanted her to say something happy and good. I wanted her to open some door, let us in, share her feelings, so we knew that the last painful, lonely, frightening twenty-three days were *working*. That she was on the path to something better. Dr. Bowman was patiently looking at her, waiting for her to say anything. The maple tree outside his office was brilliant, and I watched as a single leaf blew slowly away, floating and spinning in circular eddies.

"Well," she began. "I was saying that last year, when my grades started to go down, it was kind of like a relief." She looked up at me and then back down at the carpet.

"And that I'm not blaming anybody or anything, but like trying so hard all the time and getting those grades felt like I was always supposed to be perfect—"

I interrupted, "Oh, honey, we never—"

Dr. Bowman interrupted me. "Let's let her finish her whole thought, if that's OK." He gave me a thoughtful look.

"And when I stopped trying and then I became friends with Gina, it just felt kinda good, you know? Like Gina isn't such a great person, I know all that, but Gina wasn't afraid of anything, and there was this total freedom thing she had that I kinda liked."

William and I were both leaning forward in our chairs, our elbows on our knees.

"And once the grades started to go, I felt like air was going out of a balloon, and I wasn't gonna pop anymore…I'm not blaming Ty or Gina and Bex for anything. We've been talking about 'owning' shit…sorry, stuff. I started drinking. I started smoking. I used Xanax. And then those things just made me feel totally chill. And I had a place with those new friends. They liked me. They were cool. I felt like a part of something. Kinda like a family."

I looked at William.

Dr. Bowman added, "And do you remember what you said last week about your friends?"

"Yeah, I was thinking about how my friends and I just started doing worse and worse, and it was almost exciting. Like a thrill." She looked down at her clean, unpolished nails. "But then, like, I don't think Gina cares if she never goes to college. I don't even know if she cares if she lives or dies. And same with Bex and same with Tyler. And now that they're kicked out of school, I don't really know what they're gonna do. And I always wanted to go to college and do something good with my life. So I felt like I was different from them at a certain point but I still kinda liked the partying. It felt good. It felt really good. Then I didn't know how to stop everything." She looked out the window, squinting at the brightness.

Dr. Bowman said, "Could you talk about this past summer a bit?"

I took a deep breath and sat back. I braced myself. Hazel breathed in and out really slowly through her nose. "Yeah. This past summer totally sucked. Totally." She was directly addressing William and me now. "You guys were fighting all spring, which totally sucked, and I don't even think you know how bad it was to live in the house. It was like the air was dirty. And then when Dad moved out, I really wanted to go with him."

That really stung. The tears pooled in my lower lids. I started to ask something and Dr. Bowman held up his hand. "Go on, Hazel."

"Mom, I just feel like you're so *angry*. You're so pissed at Dad, and I get that he messed up with the job and money thing, but it's like you *enjoy* punishing him. Like you kinda get off on that. And I know you guys are separated or whatever, but you agreed he would come to the Cape on weekends to spend time with me, and the few weekends he came up, you fought or ignored each other. The rest of the summer, you were buried. You never even looked up when I came in the room."

"Honey, I—"

"And getting fucked up...sorry, messed up. Well, it feels good. Felt good. I liked it." She was worked up, and then she stopped. She sat back, pulled her feet up, and sat cross-legged on the chair. "Sorry."

"Don't ever be sorry for expressing your feelings," Dr. Bowman said. "What you're saying is your truth and it's real, no matter how it comes out, OK?"

"OK," she said. Then she added, "Another thing I realized is that I was so afraid before. Like afraid of failing or making a mistake or of not being perfect, and when I messed up so bad and that whole perfect thing was gone, I actually felt better. Like actually better."

William was gazing at Hazel with so much love in his heart. It was radiating across the room in warm pink waves. And I felt like a total shit. I was the bad guy. How did it happen that I was the bad guy here? *William* was the bad guy, wasn't he? I've never been the bad guy. Hazel had no bad feelings for him, only for me. She felt *he* was victimized by *my* anger, but I don't really think she understood the extent of what he had done to me, to our family. I had *every right* to be angry with him. *Every right.*

Regardless, she did "speak her truth," and her truth was that she had let go of a pressurized high-performance way of living, with A-grades and high test scores and excellence in sports and piano, and she had succumbed to hanging out with a group of friends who made her feel OK about not trying any more. That did make some sense to me, and the good news, the amazing news in all of this was that she was finally talking, really talking.

Hazel then said, "I'm not mad at you, Mom. I'm just talking."

"I know, Haze. It's OK. I'm glad you said it." There was a tightening in my chest.

At the end of our session, we hugged Hazel and told her we loved her. I said, "I'll see you Thursday, OK?" I didn't hear her reply as she turned to walk back down the hall to her room.

As we walked back down the hall toward the exit doors, William and I both stopped at Penny's office door. William said, "Hey, Penny, congratulations on the new job."

Penny brightened when she saw him. "Thanks, Willum. It's so, so great workin here at Edgehill Hostipal. I's doon a lotta, lotta stuff. Boy, they's lucky to has me!"

"That's the truth, Penny. Say, how about an early lunch? The three of us?"

I looked at my watch. "I can't. Sorry. I have an eleven fifteen call with Richard." I was still reeling from Hazel's comments and didn't really want to spend any more time with William right now anyway. His disappointment in my "no" was evident.

"Penny, how 'bout you? Can you have lunch with me?" William smiled at her.

"Yes, Willum. I's gonna do it. K? Let's has lunch."

I left them at her office and headed out to the car. I called Richard from the road and Darlene put me through. He picked up quickly, "Hi, Fez. How are you? How's Hazel doing?"

"Actually a little better, I think. Thanks. We just had a family session. She's getting there. Long road, but I think she's in the right spot."

"That's great. Glad to hear it." I could hear him moving papers around.

"So, Richard, what's on the agenda for today?"

"Janet just called. Good news. You have an offer on the Crow's Nest, and it's quite low, but it's a good sign that the fish are biting. I'm going through your financials now. Do you want to come in? Or should we just do this over the phone?"

An offer on the Crow's Nest? Already? I didn't think she was going to be able to get everything done this fast. I left the house a complete mess, handed her the keys, and peeled away. She had already had it cleaned and staged in this short time? Shit, this was actually happening. The house was really going to go. My heart sank deep into my ribcage.

"Wow, an offer already. That's so fast. I'm stunned. Unfortunately, I can't come in right now. Sorry. I told my agent I'd send in a draft of the book today, and I'm heading back in to Belmont to get Penny later. What's the offer?"

"All right. Got it. So here's the deal. Here's the number." He cleared his throat and told me. It was a really, really low offer. Richard explained that it was significantly below the asking price because the potential buyers thought that the house needed new "everything." Janet had told Richard that the prospective buyers wanted to completely gut the house and redo every room. What the hell was wrong with the Crow's Nest? Who were these people? What was wrong with charm and character and patina?

Richard continued, "I spoke with William earlier and got all the information regarding the loans he took out against the house on the Cape. I think I have a good understanding of his current income, which is obviously significantly lower than it has been. He told me he'll be starting a new job within the month, which is good. Also, I know you're finishing up a book, but I don't know if that has any potential or guaranteed income..." He paused for my reply.

"Sorry, Richard, I just don't know that yet."

"OK, and as far as upcoming Crow's Nest bills, I just got off the phone with the Chatham assessor. Your annual taxes have increased a bit and will be due in January, as usual, as well as the annual water and sewer bills. Finally, I don't know what the expenses for Hazel's stay are, or what insurance will cover."

The tightness in my chest was making it hard for me to take a deep breath. "Richard, what exactly are you saying?" He was piling up a big, fat list of bills and a lot of bad news.

"This offer on the house is low, but often, your first offer is the best offer, or at least a pretty good one, and I think you might want to consider countering this. You're going to need to sell quickly. It can't hurt to negotiate." No way. I wasn't going to negotiate anything. I was insulted by the attitude of these people. The house I loved and adored was not going to be purchased by some unsentimental nouveau riche assholes. Despite the fact that we were in deep financial trouble, I knew we could do better. I knew we could.

# CHAPTER 21

# PENELOPE

Today was a fun, fun day. I gots taked out to lunch by Willum! He was in the hostipal seeing Hazy with Fuzzy, but then their session was over, and Fuzzy looked all grumpy and sad to Willum *again*, and she marched off all loud and cranky, and Willum made his soldiers go up to his ears and said, *Oh well.* He watched her walk out and didn't stop watchin til she was all gone down the hallway.

I asked Ellie if it was OK for Willum and me to goes to lunch, and Ellie said, *Of course,* real friendly and happy, so Willum taked me to a real restaurant, not even just the Edgehill Hostipal cafeteria. We gotted into his shiny blue car, and we strapped in real goodly, and we drove to a place called the Belmont Café.

It was real nice with fancy white real cloth napkins and a nice lady with a black-and-white-checked apron on and with a funny accent, like she said, *What may I get forrrr yuh?* William said she was *French* from a place called *Frantz,* which reminded me that I wanted french fries cuz I loves them so, so, so much, and the lady called them *freets,* so Willum and me laughed about freets for a while, but then they came and they was the bestest freets in the whole world. I ain't never gonna eat french fries again. Only freets. Then I asked the lady what else she called stuff cuz she said words so funny.

She was nice. So water is *low* and milk is *lay*, and Willum and me laughed pretty hard about low and lay. Then I almost barfed from laughing when Willum ordered us meats and she said *biff-teck.* Her mouth went all funny when she said *biff-teck*, and I almost barfed from laughin. After we ated all of our freets and low and lay and biff-tecks, we gots fancy cookies: *beez-keets.* It was the funnest lunch ever cuz of the fun new words and the nice lady with the funny mouth and red lips and weird words, and Willum is so nice, and he has the funniest laugh ever. His whole body laughs, not just his face like Fuzzy. He laughed so hard he said his tummy smarted. Somethin about his gut getting busted. That sounded kinda scary, so I tried to stop the laughin when I heard that.

*Willum,* I said when we was eating the crumbly beez-keets.

*Yes, Penny?*

*When you comin back to live at the house with Fuzzy and me and Hazy?*

William stopped eating his beez-keets and took a sip of his *kaff-ay-O-lay.* That's jus *kaff-ay* with lay. *Well, Penny,* he said. *I don't really know.* He made a sad face. His lips made a upside down *U. Can I tell you a secret?*

*Oh no,* I thought. *Here we goes again with all the secrets.* I shooked my head real fast. *No, Willum. No more secrets. I gots all kinda secrets in my head from my mommy, and I ain't doon it no more.*

He smiled. I don't know why. He did, though. *OK, then. This is* not *a secret. I want to come home. I'm sick of living at my brother's house, and I think my sister-in-law is ready for me to go, and the guest bed is lumpy, and I miss my house. More importantly, I miss Hazel, and I miss Fez.* His face got kinda pink when he says that last part about Fuzzy.

*You missin Fuzzy? Cuz you guys is besties and you don't gots her around so much no more?*

He nodded slow; then he gots water in his eyes a little. He didn't make no noise, but that water all around his eyes and his chin got kinda shaky. I took my *serve-ee-ette,* and I handed it to Willum in case the waters came down. *Willum, I gots to tell you something too: I been living in that house at 30 Marlborough Street for a thirty-seven days now. And I knows Fuzzy missin you too.*

He put down his fancy *coop* with the tiny *koo-yare. Really? You think so? You sure? Kinda hard to tell these days.*

*Willum, you don't needa worry bout nothin. I knows things, and I knows what I know.*

*Well, that's clear then,* he said, smiling funny.

*Really, Willum. Everything's gonna be OK. I know Fuzzy likes it when you sings your silly songs at the shower times cuz she said it's so, so quiet in the bathroom now and she doesn't like it so goodly. Also, Hazy's gonna get better, and Fuzzy's gonna get smilier, and you's gonna come home soon. And I's gonna have fun at turkey time, right?*

*Yep. You sure are.* Then he looked serious, stirring his kaff-ay. *Hopefully, we'll all be a little better by Thanksgiving.*

*Don't you worry about nothin, Willum. It's all gonna be good.*

# CHAPTER 22

# FESSENDEN

After my conversation with Richard, I didn't know what the hell I was doing. I was all worked up. I drove so fast on the way home, I got a speeding ticket on Soldiers Field Road. As I was making a turn and taking the corner too quickly, my purse slid off the passenger's seat and every single item spilled out on the floor of the passenger seat. My travel mug wasn't fully closed, so dregs of leftover coffee spilled all over my lap and handbag. When I got home, I marched straight upstairs, threw my coffee-stained handbag in the tub to clean later, and stared at my exercise bike. Fuck it, I thought; I took off the plastic wrapping and got on that damn exercise bike in my bedroom. I couldn't go to bed another night with that plastic-encased thing staring at me. I pedaled on the lowest possible setting and set the program for thirty minutes, which was all I had in both time and energy. But when I was riding that bike, a strange thing happened; I got to thinking about what Hazel said about my anger and what Richard said about our finances, and I wasn't mad. I wasn't hurt. I wasn't scared. I was a little ready. My legs were going around and around, and my muscles were tired and burning. The thought that kept going around and around in my head, right along with the circling pedals, was, *Make a change.* Make a change. Make a change. I was tired of things happening to me. It was time for me to happen to things. I finished on the bike, took a quick shower, and then, calmly, quietly, I went to sit on my bed with my laptop and reread the chapters I had finished writing.

As I was reading it, I began to realize something: This book might be OK. Maybe even good, and I actually felt proud of the work. I had done so much more than I thought this summer, and when I finally sat down this fall in Boston and really focused on the compilation, putting all that hard work together into something cogent was easier than I thought. The longer I read, the more excited I became, until three hours later, I set the laptop on my bed, got up and jumped up and down saying, "*Yes, yes, yes!*" I finally, finally, *finally* managed to officially complete the first draft of the book. I pressed Send to Caroline and threw myself back on my bed, stretching out in a pose of pure joy and gratification.

My cell phone rang. It was Ellie. "Guess what?" she asked like a very excited child.

"Did you get it?"

"Yup! I'm holding a sealed envelope of your mother's medical records. Can I bring Penny home and come over and bring them to you?"

"Yes, yes, yes! Oh my God. Finally. Another Wright family mystery will be solved. About time."

"Cool. We'll be there in about an hour. Gotta finish up a couple of things."

Ellie and Penny walked into the door laughing an hour later. I could hear them talking about "freets" or something.

Ellie said, "Penny, you're so funny. I love your stories."

Penny said, "Fuzzy! Hi, Fuzzy, I had such a hards day at the office."

"That's good, Pen! Sounds like you're being a huge help over there."

Penny nodded. "Yup, I is. Oh! And I had the bestest lunch with Willum. We laughed and had a nice, nice time, and they had growed-up napkins and glasses on the table and everything. It was like a real fancy place, Fuzzy."

I couldn't picture the two of them laughing over lunch. I guess William was really letting his hair down. "Sounds good, Pen. I have to read some papers with Ellie for a bit. Can you wait for dinner for about an hour?"

"Sure, Fuzzy. I gets Ritzy crackers while I's waitin." She took the red box of crackers and headed into the living room. I heard the crinkling of the wax paper sleeve and the cartoon channel on, very loud. It sounded like Tom and Jerry.

Ellie put the closed brown envelope on the kitchen island. I came around to her side and put my hand on it. It looked ominous.

"All of a sudden, I feel sort of scared," I said.

"Why?"

"Oh, well, I don't know, like, I guess I'm just afraid of feeling something worse than I already feel about Mom."

"Like what, Fez? You already have such a hard time talking or even thinking about her. What else could there be that could make your feelings about your mom any worse?"

"Well, OK, here's an example. Do you remember when Mom got really sick? When we were freshmen, in the fall?"

"God, I'll never forget it."

"OK, so remember when we were in my room in James Dorm hanging out, and the hospital called me to say Mom was failing?"

"Yeah, I remember. Awful."

"Well, did I get in my car and drive to Boston?"

Ellie shook her head.

"No, instead, we went to Glenn's room and drank cocoa and Schnapps at that stupid party until my aunt Bunny tracked me down, four hours later on the Morrow Hall telephone in Glenn's dorm to tell me my mother had died. Remember?"

"I do. And you know what I remember about that, Fez? You didn't even *react.* You went to the hall, took the call, came back to the party, and told me about your mom like you were reporting on the weather. Even when you came back after the service, after the long weekend, I don't ever remember you ever losing it. Like, no tears or anything."

"You're right. I didn't. I had already mourned her my whole life. I felt so together. I genuinely felt relief that she was gone. So here's my point: This summer, with the Crow's Nest bullshit and Hazel being absent and William being gone, it was like my mother came back. Like she rose from the dead or something. She kind of haunted me. And for the first time ever, since fucking 1980, I'm mourning her a little. Or something. I mean, she was a terrible drunk and a terrible mother and all that. That's still all true; I'm not glamorizing her, but I've just been thinking about her. She's in my head."

"Fez, that's good. That's a good thing. It's time. *Finally.*"

"I guess, yeah, but if—*when*—I open up this file, am I unleashing more of those ghosts? I know I'm curious and I did ask for this, but I'm scared of what I'll find and what I'll feel. Can I handle whatever is in that file? I mean, I've already been losing it a lot lately, crying and stuff, and that is *so* not me."

"I get it. It's scary stuff. But Fez, it's *good* scary stuff. You've been handling stuff in your own hyper, disorganized, ever-busy, frenetic way. You're awesome, and I love you, but I think you have a long way to go in actually dealing with all those ghosts from your past. So I say open the file. But I respect your decision either way. What do you want to do? Do you want me here? Do you want me to go or what?"

"No, no, definitely stay. I've got a chilled bottle of Sancerre. I forgot we had it. I think William got it from a client this year. I just need a minute to figure out where I want to read it and if I want to be alone. I can't believe after all this time, and my needling you and then you needling the records department, that now I'm hesitating."

"No worries, Fez. Let's have a drink, and you'll figure out when you're ready...when you're ready. There's no rush. This file isn't going anywhere."

This wine looked and smelled delicious. I poured two glasses. I put a chunk of Jarlsberg cheese, crackers, and green grapes on a plate and set that out on the island too.

Ellie was checking her phone for messages while I stared at the file. I took out the store-bought rotisserie chicken and a bag of baby romaine lettuce and set those on the counter for dinner preparation. Then I looked at the file again.

"Nice seeing William today," Ellie said, taking a long sip of wine. "Oh, damn. That *is* good."

I took a sip of mine too. "Nice. Very nice. Maybe if I just hold the file in my lap, that'll make it less scary."

"Good thinking," Ellie said with a smirk. "That is known to ease the fear of opening files."

I sat on the counter stool next to Ellie and slid the file over and onto my lap. I held it. It was quite thick and weighty. "In here are the facts of my Mother's stay at Edgehill."

"Mm-hmm," said Ellie.

"And once I open this file, I can't ever unopen it. I will *know* things."

"Yep, you will."

"Seriously, it's kinda weird. I don't like it."

"I know, Fez. I'm not trying to diminish your fear of learning about your mom's mental health. But what I am trying to say is that maybe *something* in there is OK. Plus, I believe that the truth is always better than a mystery, or worse, an untruth."

"True. Very true," I agreed. I put the file up on the island again. I slipped my finger under the sealed edge and very slowly unsealed the gummy edge.

"Yes, it is."

I pulled out the stack of papers, maybe thirty or forty pages, handwritten in places, typewritten in others. I took a deep breath. "I'm going to start reading. Do you mind just kinda sitting there?"

"Not at all. I'll be here sipping."

*INTAKE FORM*
*Elizabeth Fessenden Wright*
*Case Record Folder 16-806*
*Provisional diagnosis: Psychoneurosis: Mixed type*
*Determined diagnosis: same.*
*Admission age 28*
*Female, Married, Address*
*Total net duration of hospital residence: 43 days*
*Admission: Friday, December 26, 1953*
*Discharge: Saturday, February 7, 1954*
*Condition: Improved*
*Nervous breakdown December 1953, Mental illness*
    *Patient did not wish to have hospital treatment.*

    *Neatly and suitably dressed. No scars, wounds, or burns. Behavior: Appears depressed, crying frequently, objecting strenuously to ward procedure. Height: 72", Weight: 127 pounds. Pulse: 72. Temperature: 99.4. Respiration: 16…Remarks: Very distressed and unhappy to be admitted. Does not wish to meet other patients.*

The details were so clinical and cold; it was hard to imagine they were about a real person, my mother.

    *Mrs. Wright was referred to this hospital by Dr. Jackson Thomas because of difficulties with her child, fears about her health, and inability to perform her daily duties. The patient came to this hospital on December 26, 1953, and signed a voluntary application. She has followed Dr. Thomas's advice in coming in, but as soon as she was admitted, she thought the best thing for her to do was to leave the hospital, think the matter over carefully, and then decide to return on her own accord. At first she showed evidence of hostility against her environment, the nurses, and the doctors, and stated that unless she came on her own accord, she would not be able to adjust to the hospital life. No full history was taken. Briefly, this is what the husband, Mr. Wright, had to say about his wife's illness:*

*"My wife has always been shy. When she is not well, she is practically unable to deal with her household activities or take care of our child and the only thing she does is lie in bed all day. When she is well, she is intelligent, interesting, thoughtful, and able to carry along and do everything well. Since the birth of our child, her condition became progressively worse. Going out or making plans for the future has become particularly difficult. She has spent more and more time in bed, withdrawing from her surroundings. This has caused me to do most of the work in the house both in the morning as well as in the evening."*

*It appears that these so-called attacks of inactivity have occurred more and more often, and the patient finally, through a lot of urging on the part of the husband, agreed to go and see Dr. Thomas about two weeks before her admission. Having failed to improve during this time, she again went to see Dr. Thomas, who recommended her admission to this hospital.*

*No detailed family history or medical history was given. In her past history, it was mentioned that the patient was an intelligent woman who was able to graduate from Smith College. She got very good grades but was extremely awkward socially; however, she managed to get along in her "shy way." During her college years, she did not go out often and did not have many dates but managed to adjust fairly well to the college atmosphere. After her marriage she became more and more withdrawn and developed more fears. She was often unable to go out, and whenever she did, she would develop periods of anxiety and panic, necessitating her return home.*

*She became at times depressed because of these fears and felt that she needed help by doctors. That was the reason she went to see Dr. Thomas.*

*The physical examination was essentially negative.*
Peter S. Athens, MD

Ellie said, "You OK, Fez?"

"I don't know. This is really sad."

"I know. Want to take a break? You could read the rest later."

"No, El. I'm going to keep going."

The next page quickened my pulse.

*TREATMENT CONSENT WAIVER*

*To the director of Edgehill Hospital: We hereby request that Mrs. Elizabeth F. Wright be given the electric shock therapy or insulin RX for the treatment of her mental symptoms or conditions. A charge will be made for the extra professional and nursing care required during this treatment. We are fully aware of the dangers of such treatment and agree to indemnify and hold harmless the hospital and its agents against any and all claims that shall arise out of such treatment.*
*Sullivan A. Wright*
*Witness, Dr. Peter S. Athens.*

I told Ellie what I was reading, horrified that my father consented to electric shock therapy. "That's awful. But they used to do that a lot. It's actually still done."

"Really?" I asked her. "It's so brutal, though. So medieval."

"Then there's a signed form from my dad and that same doctor to do a lumbar puncture, X-ray examinations, and teeth examinations. Then it looks like a lot of medical charts. Not even sure how to read those."

Ellie looked over. "I think those are the nurses' reports. Like blood pressure, pulse, daily mood, stuff like that. They would have probably taken all those stats throughout the day."

"This sheet at the end looks like it's kind of a summary report or something. Yeah, it's the notes for her discharge. It's called 'Doctors' and Nurses' Reports on Patient's Mental Status.'"

*MENTAL STATUS/PROGRESS REPORTS*

*Mrs. Wright is a well-developed, thin young woman who is superficially talkative but appears somewhat depressed and annoyed. When asked what was the matter with her, she answered, "Oh, I am not going to go over it again." She signed a voluntary application for admission but made a sarcastic remark about section 86, chapter 123 of the general laws. "Does that mean that you can keep me here against my will?" When seen later on the ward, the patient was sitting in a chair, crying. Her appearance was neat and clean. The patient spoke in a monotone and in a low voice. On some occasions, particularly referring to the locked doors, she would get excited and show evidence of good sense of humor. Generally, though, her mood was depressed, though not catatonic.*

*Content of thought showed mostly preoccupation and fears about her being in the room with the doors locked. Fears of being unable to cope with her difficulties and fears that something might happen to her predominated. She complained of being left out with nobody to take care of her. She mentioned that she realized she required hospitalization and treatment but had always thought that hospitalization would mean freedom of action. After she was reassured, she appeared to be much calmer, and her fears seemed to improve. Her judgment, orientation, and memory were intact, and insight was fairly good.*

*At about the third week of treatment, Mrs. Wright became extremely agitated at the memory or thought of an event, unspecified. In therapy sessions, we spent a great deal of time trying to coax the information out from this event or series of events. But her reactions were dramatic and even violent when prompts brought this unclear event to the forefront. Neither I nor the other doctors on staff were able to get a satisfactory understanding of what may have happened.*

*Mrs. Wright's nightmares came sporadically during her six-week stay. Her only reference was to "monsters" or a "monster." No other details could be flushed out.*

*She recognized that her breakdown was, in part, related to the institutionalization of her mentally retarded daughter, Penelope, at the age of four. But the monster or monsters in her dreams, and in the other event she referred to, are seemingly separate from this.*

*Diagnostic impression was that of mixed neurosis with obsessive-compulsive and anxiety features, also some elements of depression.*

*The patient was seen by Dr. Thomas, who tried to stress the importance of her staying in the hospital for a full six-week course of treatment, but the patient decided that if she had to stay, it should be her own decision. She preferred to go home, think the matter over carefully without being influenced by the outside, and then eventually come back. Dr. Thomas saw the patient again the next day and tried to impress on her the necessity to stay. The patient was very thankful but appeared to have made up her mind to go home and think it over carefully. It was not until a long conversation with Mr. Wright that Mrs. Wright agreed to stay for the full course of treatment.*

*Peter S. Athens, MD*

The majority of the file was filled with medical checkup reports and daily logs of her vital signs, sedatives taken and when, which I didn't want to read. I closed the brown folder over all the papers and rested my hands on the file. I took a sip of my glass of wine and said, "That's the start of it. There's a lot more, but I can't really do any more. That's fucking exhausting."

"Can you summarize?" Ellie asked.

"Yeah. I think Mother had a nervous breakdown right about the time Penny went away. That makes sense, right? December 1953. Just what Penny said."

"How terrible. I cannot fathom losing a child at four to an institution."

"I know. That makes total sense to me too, but then there's this whole other thing about another event, which is unrelated to the Penny thing."

"What was it?"

"Unclear. The doctor's report recognized the nervous breakdown after Penny left, and then suggested that there was *another* separate event or set of events that led to her extreme distress, including nightmares about monsters. Sounds like she kinda freaked out about something else."

"And the doctors couldn't figure it out?" Ellie looked as confused as I felt.

"No." What was the other event? She told Penny that a monster "destroyed" her. I wondered if she had had a bad relationship breakup or a broken engagement before she met my father.

"Those files usually show the visitors' logs. Can you see who visited her?"

I reopened the file and scanned back through the pages. The second-to-last page was a copy of the visitors' log. The only three people who visited my mother during her six-week stay were my father, every day at six o'clock when they shared supper; Mimi on nine occasions; and my mother's sister, Bunny, who came every Saturday at noon. Her father never came. Not once.

I told Ellie. "Well," she said, "since your dad is gone, and you're not in touch with Bunny anymore, it's going to be tricky getting any more answers. Or maybe you're OK leaving this mystery unsolved."

But I wasn't OK with that. I could find a way to reach out to my aunt Bunny, a woman I hadn't seen or talked to since my mother's funeral in 1980. Was Bunny even alive? And how could I reach out to her after all this time and after the enormous lapse in communication we had had? I would have to overcome my embarrassment at letting her go. With all the unrest in my life right now, I needed to answer questions and resolve something. Then I could put this file *and* my newly resurrected mother to rest, once and for all.

# CHAPTER 23

# PENELOPE

*Tom and Jerry* was the bestest. They was always chasin and chasin, and you know that smart little mouse always got away. Always! He was foolin that cat a lot too, which was a good thing cuz that cat was a big ol bully. The mouse had a friend who was a big ol cranky bulldog too, but he was a nice bulldog cuz he loved that mouse so, and he was helping the mouse cuz that bulldog didn't like that cat so goodly. This episode was the funniest cuz the mouse made his self *invisible. Invisible!* And that cat tried and tried to find him and then hit him with a frying pan, and then you know what the mouse did? He hit that cat right in the fanny with a golf club! I almost barfed laughin when I seen that. A mouse hittin a cat in the fanny with a big ol golf club!

Fuzzy found me a special TV station called channel 56 that had only cartoons all the times, and *Tom and Jerry* was on for a whole hour straight, and I would jus laugh and laugh and laugh. Dottie used to love it too, and we would laugh, and she'd make her funny snorty laugh too. But we only gotta see it on Saturday mornings before. Fuzzy gots lots more times of *Tom and Jerry* now.

Ellie and Fuzzy was in the kitchen drinkin their yellow juice and talkin and talkin. I looked in, and Fuzzy was reading something, and they was all serious. Not so laughy as usual. Then my *Tom and Jerry* ended, and somethin called *teen-toons* came on the TV, and I didn't like that so goodly, so I turned off the TV with the special magic wand Fuzzy had called the *remote*. My old TV didn't has a remote. Dottie and I turned it on and off with a buttin on the TV.

I got my knittin out of the Stitch by Stitch bag, which was my bag and not Hazy's. I was thinking about when Hazy was coming back home after Edgehill graduation, which was sometime before turkey time. Turkey time was gonna be so, so essiting. This was my first year havin turkey time with my family. Before turkey time was just me and Dottie or me and Dottie and all the peoples at the Center. But now it was a big essiting thing, and Fuzzy said she went kinda crazy makin food for turkey day. We was talking about it this morning.

I said, *Like what, Fuzzy?*

She said, *It's a long list. Are you ready?*

And I said, *Yep, Fuzzy. Tell me the long list of foods for turkey day.* This is what she tol me:

Turkey

Gravy

Stuffin with sausage

Stuffin without sausage

Cranberry sauce

Other kinda cranberry sauce

Beans

Squash and carrots smushed together

Punkin muffins

Salad cuz Fuzzy loved salad, even though it wasn't such a turkey day thing

Punkin pie

Praline punkin pie

Pecan pie

Apple pie

I was starin at Fuzzy like she was the hungriest lady in the whole world. *Fuzzy, is a gajillion peoples comin over?*

*No, that's the funny thing. It's just going to be William, Haze, you, me, and Ellie.*

*Hunh,* I said kinda confused. *Willum's comin over?*

*Uh, yes, I invited him for Thanksgiving,* Fuzzy said.

*How come you invited Willum?*

*I don't know. I guess I thought it would be nice for all of us to be together.*

*So you's not so mad to Willum?*

*I don't know. Everything feels a little different since Hazy went away.* She picked at a piece of skin next to her fingernail. Fuzzy was bein kinda serious.

*Yep. That's the troof. And you's gonna cook all that foods?*

*Yes, we are. We.*

*We, Fuzzy?*

*Yes, Pen. What do you want to make?*

*Well, I never really cooked before, Fuzzy. Dottie made most of the foods at our apartment.*

*Well, that's OK,* Fuzzy said. *I'll teach you how to make something. Why don't you pick something that I mentioned?*

I thought for a second. *I wants to make apple pie, K, Fuzzy?*

Fuzzy said, *Awesome. I'll teach you, and that'll be your responsibility.*

Boy, I sure liked havin *asponsibilities.*

I was thinking about that conversation I had with Fuzzy, and it was makin me so essited for turkey day and all the peoples comin home and us being a family and everything. I was knittin all quiet on the sofa, and I didn't mean to listen to Ellie and Fuzzy, but I did hear them talkin.

They was talkin about my mommy and all about her stay at Edgehill. That part was OK cuz we was all talking about that before, but here's the bad part: they was talking about *why* my mommy was at Edgehill. Fuzzy was always trying to figure out why. With everything. She was the most curiousest person. She was always asking me about my Dottie and my life before and my job at the hostipal and the people I used to work with. Now, she was asking all about why Mommy was at Edgehill.

She was reading something the doctors had written about Mommy, and she was talking about *events* and about Mommy's bad dreams and about the monsters. She was telling Ellie she wanted to figure it out. She wanted to find out what happened to my mommy. She was maybe gonna call our aunt Bunny. She was gonna try to find out the secret. That made me real, real scared and sad. I made a promise to my mommy a long time ago.

But then I was thinking about my mommy and how my mommy was dead and she ain't never comin back, just like my Dottie. Whatever bad dreams my mommy had about monsters was probably all burned up with her. No way Fuzzy was gonna find out Mommy's secret. Maybe Bunny forgotted things. Maybe the secret would stay in my head forever, and ain't nobody gonna gets it.

I started membering the day, a long, long time ago, when my mommy was visiting with me, and she didn't seem so goodly. She was in a sad mood, and she wasn't laughin so good, and she looked kinda wavy and tippy. It was the falltime, and it was cold out. I member they was no leaves on the trees, and everything was dead and brown, and the light came in my windows gray and slow. She was wearing a thin brown coat. Brown like sand, not brown like mud. Her stockins had thin, thin holes in them that ran up and down her legs. They was called runs. She kept the coat on the whole visit on accounta her being too thin to warm her own bones.

She finished her whole thermos of happy juice, but it didn't even work; she was *not happy* but so, so sad, and her words sounded funny and slurpy. She was blinkin real, real slow. I said, *Mommy, why you so sad?*

She had her eyes closed, and her face was kinda purply like mums flowers in the falltime. She sat that way for so long, I thought she had fallen asleep right there in the chair. She started talking so soft. She kept her eyes closed when she was talking, like she was seeing the story inside her tired head. She told me a long scary bad, bad story. It made me kinda shiver all inside my body and made my bones hurted. Especially my head hurted. I was listenin real good, and she was talking and talkin real quiet and sleepy. Then she stopped talkin and opened her eyes like she was wakin up from sleepytimes. She said, *Now, Penny, you don't tell anyone my secret, OK, honey? That's a secret that must never, ever be told.* I nodded at my mommy real fast.

*I ain't telling no one your story, Mommy.* Mommy knew I was the bestest secret keeper in the world. I wouldn't never tell.

An old scratchy branch blewed up against the window. Mommy looked at it and then said all kinda messy, *My sister, Bunny, doesn't even know.*

*OK. Mommy,* I said all growed up cuz this was serious talking. *I love Aunt Bunny, but I hasn't seen her in a long times.* She used to visit me sometimes before she got all old and creaky. That's what she called it: *old and creaky.* But she used a send me lots of cards and letters, and that was so fun.

*I know, dear. We used to come together. Bunny hasn't been well, and she hasn't been able to travel. That's why you haven't seen her. Anyway, I'm not even sure why I'm telling you all this now,* she said lookin at her empty thermos. *I guess I can't seem to let it all go.*

I reached over and put my pink hand on Mommy's scratchy knee. *You can let it go now, Mommy. I's gots your secret, and you can let it go.*

232

# CHAPTER 24

# FESSENDEN

I stared at my cell phone, trying to summon up the courage to call my aunt Bunny. So much time had passed. I was embarrassed at the gaping hole of time since we had talked or seen each other. We had both dropped the ball. No, *I* had dropped the ball. Neither of us was communicating, but now, with Penny in my life, our lives, I had a new and budding sense of family loyalty. Plus, I wanted answers.

I played a game of Free Cell on my phone. Then another. Then a third. I checked my e-mails, looking for a reply from Caroline about the manuscript I had sent, but there was nothing, which discouraged me and made me wonder if anything would become of that gargantuan effort. I deleted junk mail. I replied to other mail. I cleaned up the breakfast dishes. I took out the trash. I looked at my phone again.

If I was ever going to get any understanding of what may have happened to my mother, I was going to have to overcome my reluctance, my shame, and call Bunny. But how could I begin to bridge the gap of thirty-five years of silence? I forced my memory back to Mom's funeral and my last conversation with Bunny.

On that rainy spring day, after Mom's memorial, fittingly on Memorial Day, there was a catered lunch back at the house, generously organized by our neighbors. Bunny approached me.

"I'm so sorry about your Mom, Fez. You are much too young to have lost your mother." She was holding a wine glass with a cocktail napkin wrapped around its base and an empty toothpick between her fingers.

"Thank you, Bunny, I'm sorry too. This is all so weird." I wanted to talk about the will. The reading had been held two days after my mother's death. Bunny and I sat in Richard's glassy office while he read out loud that I was bequeathed the Crow's Nest and all of Mom's money in a trust fund to be meted out in thirds: now, for tuition; at twenty-five; and at thirty. Mom gave Bunny some jewelry, a box of diaries, and a family portrait. Richard would continue to manage the investment of the trust and the payment of my bills. I was only eighteen. I don't think I thought about what it meant, to have all that as a freshman in college. I didn't think to ask why my grandparents had given the house to Mother, a hopeless drunk, and not to Bunny, her smart and together sister.

Until that rainy day in May, standing in the gloomy living room of the Crow's Nest, eating deviled eggs and watercress sandwiches, it didn't cross my mind that Bunny would have felt hurt, betrayed. I just didn't think about anything but my own feelings and reactions. Somehow, we should have shared the house, or at the very least I should have had Bunny come stay every summer, or at least ask her up at all. But I didn't. I never did. I just let the time lapse, some guilty thing gnawing at me, but I was unable or unwilling to address it.

And now, decades of silence.

I stared at the phone. I googled Barbara Cushing, Weston, Massachusetts. I got a hit with the online White Pages for her address and phone number. Same after all these years. I stared at the number. I made a cup of tea. I emptied the trash. I e-mailed Caroline. Then, finally, finally, finally, after I couldn't bear another minute of delay, I called Bunny.

I half expected it to be a wrong number, an outdated listing, or for the phone to ring and ring and ring, but on the fourth ring, a voice, elderly and gravelly, said, "Hello?"

It was her. "Bunny? Is this Bunny?" I asked.

There was a long pause. "Yes, this is she."

She sounded very far away. "Bunny, hi, it's Fez."

Another long pause and a deep breath. "Hello, Fez." She offered nothing else.

"Well, it's been such a long time…"

"It certainly has," she said coolly.

"I was wondering if I could come out and see you." She didn't say anything. I thought she had hung up. "Bunny?"

"I'm here," she said.

"So would that be OK? If I came out?"

"I don't know. I'm not well."

"Bunny, I'm so sorry. I didn't know…"

"Well, of course you didn't." It sounded like she put a spoon into a teacup. She stirred something.

"Do you think I could come out? A very brief visit. I promise not to stay long." I started rambling, the words spilling out faster than I could organize them. "I know it's been ages…so I was thinking…I mean…I can't believe how long…"

She waited for me to stop my awkward stumbling. "OK. When is it that you'd like to come by?" She sounded resigned.

"Is tomorrow too soon? Maybe for lunch? I could bring something."

"Tomorrow is fine. Twelve o'clock. Don't trouble yourself with bringing anything. Maria, my aide, is here helping me. I get tired. You'll have to make the visit short."

I agreed and hung up. Tomorrow. That was good. Penny worked tomorrow, so I could visit Hazel, leave Penny there in her office, and then go see Bunny.

The drive to Aunt Bunny's house was only about fifteen or twenty minutes from Edgehill. Bunny still lived in a spectacular, symmetrical grand center-hall colonial of white clapboard and black shutters in Weston, Massachusetts, on a dozen acres of land on the Weston reservoir. Her property had an apple orchard and a formal rose garden. There was a pool and a pool house. There was a tennis court and a three-hole putting course. Her deceased husband, Buck, had raised German shorthaired pointers for bird hunting, so there was a cottage big enough for a caretaker and the attached pens and runs. There were open fields and a wooded area where I used to camp out with girlfriends when I was in elementary school and then boyfriends and girlfriends when I was in high school. I drove down that same beech-lined driveway in the dappled morning sunlight splashing all around the trees. The place looked like it was being maintained beautifully.

I parked next to Bunny's old boxy navy-blue Mercedes wagon and went to the shiny black front door with its big brass lion's head knocker. A woman, whom I assumed to be Maria, clad in a starched white housekeeper's apron, opened the door, greeted me, and led me through the entry hall, past the round front hall table with the enormous white floral arrangement of roses and twigs and hydrangeas. Into the living room with its warm well-waxed mahogany furniture, oil paintings by Hassam and Breck, Andrew Wyeth watercolors, and refreshingly bright and unexpected lime-green carpet. The vacuum lines were fresh. A silver vase gleamed on a table next to Bunny, filled with more white flowers. There sat Bunny, looking thin and frail.

She stood up with the help of a slender silver-tipped wooden cane. "Oh, Fez. Hello."

"Hi, Bunny." I hugged her gently, feeling her ribs, a delicate, breakable birdcage. Maria brought in a tray with cups and saucers, a carafe, tiny pitchers of cream, and a bowl of sugar with tiny monogrammed silver spoons. A plate had an assortment of mini croissants and scones and muffins. White linen napkins were folded and fanned out on the game table in the living room for our lunch. I walked with Bunny over to the table.

"I hope breakfast is OK for lunch," she said, looking at the table. "I don't eat much more than tea and scones anymore."

"Bunny, it's great. Thank you." I took a buttery bite and then dove right in. "I would like to apologize for my behavior."

Bunny didn't say anything. She looked at me sadly and waited for me to continue.

"I don't really know what happened, except that I simply didn't make an effort to stay in touch. I didn't think. I got busy and lost track of time…Well, no excuses. The plain truth is I behaved badly, and I am terribly sorry."

She put her teacup down on the gleaming table. "Fez, thank you for that. I tried to stay in touch, as you know, but it did seem to go unrequited. It seemed that you didn't care to keep a relationship with your old aunt."

"No, Bunny. That's definitely not the case." I looked out the window at the garden in the fall light. "I was just selfish, first buried in my college life, then in my new life in the city, then in my marriage and…I think I lost track of time, and then the more time passed, the worse I felt. Then, all this time later, I was thinking about the Crow's Nest, and I don't know why we never invited you up. You should have been visiting every summer, and I never extended an invitation. I don't even know why that house wasn't yours to start with. I'm terribly sorry."

"Fez, I never wanted anything from your mother or my parents. Especially not that house."

I was confused. "But didn't you love that house? I remember you were there all the time."

Bunny laughed. "God, no, dear. I hated that place. Buck too."

I was stunned. And something like relief started to creep in. "Really? Hated?"

"Absolutely *hated*. I wouldn't have visited you even if you had asked. I really just went to be with you and your mother."

Now it was my turn to laugh. "Well, that certainly makes me feel a little better." I told her we were going to have to sell the house.

"That makes no difference to me. Sell away. Good riddance. Still"—Bunny became serious again—"still, I would have loved to hear from you. We are *family*. There are too few of us left."

"Yes, I completely agree…On that note, I have news."

I told Bunny all about the call from Richard in early September and Dottie's death, about moving Penny in with us. Bunny covered her mouth with her hand.

"I never thought you two would ever meet. My God, Fez. My God." She kept staring at me. "Dear Lord, I'm at a loss for words. I used to visit her occasionally, and then after Buck died, and my health started to decline, I just couldn't manage it. But we have been good pen pals. What a darling. Is this why you've come to visit? To let me know about Penny? I'm just thrilled."

"Not just that. But I'm very glad to let you know that we sisters are together, and she has been wonderful, but I actually wanted to ask you about something regarding Mother. I just got the report from her stay at Edgehill in 1953," I said, searching her face for a reaction.

Bunny put down her cup. "I see. Well." She played with the cup handle and examined the tiny ring of tea in the saucer. "How did you know she was there?"

I told her about Hazel, and then Penny's memory of Mother going to Edgehill.

"Well, that's a good thing," said Bunny, exhaling. "Secrets haven't done us any favors in this family, and I'm tired of them. Good Lord, enough already. I am terribly sorry to hear about Hazel, though. In my mind, she's just a little slip of a girl from Christmas card photographs. So what exactly is your question?"

I said, "OK, I know Mom went to Edgehill a few months after Penny went to live in Providence, when Penny was only four. So it makes sense to me that she would have had a breakdown. I guess it was a nervous breakdown. Is that right?"

Bunny looked down at the napkin on her lap. She was playing with the hemstitch pattern on the edges of it, her shiny, clear nails running back and forth on the hem edges. "That's right, darling. Your mother *did* have a nervous breakdown. The winter of 1953 into 1954. I spent New Year's Day with her in the common room of that place. I visited her on Saturdays, as I recall. The only people who knew about her stay there were our parents and your father...and now you...and of course me. Your mother was terribly ashamed. She didn't like the idea of 'help' nor the idea of being trapped in there with 'unsavory' people." Bunny's hands were trembling. "Your poor, dear mother."

I reached over and held her hand. "I've read her medical records."

Bunny looked right at me. "Oh."

"Well, actually, yes. It's all very hard to read. There was mention in the records of an event or events in Mother's past. Something that seemed especially upsetting or harmful to her. She had nightmares about a monster or monsters. Does this make any sense to you?"

Bunny looked awful. Her chin began to quiver. "Oh dear," she said quietly. "How I hate all these secrets. These have been nothing but poison all of our lives. I'm sick and tired of all this. All these awful, toxic secrets. And I'm looking at you, and poor Hazel healing back at Edgehill." She patted her knees with her hands.

"*The secrets stop today.* Let me get something for you to read. I don't think I can tell you this; I'd rather have you read it."

Bunny pushed back from the table and slowly stood up using the chair arms as props, allowing some time to straighten her back. She took the polished wooden cane in her hand. She walked over to a small wooden box on the table next to her lovely green armchair. She pulled out an old brown leather journal with gold scrollwork on the spine.

"When I was younger, your mother and I kept diaries. I have dozens of them. I fancied myself a writer, I think. I believe the writing saved me sometimes, living in that house with your grandparents. I started writing in it when I was in elementary school, and I never stopped. I have an entire pile of these leather books. Your mother did also and Richard gave them to me when she died. This is one of your mother's." She walked slowly back to the table and handed the book over to me. "Go sit on that loveseat and read the pages starting in 1933. This may answer your questions, Fez."

I watched her walk away, my delicate, beautiful old aunt, as light as a songbird feather. I sat on the floral loveseat and opened up the journal, the binding cracking a little. I read the following, written in a young girl's careful script:

*Crow's Nest, May 27, 1933*
*We are here! We got here last night, and we're all so excited to be back on the Cape for the summer. Bunny and I colored the whole drive in our new paper pads and Mother needlepointed a new pillow and Father drove. Today, we spent the day on our little beach, digging and making little castles and watching the crabs. We had a delicious lobster salad lunch and the weather was sunny and hot. Yay, summer!*

*Crow's Nest, June 1, 1933*
*It was another beautiful day, blue skies and puffy white clouds, and we took the boat out to Nauset Beach to play in the big waves.*

*Bunny and I had so much fun playing at the big beach, and we rode the big waves, but Mother said I had to stay closer to the shore because of my being smaller than Bunny. I get tired of being the small one all the time. Mother made another lovely picnic, and Father had too many beers, which is what Mother said, and then Mother was quite nervous about father driving the boat. He was very snappy to us. Mother says he has a lot on his mind right now.*

## *Crow's Nest, June 5, 1933*

*Last night, when I was sleeping, something happened. Father came into my room and stood right at my feet. It was very late because I had already been asleep. I could smell the whiskey and the smoke on his breath and in his clothes. He just stood there, staring at me sleeping. He was tipping over a little. Then he left. He never, ever tucks me in or reads me stories. So I don't know what he was thinking.*

## *Crow's Nest, June 17, 1933*

*Last night, it happened again. I was sound asleep, and it was very late. I don't remember hearing crickets or any nighttime critters. Father came in, as quiet as a mouse. I could almost smell him before I saw him. He stood at my feet and rubbed them. I said, "Hi, Father," and he acted like I had awakened him. Then he left. I think he might be sleepwalking or a little bit sick.*

## *Crow's Nest, June 27, 1933*

*Father came in again last night, but he wasn't sleeping. He was wide awake. He stood there for a few minutes. Then he sat on the side of my bed. He was looking at his slippers. He was in his pajamas. The light-blue ones. I asked him if he was awake. He just turned and looked at me as if he didn't know who I was. Then he climbed into bed with me. My bed is just for one person, and a little person, so we were very close when he climbed in. He was facing me, rubbing my head. Smoothing my hair. I asked him if he was OK. He only said to close my eyes and sleep. So I did what Father said. I closed my eyes and then his hand went onto my shoulder and onto my tummy and onto my privates where no one is supposed to touch. I whispered, "Father," and he said for me to not say a word. I was so scared that I said nothing. He made his hands go all around me, and I said nothing. Then Father left.*

## Crow's Nest, July 5, 1933

*It's happening more and more. Father is visiting me on most nights now. Last night, he drank a lot of whiskey at the fireworks party. I sat very close to Mother. When Father came near, I sort of shivered, and Mother said that I must be cold. But I wasn't cold in the least.*

*In bed, I waited. I couldn't sleep knowing he might be back. I just lay awake in bed, waiting. He came in and did the same thing. He climbed in and smelled very, very strong of whiskey from the fireworks party, and his hand did the feeling under my nightie and his other hand was feeling his own privates and we lay very, very quiet. When he stopped his deep breathing, he said I was a very, very bad girl. Father was right. I agreed with him. Then he said I should never, ever speak of this. He whispered very angrily. I whispered back at him that I was going to be quiet. He said all mad and scratchy that I would be sorry if I did. I wasn't going to tell anyone. I didn't want to be sorry.*

## Crow's Nest, August 15, 1933

*I'm writing in bed with a flashlight so I don't wake Bunny. She moved into my room this morning. We're going to sleep together now. Her bed is so close to mine, and I don't want to bother her. I'm not used to her sleeping right here. I could reach right across the space and touch her hand. She's that close.*

*Last night, Father came in again, and I started crying. I didn't mean to cry, but I was scared and sad, and I didn't want to be a bad girl anymore. Father said to stop my crying. But he said it all wet because he was filled with whiskey again. I tried to stop my crying, but I couldn't. Father climbed into bed again. I lay very, very still, the tears coming and coming, and Father's voice was loud. I think he forgot about the whispering. He said to stop it or I would be in big trouble. But I couldn't stop. I said too loudly, "I can't stop. I can't stop." I know I'm a bad girl, but I couldn't stop my crying.*

*Lots of nights, I had this one same dream and in this dream, I would see Father in my tiny bed, his hand on my tummy, his pajama pants untied. His privates outside. In my dream, my big sister, Bunny, would march right up to Father and put her little face right next to him and yell at Father to leave me alone.*

*In my dream, Father looked at Bunny and whispered in the meanest, meanest way you could ever whisper that she wouldn't dare.*

*She was so brave. In my dream, she'd say, "Wouldn't I? Wouldn't I, Father?" Like she was daring Father. She just stood there getting bigger and bigger like a magic genie and stared at Father, lying there with his privates out. Father put his pajamas back over to cover his privates. Bunny wasn't afraid of anything.*

*In my dream, Father tied his pajamas up and left. Bunny sat on my bed. She hugged me close and rubbed my hair and said I was her poor little baby sister.*

*I told her I'm a bad girl. I'm just a bad girl.*

*Bunny said I wasn't. She told me I was the sweetest, best girl in the whole world. Then she said that Father was a monster. That was my dream. It was always the same.*

### Crow's Nest, August 27, 1933

*I asked Bunny to move into my room forever because I said I was scared. I didn't tell her why. She said she is going to protect me from monsters, and I was having bad dreams, and she said she could hear me crying in the night. Bunny said she wanted to sleep with me so I wouldn't get bad dreams anymore. So I guess she's going to protect me now. I don't remember any crying in the night, but she said she could hear it. So she's here now. I like it.*

There was no more writing. She must have stopped keeping diaries. I closed the little journal. My God, what a heartbreaking thing. What a terrible, sordid, awful thing. What a disgusting, sickening thing.

I looked up at Bunny. The light coming in from the window behind her lit her wiry hair, making a white halo of light. "Bunny, my God. When did you know?" I asked.

She looked so sad, so old. "I found out when I got the diaries, after she died." She spoke quietly and slowly. She looked deep into my eyes. "I wish I had known. I wish I could have helped her."

"Bunny, I know. I know. I don't even know what to say. This is so awful. That poor little girl. My poor, innocent mother."

Bunny was twisting a ring on her bony, arthritic finger. "She never told me. I can't tell you how awful I feel. The shock and the guilt. The horrid feeling in realizing that she suffered and that I was somehow spared. Father, your grandfather, never touched me. Never. But he must have known your mother was young enough, or scared enough, or sweet enough for him to carry on with her." She looked down at the floor. "I guess I was the lucky one."

I thought about how Penny *knew* of this terrible secret, this secret of monsters, our mother's secret, and Penny was the only one to know this when Mom was still alive. I thought of the fact that Bunny and Mom were sisters and one was spared and one was so deeply hurt. Then I thought of my own relationship with Penny, my sister, and the parallels to my mother and her sister. Sweet innocent Penny was sent away, sent off to live in a series of institutions. In a way, I guess I was the lucky one too.

I could see her, my mother, the little girl whose photographs hung in the hallways and stairways of the Crow's Nest. A beautiful little girl with wispy blond hair and big round eyes. Thin as a reed, wearing cotton dresses with thick silk sashes and huge satin bows in her hair. I remember the old sepia photographs of her with Bunny, Bunny's protective arm around my mother's narrow shoulders. I could see the family portraits, taken in the thirties, maybe even when this was going on. Grandpa looking seriously at the camera, Mimi seated upright, Bunny and Mom sitting on the floor, Mom's ragdoll lying limp in her lap.

My grandfather and I were so close. He had always been my caretaker, my hero, my savior. For years, we took boat trips and went on clamming expeditions and went bookstore shopping and for peppermint ice cream, and I adored him. He made my summers bearable, fun, *normal.* My mother, often drunk and sagging and tired, would always come along on these trips. I now knew she was there to protect me from being alone with him. How did I never know, never pick up on the fact that he abused my mother? How did I miss this? Shouldn't there have been some clue? Some hint of their awful secret? How would I have known? I was sickened by the thought that I had spent hours and hours with him, enjoying his company, the smell of his pipe, and the clean and soapy smell of his skin. But he had never touched me. Never. Not an inappropriate gesture. Not even an inappropriate glance. My mother had always been there.

I asked Bunny, "How could my mother bring me to that house every summer? How could she ever see her own father?"

"I don't know, Fez, but I think your mother loved and needed her own mother, and I can't believe my mother was aware of what happened; I'm sure she knew nothing. Also, your mother needed money, which they provided; she wanted a nice place for you to go in the summers. I don't know how she managed to go there and be in the same room as him. I don't really know. But I do know that the drinking, the pills, the sleeping, the hiding in her bedroom, those must have been her escape."

My mother was molested by her father; the thought ran through me over and over and over and over and over. My grandfather molested my mother, my little girl of a mother. She was only nine that summer of 1933. She was young and happy, I think. Even the early diary entries of that summer revealed her young happiness, her hope, her brightness. When Bunny moved into her room, unbeknownst to her, she became her protector, her brave little soldier. And she was only twelve. Bunny had been her guardian against nameless monsters from that terrible day on, sleeping vigil by her side, not knowing that the real monster was their own father. After that, he must have left her alone, my poor, sweet, manipulated, abused, innocent mother. My God. No wonder she drank. *No wonder.*

During one of her visits to Marion or Plymouth, lost in the dank cave of sordid memories, I suppose Mother must have told Penny that story or some version of it. She was talking about monsters to Penny and to the doctors at Edgehill, the monsters of her dreams and her memories. There was really just one monster: her own father.

I excused myself from Bunny's sunny living room, walked outside through the french doors. I walked back, back, back. Past the slate terrace with its potted boxwoods and climbing wisteria, past the cluster of apples trees, through the open field, and through the small, dark pine woods. I walked right up to the clean, clear reservoir. I looked at the reflections of the trees in the perfect glass surface: the azure blue sky, the white clouds, the verdant trees. I sat on the bank, dropped my head, and cried.

# CHAPTER 25

# PENELOPE

Last week, Hazy had her graduation from Edgehill. She finished all of her special schoolwork there, and then they gave her like a little party to say *Gatulations*. Willum and Fuzzy and I went to go pick her up, and Ellie was there of course, and we all hugged Hazy and Dr. Bowman, and the other peoples at Edgehill who had helped Hazy was there to say, *Great job,* and *Good work,* and *Good luck,* and *Stay in touch,* and *Remember all the good things you worked on,* and *Keep up with your meetings,* and stuff like that. She even got a fancy piece of paper with a gold seal on it saying she had completed her *Intensive Inpatient Program.* Hazy seemed pretty essited to be comin home, and so did Fuzzy and Willum. But *nobody* was more essited than me, cuz Hazy and I is like besties now. That's what Hazy calls it: besties, cuz we're like bestest friends. That's so, so, so nice cuz after my Dottie died, I never, ever thought I'd have another bestie again. But I do. I gots my Hazy.

Today is the bestest day in the whole world. It's my first turkey day with my sister, Fuzzy. Ellie is coming over, and Bunny is coming over, and Willum will be here. So it's gonna be our whole family plus Ellie, who's kinda like family too. She's kinda like my boss too, but she's not so bossy at all.

I been workin on makin that apple pie, and I gots to make a few *practice pies*. Fuzzy says it's always good to try out new recipes before you have to make them for something special. That turned out to be really goodly advice cuz the first pie I made tasted bad, bad, bad. Like the ocean. Cuz I putted salt in instead of sugar. Salt and sugar look a lot the same, and I forgotted which jar had which thing in it. The next pie, I membered about the sugar, but I forgotted about the timer, and I gots to knittin, and the next thing I knowed, the smoke alarm is beepin loud, and the pie was practickly on fire cuz it cooked for too many minutes. So the third time, I membered about the sugar and I membered about the timer, and the pie was so, so good. So I's makin that pie jus like that for today, and it's gonna be delicious, and everyone's gonna be like, *Oh, Penny, this pie is delicious,* and *Did you make this yourself?* and *Good for you,* and things like that.

I gots to talk about Fuzzy a little bits cuz ever since she got back from seeing Aunt Bunny, she's been kinda different like. She told me that Bunny told her about how our mommy was hurt when she was a little girl. There was kind of a monster, Fuzzy told me.

I said, *I didn't tell nothing. I didn't tell Mommy's secret about those monsters.*

Fuzzy said, *I know, Pen. Bunny told me all about it, and I'm just glad we all know because secrets aren't good for anyone.*

I took a big breath in and out and said, *That's for sure. I hated keeping that secret. It was hard.*

Penny said, *I bet. So now you don't have to anymore. OK?*

*OK, Fuzzy. So, Fuzzy, I don't wants to talk about it no more, though, K?*

*Me neither,* Fuzzy agreed with me. Monsters are scary, and I don't like thinking about them.

We wasn't talking about it no more, but Fuzzy seemed different. Even though she heard that bad news about our mommy and the monster in the nighttimes, Fuzzy said it explained things. I asked her what kinds of things were explained by that story about the monster, and Fuzzy just said, *Well, Pen, our mommy makes more sense to me now.* I had no idea what that all meant, and I really was sick of monsters and not talking about monsters and now kinda talking about monsters. I was just gonna stick to my knittin and my apple pie makin, cuz those things made lots of sense.

So early, early on this turkey day morning, I walked into the kitchen to make the apple pie, and Fuzzy and Willum was there drinkin their coffees. Willum hadn't been over in a whole lotta weeks cuz he was busy starting his new job on State Street in *BeautifulBoston.* He was here now, though.

*Hi, Pen,* they both said at the exact same time.

*Hi, Fuzzy and Willum,* I said. *I's gonna make the pies now, K?*

*Great, Pen. Thanks,* Fuzzy said. They stayed there on their stools drinkin coffee and talking.

Fuzzy and Willum kept on with their talking. I didn't bother them no more; I just took the *granny's mitt* apples to the sink to wash them and peel them and slice them into the bowl. Willum said to Fuzzy, *Well, now that you know, how do you reconcile the grandfather you remember with the grandfather you now know, from that journal of your mom's?*

Fez added more milk to her coffee and stirred. *I don't know. I've been wrestling with that so much. I always thought he and I were so close. He really did feel like a father to me, a hero even.*

*Hmmm,* Willum said, reaching for a donut. *And now what? Now, how do you feel about him?*

*The whole thing just makes me sick. He was, truly, a monster. I could never see him in any other way.*

*Oh no,* I thought, *here we go with those monsters again.* But I just kept on peelin those pretty green apples and keeping my head down, lookin in the sink. I had fourteen to peel cuz I was makin *two* whole pies.

*I agree. It's horrific, really awful. Sickening,* Willum said. *And how does it make you feel about your mom?*

Fuzzy was quiet for a long time. I turned around to be sure she wasn't choking on her breakfuss. She wasn't choking, just kinda lookin out the window at the empty branches all scratchy up against the window. *Well, look at you, asking about how I'm feeling.* She smiled at Willum. *I guess I...I guess I just feel incredibly sad. Mom was so young and innocent.* Her voice kinda got really soft. *I don't know. She was just a little girl.*

*Yes, she was. She was a victim. Truly,* added Willum. *Maybe all that drinking and pills and despondency makes a bit more sense now. But I don't understand how your mother could even be with her father after that, going to the Crow's Nest in the summers and spending time there, and also letting you be there in that house with him.*

*I know. Bunny explained that Mom continued going there because she was basically helpless and that she went to be with her mother. Bunny said she needed her mother, the way a child needs her mother. Also, Bunny told me she didn't think my grandmother ever knew about the abuse. Bunny said between Mom's reliance on her mother and her need for financial security, she continued to go to that house, every summer. But her mother and Bunny surrounded Mom and me and I guess Mom never spent time alone with her father ever again.*

Fuzzy was quiet again, and I hadda check to be sure she was breathin. *You OK, Fuzzy?* I asked her. I wiped my hands on my yellow-checked apron and turned around to see her.

She nodded, but she didn't seem OK. Her elbow was on the table, and she put her cheek down on her hand and she looked at me, then Willum, and her mouth went down like a sad mouth. *Yeah, I guess that does make sense, the reasons Mom might want or need to be on the Cape.*

Then Willum kinda patted her light-brown hairs and said, *I'm so sorry, Fez. This is really tough.*

She looked like she was seeing a ghost all kinda ascared, and she said, *I've been thinking about this for weeks now. Ever since that visit with Bunny. I feel like I've been angry with the wrong person all these years.*

I walked over to her, and I started patting her hairs too, and then she was lookin at Willum and me pattin her hairs, and she put her head down on her hands on the island and cried and cried and cried, and the tears made a little puddle right on the wooden counter, and there was snots everywhere on the wood, which was kinda asgusting, but we just kept right on pattin. Then Hazy came downstairs, and she was doon the pattin too.

Later at turkey day lunch, things gotted much, much better. First of all, Fuzzy stopped cryin, but she gotted all pink and blotchy, and she didn't look so pretty from all the cryin, so I putted makeups on her. Macscary and eye powders and lickstick and rooj. And when we came out of the bathroom, Hazy and Willum were there, and they was smiling so, so big and were so like, *Wow, Penny, that sure is a lotta makeups,* and *Wow, Penny, Fuzzy sure has a lotta colors on her eyes,* and *Wow, Penny, we've never seen Mom so colorful,* and stuff like that. I think they was pretty proud to me, but then Fuzzy did take some of it off like the blue eyeshadow and the lavender eye shadow and the seafoam eye shadow cuz she said it was *a bit too much.* But I thoughted she looked like a beautiful fairy princess Barbie doll, and I was so proud to me, but that's OK if Fuzzy didn't like alls the powders.

Then Ellie came over, and she had drived Bunny over, who had her fancy cane, and it was so fun cuz Ellie's so nice and funny and smile-y, and Bunny was so essited to see me cuz she said she hadn't seen me since *I was a wee bit of a thing,* which I'm thinking was a long time ago since I don't member ever seeing her for a long time. Plus *wee bit* sounds tiny. She looked a lot like my mommy but much, much older and with white hair kinda short and polka-dotty hands like Dottie useda has, and she smelled pretty like roses.

A gajillion things happened that was so fun at turkey day. The food was so huge, and it filled the table and the kitchen. The turkey was big and golden and yummy. So was all the foods, and I thought I was gonna barf from all the eatin, but when it was dessert times, everyone took a slice of one of my apple pies. *Everyone.* There was lots of other pies, but everybody took slices of *mine* and said all the nice things that made me so proud and happy to be part of this family, which was getting bigger and bigger.

Then Fuzzy picked up her glass of bubbly water, which she was drinkin now with no happy juice cuz Hazy wasn't doon that, so she wasn't doon that no more neither. She clinked it to make a noise, and she said, *Everyone, William and I have an announcement.*

And everyone gots all quieted, and Fuzzy said, *First of all, Happy Thanksgiving to all of you.* Everyone said Happy Thanksgivings, and they was clinkin their glasses and waters, and I was clinkin and sayin all the happy things, and she kept on goin. *I wanted to share something with you. I, we, got this news earlier in the week, but I thought today would be a good time to tell you.*

We was all quiet waitin for Fuzzy's news. She looked kinda serious. *We have accepted an offer on the Crow's Nest.* I didn't know what *accepted an offer* was, so I just looked around at everybody. I didn't know whether it was good news or bad news.

Willum said, *Yes, we did.*

Fez's little smile turned into a big wide smile, like her face was gonna split open from the smiling. *Yeah, it's great news. The best. It's a good offer. Nice family from New York. Westchester County, I think.*

Bunny smiled at that and said quietly into her grape juice glass, all quiet and kinda like a crazy lady, *Oh, how Father hated New Yorkers. How fitting. How wonderful.* Fuzzy heard her and smiled at her like she understood that crazy talking.

Hazy was lookin kinda sad on accounta her loving the Cape Cod house. We was kinda quiet for a second, and then Bunny said, *Well, I for one am thrilled. I hated that damn place.*

Fuzzy smiled at Bunny like they was sharin that same secret and said, *Yep, I guess me too.* Then, I's not sure why, but we all started laughin and laughin. I guess selling that house was kinda funny after all. I was lookin round at all the faces, and all the faces was laughin, and it made me feel so happy and silly and giggly.

Bunny was sitting right next to me, and after all the laughin stopped, she reached into her shiny black handbag, and she handed me a little box. *I think you should have this, dear.*

I opened the blue velvet jewelry box and opened my mouth as wide as I could ever open it, and I said, *Wowowowowow!*

Bunny started to tell me all about the story of this pearl necklace that I was now holding right in my hands. *This was your great-grandmother's necklace, Penny. And she gave it to me when I was eighteen, telling me I had a sparkle and a glow and that I should have a necklace that sparkled and glowed. And when I think of you, dear girl, I think you have that sparkle and glow. Yes, and your great-grandmother would be absolutely thrilled to know this necklace lived on with someone who loves it as much as you already do, Penny.*

*I's loving it, Bunny. I's so essited to has it. Thank you very much.* I was running my fingers over the big smooth, round, white pearls. There was a bunch of tiny sparkles on the part that connected.

*And here's a fun little trick, Penny. Very gently, run your teeth over the pearls.*

I held the necklace up to my smiling mouth, my teeth shiny and big, and dragged the pearls across my top teeth. *Oooooh, kinda scratchy.* It felt like the sand at the beach.

*That's right, darling. That's how you know they are real. Real pearls are made from sand, from sandy irritation inside an oyster shell.*

I was so, so happy, like it was my birthday and not even just turkey day, with my new special prezzie from Bunny. *It's funny how something so pretty and shiny and fancy comes from something like a scratchy piece of sand.*

Bunny put her old spotty hand right on mine. *Yes, dear girl, it is.*

# CHAPTER 26

# HAZEL

I was so damn happy to get out of Edgehill, but the anticipation of the first day really bummed me out. I guess Mom guessed that it was gonna be tough, cuz she walked me to school like she used to when I was little, and she was really nervous and chatty and we stopped at Starbucks and got venti lattes, which was obviously a huge treat. I didn't say much on the way over. My stomach was full of blackness, and I was really scared about how everyone was gonna be. I didn't know who knew what, but every single time someone left school for any reason, everyone seemed to find out why. So now I was gonna be the freak who drank and smoked and popped pills and was an addict and was depressed and anxious and cut herself. I was gonna be the kid who went away to fucking Edgehill. But whatever. This was my choice; I told Mom and Dad I wanted to go back to my old school. I think it would have been as hard or harder to start at a brand-new school, so I just decided to make it work where I had been.

Mom left me at the door of the school and hugged me so hard, I thought I might have dislocated my collarbone or cracked a rib or something. When I saw her walk away, I could tell by her stooped posture and the shake of her shoulders that she was crying hard and probably feeling as bad as I was. That actually helped me a little for some weird reason.

I stood at the bottom of the large stone stairs, looking up at the doorway, and put one foot in front of the other. I went into Dr. Sanderson's office first cuz she asked me to check in with her, and she gave me a huge hug too. She had tears in her eyes. Everyone was so damn weepy these days. "Hey, Dr. Sanderson."

"Hi, Hazel. Wow, am I happy to see you. You look so well. Like a new person."

"Thanks," I said. "I'm happy to see you too." I kinda was.

"How are you doing?"

"I'm better. Much better. That 'day at a time' thing is true, though. Some days aren't so good. Like today, I'm kinda not feelin so great. I'm really nervous."

"I'm sure you are. How can I help you?"

I shook my head. "I don't think anything. I'm just going to have to figure it out."

"I'm sure that's true. You have been through so much. I want you to come talk to me as often as you want or need. My door is always open. OK? And I have your schedule here. First bell is in fifteen minutes. Your locker is the same. Do you want to stay here until first period or get settled at your locker?"

"I guess I'll head down and get settled." She hugged me again and I left her office, her secretary looking at me like I had stage-four cancer.

When I walked into the hall from her office, the first kid I saw was Janie. My old friend. My oldest friend, actually. The one I kinda dumped last year for the stoners. We both just froze and looked at each other like we didn't even know what to do. It was incredibly weird. We both started to say something and interrupted each other. Then we started to say something else and interrupted each other again. Then she laughed and came right up to me and gave me the biggest, squeeziest hug ever. Even harder than Mom's. She started crying when we were hugging, and then I started crying, and then we both pulled away and wiped our faces really fast cuz other kids were starting to come into school.

"Jesus, I've missed you, Haze."

"I've missed you too, Janie. A lot. I'm so sorry—" I started to blubber out a whole apology thing, but she put up her hand.

"Nope. No sorries. Seriously."

"OK. OK."

"Are you going back to your locker? Do you have the same locker?"

"Yeah. I am. Just kinda nervous."

"I bet. Well, I'm going down there now, so let's do it together."

One of the things we worked on at Edgehill was forgiveness, making amends, and all that kinda stuff. I was walking next to Janie, seeing her completely wave off my attempts to explain my shitty behavior. It was pretty cool. I mean, last year, I totally blew her off and treated her like shit for an entire semester until she took the hint and very gracefully backed away. She never got mad at me, never confronted me, never treated me badly. She just kinda moved out of the way, and that day when I came back and felt like total shit, she took me right back. Like nothing had ever happened. She turned out to be the perfect example of moving on, healing, graciousness, and I was so grateful to her for that.

She made my first day back actually decent. Not perfect in the least, but decent. Almost everybody else just stared at me, or said hi about an octave higher than usual or completely ignored me, but I had kinda expected that. Turns out Janie and I didn't have any classes together or study hall or even lunch period, but knowing she was in the building was cool. I felt like I had a sister or a guardian angel just around the corner.

# CHAPTER 27

# FESSENDEN

I walked to Hazel's school for the last day of the semester. She was back at her old high school: Dr. Sanderson agreed with the staff at Edgehill that she had made significant strides and was absolutely ready to come back to school, reintegrate, reenter, refocus. She was way behind her class and had a lot of catching up to do, but both Hazel and her teachers felt she could catch up with the help of tutors and not have to repeat the grade. She was adjusting after her eight weeks at Edgehill, but it was hard. She was navigating the treacherous waters of the challenging academics and had few friends; her newer friends were no longer students there, her older friends had drifted away, maybe betrayed by her earlier disloyalty or maybe unwilling to forgive or make an effort. I guess her old friend Janie came back into her life, which I think was a great comfort to Hazel. Hazel said she felt like a pariah, since everyone knew what had happened and where she had gone. She ate alone at lunch, she sat alone at study hall, and she was usually not chosen early or at all for lab partner or for group assignments. She was lonely. While I would never have wanted her to feel anything like loneliness, I was grateful for this new time we spent together. She was home every afternoon, doing homework, asking for help. She helped with dinner. She helped with cleanup. She needed and wanted activities, and she and I both went to concurrent AA and Al-Anon meetings at five o'clock at Trinity Church. I started going simply to support her, to walk with her to and from the church, but then I started liking being in that space, in the quiet church basement, in the quiet support of people sharing relatable stories.

She was walking home from school alone, and I happened to see her on my way back from an errand. We got to talking about her Christmas vacation and what our plans should be.

"So, Haze, tomorrow Paul is coming up to visit with Penny," I said.

"Oh, that's cool. They haven't seen each other in a while, right?"

"Yeah, not for about a month. He's picking her up in the morning and heading back down to Marion. They're going Christmas shopping together and out to lunch at Penny's favorite place and going to put a Christmas wreath on Dottie's grave. I think Penny knit him a yellow cozy."

"That's adorable. She is so damn cute. That all sounds good. Penny will love that."

"Yep, and I have a brilliant idea for you and me tomorrow."

Hazel looked at me skeptically. "What? Brilliant ideas scare me."

"Do you have plans tomorrow?" I checked.

She just looked at me like the answer was too obvious to utter. "No."

"OK, OK," I continued. "Tomorrow you and I are going to paint Penny's bedroom."

"Oh God. I'm assuming yellow." Hazel smiled.

"Absolutely. *Yellow.*" I smirked at my own brilliant idea. "I actually got the name of the paint color of her old living room from Paul. It's called Mellow Yellow."

"I can't believe she's been living in that antiseptic white bedroom for all these months. You *know* she hates that white. It's about time."

"I know. I know. I'm really psyched. But we have to work quickly. Paul will only have her from nine thirty until about four."

"Think we can do it?" Hazel asked.

"Yes, definitely. You may not know this, but I am an excellent painter." I smiled at her. I was *not* an excellent painter; I was a sloppy and careless painter, but I was committed to being organized and efficient for the sake of Penny's surprise.

The next morning, I woke up and made coffee before I was to awaken Hazel. As I drank my coffee in the still of the dark, wintry morning, I got a text from William: *Can I swing by and see Hazel tonight?*

I wrote: *Of course. Any time.*

William: *Can we continue our conversation?*

Me: *Sure. Wanna talk now? I'm alone.*

William called right away. "Hi."

"Hey," I said.

"So," he said, faltering. "I don't want to presume anything, but it feels like we've been so much better lately."

I agreed.

"I'm just wondering if you think we could talk about my coming back home. I mean, for good. Not just staying over in my office."

This was a conversation we had started and stopped many, many times in the last month or two. I agreed with him. Things were so much better. We didn't fight at all, and we had been behaving like friends. We showed and felt mutual respect. I genuinely felt like William was my friend again.

"William," I began, "I think we're ready."

"I think so too, Fez." He was driving. I heard the blinker. "I miss you."

"I miss you too." I was trying to think how to phrase this next bit. "I'm just afraid that we'll go back to what we were last winter. I don't think I could handle that. I still feel raw from Hazel—"

He interrupted me. "Fez, I get it. I understand. I thought you might say that because I've been thinking about that too. We've come so far, we've learned so much, and we're being so careful with each other. Maybe the separate living has taught us to be more thoughtful and loving. Maybe?"

"Yeah, maybe," I added. "I guess I'm just afraid that now that we've become so thoughtful with each other, that somehow, going back to our marriage as it was before will just mess it up. I've really enjoyed *us* lately."

"Me too," he said. "But I want more. I want a *marriage.* I want *our marriage.*"

I realized suddenly what I was afraid of. "William, I just don't want to be that angry person anymore. That's how I was. I was furious all the time. It was exhausting. I don't even really remember what I was mad at, but I think pretty much everything. I don't want to go back there."

"But that's just it, Fez. I don't think you're that person anymore. Something changed in you. With everything that's happened this fall, you're different...in a good way. Truly."

"Really? How?" I asked, but I didn't even need to. I felt different.

William paused. "Fez, in so many ways." He was thinking. I didn't interrupt. "You're quieter. Like, not like you were loud before, but it's like this horrible stuff with Hazel kind of broke you in a way. And you just kinda seem like it humbled you or you gave up the angry fight or something. Then the way you reacted to the news of your mom."

I didn't say anything. He kept going.

"Like the energy that used to make you run before was angry and toxic, and now you just seem tired and a little beaten, but not in a bad way. In kind of a sweet way. Hard to explain...and you seem grateful for little things now. Please don't ask me for examples. You know I'm bad at remembering examples in the middle of a conversation."

I laughed. "That's for sure." When we used to fight, he'd accuse me of something sweeping like, "Your anger is infecting this whole household," and I'd ask him for specific examples and in the middle of the heated conversation, I knew he'd be unable to do that.

"So, please, may I move back in? Before Christmas? Please, Fez. We'll take it slow." I was smiling as he added, "Plus I think my brother and his lovely wife are sick of my company. My leaving would be the best Christmas present I could ever give them."

I was smiling bigger now. "Well then, let's give Eddie and Suz what they want."

"Really?" He sounded like a little boy, a sweet, excited little boy.

"Yeah, let's see how it goes. But just know, understand that this scares the crap out of me. Please, please, please let's take it slow. I'm fragile. We're all fragile."

"Yeah, OK. I know. I understand. Great. Awesome. We'll figure out timing, but soon. Very soon. I love you, Fez." He was happy, bright.

"I love you too."

Paul knocked as I was hanging up. It was precisely 9:30 a.m. The minute we watched Paul's car pull away with Penny strapped in next to him, Hazel and I tore upstairs to begin prepping and painting Penny's bedroom. We moved the furniture into the middle of the room and covered everything with clear plastic tarps, and I opened the first can of paint.

"Jesus," I said. Hazel leaned over to look in the can.

"Jesus is right," Hazel said. "That is one bright yellow. Is that the right color? Isn't it called 'Mellow Yellow?'"

"Sadly, yes," I replied. "I must have blocked out the memory of the yellow she had in her apartment. I just totally forgot it was so extraordinarily...*yellow*."

"Wow," Hazel added. "I thought you said it was 'butter.' This is like 'electric banana' or something."

"Well, this *is* the right color. Paul confirmed it. I do kind of remember it being bright. We'll just have to wear sunglasses when we visit her up here in the future."

We began painting, taking turns doing the edges with brushes and rolling out the walls. The work went quickly.

Hazel asked me, "So, Mom, have you heard from Caroline about the manuscript?"

"No, Haze. Nothing. It's been a few weeks since I sent it, so I'm afraid it's probably not great news. I know she's really busy, and I know she was going to get to it, but I missed so many deadlines, and now I'm afraid to even call her. I feel like I really let her down...and myself too."

"Mom, just call her. As Penny would say, 'Jeez.'"

"Yeah, I guess. I'll give it some time. I don't know, I just feel bad about the whole project now. It took so long and the summer when I was working on it was so tough. And all that thinking about Agnes Williams Black and the sick, sadistic murder of her husband...I thought it had some sordid thriller potential, and then by the time I sent the manuscript, the rough version, I had lost all confidence in it. I'm actually afraid it might be total crap."

"Mom, you're a great writer. I'm sure it's good. Just call Caroline." Hazel had paint on the tip of her nose. She put her finger in the paint can and put a dot of paint on my nose. "There. Now we're both 'mellow yellow.'"

We finished the paint job at about three o'clock, with plenty of time to clean up before Penny and Paul got back. We were washing out the brushes and roller in the kitchen sink, "Oh, and one more thing. Your dad's moving back in before Christmas."

Hazel looked at me and said, "Really? That's such incredibly good news." I hadn't heard this sound in a while, but at some point

Hazel started singing quietly. I realized it was the song I used to sing her at bedtime, when she was really young.

See my candle burning,
With its golden light.
Shining through my window,
Far out in the night.

I can light a candle.
God can light a star.
Both are very helpful
Shining where they are.

# CHAPTER 28

# PENELOPE

Christmastime was Jesus's birthday party, and it was so much fun with my brand new family. On December 17, 2014, Paul came to visit me, and he taked me down to Marion to visit Dottie's box in the grass, and he and I put a pretty pointsetter plant at her grassy part cuz she loved those plants at Christmastime. Then he said he wanted me to pick out something fun at the store called Ben Franklin, which is the bestest store in the whole world, and there's a gajillion million, million things in that store, and everything is bright and sparkedly and fun, and I could spend so much time in there looking at all the stuffs. They has stuff for the beach like rafts and blow-up balls and pails and shovels in all bright colors, and they sold the beach toys all year, even in the wintertime. There was toys and games and arts n crafts stuff, and Paul said this was gonna be an early Christmas prezzie that I gots to pick out myself. I walked up and down all the aisles, and I couldn't decide, and then I seen that Paul was sitting in a foldable beach chair by the front of the store with his eyes closed and his mouth open, and I thought maybe I was takin so long to decide about the prezzie that Paul had gone sleepynights. I decided I better pick something pretty soon, so I picked a wooden sign that said, *Jesus Love You,*

264

in pink and yellow and bright green all flowery, and I also gots a poster of a baby with spaghetti on his head that made me laugh, and I used to has it when I was with Dottie in our old apartment. So I got those two things that I picked out myself. He said he had another prezzie for me that he'd give me at lunchtimes.

On the way to lunchtimes, Paul taked me to say hi to all the peoples at the hostipal where I used to work before. We walked into the hostipal, and I guess Paul had tolds them I was comin cuz they had prezzies and cards for me, and it was like a mini Christmas morning party, and I loved it so much. Marsha bought me a tiny *figurine* of a yellow ballet dancer made of china, and it was so pretty and special, and it was wrapped in tissue paper on accounta it being breakable. And you know what else? Even Shannon boughted me something. She boughted me a beautiful coloring book of stained-glass window designs from churches and these kinda fancy coloring pencils, which is much more growed up than crayons, which I used sometimes. There was cards from the other nurses, and I even gots a mystery prezzie of Russell Stover Assorted Chocolates from the custodian, Walter. I knowed it was from him cuz he always said he was kinda *sweet on me*. Ain't no mystery there.

Paul and I went out to my favoritest lunch place called Friendlys, and the peoples was real friendly axually, and we gotted egg salad sammies and Coca Colas, and we even split a banana split, which was funny on accounta splitting a split. When we was sitting there, Paul handed me a pretty box wrapped in paper with red-and-white stripes, kinda like my old uniform at the old hostipal. I ripped open the present real good cuz I was essited, and it turned out it was the bestest prezzie ever. He gave me a yellow picture frame with *three* different frames, and in one part was a picture of Paul and me, an old picture of when we first metted back at the center, and we's smiling real good. Then in the center frame part was a picture of Dottie and me sittin together on a park bench near the duck pond where we used to go feed the ducks our old breads. But

I membered that sometimes Dottie would forgets about throwin in tiny crumbs, and silly Dottie would just throw in the whole bread slices, and that bread would just be floating on top of the water. Those poor duckies couldn't eat no big bread slices, so they'd just paddle by. The third picture was a picture of me and my sister, Fuzzy, and Hazy and Willum and Ellie and Bunny. That picture was from turkey day, and we was all smiling real good in that picture. And I was sitting there looking at the pretty yellow frame and all the pictures of the peoples I loved, and some of those peoples is dead, like Dottie, but most of those peoples is not dead, and I gots so happy about the not dead peoples I started crying.

*I so sorry, Paul. I's not sad. I ain't crying cuz I's sad.*

*You're happy, right, Penny?* Paul said, patting my hand all sweet. My hand was real sticky from the ice cream.

*Yeah, Paul, I's crying tears to happy.*

We came home after the bestest day ever, and you just can't even imagine what I seen. When I gots home from my long and so, so fun day with Paul, Fuzzy opened the door, and she had dried yellow paint on her nose and on her fingers, and she said, *We have a surprise for you, Penny.*

*What is it, Fuzzy?* I just love surprises.

*Well, you're just going to have to see it for yourself.* Fuzzy was smiling so big like she was gonna burst in two. So we all walked upstairs in a row: Paul, Fuzzy, Hazy, and me.

My bedroom was painted my favorite color: *yellow.* Fuzzy and Hazel worked on it all day when I was havin my special Christmastime with Paul. My room wasn't all white anymore. It was the color of butter and flowers and sunshine, and Fuzzy boughted me a pretty yellow-flowered pillow for my bed and a little yellow rug and some yellow towels for my bathroom. When I seen it and I was standing there with Fuzzy and Hazy and I was so happy and essited, I started having those happy tears again. Again and again and again. I was so essited cuz I loves yellow so much.

# CHAPTER 29

# FESSENDEN

Christmas morning, I was sitting in the living room at the brownstone. The sun was not up yet, and it reminded me of when Hazel was tiny and William and I would sneak downstairs early to assemble things, organize presents, make coffee, and sit in the predawn quiet, truly the calm before the storm. All the preparations for the holiday were done and the anticipation of the happy chaos was a magical thing. I felt a bit like that again today. I looked over at the pile of presents for Penny, Hazel, William, and a few things for Bunny and Ellie, who would be joining us later in the morning.

I had news to share with the family again. I savored that little surprise as I drank the hot coffee and looked out at the icy cold streets of my lovely Boston neighborhood. The snow was coming down lightly, little talcum powder dots floating gently to the herringbone brick sidewalks and asphalt streets. I saw a man walking down the street, his coat collar pulled up high, his scarf around his face, bent over to break the biting wind.

I thought back on a Christmas morning when I was about sixteen. My mother and I lived alone in a tired old house in the center of Dedham, Massachusetts. Dad had left for Arizona years prior and was married to Rosie. I was asleep in my room, then awakened by a noise, a dull thud, a muffled laugh. I checked my clock radio: 5:23 a.m. It was black outside still, except for the weak light coming from a dim street lamp. I looked out the window. There were fresh footsteps in the deep drifts of snow coming from a large delivery truck, not quite a semi, more like a big van, and onto the front steps of our house.

I put on my bathrobe and moved over to the landing. I heard them more clearly now, my mother and a man, laughing, stumbling into the house. I didn't even know she had gone out the night before. Closing the front door clumsily, somebody slipping on the wooden floor with the snowy boots. The small Persian rug, now probably gathered in a pile in the corner of the foyer. Then the sound of boots coming off, tossed across the room, and then a collapse of sorts. The man, I thought, maybe on the sofa, my mother clanging things in the kitchen. I was afraid to go down there, to see what I would see, but I had to. I had to see what Mother had done now.

I held fast to the railing, tiptoeing, hearing their drunken whispers careless and breathy. I entered the living room. The man, heavy, scruffy, in a red-and-black-checked winter coat, with layers of sweaters and woolens beneath. Thick, lined work pants, dark khaki, stained, and work boots. He was very drunk. He smelled like old booze, old food, cigarettes. He smelled rotten and homeless. He looked at me as I entered the room, too drunk to even react. He just nodded slowly.

My mother's coat was on the floor. I walked past the living room where the drunk man lay half on and half off the old green velvet sofa. Her snow boots were in the dining room, small piles of snow melting around each one, and she was in the kitchen, in just her ivory silk slip and gray-heather rag socks, looking into the refrigerator, "Oh, hi," she said. Drunk. Very drunk, holding on to the door simply for support. "Hi, Fez," she added.

"Merry Christmas," I said bitterly.

"Oh, is it? Already?" She closed the refrigerator door. Then her balance was off and she stumbled back into the Formica counter. "Oops," she slurred.

"Mom, why have you brought someone home?"

"Well," she said, her eyes closed for emphasis, "he had nowhere to go."

"OK," I said. I was trying to be rational, patient. "Where have you been? Where did you find him?"

"Well." She dropped her head back slowly and laughed, the laugh of a crazy witch in a Grimm's fairy tale. "At the bar, of course."

William came downstairs, and the cracks and creaking of the old stairs shook me from my terrible reverie. I was looking out the window. He put his hand on my shoulder. I jumped. "You OK?"

"Actually, I think I am."

"What were you thinking about?" He sat next to me on the loveseat.

"For some reason, I was remembering the worst Christmas I ever had."

"Well, why on earth are you doing that?" He took my coffee mug from me and took a sip.

I turned to face him. "I have no idea. But something just happened. I realize I don't feel the least bit mad at the moment."

"Well, that is a very good thing. Those memories used to make you angry. Really angry and bitter. Maybe, as you told me recently, maybe you feel sad *for* her, not mad *at* her now."

"Yeah, maybe."

"So here's an idea: Why don't you think about the *best* Christmas you ever had instead?"

"Maybe that'll be today." I liked today so far.

"Maybe it will."

"Now stop drinking my coffee and go get your own." I smiled at him.

When Bunny and Ellie arrived, we opened up their presents and I thought it was time for my announcement. I said to the group, "I have news."

Penny asked, "Do we gots another house we's sellin?"

"Excellent guess, Pen, but no. Any other guesses?"

Hazel asked, "Does it have to do with your book?"

"*Yes!*" I cried. "Nothing definite yet, but Caroline called last week, and she thinks she has a publisher for me. Her associate read the synopsis and then the first part of the manuscript, and he wants to talk about working together. It still needs a lot of work, but it seems to be interesting somebody." I told them the specifics and timing. "It's really nothing yet. I'm just happy because it's a start of something. Oh, and I wanted to talk with you guys about the idea of maybe renting a place on Crow's Pond this summer. Not a purchase. Just a rental."

"But I thought you were totally done with that whole entire place," Hazel said.

"I am totally done with the Crow's Nest. Absolutely. I'm just not sure I'm done with Chatham. So maybe it'll just be a little experiment."

Bunny said, "I think it's a marvelous idea. But this time, let's make sure I get to visit."

# CHAPTER 30

# PENELOPE

The trees outside the house in *BeautifulBoston* was all pretty light green, and all the leaves and flowers was bright and big. From the windows in my bedroom, I could see green and white and pink and yellow. Not enough yellow, but I guess it was something. The sunshine was coming in all bright, and I could hear little city birdies chirping and flying real fast, dipping down low and rising up real high. Avoiding the cars. Picking up tiny seeds off the crookedy brick sidewalk. It was springtime, and you could smell it.

On this sparkedly spring day, Fuzzy was running around crazy. Really running. Dottie used to say, *Like chickens with crazy heads.* Fuzzy was exactly like a chicken with a crazy head. She was packing and getting ready for moving from Crow's Nest cuz there was a *closing* soon, whatever that was. That's what they called the old house in Cape Cod. Crow's Nest. I don't member why. She was running up and down the stairs and talking to herself, throwing food and drinks into bags with handles, tote bags. Fuzzy called them *el el been* bags. I packed up my stuff for the whole summer. We was moving from the old house called Crow's Nest and moving into the new house, which had no name and was right down the beach from the old house, and we was going for the whole summer, not just a few days like at Thanksgiving. So I packed all my stuff, everything I owned.

Willum was staying at the house in Boston all the times now. I used to has a friend at a place I used to live before I knew Dottie, and his name was William too, but we all called him Billy. Sometimes Silly Billy, and he would laugh and laugh. *I ain't silly*, he'd say, but then he'd laugh anyway. I asked Fuzzy's Willum if I could call him Billy or Willy or Silly Billy. He smiled at me and shook his head and said, *I think we better stick with William. That's all I've ever been. I don't really have a nickname.* I shoulda known. He wasn't really a nickname kinda boy. He was kinda serious sometimes and kinda laughy sometimes, but he was nice to me, and I guess he and Fuzzy was good friends again. I didn't understand all the stuff they's talking about sometimes, but I guess they's friends now. He's been back in the house now 162 days and staying in Fuzzy's room and everything. He's gonna be at the new Cape Cod house too this summer but kinda back and forth cuz of his work in *BeautifulBoston*. It's better when Willum is Fuzzy's friend cuz Fuzzy's smilier and not so pinchy all around her mouth, like she was when Willum was at his brother's house in Welzlie. She got all scrunchy in her face before, but she's not so scrunchy anymore. Plus, she stopped crying all the times. This winter, it just seemed like she was always wet in her face. Glad that's over cuz we was going through Kleenex America's Number One Tissues like crazy. And this spring he started a thing on Sundays where we would go down to the park called the Public Gardens and see the boats that looked like big white birds called swan boats. Unless it was asgusting weather like rainin or sleetin, we would go. Sometimes just Willum and me, sometimes Willum and Fuzzy and me, sometimes Hazy too. Sometimes we gots Dem Dawgs for lunch, and sometimes we gots stuff at a diner on Charles Street, which was kinda close to the boats, or another place on Charles Street that had foods from India called curry that was yellow and kinda spicy and made my tongue all tingly and burny.

Having the packing day and driving day and moving day is a lotta days in one day, if you ask me. It was Friday, May 22, 2015. We packed up the car for going to Crow's Nest on Fox Hill Road in Chatham, Massachusetts, 02633. Everyone had to bring their own stuffs outside, and then Fuzzy would put the stuffs in the car. I didn't has too much stuffs, but Fuzzy had about a hundred *el el been* bags of food and drinks plus a lotta duffel bags and suitcases and stuff. Not really a hundred bags cuz that's too many but a lotta, a lotta bags.

I was essited for the summer at the new house in Chatham, Massachusetts, 02633, on accounta Fuzzy having a dry face and Hazy not feeling so sad and even serious Willum smiling and stuff. It just seemed like everybody was gonna has a good time.

When we packed up the car, Willum and Fuzzy and Hazy and I got in and putted on our seatbelts so the car wouldn't do that chiming-bell thing. The drive was eighty-eight miles, and Fuzzy said it was gonna take one hour and thirty-seven minutes. That's also ninety-seven minutes. I was going to get a lot of knitting done on the way down.

The air was really, really pretty, and the breeze was coming in the car kinda cool and sweet. But not cold. Willum was drivin the car, and Fuzzy satted next to him, and Hazy and I was in the back seats together. Willum always liked to drived when we went in the car, and then Fuzzy could relax. The drive took one hour and fifty-three minutes on accounta there being so much traffic in the *BeautifulBoston* part of the drive. Hazy was looking out the window and feeling the air with her hands, and Fuzzy wasn't all sad to her and asking her to close the window cuz of the noise and fast, fast wind. So we was all quiet driving down there. Me knitting my cozy and Hazy making like a wavy boat with her hands in the fast, fast wind and Willum driving and Fuzzy kinda quiet humming to herself. The whole trip was like that. It was kinda buzzy and hummy.

After a lotta, lotta quiet times, Hazy said, *So, Mom, what's the plan?*

Fuzzy smiled at Hazy. *Yeah, this is going to be a little crazy. I guess today we'll toss out all the crap we don't want to move. Tomorrow the movers come and pack and move the rest of the stuff into the new place. Sunday and Monday we can spend unpacking and settling into the new rental. Then we're there for the summer.*

*What's the new place like, Fuzzy?* I asked cuz nobody had seen the new house except for Fuzzy. Willum smiled too, like he was curious like me.

Fuzzy said, *It's a pretty, small cape, smaller than Crow's Nest, but more open and brighter. Much fewer rooms but lots more light, which is nice. The light is great, actually. Also, smaller yard, smaller piece of land. It's right down the beach, maybe seven houses away, and a little closer to town. Less private. But since we're renting, if we hate it, no big deal, we just won't renew the lease next spring. The owner said he's thinking of selling but not until next year, so that might become an option. We'll just have to see. It's just a next step, without leaving here entirely.* Fuzzy smiled and kinda shrugged her shoulders. *I just wasn't quite ready to abandon the Cape, I guess.*

When we turned into the driveway at the old house on Fox Hill Road in Chatham, Massachusetts, 02633, there was a big, huge green metal box in the driveway.

*Oh, good, the Dumpster is here,* said Fuzzy. *Wait, It's way too big. I ordered a ten-yarder, and I think this one is forty. There is no way we can fill that.*

Willum said, *Fez, I bet we can fill it.* Willum was like the neatest person in the whole world.

Hazy said, *Well, Mom is* terrible *at throwing things out, so maybe not.* Hazy smiled at Fuzzy.

*You're right, I'm awful at that, so I'm going to need you guys to be my strength. OK?*

*OK,* Hazy said.

*OK*, I agreed.

Willum looked really essited to start throwin stuff into the big green box.

Fuzzy and Willum opened their doors and gotted out of the car, and Hazy and I did too. Willum looked right at Fuzzy and said, *Today is all about being ruthless.* Fuzzy had her hands on her hips and was kinda stretching around like her back smarted her.

She looked at the house and took a deep, deep breath and blew it out. *I know, I know.*

*We's gonna help, Fuzzy. I's so good a throwing stuff out and I's so, so strong.* I put my knitting bag down and patted Fuzzy's back. *We's gonna has a throw-out party. Right, Hazy?*

Hazy looked right at me and said, *Yep, a throw-out party is what we're going to have.* She stopped looking at me and then looked at Fuzzy, who was staring at the house and kinda scared looking. *Where do we start, Mom?*

*Oh God. I don't know. I guess Crow's Nest, then the Halfway House and then Q?* Fuzzy looked tired, and we hadn't even started yet. Willlum looked like he was jus gonna let Fuzzy be the boss to him today.

We all walked down the little hill to the main house with some of those *el el been* bags of food and drinks, and we took turns putting the food into the refrigerator. We went back and forth to the car and got all the bags and put them in the right places in the bedrooms. Hazy to the Halfway House and Fuzzy and me to the Crow's Nest. Willum was doon something with the water heater or something.

When we was all done with the car stuffs, we all stood in the living room of the Crow's Nest. The light was shining in big yellow, pretty shapes on the carpet. The little, tiny, white, sparkly dust fairies were flying all around. Teeny and magical. We all just stood there for a long time; I think cuz no one knew where to start. We was just all looking around the room at the flowered sofa and the

275

big chair and the little chair and the other cushy chairs by the bay window and the old dusty TV and wooden ducks and books and the old playing cards and the *Parcheezy* board with the curled up edges and the ashtrays everywhere, and Fuzzy said, *Jesus Christ*, and sat down on the chewed-up, broken bench. Willum stood next to her and kinda rubbed her back.

*Fuzzy, I's gonna be the boss to you, K?* Jeez, somebody had to get this thing going. *How about those games? Is they all broked up?*

Fuzzy looked up like she had been snoozling and said all sleepy, *Uh, yeah, I don't think we've had a complete game or pack of cards in thirty years.*

*OK, then. Those is going in the big green box, K?*

*OK, Penny Yeah, definitely.*

So I went into the kitchen and got one of the big, dirty, white, empty *el el been* bags with the dark-blue straps and FWB on the front, and I filled it with *Parcheezy* and *Monopoly* and exactly thirteen little boxes of playing cards, and when I was in those shelves putting broked up games in the *el el been* bag, I picked up a book that smelled like soggy old water, and I showed it to Fuzzy. *This smells yucky.*

Fuzzy walked over to look at the book, *A Guidebook of Birds in the Northeast,* and she flipped it over in her hands. *God, it's totally mildewed. It's like this bookshelf had a leak or some water damage or something. Gross.* When Hazy came over to look, she picked up another book called *World War II Stories and Pictures,* and it was covered in soggy, moldy stuff too, and when we started going through all the books, they was all kinda wet and loose and smelled gross like old dirty water. *All these books are totally destroyed. But how do we throw out books? All these books? God.* Fuzzy looked like all those moldy, wet, disgusting books was gonna make her cry. Her shoulders was kinda slumpy, and her back was bent over all crookedy.

I looked right at Fuzzy. I put down the *el el been* bag of games and went into the kitchen to get a Hefty Hefty Hefty Lawn and

Leaf garbage bag from the counter where Fuzzy put them. I came back in the room big and strong. *How do we throw them out? Like this*, I said, and I put a gross moldy book called *Favorite Needlepoint Patterns* into a black garbage bag. *Just like this, Fuzzy.*

Fuzzy looked right at me like I was magical. Like a magical, powerful fairy, and really slowly, like the slowest thing ever, she stood up a little bit straighter and said, *Yeah, Penny. OK, just like that.* She smiled a big white smile, and her checks got round and pink, and without even checking titles, she started tossing wet, disgusting books into the black garbage bag. And then another bag. And then another. And another. So many filled bags of broked up stuff.

We took turns taking those Hefty Hefty Hefty Lawn and Leaf garbage bags out to the big green box, and once Fuzzy membered that she could throw out disgusting things, she got really essited and started practically running around throwing things out like a crazy chicken. Willum was so proud to her too. Everything on those bookshelves was disgusting and thrown into the green box. Broken old games and toys and broken chairs missing legs and moldy sheets and stained and torn towels and moldy rugs went into the box. Old bottles of Prell and cracked bars of Dial Soap and brown Jean Nate and expired bottles of Bayer and forty-three empty orange, plastic prescription bottles. Fifty-seven Yardley's English Lavender soaps in Mimi's bathroom. Arm and Hammer Laundry detergent all hardened in the box. Broken plates and cups. Rusted out pots and pans. Spices yellowed and hardened. Into the big green box. Like the fastest person in the world, Fuzzy was throwing bags into the box. Her face was pink and hot, and there was dots of water all over her face, and her armpits was all circles of water, and her ponytail was wet on the bottom from the water on her back. I'd never seen her move so fast. Hazy was right there with her, and I was too. We was all watery and hot.

Then we took a rest from all the running and had ham sammitches and iced tea, sitting on those old strappy lawn chairs.
Feeling the nice cool breeze coming from the water like a salty
fan was working in our direction. We ate those sammitches like we
hadn't never eaten no sammies before. They was so good, and the
iced tea felt cold and sweet, and I could feel it slipping all the way
down my throat and into my tummy. Cold and sweet. I laughed
and patted my cold tummy.

Willum said to Fuzzy, *I know this is a tough day for you, honey. I
know we've been through this before, but I want to say this again: I am so,
so terribly sorry that we're losing this house. That you are. If I could make
it right, I hope you know I would.*

Fuzzy looked right at Willum and said, *It's really OK.*

Willum started to say, *No, I—*

Fuzzy interrupted him, *After everything that went on in this house,
after everything that happened to Mom here, I really, honestly, am ready to
move on. I couldn't possibly stay here, even if we had the money...and now
that I know the new homeowners are going to tear it down and build something new, I think it's good. That makes me feel better. It's just time to go.*

Fuzzy was looking out at the water, and she said to all of us,
*There's a couple of things I need to throw away just because. You guys are
just going to have to trust me on these next things. They have to go. And I
need your help carrying them, OK?*

Hazy and I said OK, and we all went into the house, and we
went right for something Fuzzy called *Grampa's wing chair.* Fuzzy
stood behind it and asked, *Can you guys grab the legs and back, and
Penny, can you open the door?* They lifted up Grandpa's wing chair
that Fuzzy looked kinda mad at since it was Grandpa's and he was
kinda cranky and bossy and thought he was the boss to everyone.
Well, they picked it up, and I opened the slammy screen door, and
they carried that heavy chair out to the big green box, and they
held it way high over the sides and dumped it. Fuzzy looked like
she just won a prize at a fair. *Good riddance. Now, one more thing,* she
said, turning toward the house.

We walked down the little hill past the garden and into the Crow's Nest and back into the back bedroom where Fuzzy's and my mommy slept when she was little. There was two single beds in there and pretty wallpaper with tiny pink flowers and white curtains and the brown wooden floor with a little oval rug with flowers on it between the beds. *That bed has to go.* Fuzzy pointed to the bed on the right where our mommy used to stay when she was tiny. Hazy looked like she wasn't gonna ask no questions since Fuzzy was in such a big and bossy mood. I wasn't gonna ask no questions neither. Fuzzy was gonna move that bed one way or another, and we just went along with her. In three trips, we all took that old mattress and the old box spring and the old bed frame right up the little hill and into the big green box. The last part we threw in was all the old pillows and blankets and yellowed sheets, with rips in the corners and tired elastic and an old blue blanket with satin around the edges. When we threw all the old sheets and pillows into the box, all the old feathers from the old pillows made a big, huge, gigantic dusty cloud of dirt into the air. It looked exactly like an old gray scary ghost had rised up high in the sky and then falled down again in the big green box of trash.

# CHAPTER 31

# HAZEL

The day we moved into the new rental, after the movers had put the furniture and boxes in the rooms and driven away, I plopped down on the sofa in the living room and quickly fell asleep, waking up in the late afternoon. I sat up, seeing the un-opened boxes, the unplugged lamps, the pictures wrapped in bub-ble wrap and brown paper. Mom had left a note that she and Dad were at the market getting groceries. I think this summer rental was going to be OK. Really small, but good. Fine, anyway.

The best thing about waking up now was how I felt. For months before rehab, I would wake up with a headache or a stomachache or just incredibly tired. I had forgotten what waking up feeling good felt like. Even though some days were really tough, feeling clear and good was so nice. Some days I would lie in bed trying to figure out what my mood was, and how I felt, and while my mood changed like a fuckin roller coaster, I was starting to feel a little better in my own skin.

The weird thing about addiction is it's never going anywhere. It's kinda like an annoying kid at school who's gonna follow you for the rest of your life. And you spend all your time trying to ditch her, but she keeps popping up, right when you think she's gone. She just tags along, kinda poking you and saying, "Let's hang out." When I was talking in AA about addiction kinda being like a beautiful and persistent person, the whole group was nodding like, *Yeah.* That's the best way I could ever describe it.

I felt how fast I fell in love with it, and even in the wild ride of last year, even when I was loving it, psyched, happy, flying high, soaring, it scared the shit out of me too. Right beneath the surface of the elation is a fucking scary energy saying, *What happens when this buzz goes?*

Edgehill sucked worse than anything. It's over, and I hope I never go back. I know I can never drink or smoke or take anything again, partially because one day, it would probably kill me and also cuz I fucking hated being there so bad. Dr. Bowman's got me on a pretty nice dose of Wellbutrin, and it seems to be working. I don't feel that paralyzing blackness anymore. And when I don't feel that scary hopelessness, I'm not thinking about how to climb out of it with booze and everything. I'm still seeing Dr. B on Tuesday afternoons. He's pretty cool, and I can basically bitch for an hour and blow off steam. He says one of the reasons I was able to hide my drug and alcohol abuse for so long was because, in his words, I am "highly and fiercely intelligent." I love that. Putting a positive spin on addiction. He thought I was probably pretty good at getting by in school with minimal effort and then really good at hiding the fact I was out of it for almost a whole school year.

Drugs were and are fuckin everywhere. I could eat edibles with wicked high THC levels and cruise though my day. I could pop a Xanax and just seem mellow, relaxed, maybe just tired. Drinking and pot smoking was usually during the weekends and fucking *everybody* abused those, even the athletes and people everyone thought were clean. It was just too easy slipping under the radar. Especially with my parents, lost in and distracted by finance and work stuff. Personal stuff too.

Anyway, no excuses. I own it all. I'm just saying it was easy.

So here's the surprising thing that actually kinda makes me feel way better about all this bullshit I went thought last year. My family unburied a shit-ton of secrets this year, and my two faves are these: My aunt Penny, who is really slow, like on paper, but weirdly sharp in life, is this cool new force in our house. She was tucked away in an apartment in Marion, just an hour away, and we didn't even know she existed. She came to live with us last fall, and at first, I thought my mother was insane to take her in. But Penny's awesome. If you could have told me my closest friend was going to be a sixty-five-year-old with an IQ of about the same number, I would have said you're nuts.

Second, we uncovered some stuff about my grandmother, my mom's mom. Turns out she went through some badass family stuff, like fucking *incest*, and she was depressed too. She was even hospitalized at Edgehill, about a million years ago, though. Turns out depression and addiction runs in the family. My mom says she herself has been wrestling with moods, depression, anger, anxiety her whole life but didn't really get it till I was going through this. She said going through this with me helped clarify a bunch of bullshit for her too. Now she's got her own therapist, plus she's going to ninety-minute Al-Anon meetings every Thursday, which she says she loves.

I made some tea and went down to the little beach in front of the house to sit in the late afternoon sun. Penny was already there, hunched over her knitting, her hands going crazy fast. "Hey, Pen," I said. "Thought I'd come sit and chill."

She looked up from her knitting. "Oh, hi, Hazy!" She was so damn happy all the time. She kept knitting and then added, "I gots to finish this row, then I can be chillin too." She was starting to pick up some of my expressions, which totally cracked me up.

"Tomorrow's your birthday, Pen."

"I know, Hazy, and I so essited to it!" She finished her row, put the large yellow knitting project in her plastic knitting bag, and reached over to hold my hand. We just sat there together, holding hands kinda quiet, watching the little waves coming in and out on the sand, the boats coming and going, and the birds flying everywhere. We looked over as a murder of crows alit on the dried kelp on the sand down the beach. Penny was enrapt. When the last crow landed, I watched Penny point at them with her long thin finger, and she counted silently, mouthing the numbers.

She breathed a deep sigh of relief and said, "Eight. Eight crows."

"Yep," I said. "Eight." She was really into counting shit.

"Hazy?"

"Yeah, Pen?"

"I'm real glad all the secrets are all gone now."

"Me too," I agreed.

She took a loud slurpy sip of her juice. "Hazy, I so happy to be countin eight crows today. I ain't never counting to seven no more."

I don't know what the hell she's talking about sometimes, but man, I love my Penny.

# CHAPTER 32

# FESSENDEN

I woke up when it was still dark out. Our first Memorial Day in the rental. I wanted to watch the sunrise. It was 5:37 a.m. when I looked at my phone. I put a sweater on over my nightgown and headed downstairs, carefully sidestepping the unpacked boxes to make a thermos of coffee for the beach. I wanted to sit there quietly and alone and drink in the pinks and oranges and persimmons of the sky. As I waited for the coffee to brew, I looked out the window facing the water. The sky was still a steely gray, but I could see the burgeoning colors peeking up over Crow's Pond in the east. The rental kitchen was unchanged from the sixties, I guessed, with the addition of more modern appliances within the last decade. The cabinets were Shaker style, simple white wooden cabinets. The counters were teak, oiled and reoiled over the seasons. The floor redone in the 1960s in black-and-white linoleum checkerboard. The exact same floor we had in the Crow's Nest. I could see my grandmother in front of the large black enameled cooking pot, her glasses fogged up, wiping off the steam on her ruffled apron. Smiling at me. Saying something sweet. Her words muted in my memory. I could see her thin arms and small muscles flexing as she lifted the pot to drain the steamers into the metal colander in the sink. Her veins pushing out and her sinewy arms working the heavy pot, pouring the water far away from her body, leaning away from the heat.

In the time it took to brew the coffee, the sun started to rise over the waterline with an explosion of fiery oranges and corals and hot pinks. The colors were stunning. I took my thermos of coffee and headed out through the kitchen door, stopping to put on sandy flip-flops, passing across a small grassy lawn, wet with cool dew. Down the dry weather-beaten steps to our new small sandy beach. The same four old, rusted, crusty folding beach chairs were there in a semicircle. The movers had placed them there at Penny's request.

I sat and smelled the wonderful coffee aroma before taking that first and best, delicious sip. I took off my flip-flops and pressed my toes into the cool sand, feeling larger sand grains and shells pressing against the bottoms of my feel. I heard the first optimistic chirps of the bobwhites and then the sad, lonely calls of the mourning doves. Maybe my favorite bird songs. The crows and gulls were still quiet. They would start making their avian racket a little later.

The waves were small, quiet, lapping in and out, the water reflecting all of those pinks and oranges in the sky.

I closed my eyes as the sun fully emerged from its slumber, the full circle of orange out from beneath the horizon. I kept my eyes closed as the burst of warmth and brightness covered me. I slowly opened my eyes and looked out at Crow's Pond. I turned my gaze to the place where we had scattered my mother's ashes exactly thirty-five years ago on a breezy Memorial Day, the air still cold from the winter, the spring's warmth not yet convincing. We took the urn of ashes out in the Whaler as the sun was setting over the hill behind the house, behind the quail's ridge. It was Bunny and her husband, Buck, and the Holloways from next door and me. Five of us on the small boat, and a small tin box of fine powder and chunks of bone. Bunny, with her beautiful, rich voice, quietly, reverently sang my mother's favorite hymn, "Eternal Father, Strong to Save."

On that Memorial Day in 1981, the beginning of the summer, when I was just nineteen, the words of that hymn made no sense to me. I found it strange that my mother loved that hymn, or any hymn. But now, as I sat here, in the quiet of this glorious sunrise, this choice of hymns made sense; she was asking for protection, because there was "peril on the sea." Knowing what she suffered through as a small girl, a child, and slowly, with great fear and uncertainty in her heart, she moved ahead. Step by step. Year by year. And although, in her heart, she was filled with dread and sadness and a huge hole that nothing could ever fill, she went on. She married a man even though every single man on earth might have been an extension of her monster of a father. Even though the idea of any man touching her in any way must have been terrifying, she married my father. Then she gave birth to a daughter who went away.

So today, on this anniversary weekend of the scattering of my mother's ashes, on my fifty-third birthday, on Penny's sixty-fifth birthday, I looked out at the water. I looked squarely at the place where we turned the tin box upside down and watched the talcum powder of her body be carried away by a tiny, gentle gust of wind and land softly on the surface of the water. Where we watched the small but heavy chunks of bone fall straight down and be sucked under the midnight-blue water, the irregular gray pieces engulfed as they sank into the sea. I looked right there, at that very spot, a place I wouldn't really look at before today, for reasons of anger or regret or something even darker. But today I looked. I stared at it as if I was being transported there. As if I were flying right over the surface of the water and floating right over that spot.

As I looked intensely at that very spot on the surface of Crow's Pond, something happened. The sun came up just enough to shine on the water, *in that exact location,* and in that small spot, in the middle of the pond, the water lit up like thousands of tiny pink and red and orange firecrackers. Sparkling and shimmering and popping off the water. Light jumping and gleaming and twinkling. Magical little fireflies of light. So bright, I had to squint. As I was taking in the light-filled splendor, a stunning, incredible, magical thing happened; my mother moved through me. She went through me like a hot breeze. She entered my chest, to the right of my heart, and whirled around my heart, all four chambers, and through my lungs, hot and moist, and then she exited through my throat, gritty and raspy. She exited me right where her disease had grown in her own throat. The power of her swirling and the heat of her love pressed into my eyes and pushed out hot, round tears. The tears streamed down my face, and gathered in pools in the hollows of my collarbones.

I gasped for air because she had been in my lungs, and I had been holding back the breath. I knew it was my mother; she filled me with love and relief and joy and rapture. It was goodness and absolute love and *forgiveness.* I looked at the sparkles on the pond, and thought, *I miss you, Mom.*

I recognized something like relief. Like something I had been clenching had been released, and what was left in that clenching gut was an open, sweet space. Maybe that was joy or happiness or an absence of anger, but it was lovely and good.

I wiped away the tears. I breathed in the clean, fresh morning air. I continued to look at the water, drinking my coffee, feeling tranquil and quiet, when I heard someone coming down the little wooden stairs to the beach. Hazel was there with her mug of tea.

"Thought I'd join you for the sunrise," she said in her sleepy voice. Her young face was sleep-puffy, and there were little pillow lines on her left cheek. She sat in another of the tired folding chairs, the grit of sand scratching against the aluminum legs. "Happy birthday."

"Thanks, Haze. Nice to see you, love. I never see you at this hour. Isn't it beautiful?" I was still trying to process my mother's visit.

"It really is." Hazel took a long sip of her tea, which smelled like chamomile or lavender or something herbal and earthy.

"Mom, we should get new beach chairs this season." She smiled at me.

"I totally agree. These have definitely seen their last season. I didn't mean to move them. They were supposed to go to the Dumpster. I think these have actually been around since the early seventies. No kidding. I remember getting them with my grand-mother at the five-and-dime. Maybe we'll head into town today and find some. We're due."

"Maybe we can pick up those incredible doughnuts from Marvin's…the ones that make the grease stains on the paper bag." When I was young, my father and I used to get up early and buy those doughnuts for the family. It was a happy memory. I told Penny and Hazel that those doughnuts always made any day a better day.

"We'll get them. Absolutely. It's a doughnut kind of day."

As we sat quietly watching the sky as the sun rose higher and higher, we both turned our head toward the sound of someone else coming to the beach. Penny was in her velour zip-up bathrobe and her Velcro sandals, holding her knitting bag.

"I's coming too," she announced. "I's sitting next to Hazel. Happy birthday to us, Fuzzy! I's so essited to our birthdays!"

I replied, "Yes, me too, Pen. Happy birthday to us."

Hazel pulled the folding chair next to her so the chair arms touched. "Happy birthday, Penny. We're watching the sunrise."

Penny sat down. She looked out at the water and the sky. "Yep, the sunrise is good, but I's so, so busy today. I's got a lotta cozies to finish for the Edgehill peoples. I's so busy, even on my birth-day," she said as she hunched over and started knitting. "There's a lotta peoples who need these cozies soon. I don't know what they did before I came here." Penny looked up from her knitting and smiled at me.

I said, "Penny, you *are* really important. I can't imagine what those people did before you showed up. Or us, for that matter."

She nodded seriously and then smiled broadly with pride. She bent over her knitting, focusing, moving her fingers with such alacrity, it was hard to follow her hand movements. It was just a blur of fingers, wooden needles, and butter-yellow yarn.

Finally, William came down the stairs and sat down on the chair next to mine. He was holding an empty mug. "Mornin'."

"Mornin', Wink." He smiled at my use of an old pet name. He held out his mug, and I poured coffee in, still piping hot from the thermos.

"What a day."

"Yep, we were just commenting on it. Beautiful start to the season."

We sat in those chairs for about an hour, watching the sun continue its climb, the waves lapping at our feet, the tiny hermit crabs frantic and busy, skittering in and out of the water, feeling the warmth of the burgeoning day.

Penny and Hazel got up to get doughnuts, and William left to go on a run. I sat on the beach, alone, quiet, listening to the mourning doves cooing, the gulls laughing, watching the crows flying from the tall pines, landing heavily on the beach, and taking off again. I saw the sparkles on the water disappear. I saw the sun climb, the clouds shift, the breeze move. I watched this new day start. It was going to be a good one.

# ACKNOWLEDGEMENTS

I have so many people to thank, starting with my wonderful Sargent/Swank family: Thank you all for your love, support, care, and genuine interest during this very long writing and editing process.

Thank you to every single one of my smart, funny and loyal friends for listening to me tell my stories and encouraging me to put them down on paper. Thank you also for asking me about my writing and editing progress, and then actually listening to my lengthy replies.

Thank you to my friend Lee, for introducing me to Christine Pride, my wonderful, patient, sage and positive editor, who helped me shape this book, enrich the characters and fine-tune my some-times (often) scattered thinking.

Thank you to my literary agent Beth Davey for loving this book and believing in me, both now and in the future.

Thank you Susie Stangland for your enthusiasm, energy and knowledge of the bustling, busy and unfamiliar world of social media marketing. Thank you Lucinda Dyer and Bryan Azersky for your sharp, colorful website vision and execution. I feel as if I've known all three of you for years.

Thank you Lucy, Hannah and Charlie, my beloved children, for being so strong, brave, smart, curious and incredibly, extraordinarily funny.

Finally, thank you Andrew for your unwavering support and patience.

# ABOUT THE AUTHOR

 Amy Sargent Swank graduated from Amherst College in Massachusetts and now works as a designer. Married and the mother of three adult children, she resides in Westchester County, New York.

# NOTE

This book is a work of fiction; any resemblance to people, living or dead, is purely accidental.

45448664R00168

Made in the USA
Middletown, DE
04 July 2017